OCT - 7 2011

The Woman from Bratislava

LEIF DAVIDSEN is a Danish journalist and the author of a number of bestselling suspense novels. He has worked for many years for Danish radio and television as a foreign correspondant and editor of foreign news, specialising in Russian, East and Central European affairs. He is the author of *The Serbian Dane* (Arcadia).

BARBARA J. HAVELAND was born in Scotland and now lives in Denmark with her Norwegian husband and teenage son. She has translated works by several leading Danish and Norwegian authors including Peter Høeg, Linn Ullmann and Jan Kjærstad.

The Woman from Bratislava

LEIF DAVIDSEN

Translated from the Danish by
Barbara J. Haveland

Arcadia Books Ltd
15–16 Nassau Street
London W1W 7AB

www.arcadiabooks.co.uk
First published in the United Kingdom by EuroCrime, an imprint of Arcadia Books 2009
Reprinted 2010
Copyright © Leif Davisden 2001
Published by agreement with Lindhardt & Ringhof Publishers, Copenhagen and
Leonhardt and Høier Literary Agency, Copenhagen

This English translation from the Danish, *De Gode Søstre*
Copyright © Barbara J. Haveland 2009

Leif Davisden has asserted his moral right to be identified as the author of this work in accordance with the Copyright, Designs and Patents Act, 1988.

A catalogue record for this book is available from the British Library.

ISBN 978-1-906413-35-4

Typeset in Minion by MacGuru Ltd
Printed in the United Kingdom by CPI Cox & Wyman, Reading, RG1 8EX

This translation has been sponsored by the Danish Arts Council Committee for Literature.

KUNSTRÅDET
Danish Arts Council

Arcadia Books supports English PEN, the fellowship of writers who work together to promote literature and its understanding. English PEN upholds writers' freedoms in Britain and around the world, challenging political and cultural limits on free expression. To find out more, visit www.englishpen.org or contact
English PEN, 6-8 Amwell Street, London EC1R 1UQ

Arcadia Books distributors are as follows:

in the UK and elsewhere in Europe:
Turnaround Publishers Services
Unit 3, Olympia Trading Estate
Coburg Road
London N22 6TZ

in the US and Canada:
Dufour Editions
PO Box 7, Chester Springs
PA, 19425

in Australia:
The Scribo Group Pty Ltd
18 Rodborough Road
Frenchs Forest 2086, Australia

in New Zealand:
Addenda
PO Box 78224
Grey Lynn
Auckland

in South Africa:
Jacana Media (Pty) Ltd
PO Box 291784,
Melville 2109
Johannesburg

Arcadia Books is the *Sunday Times* Small Publisher of the Year

'It may be strange and it may be irrational, but history means a very great deal, especially somewhere such as the Balkans.'

Velijko Vujacic, historian

Prologue

IT WAS A STORY often used by security-cleared lecturers in the civilian branch of FET, by serving officers of a certain rank and other trusted members of staff with PET when briefing new volunteers on the special conditions under which the secret services had to operate in a post-communist world. Right at the start, the importance of absolute confidentiality when dealing with classified information and documents was impressed upon the young and somewhat self-conscious new recruits, who always looked forward to the talk on what was referred to simply as *the case*. In other words, this story was not for repeating to their 'partners', as they were termed in politically correct Danish, along with other pillow talk. Historians have an ingrained disrespect for any information which is not at least seventy-five years old, so as far as they were concerned this particular case was still current. The new recruits, on the other hand, tended to regard it as belonging to some strange bygone time. But then, their temporal perspective seemed to extend little further than from one TV news broadcast to the next, or at least, not much beyond the German occupation of the country, the hippie era and that time back in the bizarre seventies when the students were crying out for a socialist revolution. To these young people the chronology was often a bit muddy. For their elders, the youngsters' lack of historical knowledge was a regular topic of conversation in the canteen. It was inevitable, therefore, that lecturers on the courses for prospective analysts run by the civilian branches of the Danish Military Intelligence – FET – and Security Intelligence – PET – were given to introducing elements of storytelling into their teaching. In the academic world this would have been frowned upon, but for the budding

| vii |

spymasters and counter-spies such narrative techniques only made the lectures – and, not least, this particular story – all the more interesting. To put it bluntly: these secret agents of the future simply paid more attention.

Since the case in all its details was known only to a trusted inner circle and had, with typical, autocratic Danish common sense, been consigned to the archives for the next seventy-five years, only the most seasoned members of staff, those with complete insight into the matter, were allowed to lecture on it. It was mainly for this reason that *the case* carried so much prestige. That and the strangeness of the alliance. That two such diverse ideologies should have become bedfellows. First and foremost, though, *the case* was used as a means of making it clear to future spies and counter-spies that secret agents had existed since before biblical times and would go on existing for all time. *The case* also served as proof that the services' budget demands were well warranted. Berlin Wall or no Berlin Wall. There is treachery and there is loyalty. Every day there are men and women who make a choice. People are easily tempted. There is no risk of unemployment in this job. That was the message. We deal in facts. Nonetheless, even those PET and FET lecturers with the highest security clearance could not resist adding the odd fictional flourish to their presentations. It always heightened the class's interest. It was a common ploy to open with a description of the situation in the new, democratic Republic of Estonia, despite the fact that no one could say exactly how things stood there. Even when one is dealing with individuals who have willingly applied to join the secret services, with all their limitations, a couple of colourful, emotive adjectives has never detracted from the solemnity of the proceedings; adjectives of the sort with which Jytte Vuldom, the big boss and guru, often began her sermon on those occasions when she managed to escape from her administrative prison to teach the future defenders of the nation's secrets.

Vuldom had survived just about everything; she knew how to

handle the politicians, was a friend to her lads and the service's steadfast, erudite champion in the face of the voracious, ignorant media. Vuldom often commenced her baptism of the new initiates by invoking her right to present her own interpretation of the ostensibly innocuous image of the times and the normal situation; and so occasionally, if she considered a fresh crop of Danish men and women ready to enter the unique brother- and sisterhood of the secret services, she would begin with the story as seen – as they say in the temples of dramaturgy – from Teddy's POV. The aim was to give these future interpreters of the merchandise supplied by the dealers in secrets, these prospective analysts of the invariably double-edged nature of treachery, an initial insight into university lecturer Theodor Nikolaj Pedersen, his ambivalent part in things and the significance of history and of family ties. Or possibly to discreetly underline the fact that the gathering of information and, not least, the interpretation of same, always entails a considerable degree of subjectivity. In the end it all comes down to the unpredictability of the individual. These are the sorts of words which Vuldom used even when she was meant to be teaching new recruits how to predict a person's many weak spots. She would run an eye over the handpicked gathering at the National Police Training Centre in Avnø near the south-western tip of Zealand, at the recruits with their notebooks on their desks and ballpoint pens or felt-tips hovering expectantly, all set to record her words of wisdom and the overhead projector's instructive graphs. But Vuldom rarely took the overhead's easy way out. Instead, she often began by describing a scene:

A small group of people stands in a forest west of Narva in the now independent Estonia. It is a day in early June. Everything is lovely and green, the singing of the birds the only sound. It has rained during the night and drops of water hang like exquisite little pearls from every leaf and blade of grass. The group consists of six men and a woman. They stand quietly, gazing at a granite stone. One of the men supports himself with a stick. There are tears in his eyes. With his high, bald pate and small, sunken eyes he must be close on eighty. His skin is thin and wrinkled, it looks as though it would tear if one scratched it. But he still stands straight and tall. The other men are in their fifties, all in the middle-aged male's various stages of decline. There are bald patches and pot-bellies, but also a certain firmness of purpose, as if they have come a long way and have now, finally, reached their goal. The woman stands out from the rest. She must be about sixty, but if her body too is marked by age then her elegant trouser suit hides any signs of the decay. She has short, greyish hair, very lightly tinted, strong, beautiful lips highlighted in red and keen green eyes set nicely in a face that is well-proportioned, if a little irregular. Her figure is slim and she stands with her head only slightly bowed. She is holding a bouquet of roses. It is very quiet. Only the birdsong and the swish of feet on damp grass. In the distance, the sound of a plane cutting across the blue sky, somewhere up there among the scattering of fluffy white clouds in the stratosphere. The woman takes a step forward and lays the bouquet at the foot of the rough-hewn, brown granite stone, gently, as if it were of porcelain. The red roses stand out brightly against the green grass and the mound of black soil left over from the setting of the stone. She steps back a pace again, seems to be studying the coat-of-arms with the Dannebrog cross and the legend beneath it, as if to brand it on her memory. She already knows it by heart, though. It seems to me that a look of peace descends upon her face as she reads it aloud to herself, like a little child who has just discovered the magic of words, but has to recite them in her head in order to make sense of them.

"'The Danish Regiment. Croatia-Russia. Estonia-Lithuania. Courland-Pomerania. In memory of those who fought,'" she reads to herself, without moving her lips.

They stand for a moment. A group of well-dressed modern individuals in a forest near Narva in Estonia.

'That's that, then,' the oldest of them says.

'Yes, that's that,' the woman replies. 'And it was about time.'

'It was indeed,' the old man says and then, shifting the emphasis to the last word: 'It was *indeed*.'

Then once more there is only silence and the birds and after a while the sound of feet on wet grass as they turn, on the word of command almost, and wend their way out of the Estonian forest.

Thereafter, another picture would be presented. Vuldom would pick up a sheet of paper, run the eyes behind her narrow reading glasses over the rapt assembly, before looking down at the white sheet in her hand and reading out loud, like a mother to her eagerly attentive children:

It is a picture of a white house. A large house surrounded by beech and elm trees. The tiled roof is red. The house is pictured from above, but even so the white walls are clearly visible in the soft, limpid light. This is an aerial photograph ordered by a proud householder. It is summer and there is a black Ford van in the courtyard. There are no other cars to be seen, only a team of horses pulling a combine-harvester in a neighbouring field. Here, only a few years after the war, Denmark is still a horse-drawn country and tractors are not yet common. It must have been in August that the plane flew over the white house. One can both sense and see that the sun is shining. There is a patch of blue sky. The colours are still bright, though tinged by the years, which have lent them a patina befitting those frugal times. There is a courtyard to the front of the house and a large garden at the back. It looks as if there are fruit trees in the garden, which is surrounded by a neatly-trimmed green hedge. There are five people in the picture, which is framed as if it were an oil painting. A man and a woman. The man is clad in white with a tall baker's hat on his head. The woman has her arms crossed over a floral-print dress. Her black hair gleams in the sunlight. Both have their faces turned up to the pilot's camera. They have waited a long time for him to fly over this home of which they are now the proud owners. Behind them stands a half-grown boy, he too in white baker's garb, but bareheaded. Next to him is a girl of about the same age in a pastel-coloured frock. Her arms are bare and her hair hangs in two long, dark braids. They look alike, as siblings tend to. The aerial photograph is so sharp that the features of their faces can almost be made out as they gaze up at the plane swooping overhead. There is also a small boy in the picture. He is standing next to his mother, peering up at the aircraft, waving to it. His hair is curly and almost white and his bare knees can be seen peeking out below his short trousers. It is a very Danish picture. A picture which radiates security and comfort. A picture which speaks of good times just around the corner. The little boy in the photograph is me. This is the only thing left from my first childhood home and without it I would have no memory of that white house. I was almost four when the picture was taken in a fit of hubris. The following winter my father was forced to close the bakery when a certain matter came to light and his customers learned of his past. All this I have been told, but I do not remember it. I remember only the scent of flour and the sound of the delivery man whistling as he hopped up into the baker's van, off to deliver crusty white bread to the customers. And sometimes the rich aroma of the pork, duck and geese with which my father filled the big, black ovens on Martinmas Eve, or on Christmas Eve when the whole village brought their Christmas roasts to the baker: the ovens of their coal or coke fired stoves too small to cope with the plump festive fare. Otherwise it is all a blank, and my first clear memories stem from the time after we moved to a small town in Jutland. By then my father was no longer a part of our lives. All in all, I have only the haziest recollections of him. And I am not sure whether those things I do remember are the result of personal experience or memories derived from family anecdotes and a handful of photographs. He left his family because he was ashamed that he could not provide for them properly and died, so legend has it, two years later in a bar in Hamburg. But the past did not die with him. It lived on, and the ripples from it spread all the way to the end of the century, that century which can only be called the century of the victim. But was he victim or executioner. Or both? This was the question with which the family had to wrestle over the years that followed. It had no real bearing on me, but it shaped the lives of the other two children in a way that was to prove crucial for them. It became for them the great secret of their lives and was guarded more carefully than the most clandestine love affair. Denmark entered the modern world and the majority of people forgot, but a few tended their memories and kept them burning so fiercely that these same remembrances eventually consumed them from within.

Who am I? Vuldom would ask in her cool, slightly husky and often quite sexy smoker's voice.

Who is the 'I' in this story? Who is the 'I' in any story?

That gave them something to think about over the coffee break.

Part 1

TEDDY'S ACADEMIC LIFE

Oh, sister, am I not a brother to you
And one deserving of affection?

Bob Dylan

1

I FIRST NOTICED the woman in Warsaw. She showed up again at a couple of gatherings in Prague, but she did not make herself known until Bratislava, and my meeting with her is, I suppose, as good a place as any at which to begin my story. She presented herself at my door with her staggering secret at an inconvenient moment: a surfeit of alcohol was still working its way through my system and my mind was awash with self-pity.

I had got drunk, and when I did that I missed the Soviet Union as badly as a slighted lover can miss his faithless sweetheart. I actually did not drink that much any more and seldom got really plastered. Partly because it gave me no pleasure – the booze was more wont to make me drowsy – and partly because after the fourth whisky I usually started thinking about my third wife and then I got depressed because in my own clumsy fashion I did in fact love her, but I was afraid that she was drifting away from me. I belong to a generation which bandies the pronoun *I* as freely as our parents used that discreet word *one*, and I make a living out of analysing things; nevertheless, in that cold, war-torn spring of the century's last year I had seemed incapable of figuring out why, more and more often, I found myself feeling jealous and afraid of losing her. And the process of analysis is very important to me. Besides being my job, the ability to deduce, to discern connections is the crucial difference between us and animals. And if I am totally honest – and why should I not be – the capacity for reflection and analysis is also what separates the intellectuals from the rest, who simply take life as it comes rather than doing anything about it. In this, the final spring of my arrogance, I regarded myself as a man with a sincere desire to behave with dignity, but also with discernment in every stage of existence. This was indeed how I had always seen myself: as an individual in control of his life, both the professional and the private, despite the fact that both were, in truth, a shambles. I liked to think of myself as being smart but casual. The neatly pressed seams – the real and the imaginary – had to be there, though without being too obvious. Both sorts were, however, becoming more and more creased as time went on. The ability to fool oneself, to view oneself in the wrong light is, after all, only human. Too much self-awareness can lead to suicide. Another annoying side effect of drinking too much was, quite simply, the ease with which I succeeded in staining my clothes and making an unholy mess of my life. I had not wanted to get drunk, nor had I really wanted the Soviet Empire to collapse, and these two things were in a way connected.

Not to put too fine a point on it: I was lying fully clothed on a bed in a spanking-new, ultra-modern hotel in Bratislava, in Europe's youngest state, Slovakia, yearning for the cold war and the great Empire. I missed the dear old terminology: Politbureau, Central Committee, Satellite States, Iron Curtain, East-West, Rearmament, Middle-distance Rockets, Summit Meetings, Berlin Wall. Being one of the few capable of reading between the lines of *Pravda* and being invited onto television to do just that. I missed the hammer and sickle, the cobbles on Red Square in the days when the Kremlin was a power centre, and longed to see the snow on the frozen canals in the beautiful, ramshackle city once known as Leningrad. Back when life consisted of great existential questions and not, as now, when the three main topics of discussion in the media and among one's own acquaintances were early retirement, pension schemes and the smoking ban – this last debated so hotly that you felt you had been transported back to a time when all the talk was of the necessity for revolution and the imminent triumph of the working class. The world no longer made any sense, and no one now was interested in the knowledge I possessed. I was like a sculptor who had once been awarded first prize for my socialist ability to sculpt a splendid Lenin out of cold marble. The things I knew and could do were of no use today.

Only those small groups at the university who could be bothered to study the history of the Soviet Union were still keen to know who Malenkov was, or Berija, or Breshnev. Who nowadays wants to read up on Gosplan's abortive twenty-second Five Year Plan or is interested enough to pick my brains on the twenty-sixth Party Congress? Capitalism had won the battle. The triumphant progress of the free market was not conducive to Utopian scenarios or momentous decisions. And the fruits of victory were as bitter as a mouldy lemon on a dark November day in a bygone time in a Moscow which, with its Coca-Cola ads, Marlborough Men, an inane, babbling Yeltsin, *nouveau riche* mafiosi and small boys begging on the streets reminded me more of a Third World country. It could just as easily have been Brazil. Or Upper Volta. The only real difference were the nuclear weapons. Were it not for them it is unlikely that anyone would have taken much notice of Russia now. There was nothing special or ferocious about Moscow or the Russian bear. It was all just a big mess, one which really did not concern the rest of the world.

I was sick of this new, melted-down order and I was sick of myself. I lay on a big bed in a modern hotel in Slovakia's impoverished capital, knowing full well why I was feeling so bloody sorry for myself. Why, after dinner, I had stayed on in the bar to drink first cognac and later whisky. It was the meeting, two days earlier, with the former prime minister of the Czech Republic that had ruined the trip for me. My mood was not helped by the fact that I had toothache. One of my back teeth was giving me gyp. It acted as a constant reminder that this old bag of bones was very much the worse for wear. That I was, in every possible way, going downhill. Less hair, fewer brain cells, deteriorating teeth, shortness of breath on stairs, a waning libido. I had to admit, though, that it was the former Czech prime minister who had destroyed my last vestiges of good humour.

There I was, lying in that modern hotel with toothache, hearing in my head again and again the leader of our delegation's deliberately spiteful introduction of me. With a couple of well-chosen words he got his revenge for the Research Council grant I had snatched from under his nose twelve years earlier. In academia we never forget a slight.

In his atrocious English he had said:

'And now here is Mr Theodor Nikolaj Pedersen. One of our leading experts in and researchers into Soviet affairs. Particularly the Breshnev years.'

The former prime minister, with his beautifully cut hair and immaculate suit, had looked at me with his ice-blue fish eyes:

'What a lot of useless information you carry around in your head,' he said. Then he turned his X-ray gaze on young Lena, she of the long legs and the useful degree in 'Transitional problems in the phase between plan economy and the global market. A study in options.'

'Extremely helpful findings – for us too,' the arrogant bastard had said, holding both her hand and her eyes for just a little too long before releasing her fingers with a glance at the hidden and yet so obvious secrets of her Wonderbra which made the normally hard-nosed Lena blush. Power is a tremendous aphrodisiac and the Czech was outrageously well-preserved.

Fuck them all! Fuck the modern world! It sucks! As one of my numerous offspring would say. But I too had blushed, because he had hit me where it hurt. I had stood there trying to take comfort in the knowledge that I had had a fine academic career and no one could take that away from me. I had my history doctorate. My thesis had been described as a brilliant study of stagnation phenomena in the Breshnev era. It had been widely cited in international history journals and had earned me a guest lecture at America's Harvard University in 1981, the year before the old bugger died. Unfortunately, my thesis had arrived at the conclusion that the inherent strength of the Soviet system outweighed its structural weaknesses. Reform was possible. The Soviet Union would enter the next millenium fortified and reinforced. The bi-polar world dominated by the two big players, the USA and the USSR, was here to stay.

I got a couple of good years out of Gorbachev, but after that there were no more invitations from the major universities in the US and Europe. And I was no longer a regular guest in the blue television news studio, providing clear, concise answers to the presenter's carefully rehearsed questions. Because the whole flaming set-up had collapsed! I had actually got it wrong. And my fellow academics knew it. No journalist was likely to read every line of a doctoral thesis which came to the wrong conclusion, but my colleagues had memories like elephants, a fact of which I was reminded by the sound of their barely suppressed, gleeful sniggers when the former prime minister made his spiteful remark. They knew that I knew that at the time when I completed my highly acclaimed thesis and was able to put the letters Ph.D. after my name I was still far too young. Added to which, there had been no vacant professorships at the time and now it was too late. My knowledge was sadly outdated. I would never be able to boast the coveted title of Professor. For the rest of my days, until I started drawing my nice, fat pension I would have to make do with calling myself Lecturer in History. Trailing out every day to the south side of the city and the University of Copenhagen's concrete jungle, where the thinking was often as low-slung as the ceilings in the hideous classrooms. Here, Teddy, as I was known to everyone, high and low, went around feeling sorry for himself, without of course knowing that he was doing so. Here, Teddy made a half-hearted attempt to teach and do research, in order, at least once in a while, to publish a scholarly paper. Here, Teddy gave guidance to future generations, fitting them to take over the bastions of power. Here was Teddy, an academic relic, who, for some strange reason, society was still paying. And paying well.

I lay on the bed, fulminating, the alcohol in my blood causing my already well-developed talent for viewing my life and my career as an exercise in martyrdom to increase to the point where it gained the upper hand. *I* should have been leading this delegation. Instead I was merely a member, paying all my own expenses – although I was sure to find some loophole whereby the Institute would end up reimbursing most of my costs.

There were forty of us on this trip organised by the Danish Foreign Affairs Association. The majority were elderly tourists for whom this offered the opportunity of an organised cultural tour of Central Europe. Because these were not your ordinary charter tourists. No, no. They travelled in order to broaden their minds. Six of us would be speaking at various symposiums and conferences to politicians, journalists and civil servants; giving talks inspired by the tenth anniversary of the transformation of Eastern and Central Europe, but since NATO planes had bombed Yugoslavia a couple of days after we left Denmark our conversations often ended up revolving around the war which we were not supposed to call a war. At heart we were actually all agreed that NATO had taken the only logical step, but that it had simply come to late. Just to be contrary, though, I doggedly maintained that it was immoral not to send in ground troops. That this was a clear sign of just how pampered and egoistic we were in the West; we were more concerned about not getting killed ourselves than about not taking the lives of others. Our style of warfare was a logical consequence of our civilisation. The safety of the bomber pilots was more important than the sufferings of Kosovo Albanians. We could not cope with casualties within our own ranks. Our politicians could not stomach the thought of Western men being killed and they refused to countenance the media's pictures of such things. What we wanted was a cartoon war. A real-life version of *Star Wars*. But my heart really was not in this discussion. Milosevic was simply another villain in history's long line of villains. I ought to have studied Stalin instead, like my friend and colleague Lasse. As he so rightly said: pure evil and the endeavour to comprehend it never go out of date. Lasse too was only a lecturer, but with all the newly opened archives on the Stalin era he was in seventh heaven. He now had enough material to keep him busy for the rest of his natural. Not only was he a great guy, he was also a true scholar who loved his subject. I really envied him. He was still married to the same woman. He had children only with this one woman. They had a good life and try as I might I could not convince him that he was not happy. Like me he was on the wrong side of fifty, but with something as rare in our circles as a silver wedding celebration to look back on and his beloved archives to look forward to it was also hard to persuade him that, on the whole, life was turning out to be rather like a bad movie. Another thing that annoyed me was his refusal to face the fact that, deep down, modern man was in a hell of a mess.

We began our tour in Warsaw. The Polish capital lay cool and clear in the spring light. The city had changed a lot in ten years. Stalin had given the poor Poles a yellow wedding-cake skyscraper to remind them every day of who was in charge. Now, though, hemmed in as it was by modern skyscrapers in glass and concrete, Stalin's gift did not dominate the skyline in quite the same way. Warsaw was teeming with cars and mobile phones, advertisements and neon signs, nightclubs and beggars. It had it all. The reek of low-octane petrol was gone. The limp salami of communism had given way to imported Danish hams and French cheeses. The party's lies to the horse-trading of democracy. A normal country which was happy to be a member of NATO and hoped that Russia would eventually pull back to a point somewhere beyond the Ural Mountains, to that Asia to which it belonged, even though the Poles realised, of course, that it probably was not going to be that easy. We met all the right people, everybody said the right things, the tourists made notes and asked tentative questions and during the long, tedious meetings I thought of Lena's breasts, and neither the talk nor the breasts excited me in the slightest.

The leader of the delegation, Klaus Brandt by name, chivvied us about as if we were a bunch of schoolkids on a class outing. He told us off if we were late for the bus and looked aggrieved if we did not go into raptures over his meticulously planned schedule. He had a way of looking like a mother who is not angry, but disappointed, if we skived off a meeting at which some bureaucrat was to deliver yet another deadly dull speech. As Lasse and I in fact did one afternoon, opting instead to take a walk around the city, past the monument to the gallant Polish soldier, through the streets and down to the Old Town, rather than having to hear about the in-fighting within the Polish government. The ochre-coloured buildings of the Old Town – which was in fact brand new, having been totally rebuilt after the war, and ought therefore to have been called the New Old Town – were bathed in sunlight and looked quite charming. Lots of pedestrians were unbuttoning their coats and doing as all we northeners do in the early days of spring: lifting their faces to the blessed sun.

We ate a hearty lunch at a small restaurant. That meal would have cost a Polish academic a day's wages, but we consumed our roast wild boar with great relish and not a twinge of guilt; we drank Californian wine with the food and Czech Becherovka with the strong coffee, and I was smitten by Lasse's sincere delight that everything had gone so well ten years earlier. That for the first time in history the Poles had the chance to be the masters of their own destiny. All of a sudden in 1989 a cat-flap had been opened and the Poles had realised, along with everyone else east of the disarmed Iron Curtain, that they had to seize this opportunity. Lasse had never flirted with socialism or Marxism. He had studied his Stalin too well for that. It had immunised him against any belief in a Utopia. And a year on a student exchange to the University of Moscow had dispelled any illusions regarding the possible blessings of the so-called Really Existing Socialism. Not that I had cherished any such illusions either, but I had leaned more to the Left in the seventies. It had simply been easier, even though I too had done my obligatory year in Moscow, living and working in conditions that would have caused any Danish student to rebel. But in the long-ago seventies it had been less trouble just to go with the flow. Those years had not been so easy for Lasse. As a conservative he had found himself pushed out onto the sidelines and had for a spell been faced with half-empty classrooms when he was boycotted for having said in a newspaper interview that basically there was no difference between the aesthetics of communism and of Nazism. Such statements did not go unpunished twenty years ago. Now he was a highly respected lecturer and students were queueing up to have him as their guidance tutor. He was that rarity in the academic world: an honourable man with no hidden agenda. Unlike the rest of us, he did not need to keep getting his name on this and that scholarly article as a way of masking idleness and intellectual burnout. For many years I thought it was all an act, that he had chosen to play a part, but I had come to see that he was that most uncommon of creatures, a good person. I cherished him as my friend.

We ordered another round of Becherovka and coffee, savoured the cinnamon scented liqueur. There were not many people in the restaurant. The tourist season had not yet started, and the Poles could not afford it. Brisk little waitresses flitted about, sweeping crumbs off the blue-checked tablecloths. The place was redolent of the spirit of Central Europe, that and red cabbage. I leaned across the table and eyed my friend. Lasse wore his years well. He was tall, with a slight stoop, and as always he was wearing his drab grey tweed jacket. He had fine-drawn features and a full head of hair. Only now it was grey. He wore narrow-framed glasses and had a rather feminine mouth, wide and soft-looking. His teeth were very white. I lit a cigarette:

'Shouldn't you be giving that up,' he remarked placidly.

'Yes,' I said, blowing smoke in his face and making him waft the air impatiently with slender hands marked by the first liver spots.

'Why did you really come on this trip?' I asked.

'I had some time to spare. And I wanted to see how things had been going here. Take my nose out of the archives. Look at real life instead of the relics of the past. Broaden my empirical horizons. Anyway, Lisbeth's in New York.'

Lisbeth worked within the broad field of IT. It was a gold mine. She had originally trained as a teacher, but the world of computers had got to her, rather like one of the viruses she was so skilled in combatting. For people like Lisbeth the advent of the new millenium was a licence to print money. IT specialists are the crusaders of our day, travelling the world, ridding worried businesses of heathen foes, real or imaginary, known as computer viruses. She earned at least twice as much as Lasse. Not even that seemed to bother him, I thought peevishly.

'So – what have your archive-weary eyes observed?' I asked.

'Well, most of it's positive. It's very healthy to come to a country like Poland. People's hands don't shake here when they talk about democracy and freedom. They're just so happy to have these things. It's quite ridiculous, really. I mean we're all free. That goes without saying, right. But not here. Here they don't take it for granted.'

'Not yet maybe, but they will.'

'With any luck. That's what it's all about, after all,' he said and took a sip of his Becherovka.

'In any case, this is excellent, and I get to spend time with you,' he said.

'Daddy won't be pleased,' I said.

'Yeah, well. That's his problem. We're grown men, aren't we?'

'Well, you are at any rate.'

'What's that supposed to mean, Teddy?'

I drew on my cigarette, considered him for a moment.

'How many women have you actually slept with in your life?' I asked.

Lasse stared at me in amazement. When he was baffled a horizontal crease appeared between his eyes. He must have gone through life in a constant state of bafflement because the crease was now permanent, merely deepening when something took him by surprise.

'That's an odd question, I must say,' he replied. 'How many have you slept with?'

'Other than my three wives I haven't really kept score.'

'And you're proud of that? Sort of like a big-game hunter?'

'Not really. It's just that my dick has always been one step ahead of my brain,' I said, making him smile. Then he grew serious.

'Seven,' he said.

'You know the exact number?'

'I remember every one of them. You don't remember all of yours. What's better? One unique experience or loads of superficial ones?'

'Point taken, Lasse. I'm just amazed by you and Lisbeth. Your fidelity to one another. Over twenty-five years with the same woman. How the hell do you keep the spark alive? Can you really manage to keep your eyes off Lena's tits? Never imagine her lying starkers on your big hotel bed?'

'Numbers six and seven were after Lisbeth.'

Now it was my turn to be surprised.

'Does she know?'

'She knows about number seven. That lasted some months. Number six was just a one-off,' he said quietly and drank his coffee, as if we were simply discussing how many millions Stalin had left to starve to death.

'When was this?'

'Fifteen years ago.'

'And afterwards?'

He regarded me with his soft, brown eyes:

'We never spoke of it again. And I made a decision. It was either Lisbeth and our kids or the other woman, or women. And I've never regretted the choice I made,' he said.

'Sounds like a pretty simple choice to me.'

'Nobody says it was easy.'

'You make it sound as though it was an existential choice,' I said.

'Spare me the sarcasm. It was not an easy decision to make, but I've never looked back. Maybe my sex-drive just isn't that great.'

'I never noticed a blind thing.'

'Ah, well,' he said with that soft smile that made his Ph.D. students go weak at the knees with gratitude. 'I'm not as much of a talker as you. You could always smooth-talk your way to good grades, and into girls' beds. I don't have your gift of the gab.'

'I wonder if Majken knew,' I said, more to myself.

'I think it was her who told Lisbeth.'

'Bloody women, always sticking together.'

'It all turned out okay, Teddy,' was all he said.

'What about Lisbeth?'

'What do you mean?'

'Has she ever ...'

'Ever cheated on me? Is that what you're asking?'

He was getting a little rankled, I could tell. We were friends and we talked about all sorts of things, but here I seemed to be getting a little too personal.

'I don't know. I've never asked her. I have no reason to.'

I stubbed out my cigarette, lit another and, wise man that he was, he asked:

'I don't suppose all of this could have anything to do with the fact that yet another marriage is on the rocks?'

'I don't have anything going on the side,' I said.

'Well, you usually do, but I'm not going to get into that,' he said. 'There are two sides to every story, you know.'

The other side in this case being that of my present wife, Janne. She was an assistant lecturer at the Institute and I had fallen head over heels in love with her five years earlier, when she started as a Ph.D. student and I was growing tired of living alone. She had been married at the time, only in her early thirties; she left her husband and brought two small children into my life from that first marriage. It had not exactly been plain sailing. I felt I had had my share of small children. They took over the whole flat. They robbed me of my freedom, but if I wanted her I had to take her offspring too. And I was in love. Or at least: in love with the thought of being in love again. Of experiencing the grand passion. Although it was probably also a symptom of a midlife crisis. It's not easy when the magic five-oh is looming on the horizon. Part of me did still love her, of course, but there was no passion to speak of. Our days followed a routine pattern punctuated by fights and icy silences. So it had actually been good to get away on this trip, even though Janne had gone on about the kids and who was supposed to see to them? And how she always got stuck with all the household chores. She had her work too. I had expected her to complain. But I had not expected her to give in so quickly, saying only that she supposed I'd better go then. I immediately began to wonder whether she had met someone else. To be honest I couldn't have blamed her. Our marriage, if you could call it that, was stuck in a rut.

'Did you hear what I said, Teddy?' Lasse asked.

'I don't know whether it's going to last between Janne and me,' was all I said, and I could see that this did not surprise him. It was no secret between us that Janne and Lisbeth did not get on well. They were civil to one another, but no more than that. My previous wife, Majken, and Lisbeth were the same age and still saw a lot of one another. They were friends. My first wife and I had been teenage sweethearts, we married in order to get a flat. Five years and two children later it was over. Our divorce had been a relatively painless, amicable affair. These days we could run into one another, pass the time of day, without feeling any emotion, great or small. I think we both wonder what we saw in the other. The children had been a bond of sorts between us. Now they were grown up, married themselves, had provided us with grandchildren whom we saw separately. We very rarely met. Majken and I were married for almost twelve years, but the divorce was a nasty business. She had had one child from her first marriage and together we had three in rapid succession before it all fell apart. I cheated on her and she eventually found out. Both she and the children went ballistic and I don't think any of them has ever really forgiven me. We imagine that we live in an age when our hearts cannot be broken, but betrayal and broken promises hurt as much as they ever did. Our youngest was eighteen now, we could have a polite conversation, but I was still not very popular. What annoyed me most was that it bothered me and affected me more than I was prepared to admit. Majken had remarried. She had had another child, late on. Her new husband already had two of his own. Just as well Majken was a mathematician. Because it took a mathematician's brain and methodical mindset as well as a hefty diary to keep track of all the birthdays, the Christmas and New Year holidays, when you had to allow not only for your own offspring but also for all the various step-children. We belonged to a generation which had not gone through life quietly and unremarked. To be honest I don't think we had ever thought about anybody but ourselves.

'Do you even want it to last?' Lasse asked.

'Of course I do,' I said. 'But let's talk about something sensible, like Poland or NATO...'

He laughed.

'You started it. Lunch is on me, seeing as you're paying all that child maintenance.'

'Thank heavens my own two are over eighteen now,' I mumbled morosely and we both laughed again, possibly as a way of covering up a growing awkwardness, and I felt better.

We strolled along the narrow streets like two gentlemen, coats open and arms swinging. All we needed was a couple of top hats and somebody to tip them at and we could have been in a Hollywood musical. Horses' hooves clip-clopped over the cobbles, but as yet there were few passengers behind the drivers in the carriages they drew. Down by the old Town Hall, where a hot-dog stall emblazoned with the evocative name 'Dania' struck a strangely tasteless note, Lasse suddenly stopped short and put a hand on my arm.

'Don't look now. Remember the old days in Moscow ...'

I knew what he was getting at. I bent down, pretended to be tying my shoelaces. I glanced back. There were about a dozen people behind me.

'There's a woman, d'you see her?' Lasse said. 'Blue coat, chestnut-brown hair, sensible shoes. Good-looking woman in her early sixties. Maybe a bit younger. Well-preserved, but still ...'

I scanned the street, then I spotted her. She stopped short, made a big show of looking in the window of a sports shop, then she glanced towards us, turned on her heel and strode off briskly down a side street.

I straightened up.

'What about her?'

'Old habits die hard when I'm in this part of the world, even if the country is a member of NATO and about to join the EU. I can't help looking over my shoulder. You remember how sometimes in Moscow you could simply sense that you were being followed?'

I nodded. I remembered. We had not spent all our time with our noses buried in dusty books in the endless reading rooms in the yellow palace of the Lenin Library. We had also *met* people. We had visited the homes of the hospitable Russians and we knew that they knew that an eye was kept on dangerous foreigners who were liable to spread noxious ideas about democracy and freedom.

'What about her?' I said again.

Lasse looked after her, but she was long gone. Then, as he took my arm and led me away, he said:

'She was in the back row at the Institute of Economics when I was speaking there yesterday. I thought about it when I saw her this morning, sitting in the front row at the Institute of History, when you were giving that talk on stagnation phenomena ...'

'Oh that – I had them snoring in the aisles during that one.'

'Don't be so hard on yourself. You're a good speaker and the history students have need of your insight.'

'Okay – and ...?' I said, as we walked on in the now somewhat chillier late-afternoon sun. It was still only March. Spring was not quite here yet.

'She was in the hotel lobby, and now here. It's too much of a coincidence.'

'You're seeing things,' I said. 'The Cold War ended a long time ago. And we won. The Poles won.'

'You're probably right,' he said. 'She's probably just a tourist. There aren't that many sights to see here. I just think it was a bit odd. There's something professional about it. You get the feeling that she's been trailing us for a while and has finally decided to let us know about it. The way the KGB used to do, in the old days.'

'Those days are over,' I said.

But she showed up again in Prague. During the symposium at Charles University, when we were all lined up on the platform, boring the pants off each other and the audience in the large auditorium. I sat there half-asleep while Lena held forth and Klaus Brandt, the leader of the delegation, got himself tangled up in long-winded expositions. Again she was seated in one of the back rows, high up. Lasse and I spotted her at almost the same moment. She was wearing a plain blue dress with a simple white necklace. She appeared to be listening intently. Made notes and looked for all the world like a refined middle-aged lady taking some extramural course: her husband is gone, the children have flown the nest, now she can devote herself to learning and culture. At the interval I hurried down to confront her, but she had vanished. As mysteriously as she had appeared – I had not seen her arrive and I did not see her leave.

Afterwards there was a reception at the Ministry of Foreign Affairs and the former prime minister made his remark and my evening was ruined. I had too much to drink in the bar, but did eventually go up to my room. I called home – no answer – and fell asleep with a sour taste in my mouth that no toothpaste could dispel.

The next morning Klaus hustled us along like a bunch of little kids and I could positively see his blood pressure rising when I deliberately did not turn up until the last minute, then took my time finishing my cigarette before climbing into the bus that was to take us to Bratislava. Thus prompting the other smokers to get back off. Anarchy threatened, and at the sight of our leader's puce face I climbed aboard feeling slightly more cheerful. Lasse had of course observed the whole performance.

'How childish,' he said as I sat down beside him.

But the Czech politician's snide comment still rankled. At any rate I was too sunk in gloom to enjoy the sight of the budding Bohemian countryside, dotted with sunken haystacks. The landscape and the little farms reminded me of Denmark in the fifties. It had an old-fashioned air about it. We had to sit in a queue at the Slovakian border and Klaus got my back up even further by archly calling out to Lena:

'Well, Lena – we're about to leave the shelter of NATO protection behind us. I hope you're not feeling too nervous.'

'Who's being childish now,' I muttered to Lasse.

Things were bound to go wrong. And so they did, after another few days of tedious meetings. It was late in the evening. I had had too much wine with dinner and too many drinks afterwards. On top of everything else my teeth had started hurting, or rather – according to my dentist – my gums. They're going to rot away if you're not careful, the heartless money-grubber had declared. I got into an argument with Klaus. I maintained that it would have been better if Gorbachev had been allowed to reform socialism a little at a time, instead of having the system suddenly collapse like that. Not that I actually believe this. I am glad that the rotten Soviet system came tumbling down like the vile, absurd house of cards that it was, but I knew exactly which buttons to push to get Klaus going. So we sat there yelling at one another like a couple of idiotic teenagers while the more sensible members of the delegation took themselves off to bed and eventually Klaus stomped off in high dudgeon leaving me alone, like the stupid fool that I was.

| 19 |

So there I was, caught in the straitjacket of toothache, with my earlier inebriation reduced now to a raging hangover, when there came a knock at the door. It was long past midnight. I got up off the bed, peered through the little spy-hole. Outside was that woman. My first thought was to just leave her there, but then I opened the door. She stared at me. I stared back at her. For a moment I thought I was seeing things. She looked like my older sister. They had the same ears and nose and the same dark green eyes. The same features one saw in the few pictures of our father.

'Yes,' I snapped.

She gave a faint smile, as if she were shy, then she put out her hand and said in slow, heavily accented, but perfectly lucid Danish:

'Good evening, Teddy. My name is Maria Bujic. I plucked up the courage to come here. I almost didn't dare to, but I did so want to meet my brother.'

| 20 |

2

IT TOOK ME A MOMENT to grasp what she had said. I was still a bit woozy. Normally the only people likely to come knocking in the middle of the night in Central Europe are hookers, but she did not look like a hooker. She bore an astonishing resemblance to my older sister Irma. She was possibly a couple of years younger. It was the mouth mainly, and that piercing green gaze, with which Irma had a way of transfixing her students. I stepped aside and invited her in. Even at this late hour she looked fresh and almost youthful, her skin clear and with the usual age lines, neither overly pronounced nor invisible. Which was just as it should be. One should be able to tell by looking at a person that they have lived. The short hair curling and waving softly around her head looked almost black. Did she dye it, I wondered. She wore a smart skirt and a shirt-blouse, with a small string of pearls at her throat. She was carrying a good-sized briefcase in soft calfskin. She could almost have been a successful modern businesswoman, the sort you see on any morning flight to Århus, but only almost. Because there was an emptiness in her eyes, a look of coldness or pain which at first glance was hard to fathom. I did my footman act, waved her into the spacious hotel room. The bed was unmade, but I shifted some newspapers and offered her an armchair.

She shook her head. We stood facing one another. Both uncomfortable with the situation.

'What the hell is all this?' I asked, with anger in my voice.

She looked me in the eye.

'Could we possibly speak Russian or English?' she said in Russian, fluently and with hardly any accent as far as I could tell. My own Russian is excellent, although I read it better than I speak it.

| 21 |

'Fine by me,' I said in English.

But that too she could speak without any difficulty.

'Who are you?' I asked.

'May I sit down?'

I motioned again to one of the armchairs and she took a seat, perching on the edge of the chair with the briefcase in her lap. She looked as if she was attending a job interview.

'First I must tell you how sorry I am about the death of your, our, father,' she said.

'Now hang on a minute!' I said. 'What are you talking about? My father died almost fifty years ago. I never really knew him. He left us when I was very young. A hundred years ago, it seems like. In another time.'

With neat, efficient movements she opened her bag, produced a large manila envelope, removed a black-and-white photograph from it and handed it to me. In the picture was a young man; he was smiling the smile which Irma and Fritz shared with him. His hair was black and he was smooth-shaven, he had a little, triangular chin and a fine, high brow showing beneath his German army cap. The SS runes were clearly visible on the cap and on the old-fashioned, black uniform jacket. I'm no expert on SS insignia, but going by his badges I guessed the man in the picture to be a *Sturmbannführer*. My natural father, a major in the Waffen-SS. But that couldn't be right. The face was most definitely that of my father, whom I could not remember, but of whom I had seen pictures. The SS uniform knocked me off balance momentarily. I broke into a sweat. The woman was eyeing me intently, she handed me another picture.

This one was in colour. It showed the same man. Some years older now. His hair a grizzled salt-and-pepper, but still thick. He had his arm around a rather plump little woman wearing a summer frock in a large floral print. They were standing in front of a yellow-painted house. Vines were visible in the background. A patch of blue sky. An array of brightly-coloured flowers in pots and vases. Leaning against the man was a young woman, she had on a simple yellow dress, the skirt of which had been lifted slightly by the breeze, revealing something of her bare, brown legs. It was a younger version of the woman sitting across from me in this hotel in Bratislava. She had been an exceptionally beautiful young woman. It was a nice summery, idyllic picture. I gave the photo back to her without a word and, just as wordlessly, she handed me yet another.

This one too was in colour. It was the same man, but on his deathbed this time. His hair was sparse and white, his features very pronounced and the skin so thin that one felt one could see right through it to the bones of the skull underneath. He was dressed in a white shirt. His eyes were closed. His hands folded on the emaciated chest. Death had taken the big, strapping man whom the woman opposite me claimed was father to us both.

I did not know what to think. Every family has its myths and legends, its secrets and skeletons in the closet and my own had plenty. My family's history was a tragic one, but it had also been a success story. My parents' bakery went bust because people began to talk: 'Seems the baker was on the wrong side during the war. Decent people had better find somewhere else to buy their bread.' But as a child I was never told exactly what it was he had done. It seemed to have something to do with him having gone to work in Germany. But a hundred thousand others had done the same. It was either that or lose their unemployment benefit. I knew his name was in the Bovrup Files. He had been a member of the DNSAP – the Danish Nazi Party. But so were forty thousand others. And it was not as if it was against the law, although just after the war ended it did mean you were a marked man. As a small boy I had pondered this a lot. I was the baby of the family, a bit of an afterthought, hopelessly spoiled by my mother and step-father and by Irma and Fritz. I was also too young to really understand the marital breakdown which followed in the wake of the social disgrace. I knew that it had been an extremely traumatic experience for my sister and brother. They did not like my mother's new husband, but I thought of him as my father and continued to do so right up until his death five years ago. We three children had all done well for ourselves, two of us within the academic world. I was a historian, as was my sister, but she was also a professor of comparative literature, specialising, not surprisingly, in feminist writing. Fritz had originally been a baker, of course, but had gone on to set up his own bread factory, mass-producing all sorts of bread and rolls, which were sold in the supermarkets as home-baked, even though they all came off a conveyer belt. But he had soon discovered that image is everything. And that a good advertising campaign can do wonders for sales. He instinctively understood, long before the media researchers got round to formulating the concept, that we do not buy goods but experiences, stories. He was also quick to spot the organic trend and latch on to that. He was the wealthy member of the family. We came of age just as consumerism was really taking off and we were doing very nicely, thank you. A pretty ordinary story, really, when told in a few words.

I must have become lost in my own thoughts, she seemed to be repeating a question:

'Could I have a glass of water?' she said.

'Oh, I'm sorry,' I said, as if I were a bad host neglecting an invited guest. And not some strange woman who had knocked on my door in the middle of the night in Bratislava. 'Can I offer you something else, perhaps? From the minibar? A glass of wine?'

'Wine would be lovely,' she said.

There was a small bottle of red wine of dubious quality in the minibar. It was also very cold. Nonetheless, I poured two glasses for us and set them down on the ugly, little modern tile-topped table between the two armchairs. I was no longer feeling the effects of the alcohol I had consumed earlier in the evening. I was tired, but my head was clear. I think that already at that point I had subconsciously accepted her story as being true, even though my analytical super-ego still regarded the whole thing as absolute rubbish, a pack of lies.

I offered my cigarettes to her and she took one.

'I've actually given these up,' she said.

'Haven't we all?' I said, giving her a light before firing up my own. I picked up my glass of red wine, raised it wryly to her.

'What should we drink to, madame?' I said. 'To death?'

She winced, but her eyes remained empty of expression. They were remarkable eyes: green as a sunlit lake. But it was the glacial green of a mountain tarn.

'I was actually very fond of him,' she said.

'Sorry, that was too flippant,' I said. 'To life, then? Or to the past?'

'To the past, may our lives not be ruined by it.'

So we drank to that and gently set down our glasses.

'Might I hear the whole story from the very beginning,' I asked in my best university lecturer tones.

So she told me. Presenting the facts as dispassionately as if she were delivering a lecture herself, or making a statement to the police. Even so, it took quite a while. At my age one is past the stage of breaking in with a 'Really!' or 'You don't say!' every time something surprises you, and her story did surprise me. It did not really upset me, though. As I say: I never knew my real father. If she had been talking about my step-father, Poul, it might have been a different matter, and the story might have caused me greater mental and emotional upheaval than it did at that moment.

'My father came to Croatia at the beginning of September 1943. He was just a sergeant with the Danish Regiment. His company made camp at the village of Sisak, fifty kilometres outside of Zagreb. My mother told me that the Danish soldiers' nerves were in a bad state, they were thin and exhausted. They drank too much of the excellent Croatian brandy. As if the alcohol could chase away their memories. The Danish Regiment had been formed in part by soldiers from the Danish Legion, which had been disbanded by

| 25 |

the SS along with the other foreign legions. The men were angry about this, but that was not what drove them to drink. No, it was the memory of the bitter fighting in Russia, at a place they called the Demjan Cauldron. It was the memory of returning home on leave to a Denmark where they were not welcomed as heroes, but spat on and denounced as traitors. My mother was twenty and worked as a secretary at the local town hall. Croatia was a free country, though possibly fascist. Or so it was said after the war. The country was not occupied, but cooperated with Germany in order to remain a sovereign nation. We called our army the Ustashi. They fought against Tito's partisans, who were all over the place. The Danish Regiment was actually only meant to be in Croatia for a few months for training, along with the other units from the Nordland Division, but they were immediately dispatched to fight the partisans. It was a terrible conflict, with no mercy shown on either side. Partisans hung from every lamp post. German soldiers who were taken prisoner were killed and castrated. None of this did my father's bad nerves any good. Only one thing kept the soldiers going: there was plenty of food in Croatia – the Good Lord has blessed us in this respect. They loved the Croatian fruit and vegetables. And they loved the dancing in the square at Sisak on a Saturday night. This was sometimes possible, despite the war. The soldiers danced with the local girls on the warm summer evenings and that was how my father met my mother. At a dance in the soft darkness of a Croatian night in the middle of the war. One tends to forget that pleasures are most intense when the horrors of war are at their height. When were Sarajevo's women loveliest? When was their make-up most immaculate? When were their dresses at their most elegant? During the worst bombing raids. Mankind's gift for survival never ceases to astonish me. It's such a banal story really. At a time when death and rape were as certain as the fact that the sun rises in the east, they fell in love. Throughout their lives they would tell us children how blissfully in love they had been, despite the sounds of gunfire in the night. Despite the indescribable horrors they experienced and the blood there must have been on my father's hands. I have a picture of them. They look so happy. My father was a fine figure of a man. My mother was a beautiful young woman. The Danish Regiment was transferred to the Russian front in the November. By then I was the tiny, growing fruit of their love.'

I sat there, rapt and expectant. I had a number of questions I would have liked to ask, but I was so intrigued by her account, although it was, in fact, a fairly common wartime story. There must be thousands with similar tales to tell. It had all happened so many years ago that it hardly seemed to have anything to do with me personally. She asked for another cigarette, took a gulp of her wine and continued in the same soft voice. She had a habit of tugging her right ear lobe, usually when she came to a part of her story which seemed to affect her. Otherwise she appeared to have full control over her emotions and the narrative devices she was employing.

'The outcome of the war was, of course, a foregone conclusion. Germany lost. Tito won, and Croatia was incorporated into Socialist Yugoslavia. Some said that Tito the Croat had betrayed his own country. But maybe it was the best thing that could have happened. For a few years at least. Although it was no fun being on the losing side. My mother had not been directly associated with the Ustashi, but still. She had been a secretary for the system and she had gone out with a soldier in the Waffen SS. She was interned for a while, but even though brutality is an inescapable part of life in the Balkans, she was not abused. Maybe the guards' hearts were softened by the tiny infant at her breast. Me. What do I know? Maybe she never told me the truth. She had received no word of my father. He had written several letters to her from the Eastern front. Tender letters, but also missives from which even the censors could not delete the hopelessness and the knowledge that the war was lost. My mother accepted the protection, as it was called, of one of the new socialist officials who had taken over. She got a new job. He got her body. For a couple of years it was a good deal. I do not remember him. He may have been purged, while my mother was cleared. Or forgotten. The new job was very much like the old one, only the masters were different. I have no memory of that time, I was too young, but after 1949, when Tito broke with Moscow, it was possible to be both a socialist and a nationalist. Croats, Serbs and Bosnians had to form a concerted front against Stalin's plans for invasion. In the Balkans the past is never forgotten. History lives on in every single person. But there are times when they are very good at suppressing it. And you might think that it does not matter, but it always matters. In 1953, the year of Stalin's death, my father turned up. Suddenly one day there he was. We were living on the outskirts of Zagreb, down near the river. It was a beautiful sunny day and the air smelled of summer as it only can in Croatia. A tall, powerfully built man with a broad grin. My mother looked as if she had seen a ghost. I can't have been more than seven. But I remember it as if it was yesterday. He picked me up and hugged me. My lovely little daughter, he said in German. My mother told me later that that was what he had said. I felt so incredibly comfortable with him. Not for one second did I doubt that he was my father. Being fatherless was a fate I had shared with millions of children in the post-war world. But I think every one of those children dreamt that one day *their* father would come back from the war and take them in his arms. My mother burst into tears. She came over to us, he put me down gently and wrapped his arms around us both. That is the first time in my childhood that I can remember being absolutely happy. My father had come home.'

She stopped, drank the last of her wine, and I squeezed a few more drops out of the little bottle for her.

'And?' I said.

'I'm sorry?'

'And then what happened?'

'After that came everyday life, the sort of life that's so hard to describe simply because it's so ordinary.'

| 28 |

I stared at her. Here was this half-sister, suddenly showing up out of the past; to some extent we were related by blood. That in itself was a strange thought, but I was having trouble digesting her story. Possibly because I found it hard to comprehend. Or possibly because it simply had not sunk in. I said:

'Tell me a little bit about that everyday life. What did he do for a living, for example?'

'Baked bread, naturally. He was a baker, after all, and a baker he remained until he retired. He was a good baker.'

'How come he was allowed to stay in the country? I mean, he was a former Nazi. And an SS soldier. At Nuremberg men like him were condemned as war criminals, for God's sake.'

'There were several reasons,' she said. 'In Croatia, even under Tito, not everyone regarded the Germans and the Ustashi as fascists. To many people they were patriots, fighting for a free Croatia. For the Croatian nation and its culture. It was not as simple as the propaganda made it out to be. Some were punished, of course. Others took over the reins of government, but in some part of them they were always Croatians first and socialists second. Look at our President, Franco Tudjman. Wasn't he a socialist once? And didn't he shape the new, independent Croatia fifty years later? Who can say what he was thinking in his heart of hearts, all those years when he served socialism and Yugoslavia. And anyway, my father had taken a different name. Later he became a Croatian, or rather, Yugoslavian, citizen. Learned our language. Became one of us.'

'But how was he able to do all that?'

She considered me for some moments with those strangely blank, glacial eyes before replying:

'He never said. His old comrades fixed things for him, that was all he would tell us. After the war they helped one another. The losers helped each other to make new lives for themselves.'

The old SS network, about which so much had been written, I thought. That mysterious brotherhood of old Nazis and war veterans which had discreetly organised visas, jobs, houses. I had never really believed in it. It sounded a bit too far-fetched: the idea that the losing side should be in a position to pull strings in the ruins of post-war Europe. And once the economic boom of the sixties came along no one gave any more thought to a bygone war, apart perhaps from some old freedom-fighters or nostalgic SS veterans.

But you never could tell.

Maybe that was how my real father had come by his first bakery in Denmark. I had sometimes wondered how he and my mother had found the wherewithal to set it up. My mother said they had borrowed the money. That was why they had gone bankrupt so quickly. They had had nothing to fall back on. But strictly speaking it could also have been funded by profiteering money. There were a lot of shady goings-on just after the war ended. To put it mildly. And there was a good deal of unaccounted-for cash in circulation. Those five years were not the most illustrious in Danish history. Nor, indeed, was the period that followed them.

'Do I have any other brothers or sisters?' I asked.

'You did have,' she said, and her eyes darkened slightly. 'My father and mother had twins. Two boys. They were born in 1956. They died in 1995. Within two days of one another, at Krajna when the Croatian army drove out the Serbs.'

'I'm sorry to hear that,' I said and meant it.

'The Balkans is a sorry place,' was all she said, and we fell silent once more. All was quiet in the hotel. We heard the drone of a solitary car on the street outside and a plaintive cry that ceased as abruptly as it had begun. As if some desperate individual had given momentary vent to their pain by screaming out loud.

'Do you have children?' I said.

'I have two girls, I'm glad to say. They were spared having to fight. I have two grandchildren. Both strong and healthy. Compared to a lot of others I got off lightly. One of my sons-in-law will have to spend the rest of his days with only one leg, but that you can live with. The Serbian mine left his manhood unscathed. One of my daughters is expecting another baby. So the past ten years of war in my country have not been too hard on me. But it is a war that is still going on. In Kosovo now. And now your country, my father's native land is at war with Yugoslavia.'

'With Serbia,' I corrected her. 'I thought you were a Croat.'

A flicker of uncertainty passed over her face, as if she had somehow given herself away.

'I grew up in Yugoslavia,' she said eventually. 'I'm glad we're independent, but I worked for many years in Belgrade and I have a lot of Serbian friends and colleagues. I find it hard to get used to the idea that we are now enemies.'

'What did you do there?'

'Moved papers around in one of the ministries,' she said. 'Now I move papers around in another ministry.'

'Why are you telling me all this,' I asked, and was surprised by the vehemence with which it came out.

'It was my father's last wish. Most of this story is new to me too. My parents' wartime romance has always been a part of the nice myth of my family, but I did not hear the rest of the story, about the other family in Denmark, until very recently. It was our father's last wish. And I believe that one ought to honour a dying man's last wish.'

'One doesn't have to know every damn thing,' I said. 'Why the hell does everybody have to go confessing their sins. What you don't know can't hurt you.'

'I understand this must be hard for you.'

'I don't think you understand a blind thing,' I said. I, for one, did not understand any of it. What, I wondered, was I supposed to tell Fritz and Irma, never mind my elderly mother, who was probably too senile to grasp the fact that her runaway husband had not died in a bar in Hamburg in 1952, but had led a productive and seemingly happy and respectable, if bigamous, life in Croatia. That this whole story, in all its glaring banality, came down to love.

That my father had fallen in love with and had an affair with a young woman in a village in Yugoslavia. And that his love had been so strong that it had conquered all. That for decades he had lived happily with the same woman. On some level every modern individual aspired to that same commonplace, conventional ideal of happiness. Or hoped, at least, to find their perfect mate. They never did, though. I spoke from some experience, with three marriages under my belt. In the dead of night, when we are alone, we all dream of unconditional love. We don't ever expect to achieve it, but we dream about it. This is what we are seeking every time we look into another person's eyes. In the cold light of day we recognise the futility of the dream; when night comes we dream again.

I was very tired by now, and both my tooth and my head were aching. I could not take any more. I wanted to sleep. I wanted to go to Budapest the next day, ponder this story and try to figure out what it meant. Because that was my intellectual forte, I told myself: I was bloody brilliant when it came to thinking things through. I could analyse anything, from emotions to international politics, but just at that moment, in the middle of the night in that hotel room, my head was in a whirl.

'I'd like you to leave now,' I said.

She looked a little hurt, but her eyes still had that blank look to them which made it hard for me to gauge her actual frame of mind.

'I would like to show you some more pictures. And some letters which my father wrote, but never sent. He felt very bad about leaving his family in Denmark. Especially his little boy.'

'My father's name was Poul. He was a schoolteacher and he loved me as if I was his own son. He adopted me. To me, this ghost from the past that you've called up is not my father. He may have endowed me with a glob of genes, but feelings don't come with the sperm. They are born out of the life we share with others. And now I'd like to be alone, please.'

I was actually quite surprised to be able to express myself so clearly, bearing in mind the hour and the state I was in, but she was not impressed.

'He wanted your forgiveness,' she said.

'What about my brother and sister?'

Without a word she removed another photograph from the manila envelope. It was an ordinary, amateur colour snap, but the image was sharp enough. It showed a group of people at a funeral. They were standing with their heads bared in bright spring sunshine, watching as a simple pine coffin was lowered into the darkness of the grave. This picture shocked me more than everything she had told me up to this point. Because in this group of people, which looked, in all other respects, exactly like any funeral party in the Balkans, I saw my sister Irma. She stood with her head bowed alongside four elderly men. The photo had been taken from so far away that I could not make out the facial features of the mourners, but I was sure, beyond a shadow of a doubt, that it was Irma. It was something to do with the way she held herself, the rather boyish haircut and the pointed nose.

'He thought about them too, but you were the one he thought about most. Maybe because you were the youngest. He asked to be forgiven.'

'What about my big brother?'

'I think it was him who took the picture.'

'When was it taken?'

'On February 17th of this year,' she said. 'He did not live to see one last spring.'

'Why didn't anyone tell me?'

'It didn't involve you in the same way. You're not a child of the war,' she said.

'So why drag me into it now?' I retorted angrily.

'Is it so strange that a man anxious to make his peace with God should also wish to make his peace with the people in his life. To receive the forgiveness which we Christians are taught to grant?'

'I can't answer that right now,' I said. Although it would have been easy to do so, and I could probably have got rid of her without any more debate. But I was not going to give her, my siblings or my real father that satisfaction. They could stew in their own treacherous juice as far as I was concerned.

'Would you please go,' I said, far too imploringly, instead of simply kicking her out.

'Of course,' she said politely, getting to her feet. She offered me her hand and I took it. My own felt cold and clammy, hers was dry and cool.

'Might I see you tomorrow?' she asked, letting go of my hand.

'We're off to Budapest tomorrow,' I said. 'Give me a call. I need some time to think about what you've told me.'

'Fine. I'm sorry,' she murmured.

'Yeah,' was all I said.

She slipped the last photograph carefully back into the manila envelope and placed the envelope on the tiled table.

'Have a look at that once you've had time to digest it. You'll find my address and telephone number in Zagreb there, too, along with our father's letters. His thoughts about you and about the past.'

She crossed to the door. She looked disappointed by my rebuff, and by the fact that I had not given her my phone numbers, addresses and so on. That all I wanted was to get rid of her. But she did not fool me. She had followed me more than halfway across Central Europe. If she wanted more of me then there was nothing to stop her following me to Budapest. I did not know whether I wanted to speak to her again. All I knew was that I did not want to speak to her any more that night. In the doorway she turned, as if about to say something else, but I shut the door on her, turned the second lock and put on the chain, loudly and clearly. *Now* did she get the message?

I went into the bathroom and sat down on the toilet. The pain hit me utterly without warning, like a knife being driven into the small of my back, just above the right hip, and twisted around. I had never known pain like it. I had no idea that anything could hurt so much. A white-hot tongue of flame shot across my back and up to the nape of my neck. I thought I was going to die; not quietly and peacefully in my bed, but locked in a loo in Bratislava with some new knowledge about my past which I could happily have done without.

3

THE NIGHT WAS HORRENDOUS, the morning worse. Can there be anything more ridiculous than lumbago? Because that was what I was suffering from. A perfectly common, perfectly awful case of lumbago. But one which was to have serious consequences. I have little memory of how I got to bed. The pain encircled my lumbar region like a barbed-wire belt, but that was not the worst of it. It was the helplessness, the fact that the most ordinary, everyday actions were now almost impossible. I managed to brush my teeth, got myself undressed and onto the bed and lay there, flat on my back, staring at the ceiling and feeling downright sorry for myself. I ought to have been thinking about the story I had just been told, but I had no thought for anything but the pain. Anyone who says you can't hurt in two places at once is talking through a hole in their head. My teeth ached, and so did my back.

I woke as usual around six thirty and thought for a moment that it had all been a bad dream, both the story and the pain, but my relief was short-lived. I went to swing my legs out of bed, but could not. I lay there under the sheet and bedspread in nothing but my underpants, unable to get up. I could hear the sound of the morning traffic in the street below, the singular racket produced by the mix of modern cars and noxious old Central European rust buckets driving along the broad thoroughfare which ran from the Hotel Forum to the Presidential Palace. There were other people in the world. Lucky people. Free to move around. Driving to work without giving any thought to how privileged they were. While the great university lecturer with so many academic works and lovely women behind him was helpless as a baby. He could not get out of bed. He could only lie staring at the ceiling, wracked by the pain in his back, wracked by self-pity, and thinking of himself in the third person, like an actor in a second-rate movie.

How I did it I'll never know. I remember nothing but the pain, but I grabbed hold of the bed-head and hauled myself into a sitting position, while three or four torturers who had learnt their trade from the grand masters of the Gestapo and the KGB drove ice-picks into my back. This manoeuvre took some minutes, then I sat for a few minutes more with my feet on the floor, bringing my breathing under control. I felt utterly ridiculous. I considered calling Lasse, but that would have been even more ridiculous. No grown man wants anyone to see that he cannot get out of bed unaided, or take a shower and dress himself before duly proceeding to pack his case and catch the bus to Budapest. It really was too stupid for words.

I sat for a moment, bracing myself for the pain. And it was every bit as bad as I had feared when, by using both hands, I first managed to hold myself upright on the edge of the bed and then, as I started to keel over like a drunk after a long night's journey into oblivion, clutched at the bed-head and hauled myself onto my feet – my torturers laying into me all the while with sadistic glee. There I stood. In my underpants, with a roll of flab around my middle, almost weeping with rage and mortification. But it helped to stand up, and it helped to have the hot water from the shower massaging the small of my back. The indignity of my handicap hit me again when I tried to get dressed. The socks were the worst. Who would have thought it could be such a long stretch to one's feet, even when seated. By some miracle I succeeded in getting into my uniform: trousers, shirt, tie, grey merle jacket. Mr Nice, Old-Fashioned Tweed. The lecturer in Russian history ready for the day. For some time he stood there, with pains shooting up his back like fiery dragons. And he could not help laughing at himself and the whole situation. Now he needed cheering up.

Slowly I bent down to reach the telephone and keyed in my own home number. I pictured the phone at home in our beautiful, tasteful, well-proportioned five-room flat in Østerbro, in Good Queen Margrethe's lovely Copenhagen. The morning rush would be in full swing, a pandemonium which I usually hated, but which at this particular moment I missed with a fervour that surprised me, in spite of my pain. Janne would be in the midst of the great morning ritual of getting the kids to eat their breakfast, put on their clothes, brush their teeth and get out the door in a reasonably orderly fashion. I always left her to see to things in the morning. While I sat in the kitchen in my dressing gown, with the paper, coffee and a ciggie, and endeavoured to ignore the inexplicable uproar that small children are capable of creating in the morning. How is it possible to fight and eat cornflakes at the same time? Janne was as grumpy – or quiet, as she put it – in the mornings as I was, but she was also a mum, so she bustled about, dishing up breakfast, making packed lunches, chivvying and chiding, and almost every morning I found myself wondering why the hell they didn't just get up earlier. I had actually come right out and said this once to Janne, a couple of months after she moved in. She had not spoken to me for a couple of days. 'Why don't you just lend a hand instead?' she had hissed. 'That wasn't part of the deal,' I replied. 'I've done my bit with my own kids.' Which wasn't exactly the smartest thing to say, either.

Amazingly, every morning the operation was successfully accomplished and the little darlings were escorted to school along with all the other poor beggars. Sometimes Janne returned home after seeing them through the perils of the morning rush-hour. Then she would sit down and have her coffee, read her section of the newspaper and we would have a nice, quiet breakfast together. Being a lecturer I earned more than Janne who was only an assistant lecturer. She, on the other hand, had more duties to attend to at the university. My lectures to the few classes I now took did not make for too heavy a workload. So she was often the first one to leave, off to join the daily migration that is the lot of your normal wage slave, while I poured myself another cup of coffee before repairing to my desk to write or do some research. Although if the truth be told, lately I was more liable to end up gazing at the big poplar tree outside the window. It is amazing how long one can spend watching a little squirrel scurrying about in some bare branches, thereby managing to put off working on a project in which you really have no faith. The writing had to be done, though, if my petty, jealous colleagues on the Research Council were to be persuaded to allocate funding to me rather than to their cronies.

But with my back on the rack I missed my mornings in Denmark. How nice it would have been to feel a tender hand on the small of my back, to be kissed and caressed. How nice it would have been to be surrounded by the morning chaos of normality instead of being here alone in a modern hotel room in a city which most Danes could not have found on a map. I let the telephone ring until I heard my own voice on the answering machine, then hung up without leaving a message. Why weren't they home? Where the hell was my family? My indignation may have been irrational, but I felt they ought to be there when I needed them. As if I was ever there when they needed me. And anyway, what could they do? Give me a few words of comfort. Tell me they loved me. Isn't that what we are all looking for in our dealings with other people? To find love. To *be* loved.

I ran an eye around the modern hotel room. I was in Bratislava. I could have been anywhere in the world, wherever today's hotel chains have moved in with their professional smiles and taste-less, efficient interior designers and decorators. Fresh colours. Fresh furniture. The only thing that wasn't fresh was the smell. Slovakia might have been in the process of putting its past behind it, but the place still smelled of the old days. Just like the memo-rial that towered over the city, testifying in all its socio-realistic monstrosity to the erstwhile Soviet Union's liberation of Czech-oslovakia. Another country which no longer existed. Otherwise Bratislava displayed all the other chaotic signs of the transition from communism to democracy. Mildewed concrete tower blocks rubbed shoulders with McDonald's and stolen Western cars. Newly renovated houses with beautiful, freshly painted ochre walls were not to be deterred by their neighbours' dirty-grey walls: the symbolic reflections of a lifetime of communism's physical squalor. This was how my thoughts ran: from backache to mornings in Copenhagen to the shambles that was Bratislava. I couldn't think straight for the pain. I stood by the telephone, trying to weigh up my options. To get some kind of grip on this godawful morning. If I could do that I would never complain again.

The room was like a tip: strewn with clothes, books, overflowing ashtrays, empty glasses, old newspapers. One unpacked suitcase, half-open, putting me in mind of a gaping mouth. The fat manila envelope lay where she had left it. My so-called half-sister, who had introduced herself as Maria Bujic. But did she even exist? Or had she merely been some bizarre vision. A pyschedelic image, the mind's way of giving me a warning: something dangerous and unpleasant is about to happen. Right now it's your back that's given out, the first part of your fifty-something anatomy to do so, but that is only the start – because, Mr University Lecturer, sir, it's downhill all the way from here. Which was also, of course, a load of garbage. The envelope was right there, after all. Stiff-legged and with my hand pressed to the small of my back I tottered over to it, picked it up and peeked inside. Sure enough. There was the concrete proof: photographs, some handwritten letters, a handful of newspaper cuttings and a few typewritten sheets of paper. That turn of the wrist, slight and subtle though it was, proved to have been a bad move. The torturers returned, digging their red-hot knives into my back, causing me to drop the envelope as if it was on fire and had burned my hand. There was nothing for it but to give in, so I did, and called Lasse before my self-pity could incapacitate me completely.

Good man that he was he came right away, quickly sized up his ailing friend's situation and showed himself to be both capable and reasonably sympathetic, although even he could not hide the fact that he felt, as we all do, that there is something rather funny about a grown man with a bad back. It is not as if there is anything to see. It is not like an open wound. He could tell that I was in agony, but I knew he was thinking: it can't be that bad. Lasse's experience of illness did not extend beyond a dose of the flu, and I was well aware that he viewed the rest of us, in whom the first warning signs of old age were already being felt, pretty much as hypochondriacs. Strong, healthy individuals who do nothing in order to keep themselves strong and healthy but simply are so, are a downright pain in the neck. Lasse was that sort of person. But he was a good mate for all that. I was just in pain and feeling sorry for myself. None of my wives have ever really seen eye to eye, but one thing on which they are all agreed is that if the martyrs of the world were ever to form a club I would be the obvious choice for chairman.

Lasse packed my suitcase deftly and efficiently while I sat bolt upright on a chair next to the small desk. I had not told him about my mysterious night visitor and when he picked up the envelope I merely motioned to the suitcase. I wanted to have as little hand luggage as possible. I had a hell of a job getting back onto my feet, pain shot up my back again. It was the last straw. My mind was made up. When he was finished packing I said:

'I'm not going to Budapest.'

'Oh?' the heartless bugger said, 'Aw, it'll pass, don't you think?'

'It's sheer agony, Lasse. I can't stand the thought of sitting for hours in a bus and then having to spend several days in Budapest, with all those lectures and rotten chairs.'

'It's only for two nights.'

'I'm going to book a seat on a flight home, so just leave my case here, I'll get one of the hotel staff to help me.'

'Well, I'm sorry to hear that, but maybe it is the wisest thing to do. And Janne and the kids'll be pleased. They must be feeling so bad for you.'

'I can't get hold of them!'

'Oh? Where are they?'

'That's the problem – I don't bloody well know!' I snapped at him with undue testiness.

'Sorry, Teddy,' he said.

'No, it's me that's sorry. But I really would like to talk to Janne.'

'Do you normally call home regularly?'

'Do you?'

'Every day. When Lisbeth's at home, that is.'

'Every day! I've called home once. I can't afford to be on the bloody phone all the time.'

He laughed and slapped me on the shoulder from force of habit, but it felt as though someone had kicked me in the back, I swore so loudly that Lasse looked quite alarmed.

'Oops, sorry Teddy. I didn't mean to hurt you.'

'That's okay. Come on, let's go down and have some breakfast,' I said and attempted to take a couple of faltering steps while still trying to hang on to some shred of dignity. He put a hand gently under my arm to support me.

'Why don't you get a mobile phone?' he asked.

'Janne doesn't feel it's necessary. All folk use them for anyway is to phone home from the supermarket to check whether there's enough milk in the fridge.'

'Well, it's a good thing to have,' the practical old sod remarked as I hobbled off. Downstairs, at the lavish breakfast buffet, I had a couple of cups of coffee and some juice, but left my plate untouched. I had filled it, a mite optimistically, with scrambled egg, bacon and chipolata sausages. I never eat much in the morning, but one feels almost duty-bound to help oneself to all sorts of things merely because they are included in the price. Lasse tucked in with gusto: egg, bacon, bread and sausages, which he would normally never touch, while he read the previous day's *Herald Tribune* which the hotel took along with a whole range of other Western newspapers. CNN in the rooms. The *Trib* in reception. There was no reason to

| 42 |

miss the old days, when there was nothing to be had but communist mis-information, and happiness was a two-week old copy of the daily *Land and Folk* or *The Morning Star.*

Again I had trouble getting up. I had to brace myself before even attempting it. My back did not hurt when I was sitting still, but I knew that as soon as I made to rise the pain would kick in. Although the pain was not, in fact, the worst bit, it was the fear and the knowledge that it would come. And that perfectly normal, everyday actions had suddenly become almost insurmountable ordeals. I saw the looks my travelling companions gave me. I looked like a man with a terrible hangover who had a hard job getting to his feet and had to hold onto the back of his chair just to stay upright. But I did not care. I would be only too glad to see the back of my fellow lecturers, not to mention the cultural tourists, always trying to engage one in urbane chit-chat of the sort designed to show just how well up on things they were.

Obviously Klaus Brandt, our glorious leader, was pissed off. He hated it when things did not go exactly to plan. He would have felt right at home in the old GOSPLAN in Moscow, where specifications were worked out for everything from nuclear power stations to the tiniest children's sock. That their schemes were untenable did not matter a jot to the planners. All they did was juggle numbers and letters about.

'Now look, Teddy, there's no way I can refund the cost of your ticket or your hotel room. Everything was paid for in advance,' Brandt fumed.

'I didn't ask you to, Brandt,' I said.

'Well, there's no need to be like that,' the moron retorted, whereupon I turned on my heel, walked over to Lasse and shook his hand demonstratively.

'Bye, Lasse. Take care of yourself.'

'You too,' he said. 'See you back home in a couple of days. Say hello to Janne for me.'

Brandt was looking daggers at me. I had mucked up his schedule.

From now on, every time he did a head tally, like a teacher counting his pupils, after yet another stop for a pee or a fag on the long Central-European highways, he would have to remember that there was one less in the party. Flapping and clucking like a mother hen, he got his brood moving. They picked up their bags and plodded out to the waiting coach. A young woman approached me. As far as I remembered her name was Charlotte. She was travelling with her father, Niels Lassen, whom I knew very well. He was five years older than me and had worked for many years with various international organisations. He had thereby avoided being squeezed dry by the greedy Danish taxman and been able to save enough to take relatively early retirement. And yet he could not see his way to paying for a separate room for his daughter. They shared a double room in order to save money.

'Teddy,' said Charlotte. 'I'm sorry you're not coming to Budapest. I heard what Klaus said. About the room being paid in advance, so I was wondering …'

'Have a pleasant night in my vacant room in Budapest,' I said.

'Thanks a lot,' she said. 'I'm so fed up with not being able to smoke in the room because of Dad.'

'Well, you can smoke all you like in mine,' I said.

She thanked me again and sashayed away. It takes so little to make some people happy. It is an enviable trait, although it could also be a sign of low intelligence and lack of imagination. Nice man that I am, I waved the coach off and watched as it nosed its way through the crowd of black-marketeers, hookers on the morning shift, ordinary bystanders and the chaotic queue of taxis that is all part of the street scene outside an international hotel in this corner of our beloved post-communist world. It swung up towards the Presidential Palace – now standing empty because the Slovaks, like so many others, found it hard to agree on anything – and then, to my great relief, my colleagues and the tourists were gone, off on their way to Budapest. Me, I was off home.

There was a travel agent's office at the hotel. I presented them with my Mastercard and my wishes. By some miracle, there was no problem: there was an early afternoon flight to Vienna and a connection from there to Copenhagen. There were plenty of seats available on both flights. It made a refreshing change from all the hassle previously involved in trying to go anywhere without booking weeks in advance – under the old communist regimes that had basically been a law of nature. Now all I had to do was to stay upright, try to get in touch with Janne again, pay the bill for my meals, drinks and telephone calls at the hotel and get myself home to my own bed. And maybe make an appointment for tomorrow with a brisk little chiropractor.

I could not sit still. It actually helped to walk a little, so I strolled down through a small city gate into the old town. It was a lovely, if slightly chilly, spring day. The old houses seemed well maintained, but I had to put out an admonitory hand to ward off a group of gypsy children who advanced upon me with grubby palms out-stretched. A policeman caught sight of the bunch of raggedy kids; all that was needed was for him to set his corpulent figure in motion and they nipped down a sidestreet and were gone as if they had never existed. I tipped my imaginary hat gratefully to the policeman, who indifferently looked the other way. I saw a beggar in a wheelchair, engrossed in a book and heedless of whether passers-by threw coins into the hat lying in front of his chair or not. Another was playing the accordion, a slow, plaintive Gypsy melody that made me feel sad. I dropped some coins into his hat. There is always music in the streets in Eastern Europe. There are plenty of elderly former members of the state-run symphony orchestras who now have to earn their bread in this way. Nowhere in the world will you find finer street musicians. And always there is a beggar with no legs, a little old lady swathed in shawls or a cripple covered in running sores. The communists hid them out of the way. Capitalism has driven them out into the open in all their pitiful wretchedness. It is easy, in today's post-communist world, to feel like a socialist. Or social-democrat rather, I had to admit to myself. Since they were the ones I voted for, although I did not tell anyone that. I was only a little left of centre, as I had always been, if one disregards the obligatory flirt with Marxism at university: two years of schooling in the need for revolution. But that was a long time ago. And it meant nothing today.

No one in the narrow cobbled streets seemed to be in any great hurry. People ambled along, the younger ones often chatting on mobile phones which were obviously the latest status symbol. I came past a pub, The Dubliner it was called. It could just as easily have been in Copenhagen or Stockholm, anywhere but the Emerald Isle; the decor mock Irish throughout. I went in, found myself a spot at the bar and ordered a pint. Nothing would have induced me to sit down, knowing as I did how hard it would be to get up again. It was only mid-morning, but the place was full of people, both Slovaks and young foreigners discussing their love lives and personal intrigues. They were all very smartly dressed. Some of them better and more fashionably turned out than this particular gentleman from the affluent West, but I was past the stage of having to advertise my prosperity. Waitresses in red T-shirts and tiny white mini-skirts teetered about on stiletto heels. The mini-skirts did not look quite right with their somewhat plumper Slovakian legs. On their T-shirts, emblazoned across their chests, were the words 'Food only'. Next to the door was a sign saying: 'Food waitress with experience wanted'. Some day the whole world will speak an English of sorts. A bent, old woman shuffled past the open door, all happed up in a threadbare coat and big shawl despite the spring sunshine. She accosted a young man with a mobile phone to his ear, reaching out a gnarled, veined hand. He passed her by without so much as a glance. When another young man standing next to me started jabbering on his mobile, the ringing tone of which sounded like 'The Wild Rover', I decided I had had enough, paid the few *karuna* I owed and made my way back through the relatively quiet streets to my hotel. Back in my room I tried calling Janne again, but again I got the answering machine. I left a brusque message, demanding to know where the hell she was, telling her when I would be landing that evening and asking if she could pick me up at the airport. She had the bloody car, after all. I called the Institute, but was told that they had not seen her for a couple of days. She was off sick, her secretary informed me, with thinly disguised glee. Well, that would give them something to gossip about over lunch.

So by the time I set out for the airport I was in a pretty foul mood. In the taxi, driving through the dun-coloured, concrete Stalinist desert of Bratislava's suburbs, I kept expecting to see a cement factory proudly proclaiming that its workers strove tirelessly to fulfil the party's magnificent Five Year Plan and wholeheartedly supported the indissoluble friendship with the Soviet Union. Instead my eyes were met by adverts for Sony and Marlboro.

The terminal was deserted. It looked more like a dismal provincial aerodrome in some far corner of the globe than an airport in a capital city. The fake marble flooring, the virtual absence of any passengers, the few departures announced on the information display boards and the smell of the erstwhile Soviet Union which clung to it, all testified to the fact that Slovakia was still a European backwater. Slovak Air Services and Russian Aeroflot fought for precedence in their own little signage battle. There were no staff at the check-in desk or in the small office underneath the fancy *Informácie* sign. Besides my flight to Vienna the departure schedule from Bratislava Airport also included a flight to Prague, one to Kiev and, strangely enough, a late-night flight to Tunis. That was the lot from the capital of Europe's youngest nation. Over in a corner I noticed a woman sitting quietly reading a magazine. In a minuscule post office an elderly man stared vacantly into space. In the tiny newsagent's I could purchase a copy of *Die Welt*, and this I did, but I did not dare to sit down. I wandered around, biding my time, and eventually a young man who spoke English appeared and checked me in along with the handful of other passengers who drifted in as departure time approached. I was like a little child, I couldn't wait to get home.

I changed planes in Vienna and landed on schedule in Copenhagen. I swallowed my pride and asked the stewardess to help me out of my seat. The pain when I had heaved myself to my feet unaided in Vienna had been so bad that I would have screamed out loud, were it not for the fact that, no matter what, a man just does not do that. My back hurt like hell. Our passports were checked by the police when we got off the plane and again as we were about to step into the safe arms of the motherland. The usual poor sods were already sitting in a huddle alongside passport control, with no hope of being allowed to enter the promised land of the EU, while I, with my splendid beetroot-red document was able to sail straight through. Now aching in three different places: my back, my tooth and my head, in order of severity.

I hung around for ages, but my suitcase never appeared. A smiling woman informed me, after pressing a lot of buttons on a computer keyboard, that it looked as though it was now somewhere over the Atlantic, on its way to Los Angeles. Apparently a small mistake had been made at Vienna Airport. Why do airport staff always regard the disappearance of a suitcase as a small mistake. It's a bloody big deal for the person whose suitcase it happens to be. And for the unsuspecting passenger on the flight to the States who was even now looking forward to soaking up the Californian sunshine in his new beachwear, which unfortunately happened to be in Copenhagen. As long as there were no drugs or other substances in my suitcase it would be sent on to me. If I could just sign here please? Certainly, anything just so long as I can go home.

Janne was not waiting in the arrivals hall, where more fortunate travellers were being greeted with kisses and flowers. I gathered up my aching bones, picked up my light holdall and went out to grab a taxi. Spring had temporarily deserted Copenhagen, as if scared off by its northerly latitude. Sleet was pelting down and the taxi driver was playing some song by Gustav Winckler. I did not see how things could get any worse.

But they could. The flat was quiet and in darkness. A couple of days' worth of newspapers and mail lay on the mat, and when I switched on a light and walked into the kitchen I found a miniature jungle of the tenderest pot plants ranged in and around the sink. The light on the answering machine blinked brightly as I poured myself a whisky and proceeded to listen to my own disgruntled tones.

4

I HEARD THE KEY in the lock and, out of habit, made to get up, but could not. I lay flat on my back, stuck there as firmly as if someone had nailed me to the mattress. The thought of how much it would hurt were I to attempt the slightest movement was quite unbearable. I lay still, listening to Janne's familiar footsteps coming down our long hallway. The kids had obviously been dropped off at school already. Gingerly I turned my head to check the digital display on the alarm clock: half-past eight. I had slept longer than I usually did. I had gone to bed feeling very sorry for myself. But the sleeping pill I had taken had done the trick. I took stock of myself as I listened to Janne's feet drawing closer: aching back, aching tooth, but at least I had managed to sleep off my headache. Then Janne was standing in the bedroom doorway. She stared at me, guilty-eyed. Served her right.

She was a good-looking woman, my Janne. Tall and slim, her medium-length hair becomingly coiffed. She had small, blue eyes which suited her rather narrow face and high, clear forehead. I had always loved her little ears. The first time I kissed her it was on the small stretch of bare skin between her ear and her throat. She had been wearing her hair up, all set to have fun at the Institute Christmas party and it had seemed the most natural thing in the world to twirl her round while we were dancing and brush that lovely, opalescent skin with my lips. It was a good move. I happened to have found one of her more secret erogenous zones. Or it had found me. That little patch of skin had been asking to be kissed. Now she stood there, keys in hand, looking at me.

'How come you're home so soon? And what are you doing in bed?' she asked.

'Hi, Janne. Gosh, I'm glad to see you too.'

'How come you're home so soon? For heaven's sake, man, get up!'

It was awful to have to lie there looking up at her. Suddenly she seemed so tall and overbearing. It was an odd angle from which to view one's wife.

'I *can't* get up,' I said.

'Don't be ridiculous!'

'I've done my back in. I can't flaming well get up. Could you give me a hand?'

Janne must have seen from the look on my face that I was not joking. I tried to sit up, but the pain that shot across the small of my back warned me that if I proceeded with this manoeuvre it was going to start hurting in earnest. She slipped her keys into the pocket of her stylish jeans, bent down and hooked her hands under my armpits, making me squeal like the stuck pigs from the summer holidays of my early childhood, when my uncle used to slaughter the beasts in the farmyard.

'What's wrong, Teddy?' she asked, seriously worried now.

'I told you, it's my fucking back, it hurts like hell. Grab hold of my hand!'

I held out my hand and she took it. Her own were strong and slender and I noticed she was still wearing her wedding ring, which was always something. I asked her to pull. By this time she was looking quite alarmed and appeared unsure as to whether she dared use all her strength. But between us we managed it. She got me up in two stages: first into a sitting position – the four torturers from Bratislava had evidently followed me to Denmark, they were going at it hammer and tongs, boring their awls, knives and all manner of medieval instruments into my back as I slid my legs over the edge of the bed and then, with another burst of effort, eased myself onto my feet. But once I was standing upright the pain subsided a little. Still holding my hand, Janne regarded me with concern and genuine sympathy. She could tell that old

| 51 |

Hypochondriac Teddy was not faking it, he actually was in genuine agony. I stood there for a moment with her hand in mine.

'How do you feel?' she asked.

'Better, thanks. It helps to stand up.'

'What did you do? How did it happen? Did you lift something the wrong way?'

'Nope. I was just sitting on the toilet. It's so stupid,' I said.

Then for a moment more we stood in silence, still holding hands. What a sight we must have made. My pretty wife in her smart clothes, clean skin and beautifully coiffed hair, and me, old Teddy, in a pair of somewhat crumpled boxer shorts with my hair standing on end.

'I'm sorry,' she said. 'You really don't deserve this.'

For a second I thought she was talking about my back, then it struck me that what she was actually apologising for were the plants in the kitchen sink, the newspapers and mail on the doormat and all the other signs which said that Teddy was a cuckold. I let go of her hand.

'I need to take a shower,' I said to break the silence. All of a sudden we were like strangers and no one wants a stranger seeing them the way I looked right then.

'I'll make us some breakfast,' she said.

'Coffee would be good,' I said, and went on as if nothing had changed:

'Are you going into the Institute? Or are you still off sick?'

'Teddy, I said I'm sorry. You don't deserve to find out about it like this.'

'Who is he?'

'Go have your shower. Can you manage on your own? Go have your shower and then we'll talk.'

And that is what we did. A shower helped, and the coffee did me good, but what she had to tell me, banal though it was, was anything but good. There was someone else: she had a boyfriend as the infantile parlance of today has it. It had been going on for some time. She had to all intents and purposes moved in with him. The plan had been to break it to me gently over a glass of red wine when I got home. She had not meant me to find out like this. I said nothing, sat almost as if turned to stone, but my feelings were, in fact, somewhat mixed. I was angry and upset, but I was also strangely distanced from the whole thing. As if it had not really penetrated. As if I had actually known this was going to happen. It had merely been a question of when. I sat bolt upright on the kitchen chair, trying to keep my back still. My tooth was aching again and I was in real Poor-Old-Teddy mode.

'Who is he?' I asked again.

'It's Peter,' she said.

'Peter! He's nothing but a lousy assistant lecturer! That's a bit of a come-down, Janne. Shouldn't you be working your way up the ladder? Nabbing yourself a professor? I mean, you've already scored a lecturer!'

'God, you're so full of bullshit!' she said.

'Peter!' was all I said. He was in his mid-thirties, prematurely balding, but unfortunately it suited him. Fashion was on his side: close-shaved head matching his equally close-trimmed beard. Athletic body. He loved hiking in the Norwegian mountains. Ran in the Copenhagen marathon. He was ambitious and, as much as I hate to admit it, he was also very clever. Like Lena, he was doing research into transitional phenomena in post-communist countries, with particular emphasis on the problems faced by the new applicant states as they endeavoured to gain membership of that club of the wealthy, the European Union. He was forever being awarded one grant or another and was also going to be taking part in one of the Institute of International Affairs' new projects. IIA work brought with it both posts and funding, while the rest of us went hungry. It was bloody infuriating and extremely hurtful. I found myself picturing them in bed together. I felt a fleeting pang of jealousy so strong that it made me forget my back and my tooth. Who the hell did they think they were? If anyone was going to be unfaithful it should be me. If anyone was going to leave it should be me. Instead we sat there in the kitchen, as tongue-tied as a couple of fourteen-year-olds.

Then, all unprompted, she said: 'He loves the kids.'

'And is that more important than whether he loves you?' I retorted bitterly.

'He loves me too.'

'Oh, God, how banal can you be?' I sighed.

'You and I – we've nothing in common now,' she said. 'You're always in a bad mood. Or you're in a world of your own. Or both.'

'And Peter's not?'

'Peter is always there when I need him.'

'And I'm not.'

She placed a hand over mine and looked deep into my eyes. They were a little moist.

'Teddy, you're as charming as ever, and you're still a dear, sweet man, but you're also in danger of turning into an old grouch. Don't let that happen. There's so much good in you. I just don't seem to be able to bring it out any more. If I ever could. Peter makes me feel alive. And the children are happy when we're with him. They say we're like a real family. "Why is Teddy always so cross?" – I don't know how many times they've asked me that in the past year. Listen to me. It's for the best. For all of us. One day you'll understand that.'

First my tooth, then my back, and now I had a pain in my gut too – the coffee had upset my stomach. I felt a powerful surge of nausea. Being sick helped, but when I bent over the toilet bowl my torturers set to again with their whole battery of instruments. That she was leaving me was bad enough. Almost worse, though, was the pity in her eyes when she looked at me. She regarded me as a poor old soul, and maybe she was right.

I returned to the kitchen. She said nothing, thankfully. I poured myself a glass of milk, stood there holding it. Why are we always so bloody civilised? Why don't we chuck plates at one another?

Maybe that was what she had really been saying. That I was always so thick-skinned. That nothing could penetrate the armoured shell I had built up around myself. That deep down I was a selfish son-of-a-bitch who employed sarcasm as a deadly weapon to conceal the fact that I was a total failure – as a scholar and as a human being.

I thought about this as I stood by the kitchen bench, listening to her footsteps fading off down the hall, then I heard the bang of the front door as Nora left the doll's house and a rejected Helmer. Thank God for literature. The unfailing resort of we ageing academics. There is nothing like a good, veiled quotation to put one's demons to flight, or at least render them comprehensible in abstract terms. The situation was, however, pretty clear. Teddy was, in all ways, down for the count.

I kept the storm of emotions at bay by doing something practical. I picked up the phone, made an appointment with the doctor, and with the dentist, both of whom could manage to squeeze me in, then I called my lawyer – Janne had asked me to do this, she had already hired Peter's – and, lastly, SAS. My suitcase had obviously decided to go globetrotting. It now appeared to be winging its way to Timbuktu or some other godforsaken place. At any rate the nice lady at the airport was able to inform me that it was not on its way to Denmark. Not at the moment, as she said. Smart suitcase. I looked out of the window. It was coming down in buckets, and so windy that the rain was hitting people head-on. Cars splashed through the puddles, splattering those sorry wretches who had dared to brave the early Danish spring with cascades of brown sludge. Finally I called my sister. She was the one to whom everyone in the family took their troubles. She was not at home. I called Roskilde University only to be told that she was attending a symposium at Lund, in Sweden. She would be back the next day. I left a message on her answering machine at home and on her mobile, then I went to see the doctor and the dentist. I should possibly have booked an appointment with a psychologist as well, but that might have been overdoing things on the treatment side for one day. No matter how hard I tried to block out the image, it kept coming back to me: Peter and Janne in bed together, slim and naked, locked in a passionate embrace. Janne's face was the worst bit. She looked so damn happy. The same happiness that she had been unable to hide as she sat across from me at the kitchen table, feeling sorry for Teddy, I'm sure, but actually glad that the cat was now out of the bag, that she had confessed her four-month-old secret.

The doctor poked me in the back and I almost hit the roof. He said he doubted it was a slipped disc, it was probably nothing more than a strained muscle. Good old-fashioned lumbago. It would get better by itself. If it did not, I should come back and have it X-rayed. In the meantime I could take some paracetamol. And take it easy. The dentist told me it was my gums that were the problem, that I ought to floss more regularly for a while; if that didn't work he would have to cut away some of the infected tissue, but he did not have time to do that today. He had to help me out of the chair. Once I got myself stretched out in it I could not get up again. I have a feeling he thought I was a bit of a joke. A wimp, as my sun-bronzed, golf-playing dentist, a man of my own age, was wont to say whenever I asked for an injection.

I beat my way through the rain, did a bit of shopping, went back to my empty flat, buttered a couple of slices of bread and fried an egg. Janne had taken the car. Well, she had the kids. I didn't mind. I had never owned a car until I met Janne. In the city they were more trouble than they were worth. As far as I was concerned she could keep it, although it was me who had paid for it. The flat smelled empty, but I would just have to get used to that. At the sight of the children's toys and books lying here and there I found myself missing the little brats and the endless mess they made. Janne's side of the wardrobe was still full of her clothes. I sniffed her blouses, they smelled so strongly of her that I promptly shut the wardrobe door and shuffled back through to the living room.

The flat was mine. I had learned one thing, at least, from my previous two divorces. The first had not cost me much because we did not have much. The second had been an expensive business. She walked away with half my personal pension and the house. This time everything was in my name. I might have been in love, but I had not been a complete idiot.

I could not settle. Why the hell had Irma not called me back? I needed to talk to my wise, mature older sister. About life in general, but also about the mysterious woman in Bratislava. I could not bring myself to read. Not even a newspaper. It was nine in the evening before I really began to relax; I made a pot of coffee and took it through to the living room to watch the evening news. The petty issues that pass for news in Denmark had a soothing effect on me. But there was also a good piece on the NATO bombing of Yugoslavia, and heartbreaking pictures of Kosovo Albanians fleeing to the poorest country in Europe – Albania. Our own worries tend to pale into insignificance when we are confronted with the misfortunes of others. But I also remembered a line from a Dylan song from the mid-seventies, one which I still had on one of my venerable old LPs: *'Didn't seem like much was happenin', so I turned it off and went and grabbed another beer.'* I kept my TV switched on, though, and in the middle of the weather forecast the doorbell rang.

Outside stood two men, one in his late thirties, the other in his fifties. The younger of them showed me his ID card and said:

'Police. We have a Theodor Nikolaj Pedersen registered as living at this address.'

'That's right.'

'Do you know where he is?'

'You're looking at him.'

'Are you telling me that you are Theodor Nikolaj Pedersen?' Again it was the younger of the two who spoke.

'Are the forces of law and order always so slow on the uptake,' I said. 'I just said so, didn't I? Teddy to my friends. At your service.'

'Aren't you supposed to be in Budapest?'

'How the hell do you know that?'

'Might we come in for a moment?' the older man asked.

'Why? Has something happened?'

'We've received a message from the police in Budapest. This evening. Earlier today the Danish Embassy down there got in touch with us. They reported that a Danish citizen by the name of Theodor Nikolaj Pedersen had been found murdered. But now our Hungarian colleagues are saying that it is, in fact, another Danish citizen. A Niels Lassen. May we come in?'

'Of course,' I said, more shaken than I let on. This was definitely not the most ordinary day in Teddy's normally so straightforward academic life.

5

THEY SEATED THEMSELVES on the edge of the sofa. I remained standing. I asked if they would like coffee. They said they would, so I fetched two more cups, poured coffee for them and told them just to call me Teddy. Everyone else does. They introduced themselves. The middle-aged man gave only his surname: Bjerregaard. He was wearing the sort of jacket I wear myself, along with shirt, tie and grey flannels. Very conservative, but dapper. The younger man's name was Per Toftlund. He was the athletic type, with the look of a boxer, or a soldier: hair close-cropped, clad in a dark leather jacket, light-coloured shirt, tie and faded jeans. He could even have been taken for an undercover cop. I had the feeling that I had seen him before. In the news, in connection with that bloody business involving the writer Sara Santanda, the one with the fatwa on her head. I could not recall all the details, but I was sure Toftlund was the name of the officer who had been hung out in the media for failing to prevent the attempt on her life at Flakfortet. If I remembered rightly the would-be assassin had got away too. Toftlund was clearly still with the police, though, so maybe he had not been left to carry the can. Or maybe he had been transferred from PET to the CID or Interpol?

'Won't you take a seat?' Bjerregaard asked, as if he were the host.

'No thanks,' I said, putting a demonstrative hand to the base of my spine. 'I have a bad back.'

'Have you tried doing some stretching exercises?' Toftlund asked. 'Lie down and I'll loosen it up for you.'

'No, that's okay. Thanks anyway,' I said, sounding more startled by this offer than I intended. But I could just imagine what those strong hands and muscular upper arms could do to my back. They would make the torturers from Bratislava seem like amateurs.

'It does help, you know,' he said.

'Why don't we just get down to the matter in hand,' I said. 'What's all this about Niels?'

'Was he a good friend of yours?' Toftlund asked.

'Not really. An acquaintance. In this Lilliputian land of ours the academic world is not all that big. Everybody knows everybody else. But what about his daughter? Charlotte?'

'How do you mean?'

'Well, she was with him,' I snapped – this whole situation was starting to get to me.

Gently, Toftlund put down his coffee cup. His movements were smooth, almost graceful, those powerful hands notwithstanding.

'We don't actually know that much. We've received a couple of faxes from Budapest. We're only here now because your name cropped up. Maybe you can help us. When did you get home?'

'No. No, dammit. I want to know what happened!'

'Sometime last night a person or persons unknown broke into Niels Lassen's hotel room in Budapest. The room was registered in your name. He was killed, either by strangulation or by a blow to the back of head. The details are still a bit vague, but according to our Hungarian colleagues it was a very professional job. The intruders then ransacked the room before making their getaway. No one saw them come or go. As far as we know.'

'Bloody hell,' I muttered vacantly. 'Poor Charlotte.'

'Yeah, poor Charlotte,' Toftlund said with something approaching sarcasm. I did not like his arrogance or his coolness, but I told them the story. About my back and how I had come home, how the room had been paid for in advance and Charlotte had asked if she could make use of it, since it was going to be lying empty anyway. They had obviously done it the other way round, though. Either that or Brandt had mucked things up and given them the wrong keys. He always checked people in. I deliberately kept quiet about the woman who had come to my room in Bratislava. That had nothing to do with the police. Only as I finished telling my story did it dawn on me how lucky I had been. Incredibly lucky, to have hurt my back and have had to come home. Toftlund could obviously tell from my face what I was thinking.

'Yes, Teddy Pedersen. Fate's been kind to you.'

'A fat lot of good it does to know that. You make it sound as if it was my fault.'

'Not at all, but I can't help wondering whether the killers simply picked that room at random, or whether there was more to it?'

He let those last words hang in the air. Bjerregaard merely sat there, hunched over the table with his coffee cup in his hand, suspended, like a little painting almost: *Still Life of Plain-clothes Policeman with Coffee Cup on Teddy's Sofa.*

I put my hand to the small of my back, which was throbbing like mad, and said:

'I don't know what you mean.'

'Oh, of course you do,' Toftlund replied. 'What could they have been looking for?'

'How should I know? I don't smuggle alcohol or drugs. I'm sure I look guilty as sin if I'm carrying as much as four cigarettes over the allowance.'

'It's an odd coincidence, though,' Toftlund said.

'Yes, exactly. A coincidence. Have you any idea how crime has exploded in that corner of the world since the collapse of communism. It's part of the way of life in the old Soviet bloc. Capitalism brought them freedom, poverty and the mafia.'

'Maybe so,' Toftlund persisted. 'But you could have enemies down there. You've done a lot of travelling in Eastern Europe.'

How the hell did he know that, I wondered. They must have run a check on me before making their little surprise visit. My name was bound to crop up in various PET files, what with all the trips I had made behind the Iron Curtain over the years. Not that I had anything to hide, but I read the papers. Something akin to a witch-hunt had been under way to unmask old Stasi spies ever since the Americans had handed over the magnetic tapes which held the key to the identities of the people behind the aliases used by Stasi's thousands of agents and informers. There was something farcical about the whole thing. Ten years after the fall of the Wall some of my fellow academics were shaking in their shoes at the thought of what might be on those tapes. Had some of their pronouncements been a little too pro-Soviet? Had they accepted a couple of gifts too many? Made some remark which was now preserved on yellowing papers along with other nuggets of intelligence information? The problem was, however, that it had been in the interests of controllers and other agents to exaggerate the importance of the information they received; that, and the fact that there was in effect no court of appeal. You were guilty until you could prove otherwise. Just as well I had kept my nose clean. A few trips to the East in the old days didn't make you a flaming communist.

'I've enough enemies here in Denmark,' I said.

'And who might they be?' Bjerregaard asked, only now putting down his coffee cup.

'My academic colleagues and rivals. All the people whom I've pipped at the post for research grants, as well as those to whom, as a member of various boards and committees, I've denied funding, because I questioned the validity of their projects. We smile at one another, congratulate one another, but what each of us really wishes for all the rest is failure, disgrace and a job teaching high school in some far corner of Jutland. But we fight with words, not knives. Or at least only the symbolic sort used for stabbing people in the back,' I said.

Toftlund laughed. He had a deep, very pleasant laugh; even the more straitlaced Bjerregaard smiled and I, too, gave a little chuckle, to relieve some of the awkwardness and indeed the unpleasantness of the situation.

'Right, then,' Toftlund said, standing up. 'We may have to get back to you.'

'Of course,' I said. 'But can you tell me ... the rest of the group, are they being kept down there? Or are they coming home?'

'As far as I know they're coming home. I would assume that they've all been interviewed – it's standard procedure. But it sounds as though the Budapest police think, as I do, that it was a robbery that went wrong. We'll be speaking to the daughter when she gets back to Denmark with the ... deceased.'

It was a grim word, and with that and a handshake they were gone. I wandered around the flat with my hand pressed to my back as if I was nine months gone, reflecting on how lucky I had been and what a really awful story it was. I called Irma again, but still only got her answering machine. So I had a whisky, took a sleeping pill, flossed my teeth as prescribed by my dentist, so vigorously that I all but sawed through to my jawbone, and went out like a light. For the next couple of days, over the weekend, I took good care of myself. I stayed indoors. Partly because rest seemed to be the best thing for my back and partly because the rain and wind were battering off my windowpanes. I read the old newspapers, a new book on Stalingrad which a British colleague had sent me, watched films on TV, drank some red wine and went to bed early. I missed Janne and the kids more than I would have thought possible, even picked up the phone a couple of times to call her at his, 'the other man's', place – talk about a cliché – but thought better of it and instead gave myself up to wallowing in self-pity. I have always been good at that. What hurt most was the fridge door. More than once I found myself standing gazing at it, bleary-eyed. It was plastered with all the usual little notes. Copies of school timetables. Reminders about swimming lessons and handball practice. Pictures of the children. A postcard or two. An invitation to a birthday party. Affixed with little magnets: hearts, dogs, a cow and a cat and a shiny red apple. Little magnets holding the secure pattern of everyday life firmly in place on a white refrigerator door. This picture could have been entitled: *Teddy Forsaken By All*.

On Monday morning, wonder of wonders, the late March sun was shining and Copenhagen was once again my beloved city with its roofs and spires, girl cyclists, little doggies and big yellow corporation buses bowling almost soundlessly along. People everywhere were tilting their heads back and gazing up at that blue sky, as if trying to drink in the light. Sunlight streamed through my kitchen window as I made coffee, and I deemed it a victory that I had managed to get out of bed unaided, without having to do it in three stages as on the previous days: first sitting up, then easing my legs over the side of the bed and finally pushing myself onto my feet. It was rather like being a three-year-old again, so pleased and proud of being able to put on one's own socks. It still hurt like hell, but in many ways I had forgiven my back, seeing that it had, in fact, saved my life. When Janne called I surprised both her and myself by being pleasant and urbane and agreeing to find a day on which to discuss the practicalities. We were civilised people, after all. Nonetheless, our conversation left a dent in my good mood.

The fact was that a couple of crucial events which had occurred during the past couple of days looked set to triumph over my highly-developed ability to block out any sort of unpleasantness, particularly of an emotional nature. One of these was Janne's desertion. I was on my own again. All the signs were that this was a fact. But did I really want to be on my own? I had to admit that it probably was not going to be as easy as it had been in the good, old days for me to score the female students. Seldom, now, did I attract any glances from the new batches of first years with their bewildered, awestruck eyes. Being single again might be a lot more difficult than I thought. And then there was the appearance in Bratislava of that mysterious woman. Who was she? And what did she want with me? If she had not simply been spinning me a yarn, that is. It bothered me that Irma had not yet called me back. I really needed to talk to my wise sister; she usually had a good explanation for just about anything. She was a tough cookie, it's true, but she could also dispense tea and sympathy if she felt that was what you needed. And poor Teddy certainly did.

For want of anything better to do I made my way over to the south side, to Amager and the University of Copenhagen and my tiny office in the monstrosity of a building which some mad architect had succeeded in getting past the planners back in the early seventies. Imagine building a concrete pile in the worst East German style to house, of all things, the Faculty of Humanities – in which we who worked and studied there were expected to think great thoughts about the meaning of life and instil in young people a knowledge of language, history and literature. The weighty matters in life. Maybe that was why most of the thoughts generated here tended to be small and muddled. We led our own life within these walls, unaffected by the society around us which footed the bill. I was not the only one to have ground to a halt in the academic world; the odd polemical piece in the newspapers the only visible sign of our existence. Every attempt to have the whole execrable edifice pulled down had failed and I had eventually come to the resigned conclusion that this travesty of a building would outlive both me and the next generation. But at least the pay and the pension were good, considering how little one had to do for it. In the canteen we tried to outdo one another with tales of how godawful busy we were. And what hell it was to be slaves to diaries which nowadays were always packed with meetings. How demanding our research was. What we did not say, we middle-aged lecturers, was that the new generation was coming up fast and that they were both ambitious and talented. Just as well we all had tenure. From the early seventies onwards we had been appointed in droves, regardless of our exam results. And the idea that anyone could be fired for incompetence or laziness was beyond the bounds of our imaginations.

There were only a couple of people at the Institute when I got there. I stopped for a quick chat with them, but not about the one thing on all our minds: they knew that I knew that Janne had left me.

The woman, Signe, was – like most of us – in her fifties, an acerbic-looking character who always behaved as if no one realised how brilliant she was. Her one concession to a world that had moved on was a touch of mascara on her eyelashes. Her specialist area was women's writing in a male-dominated society, a subject which had filled classes in the seventies and early eighties, but like mine her course was not particularly popular today. That was not why she was so bitter, though. There were two other reasons for her hatred of the world. One was that another old Marxist had landed the job of editing a major history of literature for Gyldendal, the country's biggest publishing house. They were both dyed-in-the-wool hard-line leftists, so the injustice lay more in the fact that she had lost out to someone from such a provincial institution as South Jutland University. The other was that Signe had dreamt of becoming a literary critic with *Politiken*, the leading left-wing daily, even though she always described it as a crypto-conservative paper, but since the demise of the communist *Land og Folk* along with that of the Berlin Wall and my own narrow field of academic expertise, they had no use for her. In these post-Wall times her ability to assess a work of literature in the light of the slogan 'No feminist struggle without class struggle. No class struggle without feminist struggle' was not what *Politiken* was looking for. So she had wound up working for *Information*, which was fine as far as it went, but not what she wanted – so few people read the little left-wing rag. She was, therefore, pretty bitter. She had been in the same consciousness-raising group as Irma, and tended therefore to give me a bit more slack than she allowed other men, although if the truth be told she had always viewed me as a shallow woman-iser with no concept of the singularly repressed state of the female sex. Her current lover, Jeppe, who stood there nodding through-out our conversation, was nothing but a moron. We carried on as though our teaching and our research work were of the utmost importance, but were wise enough not to actually talk shop.

Instead we discussed the news that a Yugoslav anti-aircraft unit had managed to shoot down one of the Americans' top-secret Stealth bombers. Like the majority of left-wing academics Signe and Jeppe were against the NATO bombing campaign. They felt it was immoral, possibly because NATO was intent on avoiding any losses on its own side, possibly because the bombings had swelled the stream of refugees pouring into Albania. Or possibly because the Chilean coup and the war in Vietnam had left them with an instinctive abhorrence of NATO and the United States. They were considering the one move to which Danish intellectuals always resort when they really want to feel involved: that of collecting signatures for a petition denouncing the war and calling for peace, a document which they fully expected *Politiken* to print. They had given no thought, however, to what this 'peace' might entail. Nowadays most of us were too set in our ways to go taking part in demonstrations. I got round her request to support such a declaration by saying that I was too busy. They accused me of shirking a difficult confrontation. But deep down I was of the opinion that enough was enough, that Milosevic deserved a good hiding and that we could not permit the perpetration of ethnic cleansing in modern-day Europe. Petitions could not do much to stop it. But a few missiles might. Signe said I was naive and that war only made matters worse. That the possibilties for negotiation were not yet exhausted.

I went into my office, shaking my head, and spent a couple of hours answering emails and reading the ordinary post that had piled up in my absence, some of it work-related, the rest just junk mail. Along with yet another exhortation from the Faculty of Literary Studies to sign a petition protesting against NATO's military operation. It went straight into the wastepaper bin. I called Irma's numbers again. Her secretary said she could not understand why she was not back yet, but they were expecting her that day. Her mobile was switched off. I sent her an email, telling her about the woman in Bratislava. I gave her most of the details and demanded an explanation, for God's sake. I thought briefly of phoning Fritz, but we found it hard to talk to one another. There were always long, weird pauses in our conversations. My older brother was a down-to-earth man who produced that basic staple of existence, bread, and he often found it hard to take my more high-flown academic musings seriously. His world and mine were poles apart. He was also a lot older. We had never had much in common. And I knew what he would say if I told him my story: You'd better talk to Irma about that.

I considered switching off my computer and calling it a day, instead of sitting there staring at my static-laden needle-felt carpeting and concrete walls, their drabness relieved by some lovely old Soviet propaganda posters. One of these depicted a brawny worker and a blonde woman. The overall-clad worker had his eye fixed steadfastly on the socialist horizon and his powerful fist curled around a hammer; the staunch, blonde land-girl gazed at him adoringly, her golden locks framed by a sickle. 'Together we march towards socialism. The party leads the way' it said in graceful Cyrillic script. It made you weep to think how much the world had changed.

I took a chance and called Lasse's extension and surprisingly enough he answered. He had arrived home on the Sunday afternoon and – busy, conscientious bee that he was – he had of course popped into the office early on the Monday morning to make sure that none of his students were missing Uncle Lasse or needed his help. Some of them did, but he could meet me later, he said, once he had spoken to them, relieved their anxieties about their dissertations and sent each one off feeling confident that he or she was the greatest genius the university had ever fostered. He had a gift for it. But he would love to have lunch with me.

'I've such a lot to tell you,' he said, like a globetrotter returning from distant climes.

A couple of hours later he appeared, long-limbed and smiling gently, in the doorway of one of my favourite refuges in the Queen's Copenhagen, the little luncheon establishment Restauranten nestling next to its leafy little tree on Gammel Torv. With one schnapps and one large draught beer already downed and the prospect of a herring on rye sandwich and one with roast beef washed down by another schnapps and another beer the world did not seem such a bad place after all. The small, low-ceilinged premises were wreathed in cooking fumes and the smoke from the cigarettes of patrons who were almost buzzing with the expectation of tucking into the sort of good solid grub which had not yet been banned by the health freaks. I was sitting at a table by the window to the right of the door, looking out at the winter-wan Copenhageners hurrying past. The March light was lovely, though – grey, perhaps, but with a golden cast that said April was just around the corner. Sunshine glinted off the spokes of a freshly polished bike wheel and more optimistic souls were striding out briskly with their coats unbuttoned. The solitary tree outside the restaurant was covered in swollen, straining buds, reminding me of the sex life I no longer had. My back was still acting up, but it did feel a little better. I still had to be careful when standing up, and I held my head a little too stiffly, but things were moving in the right direction and the world was, if not young and lovely, then not quite as decrepit as it had seemed the day before.

We shook hands, Lasse sat down and I ordered him a beer and a schnapps, ignoring his shake of the head. And another of the same for myself. You had to be allowed some pleasures when your wife had run off and taken the car with her.

Apparently it had all been pretty dramatic in Budapest. Niels had not come down for breakfast and Charlotte had been sent up to wake him. They had heard her come screaming all the way down the stairs to the breakfast room. Lasse had gone back up with her and found Niels lying on the floor with his head smashed in. The room had looked as if it had been hit by a hurricane. Things scattered everywhere. After that the place was in uproar. A doctor was called, then the police came; they spoke to everyone, but no one could be of any help. They had attended a meeting that evening with the foreign minister, afterwards they had had a drink in the bar and gone to bed shortly before midnight.

The hotel staff who had been on night duty and had gone home once the morning shift arrived, were woken and asked to come in.

The night porter had seen nothing. There had been only the usual traffic, as he so diplomatically put it, of young ladies visiting lonely men in their rooms, but he knew all of them. They too would be interviewed.

'It was all very confusing, Teddy,' Lasse said between mouthfuls. For my own part, I was savouring the oily, slightly acidic firmness of the fried herring, which went so well with the soft onion and the cold beer. 'They asked about one thing and another, but it was almost as if it was a routine occurrence for a foreign visitor to be murdered in the middle of the night in a top quality hotel in the middle of Budapest. It's all very odd.'

'Well, that's the new world order for you,' I remarked, raising my schnapps glass. 'Here's to life!' I said.

'Sometimes you're just a little too morbid,' he said, but raised his glass anyway.

'It could have been me,' I said. 'Did that ever occur to you?'

I could see from his face that it had not. He said nothing and we sat for a moment, letting that thought sink in. He would never have said it outright, of course, but I could tell he was glad that it was Niels and not me, who had been killed. Wrong though it was of me I could not help feeling pleased about this. To have this confirmation that he was fond of me. Because I was fond of him.

We thrashed the matter out over smørbrød with roast beef and cheese, then we had coffee. We both felt sorry for Charlotte, and obviously it was strange to think that Niels was, as they say, no more, but we had not known him all that well. And sadly he was not the only one of our acquaintance to have passed away – to use another of those euphemisms designed to make the notion of death easier to take. Heart attacks had begun to strike down our colleagues at an appalling rate. All the living we had done was starting to catch up on us. We eventually agreed that it must have been a robbery that had gone wrong. Over coffee I then told him the trite, woeful, tedious story of Janne and me. It came as no surprise to him.

'Maybe you just need a break from one another,' he said.

I shook my head.

'I don't believe in breaks where love is concerned,' I said. 'I think Janne really loves the bastard. Or at least, is in love with the thought that he lusts after her.'

'You have to learn to invest more of yourself in your relationships,' Lasse said, giving me the benefit, for the first time, of this particular insight. Although we were both products of the insistence in the sixties and seventies on expressing one's feelings, we had not been particularly vocal on that score in the past twenty years. The new man had been trampled underfoot by the yuppies in the eighties.

'Who says there are going to be any more?' I said.

'You usually can't keep your hands off women,' Lasse retorted. 'And who knows, maybe you're a little wiser now.'

'According to the women in my life that is absolutely impossible,' I said and we both laughed, happy to be in each other's company.

I was feeling like my old self again, lunch was on me. We said goodbye outside the restaurant and Lasse set off towards Nørreport at a brisk lope. I headed for Rådhuspladsen, wanting to walk the stiffness out of my back. The sun was shining and the sparrows were chirping fit to burst, and I was in that pleasantly befuddled state when the light seems to dance over people's faces. On Rådhuspladsen I glanced up at *Politiken*'s electronic headlines sign. Underneath an advert were the words: 'Dane jailed for spying for Stasi'. Another one, was all I thought, and walked on in the glorious sunshine. I felt as though I had all the time in the world and I had no great wish to return to my empty flat too soon, so I cut down to Gammel Strand and strolled along the canal. The sunlight bounced off the water, reflections of the surrounding buildings were repeated in window after window. I carried on out towards Østerbro, aware of a pleasant physical tiredness in my legs. Walking was good for my back.

The flat was bathed in rosy, late-afternoon sunlight when I got home feeling very pleased with myself. I noticed the red light blinking on the answering machine. I hung my coat over a chair, lit a cigarette and listened. The first message was from SAS. They regretted to inform me that my errant suitcase was now definitely lost. Could I please contact them in order to discuss the question of compensation. There was also a message from Janne. She had a bit of a problem on Thursday evening, would it be possible for me to mind the kids? No, I thought, it certainly would not. What the hell did she think this was? She wanted me to babysit so that she could go out with her fancy man? I had to draw the line somewhere. My spirits sank a few notches, but I forced myself to stay cool, be grown up about it. I was hungry again after my long walk through the streets, so I brewed some coffee, made a couple of sandwiches and read the two foreign newspapers I had bought on the way home. Then it was time for the television news. There was another report from the Albanian refugee camps. If NATO had been hoping to stem the flow of refugees with its bombing raids then the alliance had been seriously mistaken. There were heart-rending shots of people – soaked, frozen and starving – who had crossed the border at Kukkes. These were the sort of scenes we had become accustomed to seeing ever since Yugoslavia began its slow, suicidal breakdown almost ten years earlier. I still had not come to terms with those stony, desolate faces. They came on foot, or driving their pathetic little tractors, with all their belongings piled into the tiny trailers. What a great gulf there was between the refugees and the healthy, well-fed pilots in another item on the news, this time about the Danish F-16 fighter planes and the fact that they had not yet seen combat, but flew missions every day as air support for other NATO planes. Then it was back to Albania, where one of Danmarks Radio's foreign correspondents reported from a refugee camp set up in some old factory buildings: more distressing scenes of individuals lying in the mud under primitive awnings made from plastic sheeting while the rain poured down. There was a shot of a ten-year-old girl up to her knees in mud, lugging a stack of sodden loaves. 'Give me back the Berlin Wall' I sang to myself, thinking of that song by Leonard Cohen, although I did not really mean it. The ten-year-old girl, who had dark, tangled hair and a little cat-like face with large, blank eyes, handed the loaves to a woman, who took them with a smile. Before cutting back to the reporter the camera zoomed in on the woman's face, a fleeting glimpse only, but I recognised her right away, despite the fact that the hair under her red hat had been cut short. It was the woman from the hotel room in Bratislava. She was wearing a yellow raincoat. On it, just over her right breast, was a badge. Before I had any chance to make out what this emblem represented the reporter's hale and hearty Danish face was back on screen, telling me what I ought to think about the whole situation, but it was her. For a moment I just sat there, stunned. I had almost begun to doubt whether she had even existed. And if my suitcase was lost, then gone too was the physical proof which she had given me in Bratislava. I sat staring at the television, letting the rest of the news go in one ear and out the other. *Teddy's World Falls Apart* this picture might have been called. *Cracks Start Appearing in Teddy's Life* would also have made an excellent title for this still life, which I contemplated from the outside as it were. I was jolted out of my inertia by the trill of the phone, so sudden and shrill that it made me jump.

It was my brother, Fritz. The hardy baker did not sound quite himself. His Fünen accent was even more pronounced than normal and his voice at least an octave higher when he said:

'Teddy. It's Irma. She's been arrested ... what are we going to do?'

'Fritz! What in God's name are you talking about? Where is she?'

'The police called. They've got her at police headquarters in Copenhagen. What am I going to do?'

'Calm down, Fritz. Who's her lawyer?'

| 73 |

'How should I know, Teddy. I'm all the way over here on Fünen, what can I do? There's *nothing* I can do. What *is* all this? Irma hasn't done anything.'

'Calm down, Teddy,' I said again absently, as I tried to think.

'Why has she been arrested?'

'They won't say.'

'Well, they must have said something.'

'They say she's a spy,' my brother said. 'What's going on, Teddy?'

Teddy had no idea, of course, but Fritz was quite sure that Teddy would find out.

6

AFTER FRITZ'S CALL there followed a couple of hectic days. The newspapers could not publish Irma's name, of course. She was being held in solitary confinement under tight security, so the media were not even allowed to say what she was charged with. Only that she was being detained under the Official Secrets Act, which never really goes out of date. But the press had, nonetheless, managed to dig up some details. So they had a field day anyway, speculating on whether this was the big fish that everyone had been expecting to see caught ever since the Wall came down. In their reports they used her cover name, which was apparently Edelweiss. That very evening there had been a big item about the case on the Nine O'Clock News. And the morning papers were full of it. They had had access to some of the material which Edelwiess had passed to Stasi in East Berlin from as far back as the early seventies until the beginning of 1988. Chickenfeed for the most part, relating to Denmark's oil policy or the Danish view on security in the Baltic area, but also more crucial documents, such as maps of Danish NATO depots and plans for mine-laying in the event of war. The papers also said that Edelwiess had reported on top-secret NATO meetings. But what the hell would Irma have been doing there? She had spent her whole life inside her intellectual glass bubble with little thought for the real world outside. She had only ever had one student job, with the Ministry of Foreign Affairs. She had never had access to classified material of that nature. And even if she had applied for a job with NATO she would never have got it. She was a Red of the first water and she made no secret of this in the numerous articles on the need for revolution which she wrote for *Information* and diverse obscure left-wing journals. She

| 75 |

had been a member of a variety of different parties on the far left until rendered wiser by age (or the fall of the Berlin Wall). But she had never struck me as being a particular fan of the former GDR. As a young woman she had been more a devotee of such characters as Chairman Mao and, God help us, Pol Pot. Now she was a professor at Roskilde University. Denmark is a tolerant, forgiving little country. Words do not count for a whole lot here.

A read through the papers left me little the wiser, despite their massive coverage of the case. At Roskilde University everyone knew, of course, that they were talking about Irma, but it says a lot about how much the world has changed that her colleagues kept a very low profile. No one protested or wrote to the newspapers. The wind from the Right blew strong and keen across Denmark and the old left-wingers were sheltering from the storm. They couldn't go sticking their necks out, not now, with their pension only ten years away. They knew only too well that having taken part in a peace demo or been a member of a delegation to Moscow during the cold war, with free lunches and all, was all it took for *Jyllands-Posten* or *Ekstra Bladet* to condemn them as spies or tail-wagging communist lackeys. Time was when they had taken a very black-and-white view of the rotten capitalist society. Now the victors on the Right were paying them back in the same black-and-white coin. I did not really feel sorry for them, and yet I found it hard to reconcile myself to the bumptious, self-righteous tone of the attacks made on them. On the other hand they could have refrained from lunching with Pol Pot or writing articles extolling the Cultural Revolution. The past has a way of catching up with most people.

These were some of the thoughts that went through my head as I tried to figure out what I could do to help my sister and why she had been locked up. She had been assigned a counsel who had made a routine, but unsuccessful appeal to the High Court against the order to keep her in solitary confinement for four weeks, but I got in touch with Kenneth Graversen. He was one of those hot-shot lawyers capable of conducting a case both in the lawcourts and in today's other great seat of judgement: the media. He was in huge demand, but he agreed to look at the case. He was already familiar with it, of course, from the press and TV. He did not actually need any persuading. I had the feeling that he could already smell the publicity: the blazing flashlights, the seductive television cameras. This could well become something of a *cause célèbre* once Irma's identity became known. Graversen had a deep, rich, cultured voice. He would give me a call after he had spoken to his new client, but he wanted to make it quite clear that he would not be able to tell me anything about the substance of the case, since the High Court had upheld the order authorising solitary confinement in a high security wing. It would be against the law for him to run telling tales, so to speak, to old Teddy.

At long last I managed to get hold of the police spokesman for the case, a detective inspector, in the press at least, had sounded pretty sure of himself – as if my sister had already been found guilty. He was a pleasant middle-aged gentleman whom I had often seen on television: the very image of trustworthiness and not the sort of seedy alcoholic who tended to populate the detective novels which I occasionally read for amusement. I recognised his voice when he eventually called back, after I had left umpteen messages for him. Although that was possibly a little unfair: it was actually quite hard to get through to me on the phone. When I wasn't trying to reassure Fritz, I was arguing with Janne because I could not look after the kids, talking to curious colleagues, receiving moral support from Lasse or trying yet again to make my mother understand that her daughter was in prison, although I do not think this fact penetrated the mists of senility she inhabited in the nursing home on Fünen. My back was all but forgotten in the Kafkaesque situation in which I suddenly found myself. My tooth, or gums, had, however, started to ache again. You did not need to be a doctor or a dentist to know that this pain was in fact psychosomatic and a symptom of stress.

The detective inspector with that most Danish of all Danish names, Per Jensen, could not have been nicer. But he would say nothing about the case. He spelled out for me, as if I were some ignorant journalist, what it meant to try a case in a closed court, within prison confines and what it meant to be held in solitary confinement. In this the tiny democratic state of Denmark had a formidable weapon. Cutting an individual off from all human contact. Permitting them no communication with anyone except a lawyer. I tried to tell him that, as the accused's younger brother I had certain rights, but there was no moving him. Out of the question at the present time, was all he would say, again and again. And besides, the investigation had been taken over by another department. Which one? That he was not at liberty to say at the moment.

I also needed to keep an eye on the television news. I had to see whether the woman from Bratislava would show up again. But she did not. I searched on the Internet, found the item in which she had appeared. There was no doubt. It was her alright. Lasse suggested that I also check the news broadcasts on TV2. They often used the same agency footage as DR. I rarely watched TV2. I had grown up with Danmarks Radio and still found it hard to take the Odense based station seriously. I found its presenters too jaunty by half. Back to the Internet. And clever old Lasse was right. There she was, in two different shots. In one she seemed to be performing some sort of official role. At any rate she was seen pointing and two men walked off in the direction she indicated. Later in the same piece the two men were back again. They stood facing her, looked as though they were presenting a report. But the item had been edited without any thought for the actual sequence of events, so it could just as easily have been the other way round. The woman was merely a prop to illustrate the reporter's hackneyed spiel about the poor refugees. The trendily dressed female correspondent must have used the phrase 'humanitarian disaster' at least eight times. And informed viewers almost as often that Albania was the poorest country in Europe. First she presented her report, then she remained on-screen while the studio presenter asked inane, obvious questions and indulged in wild speculation – but that's modern TV for you.

I called Fritz and told him the whole story about the woman in Bratislava. I could hear him puffing and blowing all the way over there on Fünen and could tell from his laboured breathing that it both surprised him and yet did not. He was a heavy man in all ways and hard to get through to. I did not have the knack for breaking through his shell. When I was finished he said exactly what I expected him to say:

'You really ought to talk to Irma, Teddy.' His lilting Fünen accent made everything, even the gravest of topics, sound like an operetta. Even so, I could tell from his voice that I had hit a raw spot.

'Fritz, for Christ's sake. Irma's in prison. In solitary. I can't just pick up the bloody phone and call her, can I?'

'Well, I still think that would be best.'

I lost my temper:

'Tell me. Is this story true? Have you two been hiding something from me?'

'You were so young, Teddy. It was all before your time. You weren't even born then.'

'Do we have a half-sister down there?'

There was a long silence.

'Not that I've ever heard of,' he said at last, sounding anything but convincing.

'So what have you heard, Fritz?' I hissed.

'The bit about our father. That's true enough ...'

'What?'

'Dad fought on the Eastern Front. And he was a member of the party. There, now you know.'

I stood for a moment, listening to his heavy breathing on the other end of the line. It was quite a blow, to learn in mid-life that your father had been a Nazi and a soldier with the SS. Take that. To say that lots of families have skeletons in their cupboards is a tired, old cliché, but this was one of the darker secrets. I suppose I had had some suspicion of his Nazi past, but I had had no notion about the rest of it.

'So he didn't die in Hamburg, the way you always said he did?'

'I don't know, Teddy. I really thought he had. As far as I was concerned he died the day he left home. You'd better talk to Irma about it.'

'Why was I never told?'

'You were so young, Teddy,' he said again. 'You weren't even born. It was all before your time.'

'And hence I was not made privy to this great family trauma.'

'You use all those fancy words. But I'm not stupid. I have different talents from you and Irma, that's all,' he said, sharply this time.

'Why wasn't I let in on the family scandal?' I asked.

'You were so young. It was nothing to do with you,' he repeated.

I waited, expecting him to go on, but of course he did not, so I asked:

'Was that why the bakery had to shut down?'

'Folk were starting to talk. You know how they talk.'

'Naw – I live in a city. Nobody ever talks here,' I sniped, out of old, sarcastic habit, as I stood there with the receiver to my ear, gazing out across a city which seemed to blur at the edges and fade from my view. Possible title for this picture: *Teddy Learns of the Past Over the Phone.*

I tried to get more out of him, but he was not especially forthcoming. This much he was prepared to tell me: that our father had been an SS soldier, a non-commissioned officer. That he had been sentenced to two and a half years in prison for enlisting in the Danish Legion, but that he had been released after a few months. That 'someone' had helped him to go into business for himself as a baker. That he had left home when he became the victim, as Fritz put it, of reprisals in the early fifties. But the bit about a daughter and another life in Yugoslavia, that I would have to talk to Irma about. That he really could not go into. I had the feeling that he was hiding something from me, but I also knew that I was not going to get any further with him. So I changed tack:

'I've hired a very good lawyer, Kenneth Graversen ...'

'I've seen him on television,' the voice from Fünen said, as if this were the seal of approval. But then Fritz was not familiar with the players in the daily media circus, where everybody knew everybody else and nobody was interested in the truth, only the image.

'He doesn't come cheap,' I went on.

Another of those long pauses when all I could hear was his breathing, then:

'That's not a problem. I'll put up the money.'

'I've no idea how much Irma has in the way of a nest egg, but I've got nothing.'

'Don't worry, I'll see to it,' he said sounding a little happier. Finally, here was something that Fritz the baker could do. Where he was one up on the rest of us. Because he actually did have a nice little nest egg, although these days it was more likely to be certificates in a safe deposit box.

'Great, well I'll reassure the brief on that point then,' I said, but Fritz jumped in quickly:

'No, I'll do that,' he said, the firmness of his tone betraying that he really did have some cash stashed away. He had not got rich by being stupid. Quite the opposite. 'Give me his number and I'll have a word with him. Then we can discuss the details.' I knew what he was getting at. He would pay for Irma's defence, but first he wanted to negotiate the fee. There was no reason for the family to be ripped off by some Copenhagen lawyer. I found the number and read it out to him. There followed another of those long pauses. It struck me that we were like strangers, despite the fact that we had been boys together, for some years at least, and always met up at the usual Danish family gatherings: confirmations, weddings, funerals. At the church and later around the dinner table. But I did not know him. He was born in 1943. Irma was born in 1940, which fitted perfectly with the date of our parents' marriage.

| 81 |

At long last they could fuck without having to worry and the first baby followed pretty much as a matter of course. Fritz's birth in 1943 tied in – so I calculated after a quick recap of the dates of the occupation – with my father's first trip home on leave. The men of the Danish Legion thought they were going home to take their native land by storm. Instead they had been ostracised by almost everyone, with the possible exception of their closest family. I was born in 1948, which fitted with the time when he returned home. Or at least, was released from prison. 'He' was my father. A figure whom Teddy found it rather difficult to relate to. If the woman in Bratislava was more than a mirage in a mysterious desert then she had been born in 1944, which corresponded with my father's service with the Nordland Regiment in Yugoslavia at the end of 1943. The old man had been pretty prolific. Not like the young men of today. The past was both an obscure bastard and a database full of concrete facts – and dates which brooked no denial.

'Was our father in Yugoslavia?' I asked.

'He served on the Eastern Front,' Fritz said after a lengthy pause.

'That covers a lot, Fritz.'

'Maybe. I think you should talk to Irma.'

'I can't talk to her, goddammit. Come on, tell me!'

'I think so.'

There followed another long silence. The only one getting any joy out of this conversation was the phone company. The minutes ticked by and the meter ran as I listened to his heavy breathing. I could see him in my mind's eye: a burly, middle-aged man with a bit of a paunch, standing in his nice, respectable living room in his nice, respectable detached bungalow in a small town by the sea in which he produced the bread that had made him a wealthy man. He and Dorthe had two sons, both grown up and doing well, as they say. Hans-Peter was a long-distance lorry driver, transporting fish to Spain and Italy. They got all the top-grade produce which we were not prepared to pay for. Little brother Niels was a schoolteacher in Lemvig, married to the local vicar. They lived far away from the aggravation of Copenhagen and were the sort of provincial Danes who could not understand why anyone would willingly live in the capital. To them Copenhagen was an exotic place, inhabited by restless, confused people and prodigal Jutlanders and Fünen folk forced into exile by misfortune. Copenhagen sucked honest, hard-earned money out of the provinces. That one just had to live with, but to actually live in the big city was another matter. Beyond the imaginings of decent souls.

'Well, let's keep in touch,' I said to break the silence.

'Of course. Everything's going to be alright, you'll see. We know our Irma, right?' he said in the soft, lilting burr to which he had reverted so easily on his return to the island.

'I wish it was that simple,' I sighed. We both said goodbye at the same time and I stood for a moment staring down at the road and the traffic, missing Janne and the kids. It was at times like this that one really had need of a mate. Someone with whom to share one's troubles. I could have called her, of course, but I would not. Janne was actually a good woman, I was extremely fond of her and she was a good listener, but I did not want to run the risk of *the other man* answering the phone.

I made some sandwiches, left the coffee filtering in the kitchen and carried them through to the television along with a carton of skimmed milk. On the news were reports on the NATO air strikes. As usual things were going very well. There had been no losses, and civilian casualties on the Serbian side were minimal, so said a uniformed American general. Serbia was being systematically bombed back to the Stone Age. A Danish officer explained why it would at some point be necessary to send in ground troops, then came a piece on the stream of refugees into Albania. More grim shots of shivering, distressed people. But there was no sign of the woman from Bratislava. I suddenly remembered the words of an American officer during the Vietnam War. 'In order to save the village it was unfortunately necessary to destroy it,' he was reported to have said about a little South Vietnam village. That was then. Nowadays there was something cartoon-like about the whole thing. High-flying, high-tech jets firing off laser-controlled missiles and then zooming back to Italy for evening coffee. What must it be like on the ground? We would probably never know. Once the war was won the media would lose interest and the dead and wounded would be forgotten. Among the living nothing would be left but the hate.

The telephone rang. The voice on the other end, a deep bass, enunciated with exaggerated care.

'Teddy Pedersen? You are speaking to someone who knows who you are. I was wondering whether we could meet. It's about your sister.'

The question mark was left hanging in the air. I had reached the stage where nothing could surprise me. Why shouldn't a stranger call to ask about my sister? After all, nothing was the same as it had been only a couple of weeks earlier.

'I have nothing to say to the press,' I said shortly.

'I'm not a reporter. This is personal.'

'I don't know you,' I said.

'I think you would do well to meet me. Tomorrow perhaps?'

'What for?'

'To talk about your sister. It's about Irma.'

'That much I understand. What's this all about? My sister's in jail. And who the hell are you anyway?'

'That is of no importance.'

'It is to me. I'd like to know who I'm talking to.'

'I realise that, but I would prefer not to discuss it over the phone,' he said in that deep bass. The man was obviously paranoid.

'And where do you suggest we meet?'

'How about the new Knudshoved service area. On the Fünen side, just after the bridge.'

'You expect me to drive all the way to Fünen, pay the bridge toll and all, when you could easily tell me on the phone what this is all about? You must be mad!'

| 84 |

'I don't think it's such a good idea to discuss it on the phone, but it's about a woman in Slovakia. She gave you some papers. She told you a story.'

Now he had my full attention. Nobody knew about that except Lasse, who had shaken his head at the whole thing. Then there was the message on Irma's answering machine and an email.

'How do you know about that?'

'I think we should meet,' was all he said.

'Okay,' I said without stopping to consider. 'When?'

'Why don't we say tomorrow morning, around eleven. Park your car, go into the cafeteria and you will be contacted.'

'By whom?'

'We'll recognise you. Do we have a date?'

'I suppose so,' I said – Teddy was born curious. The bass voice hung up. Might he have been afraid that my phone was tapped? The worse of it was that I had to call Janne and ask if I could borrow my own car. She griped about it, even though it was me who had paid for the damn thing. We had kept our finances separate. It just so happened that she would be needing it the next day. What about the kids? Couldn't it wait for a couple of days. What did I want it for?

'That's none of your business. You're the one who chose not to have any part in what I do. It's my bloody car, Janne! And I'm going to be needing it tomorrow morning at nine o'clock sharp. So fucking well get it over here!' amiable old Teddy snapped and slammed down the receiver. I waited an hour, but she did not call back, so I went to bed feeling cross and resentful.

She evidently had no wish to see me. I looked out of the window at eight o'clock the next morning to see our natty little Renault parked neatly alongside the kerb. It was streaked with the muck of the Copenhagen spring and when I slid into the driver's seat at nine thirty to set out for Fünen, the petrol gauge was reading close to empty. I felt a lump in my throat when I saw one of the children's little cuddly toys lying on the back seat and caught their and Janne's scent in the car – I cursed the morning and the grey, dismal weather. Janne was dead set against anyone smoking in the car so in order to establish my rightful ownership I lit a cigarette and blew the smoke over the upholstery. But I was not used to lighting up in cars either now, the smoke soon started to get to me, so I opened a window, chucked the ciggie out and managed to get the window rolled up again before another shower swept over the rain-ridden city. *Teddy Regretting His Actions* might be a good title for this picture.

I stopped at a petrol station to fill the tank and had a cup of coffee in the adjoining cafeteria. There were only a couple of us in the place and it cheered me up no end when the young girl behind the counter wished me a nice day, although I don't know what in hell it had to do with her. Still, a little politeness does make life easier all round. The weather cleared up a little. The sun came out and sent long, shimmering rays playing over a landscape that looked green and ready for anything, bristling with signs of spring. Apart from the big, heavy trailer-trucks there was not too much traffic on the road to Halsskov. I stayed on the right side of 130 kph, while one shiny new car after another went flying past me. These people were clearly in a hurry and regarded speed limits as no more than gentle guidelines. The bridge over Storebælt loomed ahead. Its pylons reared up far off on the horizon, glinting in the spring sunlight. I did miss the ferries sometimes, but it wasn't as if I had ever used them much and to be honest like most Danes I was very impressed by the costly suspension bridge. No one gave it a second thought now, although initially there had been a lot of opposition to the project. Like every other bridge built by man, once it was finished and the dust had settled no one could imagine a time when it hadn't been there. I had driven across it often, but I still got a kick out of skimming over that blue belt of water, feeling the wind buffet the car as I passed the massive anchor cables. Sprogø disappeared briefly from view when a sudden fall of rain over the water swept across the tiny island, giving rise for a few seconds to a rainbow which arched from the edge of the island out into Storebælt. A large coaster seemed to sail, Flying Dutchman style, through the rainbow, shimmering like a mirage. *Teddy Witnesses One of Nature's Wonders* would have made a good title for this picture, I thought to myself, before driving out onto the low section of the bridge. This, on the other hand, was just a stretch of motorway running across water. Nothing to write home about.

The cafeteria lay next to the old ferry wharf. The water in the harbour was like glass, the dock empty apart from one of the Lifeboat Service's red craft and a small, covered wooden boat which I guessed must be used by local anglers. There were only a handful of cars in the car park when I got out, buttoning my coat against a stiff breeze which the sun was incapable of warming. I stretched, massaged the base of my spine. My back was better, but it did not take kindly to being stuck in a car for an hour and a half. I glanced round about. A vehicle pulled into the car park, but stopped some way off, as if the driver could not decide where to go. Or maybe he or she had been under the impression that there was also a petrol station down here.

I went into the cafeteria, bought a cup of coffee and a copy of *Ekstra Bladet* and sat down. I had drunk half of my coffee and flicked through the newspaper when a youngish man stopped in front of me and said my name. There had been a small item in the paper about Edelweiss. The spy who will not talk, the headline said, but it was merely a rehashed spin on an old story, so it left me none the wiser. I recognised the deep bass voice. I had expected him to be much older, but he could only have been in his early thirties.

'Finish your coffee, by all means, but then we ought to be on our way,' he said.

'It tastes like shit,' I said as I got to my feet and made towards the entrance, but the man took my arm politely but firmly and drew me towards the back door. It opened onto a terrace on which, in summer, patrons could enjoy their coffee or a snack. Once outside he led me towards the little fishing boat.

'Are we going for a sail?' I asked.

'Only across to the other side of the fjord.'

'What on earth for? This is absolutely crazy. Why all the secrecy.'

'Just get on board,' he said, his voice suddenly hard.

I stepped down into the boat which gave and rocked under my feet. I felt the first faint surge of nausea.

'I'm not a good sailor,' I said. 'I get seasick on the Storebælt ferry in a dead calm.'

'It's only a short trip,' he said and pointed to a small cabin containing a table with a bench seat on either side of it. Curtains hung at the windows and there was an all-pervading reek of petrol and fish. Peering out of the low doorway – for which there was no doubt some other nautical word – I saw him cast off and start the engine, which kicked into life at the first turn of the key with a cough that was actually quite reassuring. I heard a car accelerating, the sound of running feet and a shout.

'What was that?' I cried.

'You were being followed. We suspected as much,' he said above the steady, monotonous drone of the engine.

'Why in hell's name would anyone be following me?' I yelled.

'Because of your sister, of course,' he said. 'Come on up into the fresh air if it makes you feel better. I'm Karl Henrik Jensen.'

My stomach was heaving, but despite the wind there were no waves, not even when we drew clear of the old ferry harbour and cut over to the narrow spit of land extending into the water. We sailed round the tip and down the other side. Only a few minutes later Jensen pulled in alongside a small jetty. We were in a little marina. There did not seem to be anyone else around on this chilly spring weekday. Seagulls wheeled and screamed overhead, as if searching for the long-lost ferries. I noticed what looked like a golf course. Red flags fluttered in the breeze and a man was helplessly searching the ground for something. Karl Henrik

Jensen gave me a hand up onto the jetty and pointed to a car parked nearby.

'Go on over to the vehicle, I won't be a moment,' he said. I walked over to what was a perfectly ordinary saloon car. A young man sat behind the wheel. He reached behind and opened the back door.

'Good morning, Mr Pedersen,' he said. Helluva polite, they were. A moment later Karl Henrik Jensen appeared. He got into the front. Before he slammed the door shut and we drove off I heard the throb of an engine again. So they had a third man to take the little boat away again. It seemed to be a very well-planned operation.

'Who's following me? *Why* would anyone be following me?' I asked with a note of panic in my voice.

'Either PET or the CID. At any rate we saw one car turn in to the car park behind you, and there was another one sitting by the exit, in case you decided to drive out again.'

'But I haven't done anything wrong,' I said.

'Neither have we. We simply want to have a quiet chat with you, somewhere we won't be disturbed. That's all. Do you have the documents with you?'

'No. My suitcase went missing. I actually have to go to the SAS office. Apparently I can claim compensation.'

Jensen turned to look at me. In the same placid tone he said:

'That's not so good.'

'Well, there's nothing I can do about it,' I retorted sullenly.

'All I'm saying is it's not so good,' he muttered.

We drove towards Nyborg and then south in the direction of Svendborg.

'Where are we going?'

'We'll be there in less than half an hour,' he said. 'All your questions will be answered then. Just have a little patience, Mr Pedersen, and in the meantime sit back and enjoy our beautiful Fünen countryside.'

There was nothing else for it. No further explanation was

forthcoming. And Fünen *is* very pretty. Besides which, I felt safe in assuming that this small island had not turned into a Danish version of Chechnya. What would be the sense in kidnapping a middle-aged lecturer in Russian and history? So I sat back and watched the lovely Lilliputian scenery slip past until we turned off the main road, drove down a narrow side road, then made a sharp left onto a dirt track leading to a small whitewashed farmhouse with a thatched roof hidden behind a hawthorn hedge. Once parked in the front yard we were invisible from the little side road.

I clambered out of the car and stretched my back. An upright man of around sixty-five was standing in the doorway. A thick mane of white hair was swept back from his high, narrow forehead and long, strong arms protruded from a short-sleeved shirt buttoned right up to the throat. When he stepped towards me and smiled I saw a row of even white teeth, and appraising eyes held mine a fraction too long, just as his firm, lengthy handshake was a little overdone. One would have thought we were old friends, miraculously meeting after years apart. From behind him Fritz edged out and looked at me.

'Hi, Teddy,' he said.

'Hi, Fritz. I had a feeling you might be mixed up in this.'

'If only Irma were here,' Fritz said, wiping his hands on his trousers. He was wearing his old grey tweed jacket over a light-coloured shirt with neatly knotted tie and navy flannels. In his hand was his unlit pipe.

'Yeah, well, Irma can't get us out of this one,' I said.

'I'm pleased to meet you, Teddy. I'm pleased to meet Irma's brother. You're more like your mother, I think,' the upright old man said. Although I don't know why I should have thought of him as old, when I had just gauged him to be in his mid-sixties: that would make him only about fifteen years older than me. Maybe he was actually seventy? Well, at any rate we were on first name terms, while to the younger men old Teddy was still Mr Pedersen.

'I'd really like to know, Mr ...?' I said.

'Karl Viggo Jensen. Come in and have a bite to eat. Then I will tell you all about your father and my father, and about Irma's secret life.'

7

FRITZ CAUGHT THE DIRTY LOOK I shot him as we walked through the narrow door into a low-ceilinged living room. I could feel anger starting to well up inside me. Not so much over the strange secrecy surrounding this particular meeting, but also at the fact that I had for so many years been kept in the dark about certain crucial aspects of my family history: that my unknown natural father and my dear, but now totally senile mother had lived a double life, like secret agents living in a hostile country. The living room was small and very cosy in an old-fashioned way, with heavy furniture and naturalist pictures on the walls – the royal stag and the weatherbeaten fisherman. Classic, petit-bourgeois kitsch, I thought to myself, with typical academic arrogance. As if my own equally inoffensive abstract poster art was anything other than a reflection of what I and others like me considered pleasing to the eye. Were we not just as rigid in our own ideas of good taste? There was a large bookcase filled mainly, I noticed, with volumes on war and military history. In one corner a worn battered leather armchair was flanked by a small round coffee table and a black pot-bellied stove. There were three books on the table, bookmarks protruding neatly from each one. These volumes were not for decoration. This was where the man of the house sat to read and expand his knowledge. The room had the faintly stuffy air of an old man's home, overlaid with the smell of pipe smoke. The resulting odour was not unpleasant, though: a little musty, rather like windfall apples; a whiff of childhood which brought back memories of my maternal grandparents' smallholding, where I had spent my holidays as a little boy. From where I stood I could see into an antiquated kitchen where a woman of Karl Viggo Jensen's age was

| 92 |

bustling about. She gave me a quick nod and wiped her hands on her apron before coming through to the living room and offering me her hand. It was damp and cool, but her handshake was firm and the grey eyes in the wrinkled face were bright.

'Karla Jensen,' she said. 'I'm sure you could do with something to eat – it's not as if you can catch a bite on the ferry nowadays.'

'That would be lovely, thank you,' I said, ensnared by the out-moded surroundings and atmosphere. In Copenhagen one forgot that in the country another life still went on, at a different tempo and in a different tone. One in which old words and expressions continued to be used, as if television had never been invented.

'Can it wait fifteen minutes? I'd like to show Irma's little brother the museum first,' Karl Viggo Jensen said.

'There's no reason why not,' she said. 'It's only a bit of lunch. It won't come to any harm in fifteen minutes, but if the gentleman is hungry ...'

'No, I'm fine, really,' I said.

'Well in that case I'll put the aquavit back in the fridge,' she said, as if the schnapps was more important than whatever was pervading the house with such delicious odours.

The rest of us filed through another room in which a table was set for lunch, out into the garden and over to a low, whitewashed building which might once have been a pig shed. Our feet swished through the matted layer of leaves from the autumn still lying around a copper beech tree. Karl Viggo, straight-backed, led the way with me trudging at his heels and Fritz bringing up the rear, trailing his feet and panting slightly. He was not as young as he had once been and he had never been one to deny himself anything. Were the cigars and the pipe starting to have too marked an effect on my brother's lungs, I wondered, feeling genuinely worried about him. Families are funny that way: we do not choose them, they can often be a pain in the neck, and yet they are the one constant in our lives.

The room we entered was a grim one, even if it did to some

extent resemble a small local museum in that it had pictures on the walls and exhibits in small glass cases. It was the objects on display which gave the place its sinister air. This was a museum dedicated to the SS, containing photographs of officers in black uniforms with SS runes on their collars, large black-and-white pictures of battle scenes, a Danish flag bearing the words: *Frikorps Danmark* – the Danish Legion. Guns, medals, yellowing letters and documents, what looked like diaries, gas masks, military insignia, accoutrements and dog tags. All the detritus left behind on the battlefields. Maps of the battles of Lake Ilmen, Stalingrad and Narva were carefully arranged in glass cases. With arrows and little labels giving the names of the regiments and which side they were on. As if that were of interest to anyone apart from those involved. In any case, even to a historian such as myself they said nothing. We were talking minor skirmishes on a pretty horrific front line, but obviously that part of the line, with all its small victories and defeats, was of interest to those who had been there. To the common soldier war is really just a matter of the next ditch, the next sheltering hedge, the next hot meal. Here one had everything which a small museum run on the limited resources available to such local ventures would be proud to present – were it not for the fact that this was an exhibition in honour of the losing side – and hence: evil. Karl Viggo Jensen said nothing, he merely remained just inside the door while I walked round in silence, looking. Fritz stood in the corner, staring at the floor and shuffling his feet on the scrubbed floor. It was still a pig shed, I thought to myself, but said nothing. Maybe I was simply a little scared, maybe I did not want to hurt Fritz's feelings. Some of the pictures were well-known to me: the Danish Legion home on leave in '42, for example. Fritz Clausen, the leader of the Danish Nazi Party, making a speech was another familiar image. And the picture of Christian Frederik Von Schalburg, first commander of the Danish Legion, with his small son in SS uniform – that too I had seen before. But the numerous other photographs of perfectly ordinary young Danish men with the Swastika and the Danish flag on their jackets pictured at different spots along the Eastern Front were new to me. The historians had not concerned themselves much with the losers' story. For many years there had been no academic posts or grants available for research into this dark chapter of the occupation. But I realised as I wandered round the exhibit that this was not an impartial, if secret, museum. This was a shrine, cherished and cared for as conscientiously as if it were a part of modern-day life and not a testament to acts of treason committed almost sixty years before; as if there were people who wished to say: We did exist. We do not want to be forgotten. We are a part of you.

One of the photographs showed a Waffen SS officer who was the spitting image of Karl Viggo Jensen himself, albeit in a much younger version. If it was the same man then I had got his age all wrong. He was standing next to another man whom I recognised as my father.

'Yes, that's me with your father, Teddy,' Karl Viggo said. I had not heard him come up behind me. I stared at the picture with a combination of fascination and disgust. The two young men stood side by side in their black uniforms, grinning broadly beneath their garrison caps. My father had a machine gun resting on his hip – like a big-game hunter who has just brought down a wild beast. But behind the two men a whole lot of bodies were laid out in rows like the bag from a hunt.

'Russian partisans. They had killed one of our men, a Dane from Himmerland, and poked his eyes out. So we raided their village, made them sorry they ever did that. War is a dirty business, believe me.'

I said nothing. I felt sick, my nausea increasing as I gazed at the picture of my father. I had never really known him, but his blood ran in my veins. And although I did not believe that the sins of the fathers were visited on the sons, it was quite a blow to be confronted with the fact that one's father had been involved in war crimes on the Eastern Front.

'That must make you almost eighty,' I said stupidly.

'Seventy-eight,' he said. 'There aren't many of us left and most of them are drooling cabbages in nursing homes now, but the Lord has blessed me with excellent health.'

'Who's Karl Henrik, then? He can't possibly be your son?'

'He's my nephew, and the secretary of the association. But you'll hear more about that over lunch. His grandfather is over here, come ...' He pointed to a corner of the room, made to take my arm, but thought better of it when he saw the look on my face. In the corner a number of photographs were displayed alongside two service books emblazoned with the Swastika. In one photo was a man who bore some resemblance to Karl Viggo. He was sitting in an armoured troop carrier with a pipe in his mouth and a rifle across his knees.

'That's Hans Peter. This picture was taken in Yugoslavia, not far from Zagreb, where the Nordland Division was stationed in '43. Hans Peter never came home. He fell at Narva in '44. He's buried there. We found his remains a couple of years back and gave him a Christian burial. The Estonians have a greater understanding of our fight against the Reds than you find in this country. Look at the other picture.'

It was another photo of my father. He was stripped to the waist and appeared to be soaping himself before rinsing off the suds under a makeshift shower set up in a tree. He looked thin, but muscular still. On the edge of the shot was a young girl; she had her hands over the lower part of her face, but was obviously in fits of laughter at the apparent antics of the Danish SS soldier.

'That's Andrea. Your father was very fond of Andrea. And she of him. She was the daughter of one of the local Ustashi commandants who helped us to disarm those lily-livered Italians and hunt down Tito's devils ... oh, and see here.'

It was a small picture in a light wood frame, in colour. It had been taken on a summer's day in a woodland clearing. A number of people, among them my older sister Irma and my older brother Fritz, were standing around a monument on which one could make out the words: 'They gave their lives for the Glory of Denmark'. In the small group I also recognised Karl Viggo and Karl Henrik Jensen.

'As I say, in the new Estonia they appreciate the contribution we made. We were fighting against the heathen communists. We were fighting Ivan. That picture was taken on June 2nd, 1998. The stone was erected on Christian Frederik von Schalburg's birthday. We felt that was rather fitting. He was a brave soldier and a good Dane.'

'And a fucking Nazi and an anti-Semite,' I burst out, but his voice did not falter:

'Yes, and so was I, but that's all in the past. Nazism died in a bunker in Berlin in 1945. That's what the younger generation don't understand. That it's a lost cause, although national socialism was originally conceived as a means of combatting communism and a social guarantee against capitalism. But that's all over and done with. We made a mistake. We lost the war. National socialism neither can nor should be revived. That's not the point.

'Oh, and what is the point?' I said, with anger and impotence in my voice as well as a note of indignation.

'Justice. It's a matter of justice, Teddy,' he said.

I could not bear to stay another moment in that ghastly room with its grim aesthetic and its worship of evil. Without a word I turned on my heel, strode past Fritz and out into the garden, where I took several deep breaths – as if the fresh air could cleanse my soul of the distorted reflection of one side of my family which that secret room represented. I lit a cigarette, puffed on it furiously while staring up at the bare branches of the copper beech. Possible title for this picture: *Shocked Teddy With Cigarette Under Copper Beech*. And this, my usual way of observing myself from the outside and making a joke of the situation helped me to get things back into perspective. I hadn't even known my father. His blood ran in my veins, but that did not mean that I shared his views or ever would. I was Teddy, good old, sardonic, distanced Teddy. And besides, this was the stuff of history, it could be analysed coolly and objectively, so there was no need to panic. Such was my reasoning, as I smoked that wonderful cigarette in the big garden and tried to bring my galloping heart under control.

For lunch there was herring and beer and schnapps, homemade rolled lamb sausage, rib-roast and streaky pork with apple the like of which I had not tasted in years. The aroma of the tart apples and smoked pork tickled my nostrils. The marinated herring served with curry salad had just the right consistency. The pork crackling was so crisp it made my brain pop. I would have thought that I would have lost my appetite, but Teddy just loves politically incorrect food, and having lived for so long in Janne's salad, bread and pasta hell, he tucked in with a will, washing it all down with two large drams of schnapps and a couple of cold Albani beers. The lady of the house went back and forth, so it was just we four men at the table. The atmosphere was, not surprisingly, a little strained to begin with, but everyone, including Fritz, ate well – although my brother would not look me in the eye. But the old man with the ice-blue gaze and the astonishingly smooth, parchment-like skin on which only the liver spots betrayed his age, acted as if nothing were amiss and chatted with his nephew about everyday doings in the neighbourhood. About a cow that had calved, a son who had gone off the rails, a forthcoming wedding and the new vicar, who hailed from Odense. They made no attempt to include the rest of us in their conversation, but made sure that we were helped to each new dish served up by Mrs Jensen. I had several questions which I wanted to ask Fritz – (or preferably Irma) – in private, but I had no desire to involve the two strangers in our family drama. In any case, this traditional Danish fare was so good, even if the fat content of the pork and apple would have had the Danish Heart Foundation up in arms and condemning us all to a strict diet of vegetables and fibre.

A pot of coffee was placed on the table along with a bottle of brandy. I refused the latter, remembering that I had to drive back to Copenhagen. I passed on the cigars too. I preferred to stick to my cigarettes. Only once the table and the rest of the low-ceilinged room were wreathed in blue smoke did the old man get down to business. He explained, in the deep voice which his nephew had inherited in such measure, that he had no regrets, but that he admitted having been on the losing side. There was nothing to be done about that. There were not too many of the old legionnaires left. But the survivors met once a year in Austria, a country which took a more sympathetic view of the crusade against Bolshevism. There they could sit in the taverns and sing the old songs. There they could check whether the old uniforms still fitted. There they could tell war stories of the just battle against the Jews and the communists. The pork and apple turned sour in my stomach and I noticed both Fritz and Karl Henrik Jensen shifting restlessly in their chairs. The old man saw it too of course and said:

'Who says we exterminated six million Jews? Who the hell counted all those bodies?'

'There's no need to defend it,' Karl Henrik said. 'You can't defend those killings, no matter how many or few they were. One was one too many. But that's not the issue here.'

'No, you're right, Karl Henrik. You're right. I'm an old man. I have a right to take my opinions with me to my grave.'

'So what is this really about, Fritz?' I asked, but it was Karl Henrik who answered. He spoke with his cigar held up in front of his eyes, as if he were studying it. Fritz ran the glowing tip of his cigar around the ashtray until it fell off.

'It's about justice,' Karl Henrik said. 'It's about the rehabilitation of those Danes who fought on the German side on the Eastern Front. That is the purpose of the association.'

'What association?' I asked.

'The Veterans' Association, of which I am secretary. We work for the rehabilitation of the fallen, the missing, the convicted, the survivors ...'

'Of whom Dad was one,' Fritz interjected.

'That's nothing to do with me!' I snapped and he lowered his head again, but Karl Henrik went on, under the icy, blue eye of the yellow-faced old man.

Karl Henrik leaned across the table.

'We are neither old Nazis or neo-Nazis. My uncle here may never have completely given up the faith, but he also voted Conservative for years – though I suspect that these days he would be more likely to vote for the Danish People's Party ...'

'Too bloody right. It's not the Jews who are the big threat to the Danish way of life nowadays, it's the Muslims who are destroying everything that's good about this country and the old parties are failing the nation again, just as they failed us.'

'Be quiet and let me explain.'

'Don't bother. I have to be getting home,' I said, but Fritz placed a hand on my arm and said in a voice both pleading and peremptory:

'Just listen to him for a minute, Theodor. If only for my sake, and Irma's.'

I sat down again and listened, puffing fiercely on another cigarette. It was the old story of betrayal and deceit again. Karl Henrik described – with perfect truth – how twelve thousand young men joined the Danish Legion and the Waffen SS. Six thousand of these were sent to the Eastern Front. Possibly as many as three thousand were killed or went missing in action. The largest number of Danes to go to war since the Schleswig-Holstein conflict in 1864. They played their part in the first lightning victories and the last of them fell in the ruins of Berlin in May 1945. They were dispatched with the blessing of the Danish government in 1941 and condemned by the same politicians in 1945 under *ex post facto* laws. For years they were treated as pariahs and outcasts.

'We are campaigning to have their reputations restored, to see that they receive an apology for the wrong done to them after the war.'

'It was a gross injustice,' the old man said.

'You'll never get that apology, I'm glad to say,' I responded. 'These fine men you're talking about fought for the Nazi killing machine, in the SS – an organisation which was convicted as a whole at Nuremberg of crimes against humanity. You make me sick!'

Something like fire flashed in the old man's eyes and Fritz fiddled nervously with the tablecloth, but Karl Henrik continued unperturbed:

'You're part of this too. Your father was wrongfully convicted.'

'That's right, he was a soldier, not a criminal,' the old man said.

'I don't want any part of it,' I said.

'The Veterans Association is now several hundred strong,' Karl Henrik said. 'We've attracted a lot of new members over the past few years. Most of them descendants of Eastern Front combatants who now realise the injustice done to their relatives. We help one another, but neo-Nazis are not welcome – although we have been approached by some.'

'What a network,' I remarked wryly, but the irony was lost on him and the old man said:

'We would like to offer whatever assistance we can give, to enable you to help Irma. It would be better coming from you than from one of us …'

'What's Irma's part in all this, Fritz?' I asked.

Fritz glanced at his two associates before answering:

'She's been a member of the association for years. She supports its aims …'

'Irma's a flaming Marxist, or at least she was …'

'We don't discuss politics within the association, Theodor,' Fritz replied. 'It's best you speak to her yourself.'

I merely stared at him, wondering yet again how he had ever managed to make so much money. Once more Karl Henrik came to his aid and in his words I heard an echo of my sister:

'Through her Marxist analyses of the crisis capitalism of the thirties Irma has also come to the conclusion that the Eastern

Front volunteers were as much victims of the war as the members of the resistance. There were simply more of them. The real bad guys were the collaborationist politicians who got Denmark into such a mess. With their boundless hypocrisy and double-dealing they managed to push the resistance movement onto the sidelines after the war, and judged the volunteers according to unlawful principles. You know your sister. The very fact that she is a socialist means she's determined to see that justice is done.'

I clapped my hands sardonically and said what a splendid little lecture that was, but I could tell that I had better not step too far out of line otherwise a situation which was already fraught could turn really nasty.

'Look,' I said, as if I were talking to a bunch of silly, badly-behaved schoolchildren. 'This may sound trite, but it is also fairly obvious. People make choices. In this case, some chose to join the resistance movement. Others did nothing and got through it as best they could. Still others chose to pick up a gun and enlist in the SS. But they crossed that line themselves. It wasn't society's fault, dammit.'

'It was a different story when the Soviet Union collapsed, though, wasn't it?' Karl Viggo Jensen said, raising his voice slightly. 'Suddenly everyone could see the true face of communism. If the Western powers had made a concerted stand against Stalin the world would have been a different place. It was a bad, bad system. We fought the atrocious system which attacked little Finland and the Baltic countries. It was our duty.'

'Stalin was an arsehole,' I said, genuinely appalled. I was sick of the way everything these days was subject to the same moral relativism. 'On that we can agree, but the communists did not believe that one race was superior to another. They weren't fucking racists. Originally they were in fact idealists. Communism is a wonderful concept. Nazism is anything but. Even in totalitarian systems there's a difference, for Christ's sake. The Nazis were racists. They regarded themselves as supermen.'

Karl Henrik glared at me:

'I may be only an amateur historian, but it so happens that there are well-respected researchers, also at your sister's university, who see the matter in a different light. A certain revision of history is, after all, taking place these days. Giving a more nuanced picture of the occupation. The views of the resistance movement no longer predominate. The fact that in their lust for revenge they too committed atrocities is, I believe, now being accepted in certain historical circles.'

'I know. You're right, I'm sorry to say. Everyone in Denmark suffered. Some simply suffered more than others. I only hope,' I continued, declaiming like a second-rate actor, 'that our version of history doesn't end up like that presented to Russian high school students. Do you know what *they* say: Russian history is too difficult to learn – because they keep changing it.'

They did not find this funny. They hardly turned a hair, merely smiled politely. I was a guest, after all, and this was the country, where people are more prone to observe the proprieties. The old man poured a brandy for me anyway, and this time I was stupid enough not to say no. It went down well too. Fritz had got his cigar going again. Suddenly he blurted out:

'You don't know what it was like growing up as Dad's son. Or Dad's daughter. The amount of stick we had to take. How we were called Nazi brats until we moved and people gradually forgot as times got better. You were kept in the dark. You were the baby. You had to be shielded. Poul forbade Mum to talk to you about the past. Poul betrayed Dad's memory ...'

Now I was really riled. How dare he insult my good, kind, loving step-father.

'Leave Poul out of this, brother mine. *He* was my father, so you and Irma can keep your rotten Nazi, Eastern Front volunteer of a Dad!'

I could see from Fritz's face that his temper was up and I suddenly remembered that he had actually given me a hiding once or twice when I was a little boy. He had a violent, or at any rate an aggressive, streak. Maybe he had brought that to bear in the business world from which he had made his money, or maybe he was just good at baking and selling bread.

'You had no right to say that,' Fritz said at length.

'No, you're right, I didn't,' I said mildly. 'I didn't know him, my real father. Well, how the hell could I? So Poul was my Dad, okay?'

'Dad was a good man,' he said.

'If you say so, Fritz. I didn't know him. And you're right, I may have gone too far.'

'That's alright,' he said, but I could tell by looking at him that it was not. We sat for a while in silence, probably less than a minute, but it felt longer. At last the old man said:

'You met a woman in Bratislava …'

'How in hell's name do you know that?'

'She is Andreas's daughter. I told you, we support one another, we stick together. Our work also transcends national boundaries. Not in order to gain power or to bring back Nazism, simply to help one another … you met Maria, didn't you?'

'I received a visit from a woman who called herself Maria and told me some crazy story about her being my half-sister. And how my real father had not died ages ago in a bar in Hamburg, but lived happily ever after in Croatia. Is that the one you mean?'

'That's the one I mean,' he said clasping his hands on the table in front of the blue-fluted coffee cup. 'That's the story I'm thinking of and I was wondering whether she showed you anything to substantiate her story?'

'Yes, she did. Both words and pictures. Most convincing,' I said.

'And I presume that you have this material at home?'

'I do not have this material at home.'

'Don't tell me you brought it with you?' he said, sounding surprised and pleased.

'No. I no longer have it.'

There was silence around the table, then Karl Viggo and Karl

Henrik both spoke at once, their questions overlapping: had I thrown it away, destroyed it? I told them the honest truth – that I had packed the letters and photographs into a suitcase which had disappeared, as so many suitcases have a way of doing on their way from one place to another. That my suitcase, according to the information I had received from SAS, had decided, more or less of its own free will, to see as much as it could of our wonderful world and in the course of its new globetrotting life had then chosen to vanish into thin air.

They did not find my presentation of the facts particularly amusing, but I honestly did not give a shit. They might well have been hoping to add those letters and photos to their little SS shrine, but that I would never have allowed, lost suitcase or no lost suitcase. Not that I said that to them. Instead I asked to be driven back to my car. They looked at one another, then got to their feet.

I stood for a moment with Fritz in the yard. It was extremely peaceful out there. A couple of chickens strutted about, and the birds had started singing again. The unmistakable scent of spring was in the air, it seemed to send a double dose of light and ozone shooting straight to the brain.

'I don't want to be in your gang, Fritz,' I said. 'And I think you would do well to let sleeping dogs lie.'

'That's funny, coming from a historian,' he said with a sigh.

'This isn't history, it's fetishism,' I retorted and gave him my hand. 'I'll talk to you later.'

'I've spoken to my lawyer, it's all arranged,' he said, releasing my hand. 'He'll take on Irma's case, but he says that there's very little we can do for the next two or three weeks. Not until she comes up before the judge again.'

'Fair enough. And thanks.'

'It's the least I could do,' he said. 'I mean, I have the money, and she *is* my sister ...'

'Even so.'

I do not know how much Karl Henrik had had to drink, but he took it nice and easy on the drive back to Knudshoved where

| 105 |

my car was waiting. The young driver had evidently taken himself off. We did not say a word to one another the whole way. I was tired and I had a headache. My back was playing up too, although even that I was getting used to, pain and all. I fleetingly considered driving into Nyborg and taking the train. Let Janne pick up the fucking car. But that was just plain stupid – I hadn't had that much to drink, and it had been with a meal. So most of the alcohol had to be out of my system by now, surely?

I drove onto the low bridge, across the high bridge and through the toll barrier. That must have been where they spotted me. Nobody gets through there without being caught on video and it is also a good place for checking number plates, especially on weekdays when the traffic is not so heavy.

The squad car flagged me down just outside of Slagelse. A uniformed policeman came up to the car and I rolled the window down. How much *had* I had to drink? He tipped his cap politely and asked to see my driving licence.

'Have you had anything to drink today, sir?'

'A beer and a schnapps with lunch,' I said.

'Oh, at least, I'd say,' he commented, sniffing inside the car.

Cars zoomed past and I saw people sending me sympathetic or smug looks. The policeman held onto my licence and said:

'There's a lay-by a few kilometres up the road. Drive on up to it, nice and easy and pull in.'

'Why should I do that?' I said.

'Because I say so,' he replied and returned to his partner in the squad car, still clutching my licence. There was really nothing else for it, so off Teddy tootled at the regulation 110 kph with the squad car in his rear-view mirror, until he reached the small lay-by in which stood a block of toilets, a truck and a blue Ford Escort. The squad car drove past me and stopped behind the blue Ford. I stayed in my car, trying to do a quick calculation: how much schnapps and beer had I had and how long ago had that been? It did not look too promising. Not an outrageously high blood-alcohol level, but it had to be more than the limit of 0.5 per cent. One of the uniforms got out of the squad car, walked up to the blue Escort and handed my licence to a man in a dark, well-worn leather jacket. This done, the policeman saluted and, much to my surprise, returned to the squad car, climbed in beside his partner and they drove away.

There was a woman in the Escort's front passenger seat. The man in the dark leather jacket stepped out and walked up to my car. I recognised him now. It was the younger of the two CID officers who had interviewed me at my flat. What was his name again?

'Hello, Teddy,' he said.

'Hello, er … what was your name again?'

'Per Toftlund. Police Intelligence.'

'Oh, that's right. Hello to you, Per Toftlund. And what can I do for PET? I'm assuming this has to do with my sister?'

'It might. For the moment could I ask you to get into my car and my colleague will drive yours back to Copenhagen. We have a lot to talk about.'

'And if I refuse?'

'You'll have to blow into a plastic bag and then I think you can wave bye-bye to your licence, Teddy. You smell like a brewery.'

'It's just one of those days,' I said as I climbed out of the car. I had to take a second to steady myself. Per Toftlund may have thought it was because I was drunk. And I'm sure I must have smelled somewhat of alcohol, but the real reason was my back, which had seized up, as it always did when I had been sitting in the car for any length of time. I had to stand for a moment with a steadying hand on the roof until I could straighten up and regain my balance. I could have drunk nothing but milk and I would still have been tottering about as if I were pissed.

Teddy Arrested In Bleak Danish Lay-by With Toilets And Truck might have been the title of this picture, but my usual attempt to put a self-ironic distance between myself and the situation did not help much. *Teddy Out Of His Depth* was probably more like it.

Part 2

PER'S HAPPY LIFE

'All warfare is based on deception.'
Sun Tzu, 500 BC

8

THESE DAYS when Per Toftlund woke, for a brief, almost imperceptible moment he was always afraid that he was alone in bed. Only once he had reached out an arm and touched Lise's warm, bare thigh under her short nightie and felt her, still half asleep, take his hand, did he feel that daily, almost unreasonably satisfying feeling of happiness. Unreasonable, because, he thought to himself in the seconds between sleep and consciousness, there had to be a price to pay for such happiness. This northern-European sense of guilt evaporated, however, as soon as he was fully awake. And that did not take long. He had never lost the old habit from his army days of wakening early and being instantly and fully alert.

But these days he would lie for a while, running his hand over Lise's swollen belly, hearing and feeling her sigh voluptuously – and, if he was lucky, discerning a kick of life from the baby inside her. Her skin was soft and warm and moist, over her drum-tight stomach it felt smooth as velvet under his hand. The bare breasts inside her nightie were taut and ready for breastfeeding. Again he felt that dangerous surge of happiness.

'Sleep well, you two?'

'Uhmmmm …' she grunted. 'She takes up so much space, she's turning somersaults in there and I'm as big as a cow,' she mumbled.

'You're beautiful,' he said. 'You're both beautiful.' He propped himself up on his elbow and brushed a strand of hair back from her brow.

'I'm huge,' she said. 'And I'm sleepy and I've got the day off.'

'You're so sweet and lovely,' he said, as if quoting a line from a pop song. 'And it's only four weeks to go.'

'Have you any idea what the thought of another four weeks feels like in my condition. It feels like a hundred years,' she said. 'And I'm so sleepy, and now I'm on maternity leave.'

He kissed her on the forehead and the lips and she smiled, still with her eyes shut. He got up, closed the bedroom window, pulled on shorts, a T-shirt, track-suit top and bottoms, drank a glass of tap water then ran out of the house in Ganløse and up towards the woods north of the town. The wind was from the south-west and there was rain in it. The temperature was only a few degrees above freezing and the ground felt hard under his running shoes, even when he reached the woods and turned onto the paths winding through the mix of hardwoods and conifers. He soon settled into his stride, breathing rhythmically, and his mind turned to the day ahead and the meeting which his old boss had asked him to attend. He was looking forward to it, although he had no idea what she wanted with him. He was hoping, although he did not dare to admit it, not even to himself, that she might be going to ask him to come back. There was a chance, though he doubted it was very great. She probably just wanted to clear up a few points regarding yet another of their interminable investigations. He knew that he had got off relatively lightly with a transfer to Customs and Immigration after his failure to protect Sara Santander, but he missed PET and the work with counter-espionage, missed being out there operating on the fringes of the law, in that shadow world where different rules applied. Running there in the light of early March his mind also went to the new war that had broken out in Europe. NATO had commenced bombing raids on Yugoslavia and for the first time Denmark was officially party to a war of aggression against a sovereign nation. He imagined that this would mean a tightening up of domestic security and cherished a faint hope that he might be involved in this. Even if he had fucked up and Vuk the Serbian Dane had got away, that whole business had given him one gift: he had met Lise Carlsen and, wonder of wonders, she had also fallen in love with him. They had married and were expecting a baby. She had even agreed to move from the Copenhagen flat which she had owned with her murdered husband to a new house in Ganløse. The inveterate city-dweller was now a suburbanite. For the baby's sake.

He ran smoothly and easily, aware of how alive his body felt as he rounded his personal five-kilometre mark and started back down the trail. His mind gradually emptied of all thought and on the run home he simply felt light and clear and exhilarated by the lovely morning light flickering through the bare trees. April was just around the corner and you could feel it in the air. He would never see forty again, but he still felt in control of his body. And that was important to him. Per Toftlund was a very physical person. All his life he had sought physical challenges, from his days as a volunteer in the Royal Navy's special forces unit until the stringent demands made on a frogman on active service became too much even for a man in his physical condition and, with the prospect of a desk job and an instructor's post looming on the horizon, he had left to join the police. He turned the corner into the new housing estate which they would learn to call home and did his warming-down exercises by the carport. They had chosen the house because it was affordable and brand-new, so they could move straight in. The gardens had not yet been laid out. Piles of damp black soil were dotted around the little red houses. But it would be nice when it was finished. And the estate agent had told them that several families with small children had already put their names down. This had suddenly become an important factor for Per and Lise: coming to parenthood late they were looking forward to it and at the same time dreading it. The financial side was not really a problem. Lise had got a tidy sum from Ole's life insurance and the sale of his psychology practice, but the way Per saw it this was Lise's money. He had been persuaded to let the proceeds from the sale of the flat go towards the purchase of the house and other future family outgoings. But he refused to touch the rest of it, even though she would not hear of them keeping their finances separate. Some of it, at least, they would put in trust for the baby. Per preferred not to think about that money. You had to manage on what you earned. That had always been his policy. Things that came too easily had a way of going just as easily.

Per showered then had a slice of toast with cheese. He kissed a still drowsy Lise as she lay there with her big belly, smelling of bed and sleep, and drove into town, to the low dun-coloured concrete building on Borups Allé which was home to the Danish Security Intelligence Service. The traffic on the road into town was heavy and sluggish. The travelling time was Lise's biggest bugbear about suburban life. She had been used to cycling everywhere, but now if she had to be at work in the morning she was liable to end up stuck in traffic along with everyone else. Fortunately, though, that did not happen often. She would soon get used to it. The morning light was struggling to break through the dull haze and grimy drizzle that blanketed the city, making it look drab and dirty and damp. Glistening, as if someone had coated the road and the buildings with sump oil.

Seeing that ugly grey concrete block with the red windows sitting alongside the busy road, just before the big old Telephone Exchange building was like coming home, he felt. For the best part of his police career this had been his workplace. It might not possess the same sense of history as the old Police HQ, or its unique air of authority, but it probably harboured more secrets than all the other police stations put together. He knew it like the back of his hand and felt comfortable in its functional, rectilinear corridors. He went upstairs and greeted Jytte Vuldom's secretary with easy familiarity. Vuldom was the second female head of Police Security Intelligence. Her predecessor, Commissioner Jansen, had been the world's first female spy chief and in most parts of the world it was still a rare thing for a woman to be the head of a national secret service. Toftlund had always got on well with Vuldom. He felt she was good at her job and he had nothing against female bosses as long as they were professional – and Vuldom was. Not only that, but she was adept at walking the diplomatic tightrope between openness and reticence when dealing with the press and politicians; practising the transparency necessary within a democratic society while at the same time, in the looking-glass world of the secret service, hushing up those things which had to be hushed up. In order to safeguard democracy one sometimes had to break democracy's rules, as Vuldom had said at one of her rare, but popular seminars at the National Police Training Centre at Avnø.

Per knocked on Vuldom's door. The lady herself was sitting at her desk with a cigarette in her hand and a cup of coffee in front of her. The desk was clear apart from a couple of green files lying next to the telephone and intercom. Per wrinkled his nose at the acrid cigarette smoke. He had not managed to persuade Lise to stop smoking altogether, even though she was pregnant, but at least she had cut down drastically, to the point where she was now not much more than a social smoker, and only the other day she had announced that she was giving it up completely. Vuldom, in her realm, smoked as and when she liked. She was in her early fifties, a woman with sharp, shrewd eyes and attractive, finedrawn features. Her short hair was swept back from a level brow. Her make-up was subtle, matching her sensible skirt, shirt and rather masculine jacket, the overall image that of an independent woman exuding both femininity and efficiency. Lise had called her a role model for other women. Because she succeeded in remaining womanly while at the same time forging a career for herself in a world where, by and large, the men were still the bosses and the women made the coffee. Lise admired her for that. Lise saw injustice everywhere. Per seldom thought about life in abstract terms. He was better at tackling concrete tasks head-on and accomplishing them. But he could tell that Lise did have an influence on him, although she was very discreet about it, recognising, as she did, his Jutlander's stubborn streak. Nobody could tell him anything! But he did read other books now. And he was no longer so quick to come out with dogmatic statements or opinions on matters about which he in fact knew nothing.

'Hi, Per,' said Jytte Vuldom in her deep, husky smoker's voice. 'Sit down, have a cup of coffee. Long time no see.'

Per sat down in the chair on the other side of the desk. Vuldom poured coffee for him.

'I hear you're going to be a father,' she said as she filled his cup. 'Well, I never.'

'You could congratulate me, you know,' Per said.

Vuldom smiled:

'Congratulations. I just never expected it of you.'

'Why not?'

She shrugged, took a dainty sip of her coffee.

'Oh, I don't know. Lone wolf and all that? How are things at HQ?' She nodded in the vague general direction of Copenhagen, as if they could see all the way into the city centre and, down near the harbour, Police HQ where Toftlund had been stationed for the past couple of years, working mainly with the Customs and Immigration department at Kastrup Airport, known to most people as the passport police. It was a tedious and often heartbreaking job, having to turn away refugees, seeing them huddled like forlorn rag dolls outside of passport control. Or to be right out at the plane, denying them entry. Or to have to sit for hours checking tipsy, sun-tanned package tourists back into the country, listening again and again to the same few standard remarks about the weather there and here.

'It's a job,' Toftlund said.

'An important job. Very important, no doubt about it. But do I detect a note of dissatisfaction?'

'Drop the act, Vuldom,' he said, raising his voice slightly. 'I was dumped there. I could have done worse, all things considered. But it's not like I applied for the bloody job, is it?'

'Temper, temper!' she said, with a smile in her voice. 'You had to carry the can, Per. That's all there was to it. And you did make a mess of things, so to some extent it was fair enough …'

'What about the politicians? What about them?'

'Ah, now that's a different matter. And one which we public servants need not worry our loyal little heads about,' Vuldom said, leaning across the desk slightly: 'That's history, so we leave that to the historians. Our job is to take care of all the everyday crap. Which *can* turn out to be history in the making. Or a mixture of both. In which current events suddenly take on a whole new meaning. And the past, which everyone thought had been buried, forgotten, destroyed, rears its head again and – due to the sort of coincidences which lie at the heart of all intelligence work – acquires new significance.'

Toftlund grinned and said:

'Now, now, Vuldom. Are you trying to seduce me?'

Vuldom grinned too, but her eyes were cool and calculating, exactly as he remembered them:

'Would you like that?'

'Oh, I think I could be persuaded.'

'That's what I thought.'

'But my boss out at the airport won't take kindly to me leaving him in the lurch. You should see the piles of paper on my desk. Duty rosters that never seem to work out. An enormous backlog of lieu time still to be taken. And what with all the talk on the one hand about us letting too many people in and on the other about us being too restrictive, we've really got our hands full.'

'I had a word with Larsen.'

'Oh? You were pretty sure of yourself.'

'You were made for this job, Toftlund.'

Per sat back, leaned forward again, took a sip of his coffee and wafted away the smoke from her cigarette.

'What about … that other business? Are the politicians going to accept me being back here? I was the scapegoat, after all.'

'You've been on the sidelines long enough. Besides, people have short memories in this country. No one can remember *any-thing* that happened more than a week ago, the media are always coming up with some new story. They're like children. Totally

| 117 |

focused on one thing at one minute, throwing themselves heart and soul into something else the next. You won't be doing surveillance work anyway. And besides, no one outside our little family will ever know.'

'When will my transfer come through?'

Vuldom picked up one of the green folders, removed a single sheet of paper from it and pushed it across the desk to him. It was a standard transfer form, used when police personnel were being moved from one department to another. It had been completed right down to the date. If he signed it he would actually have started two days ago.

'Now,' she said. 'We have a case which we would like you to take on right away. It is what one could call urgent.'

'And Larsen?'

'He kicked up a fuss, but he had to face the facts.'

'Which are?' Per asked, as he took his pen from his inside pocket and signed the form.

'That the Police Commissioner and his political superiors felt it was a good idea. Possibly even vital to national security. You will be accorded a new rank and your old merit allowance.'

'I'm impressed, Vuldom,' Toftlund said and meant it. 'The Minister for Justice and me. Well what do you know.'

Vuldom picked up the form, slipped it back into the folder.

'None of your sarcasm,' she said briskly. 'You're one of the best men PET has ever had and I want the best. For the first time since 1864, Denmark is involved in a war of aggression. The politicians may call it a humanitarian exercise, but it still has an effect on national security and hence on our workload. We need more resources. The minister understands this. In addition, a whole lot of old cases, including some of yours, have acquired fresh relevance. The papers will be full of it in a couple of days and at that point the minister will demand a definite answer from us, the gist of which will be that we – which is to say he – are pulling out all the stops in our efforts to solve the strange mysteries of the past.'

'I stand corrected,' Toftlund remarked wryly, feeling nonetheless childishly pleased and proud. Like a fourteen-year-old who has just scored a goal in football. 'Who have I got?'

'You've got Bjerregaard, and a new girl. You don't know her – Charlotte Bastrup. They'll be your core team. Bastrup is in her early thirties, still fairly new to this field, but good. You've been allocated an operations room downstairs, number 28. You can, of course, draw on all the usual departments. If you need more resources, you'll need to come to me.'

'Right,' he said and waited. Vuldom stubbed out her cigarette, picked up the other, somewhat thicker folder which was, he could see, bulging with surveillance reports, pictures and notes. She proceeded to read aloud in the dry, but invariably precise and fascinating manner which she adopted whether giving evidence in court or presenting a case. He listened intently, conscious of a tingling inside which he had not felt in a long time. It was that sixth sense which tells the hunter: here is a quarry which can be brought down, but which can be bested only by dint of all one's skills and ingenuity.

Vuldom handed him a picture:

'Irma Pedersen, born 1940. Her father was a baker from Fünen, he died years ago. Her mother's in a nursing home on the island. Today Irma is a professor of women's history at Roskilde University. Extremely – and I mean *extremely* – radical left-winger in her youth. Way out where there was certainly talk, if nothing else, of bombs and the need for violence, as those delightful people used to say in the seventies. Hence the reason we had her on file. But for her, as for the majority of them, it never amounted to more than talk and a few articles in the *Political Review*. Divorced. Childless.'

Vuldom lit another cigarette while Per studied the colour photograph. Irma Pedersen had clean-cut features in a surprisingly wrinkle-free face. Her hair was short and cut in a rather dated, pudding-bowl style. She had narrow, nicely shaped lips, a straight nose and clear green eyes. Her brow, though high, did not

| 119 |

dominate her face. She had fair skin which looked as though it would freckle when exposed to sunlight. Per laid the photograph on the desk.

'A terrorist sympathiser, then a university professor with responsibility for future generations. What a liberal society we live in,' he said.

'It certainly is. And here's the family ...' She passed him another two pictures. One of an elderly man, the other of a younger man whom Toftlund would, nonetheless, have described as middle-aged.

'He's not that old,' Vuldom said, as if reading his mind, but Per was not surprised. Within the service, Vuldom's intuition was famous. 'That is one of her younger brothers. Fritz, who followed in his father's footsteps. Born in 1943, a baker on Fünen. Although I suppose these days manufacturer is more like it. He produces all that so-called 'artisan' bread that's sold as organic in the supermarkets. We have absolutely nothing on him. A solid citizen, married to the same woman all his life, two children both doing well for themselves, member of the Rotary Club. Did a stint as chairman of the parish council. A good Danish man. My guess is that he has some sympathy with the Danish People's Party but has always voted Conservative. Long-standing member of the party. Because that's what respectable people do.'

Fritz was a heavily built man who looked older than his years. He was rather coarse in appearance, his face notable for its high, bald pate, bushy eyebrows, big nose and puffy cheeks.

The other photograph was of a middle-aged man clad in a slightly crumpled shirt with a loosely knotted tie. He had blue eyes, light-brown hair with a dusting of salt-and-pepper and a big smile that lit up his face. He looked a bit of a rogue. Or a disarming charmer. Per felt he had seen him before.

'That's the baby of the family. Theodor Nikolaj Pedersen, Teddy to his friends. We have nothing on him either. We ran a check on him a couple of years back when he gave a talk on the aims of the new Russia to a group of our staff over in Jutland. Teddy was born in 1948. Today he's a lecturer at Copenhagen University. Currently on a tour of Central Europe with the Foreign Policy Society. Married to a woman quite a bit younger than himself, whom he scored at the univ ...'

Per could not help smiling at Vuldom's use of the imported English slang. Score! In Denmark, when he was a kid, that had still only been something you did in football. She carried on undaunted: '... but she's a bit of a gadabout and now she's seeing someone else, which makes Teddy a bit of a cuckold. She has in fact moved in with her lover while Teddy is studying the post-communist morass of Central Europe. I don't know how bad that will make him feel. Our Teddy is something of a womaniser; he may not look like a movie star, but he must have something because he's seldom short of female company.'

'He doesn't look like a ladykiller.'

'Well he is, Toftlund.'

She placed three documents in front of him:

'And here you have the surveillance warrants. We've been tapping the phones of all three. But no luck there, so far. In this file you'll also find profiles of each of them – their habits, vices, virtues. You know the routine – or have you forgotten your craft?'

'I'll try to remember all you've taught me.'

'You were a good pupil, so I'm sure you will.'

This last was said with a trace of sarcasm, but in an oddly childish fashion Toftlund was gratified by the compliment. Vuldom slipped all of the papers back into the green folder, slid it across the desk to him and sat back in her chair.

'Their biographies are by no means complete so might I suggest that you put Bastrup onto bringing them up to date,' she said and proceeded to fill him in on the background to his first new case in his new, old job:

'You know something of this from before, of course, but just to bring you up to speed on the events of the past few months: as you know, our old pal Markus Wolf and his henchmen managed to destroy a lot of the records held by HVA, East Germany's international intelligence network, before the fall of the Berlin Wall. We were, however, able to get hold of the SIRA tapes, which contain the names of hundreds of agents. Only their cover names, though. The GDR was in total chaos after the collapse of the Soviet system, and in all the confusion our dear allies in the CIA contrived to swipe the so-called Rosenholz Tape, which holds the key to the cover names. Now, more than ten years later, it has finally been possible to collate some of the data from these two records and this has paid off, Toftlund. Having the key to the secret lock really paid off. The first cover names were deciphered only a fortnight since. The last of them a few days ago.'

Vuldom lit yet another cigarette and pointed to the coffee pot. Toftlund filled both their cups and let her continue without interrupting:

'The politicians have at long last given us the green light, and the resources to enable us to check which good Danish men and women joined the Stasi payroll, whether out of idealism, financial greed, ignorance, ideological conviction, naivety or a combination of all of these. It only took ten years. But what the hell. By then the statute of limitations on most of them had expired. Isn't that just the most convenient thing about this comfortable little country of ours, where we never have any desire to look the past squarely in the eye. Better late than never. I dislike unpaid bills and old debts. I have had people working in Berlin, good moles who have burrowed into Stasi's massive archives and dug up a lot of dirt as well as pure gold. I won't bore you with all the details. But we have about fifty cover names which we have investigated more closely. That is partly why you have been brought back into the fold. These informants are named and the dates of their reports to Stasi are given on the SIRA tapes. Once the code was finally broken it became possible to find the actual reports in the archives. But only the cover names. It was, and is, a mammoth task. The matter has attracted the interest of the press and hence of the politicians. So we're working to a tight deadline. But ... one of the informants we came across was a busy little bee by the name of Edelweiss.'

Toftlund grinned broadly at Vuldom's mixed metaphor.

'What a pretty codename.'

'When you think of all the agents and informants Stasi employed, they must have had a whole department doing nothing but dreaming up cover names. Anyway, let's read on. You'll find copies in the folder.' She opened it again, handed him a list of topics. 'These are just the titles of over eighty reports in which, from 1971 until the fall of the Wall, the little flower betrayed her country. If our information is correct there is no statute of limitations on this case. Which means that once we've completed our investigation we can ask the Public Prosecutor to throw the book at this one. Take a look at that.'

Vuldom leaned back in her office chair, coffee cup in hand, and watched as Toftlund quickly scanned the long list of reports passed, over a twenty-year period, by a Danish agent codenamed Edelweiss to the Ministry for State Security in the sprawling Stasi complex on Normannenstrasse in East Berlin, in the days when the city was split into East and West, thus forming the front line in the continual, clandestine war between two systems. A brutal conflict fought on an invisible front; one in which lives were at stake and to which there was only one possible outcome: for one of the systems to collapse because in character, style and structure they were irreconcilable. In the long run a communist dictatorship and a democracy could not exist side by side, since the ultimate goal of the dictatorship was to do away with democracy.

Edelweiss's first reports had issued from the Danish Ministry of Foreign Affairs. They appeared to be copies of top secret memos from Danish embassies in such diverse locations as Oslo, Moscow and Beirut. There were some relatively harmless reports on Danish oil policy – which would, however, have been of interest to such a large oil producer as the Soviet Union. Denmark's views on the deployment of new American mid-range missiles in Europe – the so-called 'Double-Track Decision' whereby NATO proposed setting up a shield of Pershing and Cruise nuclear missiles to counteract the Soviet Union's huge arsenal of SS-20 rockets – were, on the other hand, highly confidential. There had been a tremendous political battle. The decision had given the slumbering peace movement a shot in the arm.

The Danish evaluation of the independent trade union organisation Solidarity was also perused in East Berlin and in Moscow, which would naturally also have had access to the Danish agent's material. Then the nature of the reports changed. They began to deal more with the state of play in the Common Market. Financial and political assessments. Edelweiss grew more ambitious. Also started reporting on the intentions and policy considerations of the major powers of France and Britain. Then came more reports from the Danish Ministry of Foreign Affairs. A lot about the economy, but also political appraisals of Denmark's new conservative government. As well as a report on how attempts to persuade the Danish Social Democrats to change their line on security matters and adhere to the so-called 'footnote policy' had borne fruit. Suggestions for further action to be taken. A note on the need to infiltrate the peace movement, so that those elements which voiced criticism of socialism would be brought into miscredit or excluded. Then the scene changed yet again. Once more Edelweiss was reporting on NATO business. Again her communications were concerned with matters of policy, but there were also some which seemed to indicate that Edelweiss had now attained a very high level of security clearance. These reports contained information on NATO strategy so hush-hush that even today certain passages would have to be blanked out.

Toftlund glanced up:

'Wow. I've really hooked the big one.'

'There's worse to come,' Vuldom said.

And there was one report which struck Toftlund as being

very serious indeed. It told of two Danish officers who had been arrested for spying in Estonia in 1987. It appeared that Edelweiss had been paid a bonus of twenty-five thousand Deutschmarks for supplying the information leading to their arrest. Toftlund remembered the case being in the news. He had still been with the Royal Navy special forces unit at the time, so he had not been privy to any classified information on the affair. The Danish media had made light of the matter, even though the two officers had risked being given the death penalty or, at the very least, lengthy prison sentences. During question time in Parliament the Social Democrats and the left-wing parties had demanded an admission from the government that the two officers were spies in the service of the Danish state. But to admit such a thing would have been sheer madness. These people were operating without diplomatic immunity. Luckily, the liberal foreign minister had kept a cool head, even though the lives of these agents were on the line – a fact which he could not, of course, reveal while they were working to have them released. Eventually money changed hands and the officers were freed: the Soviet Union dealing in hostages like some mafia organisation. Their names were published and photographs of them appeared in the newspapers and on television, the Danish media having acquired them from Estonian TV, which had shown footage of them being interrogated by a military prosecutor. They had escaped having to serve long prison sentences, but their lives were ruined. That wasn't the media's worry, though. It was all just a bit of cloak-and-dagger nonsense anyway. Nothing serious.

It did not seem as if Denmark's responsibilities as a Baltic member of NATO had ever been taken seriously during the cold war, Toftlund thought to himself. Nor was any recognition given to the fact that – whether through its listening station on the island of Bornholm or its network of agents – Danish Military Intelligence had played a vital role in ascertaining what was going on inside the closed dictatorships. Because at the end of the day any deviation from the normal situation could have spelled the difference between war and peace. Few people had understood that. Denmark had conducted an efficient, professional intelligence-gathering operation within the GDR, Poland and the Baltic countries. Given Denmark's geographical situation it had seemed only natural that it should have responsibility for these particular countries. NATO had no central espionage organisation. It based its decisions on intelligence received from its various member states. And in this Denmark played a key role.

Toftlund raised his eyes from the sheet of paper and looked at Vuldom. She returned his gaze without making any comment and he read on. Attached to this document was another, not directly related to Edelweiss. It was a brief memo addressed to the head of Stasi, Erich Mielke, himself. In it his Soviet comrades expressed their gratitude for his brotherly assistance in breaking a counter-revolutionary, imperialist spy ring controlled from Denmark, a country which had acted yet again as an advance post for NATO aggression against the peace-loving socialist nations.

Toftlund glanced up again as Vuldom said:

'Three death sentences, all pronounced in secret, all carried out. Also in secret. Only two years before the Wall fell. Two life sentences and one of twenty-five years. We managed to get four out before it was too late. Although it doesn't say so there, not in so many words, it was Edelweiss who supplied the information. At least according to those who survived. There's little help to be had from the FSB, the successor to the KGB. They haven't opened their archives.'

'But we're talking murder here,' Toftlund said.

'Or accessory to murder, at any rate. And there's no statute of limitations where murder is concerned.'

Per Toftlund removed the three photographs of the Pedersen family from the folder again and considered them.

'There's something here that just doesn't fit,' he said.

'I knew it wouldn't take you long to figure that out.'

'There's no way that any of these three could have had access to even a fraction of this material. A baker. A couple of academics. They simply can't have had access.'

'No, but the Rosenholz file makes it quite clear, beyond a shadow of a doubt, that Irma is Edelweiss and Edelweiss is Irma – take your pick.'

'She wouldn't have had that level of clearance. Nowhere near.'

'No, but there are no two ways about it. We've been onto Edelweiss's little game for a year or so. We've received reports, but never a name to go on. We've nosed around the Ministry of Defence and the Ministry of Foreign Affairs to see if we could come up with a profile that fitted. A career path that matched the pattern of the reports. Without success, obviously. These people move around a lot. But Irma is our little flower. It's as simple as that.'

Toftlund got up, paced back and forth. Vuldom regarded him. He looked as athletic as ever, with a lurking aggression in his movements, for all that he was over forty now. And yet, there was a greater fullness about him. Not a physical fullness as such, more a softness in his actions and in his manner which had not been there before. Maybe it was marriage that had brought this out in him. Maybe marriage was good for him, although only a few years ago she would have said that was impossible. Toftlund turned round:

'Irma wrote the reports, but …'

'But someone else dictated them to her,' Vuldom finished. 'Yes, that must be it.'

'She was guiding the pen and the man or woman. She wasn't the mole. But she controlled the mole.'

'Why do you say "was"? Why not "is"? Who says the operation terminated with the fall of the Wall? Who says the KGB didn't take over the reins? And later the FSB, who are every bit as obsessed with NATO as the communists were.'

Toftlund turned to face her:

'So that's the job, is it?' he said. 'To find Irma's source.'

'Clever boy. Irma is out of the country at the moment, but we accessed her flight booking. She gets back from Brussels late this afternoon. Arrest her. Then we'll go to court and request that she be remanded in solitary confinement for four weeks. Under tight security. With what you have in front of you there should be no problem. They'll probably appeal to the High Court, but I'm sure we'll be granted our four weeks to begin with.'

'Right.'

'And Toftlund – find the bastard.'

'Right.'

'Keep at her. Night and day. Don't give her a moment's peace. We want that name.'

'Right.'

'And preferably soon. Okay? Denmark's at war. It'll be no joke if, somewhere within the NATO system, there's a Danish citizen who cares more about certain foreign powers than their own native land.'

'He's probably retired by now. Thinks the past is dead and forgotten.'

'The past never dies,' Vuldom said. 'Well, welcome aboard. And keep me informed. Regular reports. I'm in on this too.'

'Right,' Toftlund said, wondering for the first time what Lise was going to say, on suddenly finding that, for the first time since they got married, there was going to be no such thing as regular shifts or regular mealtimes. He dismissed the thought and went off to find his new office. His heart was beating faster and he felt better than he had done in a long time. This feeling he had was not the same as the surge of happiness he felt at those moments when he woke up next to Lise, but a sensation he had also experienced on night manoeuvres: sneaking ashore, setting explosives and slipping back into the dark water without the defending troops or home guard guys ever being aware that he had been there. It was the sense of satisfaction the hunter feels when the chase is on.

9

PER TOFTLUND WAS SURPRISED by how much he had actually missed his old job. He threw himself into it with a vigour that made Vuldom pleased and happy with her decision to recall him, only then realising how he had blocked out the thought of how much it meant to him. Lise, on the other hand, found it hard to conceal her dissatisfaction with his sudden physical and mental absence. From one day to the next he went from being as dependable as a bank clerk with regular working hours to being a spouse whose whereabouts she never knew. She did her best not to let Per see how she felt: she had promised herself years before that she would not be one of those small-minded wives who henpecked their husbands and held them back. In her marriage to Ole, too, she had always insisted that it should be an equal partnership. That it was vital to a relationship for both parties to be free to get the most out of their lives, professionally and personally, as long as they remained true to one another. But in her heart of hearts she had to admit she was not happy that Per's work now took precedence over her, not least because she also saw how much he loved it. She felt as big as a cow. She missed her own work, even though she had been looking forward to going on maternity leave. And she had suddenly begun to worry that even the baby, when she arrived, would not be able to hold him. The problem was, though, that she could well understand him. And envied him his freedom. As a couple they had found their own rhythm, but this he had suddenly broken, like a melody being rudely cut off right in the middle of a beautiful note. They had created the framework for a life together. They had both been suffering from emotional shell-shock, but they had found one another and together they had built something new. They had managed to make a fresh start. But now that framework had been abruptly and fundamentally altered by him. She could tell that he was really happy. And he was under pressure. That too was clear to see. The case was constantly on his mind, but he was not stressed. He thrived on the pressure and the challenge of it, that she could both see and sense. And her feelings were complicated by the new air of reckless assurance he had about him, in which she recognised the man she had fallen in love with. The man with whom she had cheated on her husband. But it was one thing to have an affair with a man who was different and intriguing, quite another to discover that that self-same unpredictability was not really such a desirable quality in a husband. Was that the way of it?

He came back from his morning run quite literally on his toes, glowing with energy, bouncing lightly and sexily on the balls of his feet, boxer-fashion; then he would breeze whistling out of the door, leaving her with hair uncombed, her hand in the small of her back and her stomach swelling out in front of her like a shapeless balloon that seemed to fill the whole kitchen. With a figure like this why bother even trying to smarten oneself up. The worst of it was that he did not talk to her about his work. It was just like it had been before they were married, when everything had been so hush-hush: all that un-Danish secrecy and confidentiality. Although she had actually grown pretty tired of his interminable complaints about his work with Customs and Immigration – the same stories again and again – she found herself missing them within only a few days of Per's caterpillar-like metamorphosis from a dull hubby on shifts to one of Vuldom's lads. And from Vuldom in the director's office to the newest office boy they all loved their stupid secret game, in which they hunted the ghosts of the past and the spies of the present.

She had a bit of a sniffle after Per left. She did not want him knowing how she felt. She had a cup of tea, read the papers, envying her colleagues their articles, and felt the baby kicking.

That made her feel better. Pull yourself together, Lise! You're about to become a mother! You have to make this work! She got on with her nest-building: sorting out clothes, cleaning, going through the freshly-washed, sweet-smelling baby clothes from relatives and girlfriends, arranging them in neat piles, contemplating the crib, neatly ranged alongside their bed. They would make a lovely family. And she loved him so much. He was good for her and good to her. But it was no wonder that she burst into tears when he called later in the morning and announced, without any further explanation, that he was at the airport, on his way to Warsaw and possibly a couple of other cities. He would probably only be gone a day or two so she wasn't to worry. It was not so much that he had to go that upset her. But the fact that he simply up and went. That he took his passport with him to work as a matter of course, knowing there was always a chance he might have to go abroad. That he had not deemed it necessary to at least discuss this with her. She felt cross and resentful. What the hell did he have to go to Central Europe for? Had he no thought for her at all?

On the SAS flight to Warsaw Toftlund mulled over the case. So far they had got what they wanted. They had arrested Irma at Kastrup Airport, had their request for four weeks in solitary granted by the Municipal Court and this order confirmed by the High Court. They had obtained additional search and surveillance warrants and had in their possession the material from the old Stasi records with which they had confronted the accused – although she had of course denied everything. The name Edelweiss meant nothing to her. She had never spied for anyone. This whole thing was utterly absurd. Who the hell cared, now, almost ten years after the fall of the Berlin Wall, what someone might have said or done in the seventies – or the eighties, for that matter? It might be of interest to historians, but not to the police, surely? Had they really nothing better to do with their time than to hunt the ghosts of the past? To go delving into a cold war that came to an end long ago. Good God. Capitalism really had triumphed. She denied all knowledge of any espionage case in the Baltic region. She knew nothing except what she had read in the newspapers. Irma's lawyer was of the same mind. As far as he was concerned, they did not have a leg to stand on. The judge had, however, sided with the prosecution, while also making it quite clear that they would have to come up with some more concrete proof if they wanted to hold her for longer.

It was a hell of a job, despite the fact that Vuldom had allocated him more people. They had started digging back into Irma's life, dissecting it. They threw themselves into that task which is the key to all detective work: finding the connection, linking apparently random elements together to form a solid case with which to present the accused. As in any investigation they also needed a bit of luck. But without a painstaking scrutiny of the available material they would not recognise a stroke of luck when they saw it

Once the plane was in the air and the seatbelts sign had been switched off Toftlund removed a small tape recorder from his bag. He put on the headphones. The seat next to his was empty. There were only a handful of passengers in business class, while tourist class seemed pretty busy, full of OAPs taking a little city break and a high-school class on a study trip. But NATO's bombing of Yugoslavia had led a lot of people to steer clear of the alliance's newest members – the Czech Republic, Hungary and Poland – for fear that the Serbs would carry the war into the enemy's camp.

Toftlund pressed Play and once again heard Teddy Pedersen's voice. It sounded loud and clear over the faint hiss one always gets on a wire-tap. He had a nice voice – deep, mellow and not a little arrogant, even if he did sound a bit het up:

'In hell's name, Irma. It's me, Teddy, again. Where the fuck are you? Listen to your messages, for God's sake. I've got lumbago, and I need to talk to you. I just got back from Bratislava and I heard the damnedest story about Dad while I was there. This woman shows up at my door in the middle of the night claiming to be my half-sister. Do you know anything about this? Irma, old girl, do you know anything about Dad being an SS soldier in Croatia and on the Eastern Front? She had pictures and papers which seemed to support her story. And she was following me, sis. In Warsaw, Prague, Bratislava. She said her name was Maria Bujic. For the sake of your non-Slavophile ear that's spelled B-u-j-i-c. Weird, eh? And those pictures and papers? And then my bloody suitcase got lost. What sort of skeletons has our harmonious little family got tucked away in the closet? Sister, dear! Call your baby brother, or send him an email, for Christ's sake. Fritz is just being his simple baker self, he's clammed up completely. So call me, dammit!'

Vuldom's feeling had been that this was a tenuous lead, probably no more than a coincidence, but Per believed that every lead should be followed up, and that there might be some connection here. That the murder in Budapest might not be a coincidence, but part of a pattern. On what, Vuldom had asked tartly, did he base this theory? She had hooted with laughter when he pointed to his gut and said: 'This!' Some of the research work was easy enough. And the young woman DI who had been assigned to him had proved to be an efficient investigator.

One part of the story, at least, checked out. Irma's daddy was listed in the Bovrup Files, on which the names of members of the Danish Nazi party were registered. That he had enlisted in the Danish Legion in 1941 and fought on the Eastern Front at Lake Ilmen, where he was wounded, though not seriously. That he had served in Yugoslavia with the Nordland Division she had also had verified by a surviving SS man who remembered Irma's father. That he had been sent with the Nordland Division to Narva in Estonia and taken part in the great retreat to Berlin. In March 1945 he appeared to have deserted. At any rate he had shown up in Denmark in October 1945. By then the worst thirst for revenge had been quenched. He got two years, but was released after four months. His name was removed from the national register in '52 and in '54 he was declared dead, although no death certificate was ever issued. The court upheld his wife's contention that he had in all probability died in Hamburg – the body had never been identified, but from the papers found on the deceased it seemed likely that it was him. She was free to marry again. And this she had done. End of story, if that woman had not turned up out of the blue in a hotel room in Bratislava. If a man had not been murdered. Possibly by mistake? It was a lead he felt was worth pursuing. To see where it led. Such things were easier now that former enemies were allies. Sex, an approximate age, a name and computers started buzzing in the Czech Republic, Hungary and Poland and, yes, even in little Slovakia. This last-named might not be a member of NATO, but like an eager suitor who will do anything to win his beloved's favour, Slovakia would do anything to help a NATO country. His gut instinct had proved to be correct. The name Maria Bujic popped up on one computer. Warsaw had her in their system. Bujic was only one of a number of pseudonyms adopted by this Yugoslavian citizen. The most interesting thing was that the Polish security service also had a record of her having entered the country in 1995 on a Swedish passport under the Scandinavian sounding name of Katrine Ulfborg. Who was this woman? His opposite number in Warsaw would not say over the phone, but would be happy to speak to him face to face in Warsaw. Toftlund promptly booked a ticket.

He did not touch the food, took only a cup of coffee. Time was when a visit to Denmark's big neighbour had been a chancy expedition into enemy territory, into another system and another world, in which communism had turned everything on its head. Less than an hour's flying time from Copenhagen people lived a life which could have been the Danes' lot if the Russians and not the British had liberated the country in 1945. Toftlund had been there once when it was still under the communists. All he could recall of that visit was the dismal poverty and the constant sense of being watched. That lies and deceit were every rational human being's faithful companion. He did not miss the Berlin Wall. Only those who had forgotten the past could do that. He felt the pressure in his ears as the plane commenced its approach. Flat, dun-coloured fields dotted with houses came into view as they dropped below the clouds and prepared for landing. Passport control was a mere formality and he walked straight through customs with his carry-on bag.

He scanned the crowd of people waiting outside the customs area. A man of around thirty was holding up a cardboard sign with 'Toftlund' written on it. Per walked over to him. He looked like a cop, in a grey windcheater and trousers that did not quite go with it. He had rather flat features, his skin was sallow and pitted by acne, and three gold teeth glinted when he smiled. He smelled of tobacco and when he offered his hand his jacket slid aside and Toftlund saw the gun in its holster on his hip.

'Toftlund?' the other policeman said slowly, as if he had been practising saying the name.

'Yes.'

'Little English. I driver. Take you to boss.'

'Okay.'

He strode briskly towards the door. The air was damp and cold and a stiff breeze caused the bare trees to sway. He had parked right outside the arrivals hall. The car was a grey Mercedes of older date, but the engine purred as they sped along the road into the city. Toftlund sat in the back, gazing out at the grey and yellow concrete tower blocks flying past. Everywhere one looked there were large hoardings, mainly advertising American brands. In the grey haze it all looked rather bleak and half-done. As if they were in the middle of a process which had ground to a halt. Which was pretty much the case, Toftlund thought. You can't expunge the traces of half a century of communist rule in just ten years. It all seemed oddly shambolic: in among housing blocks from which the paint was flaking in great patches, sat a new, modern petrol station; a large shopping centre could just as easily have lain on the outskirts of Copenhagen. But then he saw an old woman selling

| 135 |

vegetables from a little stall by the roadside and suddenly he could have been nowhere but in Central Europe.

Then they were swallowed up by the city and the traffic grew heavier. There were a lot of new cars on the road and people on the street all looked well-dressed. The driver said not a word, but wove his way neatly and expertly around tramcars plastered in adverts. They drove past a skyscraper which Toftlund knew had been a gift from Stalin. He remembered it as having dominated the skyline with its monstrous bulk and social-realist lines. Now, though, it seemed almost hidden, surrounded as it was by modern tower blocks of glass and steel. Was he in Warsaw or Frankfurt? They turned a corner and drove past a park where people were beating their way forward, heads into the wind. Bare, exposed boughs covered with the tiny buds of April reached heavenwards as if praying for the speedy advent of spring. There were lots of people on the streets. Outside office buildings and shops sat beggars with dead eyes and outstretched hands. Two young women walked by, both talking on their mobile phones. The driver turned into a narrow side street and from there into a courtyard in which a couple of other Mercedes were already parked. The courtyard looked well-cared for. Toftlund noted the uniformed guard on the door, but there was no sign to indicate that these were the offices of at least a part of democratic Poland's security service.

Without a word the driver got out of the car and opened the door for Toftlund. He handed him his small holdall and motioned with his head for Per to follow him. They passed through two doors. The flight of steps between them was broad and freshly painted. Beyond the inner door a woman was stationed beside a bank of telephones and a computer. Toftlund's eye was also caught by a television monitor showing shots from surveillance cameras covering the various access routes to the building. The driver nodded to the woman, but she made no response. She was in her thirties, stout, with full, red-painted lips and drenched in heavy perfume. That, at least, had not changed. The habit so many women had of being too heavy-handed with the make-up. As if a layer of rouge was the mark of femininity. They took the lift up to the eighth, and top, floor and stepped out into a hallway from which Toftlund could see rows of office doors running down two long corridors. The driver knocked on the closest one and they entered a reception area in which two young secretaries sat at their respective computers. Smartly, but informally dressed, they could have been receptionists in an advertising agency anywhere in the world.

'Toftlund,' the driver said, then continued in Polish. One of the secretaries got up, went over to a heavy door and knocked on it. A voice answered and the woman beckoned to Toftlund, who dipped at the knees to pick up the holdall which he had set down on the floor.

'You can leave your bag here,' the other secretary said in excellent English.

'Mr Gelbart will see you now.' She took the coat which he had slung over his arm, put it on a hanger from a coat stand in a corner. The driver nodded to Toftlund and said something else in Polish before slipping out of the office.

The door was opened and Toftlund was surprised by the man who came out to greet him with a big smile and firm handshake. He had been expecting a somewhat older man in a tatty grey suit and bland tie. But this man was about his own age. He had black, curly hair and a narrow mouth in a pale, almost feminine face. He wore a beige, open-necked shirt and blue designer jeans tucked into a pair of pointed cowboy boots.

'Colonel Konstantin Gelbert at your service. It's a pleasure to meet a colleague from Copenhagen,' he said in flawless American English. 'I was in Copenhagen only last month. I hope Commissioner Vuldom is well. She is a formidable woman, if you don't mind my saying so. Please come in.'

'Thank you,' Toftlund said, shaking his hand. He felt rather overdressed in his grey trousers, tweed jacket and speckled tie. Gelbert bore little or no resemblance to a colonel in the secret police. He looked more like a university lecturer, or possibly one of today's computer wizards, the type who has made his first million before he is twenty-five.

His office was big and bright and dominated by a gleaming steel and glass desk. On one side of the room was a low table surrounded by a sofa and three armchairs whose tall, rigid backs indicated that this area was designed not for relaxation, but for conferences. The walls were painted white. On them hung three reproductions of paintings by the Danish painter Asger Jorn. The large windows looked onto a busy road, but the glass was so thick that not even the sound of the raindrops now battering off the windowpanes could be heard.

'I'm a big fan of Scandinavian design,' Colonel Gelbart said. 'I'm a big fan of Scandinavian art. Hence Jorn. I like your democratic system and your common sense. Your way of sitting around a table and thrashing out a compromise – rather like tribesmen, really. Compromise is essential if a democracy is to function well. The communists abhorred the art of compromise. They didn't understand anything but orders.'

Toftlund looked down at the street below. The traffic seemed to have come to a standstill. Cars were stuck in long queues. He guessed they were all tooting impatiently, but no sound penetrated what had to be bullet-proof glass.

'Ten years this autumn since democracy was introduced. Who would have imagined that in the spring of 1989,' Toftlund remarked.

Gelbert laughed. He had a reedy, high-pitched laugh. It did not sound altogether sincere. He had his hands stuck in his pockets. He could have been taken for a young student, but Toftlund saw now that he was older than he had first thought. Possibly mid-forties. The skin of his face was smooth but there were creases around the keen brown eyes.

'No,' Gelbert said. 'I took part in the so-called Round Table talks ten years ago. One of my opponents in the negotiations was our current president. He was representing the communists. In those days, in Solidarity we would have been happy just to be a legal organisation and maybe be able to publish a newspaper. Take it one little step at a time. But with Gorbachev in Moscow, the economic crisis here and the complete moral collapse of the Communist Party a window of opportunity suddenly opened up. For a country with such a troubled history as mine it was a miracle. I'll never forget the election night. We won. By a huge majority. But it was almost as if even we didn't believe what had happened.'

'And there was no way back?'

'No, not here in Poland. This isn't Russia. No one here dreams of the old days. Because the truth is that life was pretty much unbearable for all of us. There's no doubt, though, Chief Inspector Toftlund, if you were to ask an unemployed miner whether he was happy with his life he'd probably kick you from here to kingdom come. Ask me or a successful businessman or a writer who is free to write what he wants how things are for us ten years on, and you'll receive a very different answer. The whole debate regarding democracy and the market economy has become a cliché. Everybody is in favour of both. The truth is, Mr Toftlund, that we have our problems. But they are the same problems as those faced by other democratic, capitalist countries. The only difference is that we also have to contend with the legacy of Soviet lunacy, because ours is a post-communist society and will remain so for another generation. I am, however, optimistic. Won't you sit down?'

Toftlund took a seat across from Gelbert, who settled himself in his high-backed office chair. On the desk in front of him lay a manila folder. One of the secretaries came in with coffee, sugar and cream.

'What is your background?' Toftlund asked, while the secretary poured coffee and handed round the cream and sugar.

'I was at the university. Teaching English and American literature. I was one of the lucky ones, I got to study at Stanford for a couple of years when I was younger. That's maybe one of the few advantages of being Jewish. The Jewish community in the US has a lot of clout and I suppose the regime here needed to drum up a bit of goodwill as well as some funding. In any case, my parents and siblings remained here: as hostages, to make sure that I came back. I came back – and joined Solidarity. Martial law put a stop to that. I was interned for some months, like so many others. After that I did various odd jobs – street-sweeping, window-cleaning – this was in the eighties.' He smiled and stirred sugar into his tea. 'The standard career progression for a Central European intellectual who refuses to toe the party line. After 1989 I edited a Jewish magazine until Solidarity came into government and I was called in to do this job.'

'How does your rank figure in all this?'

He laughed his high, clear laugh again:

'The president felt it was a good thing to have a military rank. Some of the old habits die hard. "What would you like to be?" he asked me. "How about a colonel?" I said. And so I became a colonel.'

'I don't suppose the career policemen were too happy about you being promoted over their heads?'

'Possibly not. My main task is to clean up the service, weed out the sinners of the past, appoint democratically minded individuals. In short: to normalise the service, bring it into line with NATO and EU regulations. Democratise it, in such a way that its officers understand that we serve the people as well as the state. And that we are subject to parliamentary control and have to account for both our budgets and our actions.'

'Sounds like a tall order,' Per commented wryly.

'Like others, we have learned that a democracy, too, has its secrets, and that one does not have to give everything away. I've taken on quite a few people from the university, from the provinces and from the media – all people I trust. But I have, of course, also had to retain some of the old professional agents. What they now have to learn is that NATO is no longer the enemy and that, if there is an enemy then it's in the east they should look for it.'

'Russia?'

'It's not nice to say it out loud, but yes, the Russians are extremely active here in Poland and in the Czech state, and in Hungary, for that matter. They still look upon us as their province and now, as a member of NATO, as a legitimate target. And I have to admit, Mr Toftlund, that it has probably been easier for them to build up a network among their old subjects in Poland than it would in Denmark. They have friends and acquaintances here from the old days whose services they can call on. The situation was complicated, obviously, by the fact that only twelve days after officially joining NATO we were at war with a sovereign nation. Yugoslavia. One of Moscow's friends.'

'Everything has its price.'

'Banal, but true, of course. The price was, however, perhaps a little higher than we had expected. Not that we don't support this so-called humanitarian intervention, but we were never consulted about it. It does not have the backing of the Polish people. And Moscow is furious with us. We can actually see how they have stepped up their intelligence gathering activities here. Only the other week we very discreetly expelled two Russian cultural attachés. They have a network here, that's for sure. But I'm going to destroy it, you'll see.'

'And another one will spring up.'

'Ah, but isn't that what the game is all about?' Gelbert said. 'Playing cat and mouse?'

'The great game. There's no end to it.'

'No, and it gets into your blood.'

Toftlund nodded.

'It certainly does,' he said. 'So you've given up the academic life?'

'For the time being, yes. Come election time, if there's a change of government it'll probably be back to the university or the newspaper world for me.'

'But until then …'

'Until then I'll serve my country and do my best to defend it against its enemies.'

He drained his coffee cup, leaned forward and opened the folder in front of him. Inside were a number of closely-written A4 pages and some black-and-white photographs.

'Enemies like our mutual friend here, for instance.'

Gerbert handed him one of the photos. The woman in the picture was tall and slim. Her age was hard to gauge. Anywhere between forty and fifty, possibly older, but she looked good. She appeared to be standing on a street corner. Possibly waiting for a taxi to come along. The photograph had been taken in summertime. She wore a skirt and a light-coloured blouse. The wind was ruffling her hair. The face behind the black sunglasses was blank.'

'Maria Bujic,' Toftlund said.

'Oh, right – that's your name for her,' Gelbert said. 'We know her as Svetlana Ivanova – Russian citizen, representative for a company importing perfume. Russian women love perfume. We also know her, of course, as Katrine Ulfbjorg. My predecessor kept an eye on her too, but not until February of this year did we discover her true identity.'

'She's Croatian, I understand.'

'Possibly, but if our information is correct then her name is Ina Cukic. And she is one of Slobodan Milosevic's top agents.'

'A Serbian spy?' Toftlund said in surprise.

Gelbert sat back in his chair. He was a little like an actor, or a lecturer, Toftlund thought. Or Vuldom when she was in that frame of mind. They both had a fondness for delivering their points as if they were punchlines.

'Maybe more than that. Look at this.'

Gelbert handed Toftlund another photo. This too in black-and-white. Per recognised the man in the picture, dressed in camouflage fatigues with an AK-47 held across his chest and a big grin on his face. Behind him was what looked liked a pile of upturned earth. The man in the photograph was Arkan, leader of the notorious Serbian militia. Also discernible in the background were some other men in army uniform, but he could not make out their faces.

'Arkan?' Toftlund said.

'The man himself. Taken in Srebrenica. Need I say more? A name synonymous with bloodshed and evil. Pictured at the site of one of the biggest massacres on European soil since the Second World War.'

'Srebrenica,' Toftlund murmured, as if rolling the word around his tongue, and was conscious of a bitter taste in his mouth, as if his gorge had risen. He had seen pictures of the hundreds of bodies which had later been dug up. But could he identify with them? Could he hear the shots and the screams? Or was it impossible for a Dane to comprehend such an explosion of evil?

Gelbert let him sit for a minute, then handed him yet another photograph.

'One of my young officers found this – well, to be honest, filched it from Microsoft here in Poland, found it interesting, played about with it in his computer, and up she came.'

Toftlund studied the photograph which Gelbert had given him. It was a blow-up of the background in the Arkan picture. It showed a woman. The woman from the street-corner snap. She was wearing a beret, but the lovely mouth and Greek nose gave her away. The body, too, was the same. The straight shoulders and the full breasts under the camouflage jacket.

Toftlund glanced up at Gelbert, who nodded.

'Yes, Chief Inspector. She has blood on her hands, our little friend. So if you should run into her, watch your back. I don't know exactly what you want with her. Nor is it any of my business. But I've a feeling the people at the Hague might want to have a word with her after she has assisted you with your inquiries.'

'What business would she have with a Danish university lecturer? Why would she make up a story about being his sister?'

Gelbert spread his arms wide.

'What do I know? But as you and I are well aware, in our business it's usually a matter of information and the sale of said information. The big question is, of course, what she wants to sell and for how much.'

'And why?'

'That too, Mr Toftlund. That too.'

10

PER TOFTLUND SPENT THE AFTERNOON with two of Gelbert's men: young guys, both of whom spoke excellent English. Gelbert found a free room for them. It was sparsely furnished with a desk and phone, and a conference table on which coffee and water had been set out. Gelbert had kindly asked Toftlund if he would like to have dinner with him that evening and the Danish policeman had gratefully accepted. On the conference table lay the whole file on Maria Bujic. It was thick and appeared to be in perfect bureaucratic order, but then the Poles had learned their craft from the KGB. Once upon a time. Before these erstwhile allies had become adversaries. And now this erstwhile adversary was his ally. It was a historic fact, but Toftlund still found it a bit strange. It was not that many years since Denmark had been sending its agents into Poland; in one of his own first jobs as a newly fledged, inexperienced PET agent, Per had been charged with finding out which Danish citizens a particular Polish diplomat associated with outside normal office hours. Now, it seemed, the Poles would do anything to show, to *prove*, that they were friends and useful partners, doing their utmost to help a sister organisation in Denmark.

The Poles had had their eye on the woman for some years, but had not, of course, arrested her. They were more interested in discovering whom she met than in eventually deporting her. The woman, referred to by Toftlund and the two Polish agents for simplicity's sake, as Maria, had been coming to Poland a couple of times every year since 1995, which was when they had first spotted her – a discovery which came as a side benefit of their surveillance of a Soviet cultural attachè whom Polish counter-espionage suspected of actually working for the large branch of

| 145 |

Russian intelligence which occupied the old, screened-off floor in the big Russian embassy in Warsaw. The two had met in front of the eternal flame on Victory Square, opposite the Hotel Victoria, and on one occasion in the bar of the Hotel Victoria itself. It had not been possible to get close enough to actually tape their conversations. Maria had had meetings with several different people, some of them identified, others not. She had conducted herself like a real pro and only once had possibly detected that she was being followed. At any rate, on that occasion she had caught the first plane out without meeting anyone at all. It went without saying that she had probably been in the country at other times without the Poles being aware of it. Nowadays it was not particularly difficult to enter Polish territory by train or car. Two Polish citizens were still under surveillance, suspected of being agents for a foreign power or, possibly more likely today, involved in organised crime. Or both. The boundaries between Russian espionage and the Russian mafia had become somewhat blurred. It had not been possible to establish any direct link between Maria and any Danish citizens.

That was basically it, but Toftlund still had a hunch that there had to be a connection. Deep down he did not believe in chance connections, not in the world of espionage. He knew that coincidence often played a vital part in the unravelling of an intelligence operation, coincidence and luck. But you also had to follow every line of investigation, however tenuous. And if individuals figuring in such an investigation happened to be seen together, and when one was dealing with professionals it was no longer a coincidence, but a deliberate act. Of this he was firmly convinced, even if a pattern was not readily discernible.

The material on Maria consisted primarily of reports from the teams which had tailed her and a number of photographs taken with a telephoto lens. They had not managed to tap her phone, although they had tried – for this the two Polish agents apologised more than once.

It took time to go through the material. The two Polish offic-ers patiently translated documents and did their best to answer his questions. There was one picture which stood out somewhat from the rest. It showed Maria sitting at a pavement café in the Old Town. It had to have been taken in late summer or a day in early autumn when Warsaw had been enjoying an Indian summer of sorts. The light was not altogether summery and although the other people around the table were in their shirtsleeves one could see their coats hanging over the backs of their chairs. As if they were afraid that the sun would suddenly disappear, giving way to showers and chill winds. Maria was sitting with three elderly men. Western in appearance, Toftlund thought, possibly Danish even. He could not have said exactly why he took them for Danes, it was something about the shape of their heads, their clothes, the fact that two of the men had beards. You could almost always tell a person's nationality just by looking at them. It had become a bit more difficult, certainly, due to the influx of immigrants to Europe over the past twenty years, but every nation did still have its own small distinguishing features which marked it out from the rest.

Something about this picture was niggling at the back of his mind. He had to look at it for some time before he saw what it was. There were three shots of the same situation: one of Maria's lovely, mature features, the doleful eyes under the high brow; one showing the three men and Maria huddled over the glasses of beer and her coffee cup in what looked like intimate conversation; and a third, a wide shot taking in the whole situation – probably the first snap the photographer had taken, to set the scene. Like a press photographer or a film cameraman.

'Do you have a loupe?' Toftlund asked.

He could tell from their faces that they did not understand the word 'loupe'.

'A magnifying glass,' he said.

They smiled with relief, happy to be able to please the Danish visitor. Their new ally and friend. One of them went out and

| 147 |

returned carrying an old-fashioned stamp-collector's loupe. Toftlund pulled the photograph closer and examined it through the magnifying glass. The grainy picture dissolved into patterns of dots; the image was not very clear, but he could read the label on the bag sitting next to one of the table legs. The most striking feature of the label was what looked like a black circle surrounded by concentric white lines, but Toftlund had no trouble imagining that this circle was, in reality, blue. Because in its centre, in white, were the initials OB – for Odense Boldklub.

'Do you have a report which ties in this picture?' His voice was steady, despite the fact that his heart was beating faster, but they sensed the tension in him. At any rate, they both nodded and the report was unearthed from the pile of papers. Like the others it was dated and had been written on an old-style typewriter.

'Could you read the whole thing, please,' Toftlund asked.

'October 3rd, 1998, time 14.43,' translated the Pole whose name Per had not caught. 'Subject leaves the Hotel Victoria in the Old Town, sits down at a café and orders coffee, reads the *International Herald Tribune*. After ten minutes Subject is joined by three men, foreigners, all of whom look to be in their early seventies. Well-dressed. They appear to ask Subject if they can sit at her table, even though there are other tables free. They speak a language which surveillance agent B, who has placed himself at the next table, does not understand. Thinks it might be Dutch or Flemish. Certainly not German, although it sounds rather like German. (B understands and speaks German.) On consideration B believes the language to be Danish. Subject and the three men strike up a conversation in English. B does not speak or understand English. In any case he cannot hear a word they say because at that point a street musician starts playing the violin not far from their table. So no report on the substance of their conversation. After about twenty minutes Subject gets up, leaves the table and returns to her hotel. Nothing else to report.'

'That's it?' Toftlund said, unable to hide his disappointment.

'Well, there is an addendum,' the Pole said, and read: 'Addendum to surveillance report no. 234/10/1998. Surveillance agent T ...'

The Pole looked up from the paper:

'I'm sorry. We only have an initial here. It's standard procedure, but obviously I can find out which of our officers it was. If you would like?'

'That's okay. Just read me the rest.'

The Pole continued:

'Surveillance agent T reports that a parallel investigation has confirmed that the three men whom the Subject met are of no relevance to this case. They were members of a Danish hunting party. There is no record of any of them being involved in any criminal or espionage activities. The immigration police inform us that they had come to Poland to hunt. Due to our good relations with Denmark and according to the rules protecting citizens from illegal registration their names have therefore been deleted.'

'Does it give a date?' Toftlund asked.

'October 14th, 1998.'

'So we don't have those names?'

'Not in the report.'

'Can we get hold of them?'

The Pole hesitated, and looked at his colleague, who nodded.

'Maybe. But it will take time. For people like us, democracy is not always conducive to an efficient investigation. Naturally, though, we have to respect the law. And people's legal rights. Some things were, no doubt, simpler in the old days. So my older colleagues tell me, anyway. We don't have the names, but we can ask the immigration authorities. If these men have not broken the law in Poland then we will no longer have them on file. It's a long time since Danes needed a visa to visit our country. If they've been coming here regularly we might still have something on them from years back, under the old regime, but I doubt it. We've done a lot of clearing up.'

'Could you give it a shot anyway?' Toftlund asked.

'Yes, of course.'

'Could I have copies of those documents which have a bearing on my own investigation?'

'Of course. I gather you will be having dinner with Mr Gelbert this evening. He'll bring them with him.'

The rest of the material was of no interest to Toftlund. The dour driver took him back to the large, modern Hotel Victoria. It was still raining, but the air seemed milder. There were crowds of people on the street, moving through the twilight like damp shadows. Most were laden with shopping bags. The trams were jam-packed, their windows fogging up as the heat of so many bodies collided with the cold air outside. The hotel overlooked a grand, broad square, bounded on three sides by socialist-style concrete blocks. On the fourth side of the square two soldiers stood guard next to a memorial on which a gas flame wavered in the wind. Behind it lay a park with its paths and bare trees.

Toftlund checked in and had a shower. He thought briefly of calling Lise, but before he could do so Konstantin Gelbert called from the lobby. Toftlund was famished. He had not eaten since breakfast in Copenhagen, which suddenly seemed a very long time ago.

Gelbert had put on a tie, but was otherwise still dressed in the same casual attire. Toftlund stepped out of the lift to find him waiting in the large, high-ceilinged lobby with a beige raincoat over his arm. He shook Per's hand formally.

'I hope my men were able to help you.'

'Yes, thank you very much. They were a great help.'

'Good. Later this evening one of my people will deliver the copies you asked for. By hand. There's no point in having them lying about in your hotel.'

'Fine.'

Gelbert took him gently by the arm and suggested that they walk down to the Old Town. It was no more than a fifteen-minute stroll. The rain had stopped and the evening was quite warm for the time of year. Toftlund would much rather have driven there in a patrol car with the siren blaring and lights flashing, to get to the restaurant as quickly as possible, but he nodded politely.

He did not regret it. On their stroll across Victory Square and down to the Old Town Gelbert proved to be an interesting and entertaining raconteur. The streets were black with rain, they could hear the sound of car tyres swishing through puddles and even though there was an edge to the wind when they turned a corner, Toftlund undid the top button of his coat. Gelbert strode out smartly, almost marching, with short steps and arms swinging, while he related the history of the city in the American accented English which sounded somehow wrong coming from him, but at the same time right. They reached the Castle Square, with the rebuilt Royal Castle on the right-hand side. Toftlund was more intrigued, though, by the Danish hot-dog stall with Tulip sausage signs sitting next to the massive castle.

'The old and the new,' he remarked.

Gelbert trilled his falsetto laugh:

'Appearances can be deceptive, my friend,' he said. 'Everything around here is new. In 1945 this place was nothing but a pile of rubble. The whole lot was in ruins. But we rebuilt it brick by brick. Like a phoenix the Old Town rose from the ashes, although it is not, in fact, old at all. It is a symbol of our history. Time and again we have been overthrown, occupied, divided up by the Germans or the Russians. They have tried to seize our soul and our history, to wipe it out. But they have never succeeded. Each time we have risen from the ashes again.'

The square was dominated by a huge statue set atop a tall column. Gelbert pointed:

'Our great king, Sigismund the Third. The Russians hated that statue. He watches over Warsaw, but they did not realise until it was too late that we had positioned him with his sword pointing to the East instead of towards the capitalists in the West. We made the right choice. Then and now. Today the Germans are our allies. In all of its history, Poland has never been more secure. But the future, my friend – we Poles have learned never to take *that* for granted.'

Toftlund stood quietly for a moment, taking in the sight of the beautifully restored buildings, the people strolling past, the teenagers in their jeans and trendy down jackets, with their eternally beeping mobile phones, three clattering horse-drawn carriages, each carrying a couple of frozen tourists, and the drone of heavy traffic in the background. The wet cobbles glistened and despite the cars on the road running alongside the river the air was strangely hushed.

'But it's so quiet and peaceful here,' he said. 'Russia is weak. What could the Russians possibly do now? They can hardly feed themselves. They got their asses kicked in Chechnya. Their military is rusting up. They couldn't prevent the expansion of NATO. They couldn't stop NATO from going to war against Yugoslavia. It's the Upper Volta with nuclear missiles. Yeltsin is both blind and deaf. And anyway, they have to behave themselves. They can't afford to do anything else.'

'You're forgetting history, Mr Toftlund,' Gelbert said. 'It's always a mistake to forget history in this part of the world. It is always with us. I can smell the bodies of my countrymen in the Jewish ghetto. There are hardly any of us left …'

'But that was the Nazis.'

'Correct! But who was sitting only a few kilometres away, on the other side of the Vistula? Sukov and his mighty army. And did he come to their aid? No, he let the Nazis do the dirty work, and then he moved in. He let the Nazis destroy the Polish resistance and wipe out the Jewish ghetto. It was surrounded, fired upon, gassed and finally burned to the ground. Not far from here my Jewish kinsmen died in their millions in Auschwitz. All Jewish culture disappeared for ever from Central Europe. A great, rich and ancient culture. Lost for all time.'

Gelbert's speech had grown more impassioned. Toftlund did not like being lectured. This was all water under the bridge. And anyway, his stomach was rumbling. Nonetheless he asked:

'So what are you today, Colonel Gelbert? Jewish or Polish?'

'A Polish Jew who remembers his history,' Gelbert replied. 'Come on. You must be hungry. I'm a bad host.'

He strode out briskly again, Toftlund keeping pace with him.

'You mentioned that both the Russians and the Poles carry their history around with them. Like an old coat they can't bring themselves to throw out. What did you mean by that?'

'Our mistrust of one another runs deep. It does not fade simply because we are now free and Russia is struggling to shape a democracy.' He laughed again and went on: 'It may sound banal, but it is no less a fact. The Russians remember how the Poles occupied Moscow and the Kremlin in the seventeenth century, when we were a major power. The Russians remember how in 1920 the Polish army beat the Red Army when it was marching on Warsaw. Poland was opposed to the revolution. We Poles remember that for the greater part of the last two hundred years our country was occupied by the Russians. An occupation which did not end until 1989. A bloody occupation. We remember how Russian troops slaughtered fifteen thousand Polish officers at Katyn and blamed the Germans for it. For most of my life it was forbidden to talk about this massacre. Although we knew about it, of course. Everyone in Poland knew that the regime was lying when it denied that it had ever happened. History lives on here. Obviously we have to improve our relations with Russia. We have to live with the bear, but we don't need to trust it. Especially not if it starts to get hungry again. It is dangerous to underestimate Russian nationalism.'

They walked on in silence, then Toftlund said:

'I get the impression that the Poles feel they have always been persecuted by Russia, while the Russians see the Poles as perpetually betraying some sort of Slavic brotherhood.'

'A shrewd observation, Mr Toftlund, and quite true,' Gelbert said. 'But now Poland is a success story and Russia is a big mess. The roles are reversed, right?'

Gelbert stopped again. They had been walking through the narrow streets and had now come out into a pretty little square surrounded by lovely neo-classical buildings. There were lots of shops and restaurants. In the centre of the square a number of horse-drawn carriages stood in the darkness. Business was slow at this time of day. The drivers sat hunched inside their heavy over-coats, puffing on their cigarettes. The horses had their muzzles buried in their nosebags. The absence of cars here made the silence even more marked. The mist enveloped the scene in a bewitching light which erased all sign that the buildings were actually of con-crete and modern-built. A shiver ran down Toftlund's spine. He could not have said why he suddenly felt uneasy. Maybe it was the atmosphere. But he felt he could clearly hear muffled screams emanating from the walls of the houses round about. It struck him that they were standing on piles of skeletons, that the city rested upon the bodies of thousands.

Gelbert sensed his mood:

'History lives on here. Warsaw is just one city among many which have made this the century of the victim. You Danes live in a cosy little backwater. I envy you that. Just as people in the Balkans today envy you, because you know nothing of suffering and death. This means, though, that you tend to forget history and what it can do to people.'

'We're adept at steering clear of serious trouble and keeping on the right side of our big neighbours, not least Germany,' Toftlund said.

Gelbert smiled:

'It's history that has taught you to do that. Just as history has taught us not to take tomorrow for granted. I had a meeting just the other day with my Russian counterpart, a delightfully diplo-matic meeting. Because we are, of course, gentlemen. But there was a certain undertone to the whole thing. This was shortly after the Foreign Ministry had declared two so-called diplomats to be *personae non gratae* in Poland. Our membership of NATO was more or less a *fait accompli*. He expressed his regret about this, but I had the feeling he knew that while Russia is weak at the moment, Poland is strong, protected as we now are by the world's only superpower, the United States. When we said goodbye he shook my hand and said: "It's been nice talking to you, Colonel Gelbert. Might I ask you to remember that when a lion is sick even a monkey can beat the shit out of it. But what happens to the monkey on the day when the lion is back on its feet?" It was an elegantly worded threat, but a threat nonetheless.'

'And an elegantly worded insult,' Toftlund remarked.

'That too. This is the place.'

They stepped into a warm restaurant full of good smells. Almost every table was taken. The waitresses, in green blouses and short skirts, looked like something out of a bad operetta, but the beer was cold and foaming. Toftlund let Gelbert order for them both. He was so hungry that he would basically have eaten anything. The meal was heavy, but good. They started with a thick cabbage soup, and followed this with big wild boar steaks served with potato cakes, sauerkraut and gravy. Food like Grandma used to make, Toftlund thought. He ate it all with relish. So did Gelbert. What a metabolism he must have had, to be as slim as he was. They each had another large beer and rounded off with coffee. They chatted a little about their families, but mainly about the one subject on most people's minds that spring: NATO's war against Yugoslavia and the stream of refugees now pouring into Albania and threatening to spread to the rest of Europe.

Over coffee Toftlund said:

'It was very nice of you to invite me to dinner.'

'It was the least I could do. Denmark is our neighbour. In any case, I would always consider it my duty to help one of Commissioner Vuldom's people. As I said – a formidable woman.'

Toftlund found his use of the word 'duty' – and, in fact, his whole way of speaking – interesting. In Denmark, a word such as 'duty' could easily give rise to some wry or sarcastic comment. Despite his American English Gelbert came over as being Central European to the core.

'Can I take it that she has helped you?'

'Most astute, Chief Inspector. Not only *has* helped, but *does* help me. For someone like me, appointed to this job not because of my police or legal experience, but because I am seen as having a democratic mentality and a clean sheet as far as the past is concerned, the advice which a woman like Commissioner Vuldom has to offer is invaluable.'

'I see.'

'And a word of advice to you, before we say goodbye. If you will permit me?'

'Of course. I would be honoured.' The words were out before Toftlund had time to think about it. He was starting to talk like Gelbert. In a rather antiquated, formal mode of speech which reminded him of the dialogue from an old Danish film, but which seemed to suit the situation.

'Your case is a complex one, that's for sure. I think you should be looking at the past. Especially the distant ...'

'What makes you think that? Is there something you're not telling me?' Toftlund said, more sharply than he had intended.

'No. It's just a hunch. Possibly triggered by our conversation earlier this evening. A hunch based on the fact that Maria Bujic, as you call her, has met so many different people, and that the frequency of these meetings has intensified over the past two years.'

'There's no guarantee that she has anything to do with this business at all.'

Gelbert drank the last of his espresso and looked him in the eye:

'What's your gut feeling?'

'That she does. Somehow she is the key. I just don't know which lock the key fits.'

'You see. One more word of advice?'

'Yes, please.'

'You'll have no problem with our allies in Budapest and Prague. We've sent them the relevant documents on our friend as agreed. But later, in Bratislava, when you meet my Slovakian counterpart, if we can call him that, you should not, perhaps, be quite as open with him as we have been with one another. I don't think he has very much contact with Commissioner Vuldom. If I can put it like that.'

'Konstantin. Stop beating about the bush,' Toftlund said.

Gelbert gave his high-pitched laugh and reached a hand across the table.

'Okay, Per. Let's cut the bullshit, as they say in the States. My esteemed colleague, Eduard Findra, is a product of Meciar's special forces regiment. He may not be entirely loyal to the new left-wing government, or to NATO for that matter. He used to work for the old Czechoslovakian secret service. Had he been a Czech he would have been put out to pasture years ago. The Slovaks are not quite so choosy. They have to use whatever skills these people happen to possess.'

'Meciar? The name rings a bell, but I can't quite think why.'

'No, well, why should you Danes take an interest in the politics of some remote country in Central Europe,' Gelbert responded drily. 'Meciar is a former boxer, a gangster, prime minister, nationalist, one-time communist and far too popular with the Slovaks. Since last year Slovakia has had a new government, a broad democratic coalition. It is now racing against time, trying to get Slovakia back on track for membership of the EU and NATO. Like the rest of us. Slovakia was given the cold shoulder because of Meciar. There's to be a presidential election in Slovakia in the summer. But Meciar could still cause trouble. Mr Findra, the head of the Slovakian secret service, was appointed by Meciar. He's living on borrowed time, but he's still alive. I'm sure he is doing his patriotic duty, but duty is one thing, cronyism is something else again.'

'I'll bear your advice in mind, Konstantin.'

'Well, I just hope it's good advice,' he said and raised his hand. The waitress came over right away. Toftlund had the distinct impression that Gelbert was a well-liked and respected regular at the restaurant, although he could tell from the prices that this was not a place where ordinary Poles, with their low wages, would often, if ever, eat.

Toftlund took a taxi back to the hotel. His driver from the morning was waiting for him in the lobby. He worked long hours. Without a word he handed Toftlund a fat manila envelope. Then he bade him a curt goodnight.

Per settled himself in the room's one armchair with a whisky from the minibar. In the envelope were the photographs and the relevant reports translated into English. Gelbert's boys had been hard at it. Instead of the characteristic typewritten characters of the originals, the copies were printed in a modern, word-processor typeface. A handwritten note was attached to the pile. In English, almost as if he had orchestrated their conversation of the evening in advance, Gelbert had written:

Dear Per,
Here, as promised, are copies of the documents you requested. We cannot, of course, guarantee the authenticity of the originals. If your inquiries in Bratislava should give rise to any complications you might want to consider contacting Pavel Samson. He used to work for our sister organisation there, but was consigned to criminal investigation by Meciar. This is his private number. He deserves our confidence. Godspeed to Bratislava and my best wishes to Commissioner Vuldom for her health and happiness.

Yours,
Konstantin.

'Well, I'll be blowed,' Per Toftlund said out loud. Then he picked up his lined A4 notepad and began to work up his meticulous notes into a report, all ready to be transferred to the computer and thereby to the case file – and, not least, to Vuldom, when he got back to Denmark. He was booked onto a morning flight to Budapest and, if the day went as planned, an evening flight to Bratislava, in order to keep his morning appointment there before flying on to Prague.

Toftlund wrote down the facts, simply and clearly. Vuldom set great store by lucid prose. But she also liked a report to have a *feel* to it, or a mood: the expression on a face, an impression, such things could invest a bald case report with meaning and could always be weeded out again later when the document was filed so that, seventy-five years from now, historians and others might be allowed to dip into these top secret documents. On the other hand, one should not go any further than one deemed reasonable. There was no need to give everything away. As she said at her training courses: In a report, what is left unsaid can be both distracting and revealing. And in that paradox the truth about a person or an event will often lie hidden.

11

IT WAS RAINING AGAIN early the next morning when Per Toftlund went for a run through the park near his hotel in Warsaw, but the sun was shining from an almost clear sky when his plane landed on schedule in Budapest. Again he was picked up at the airport and driven into the city. The Hungarian capital seemed more prosperous than Warsaw, although it might have been the beautiful houses in the city centre which gave him that impression. The suburbs they passed through on the way from the airport resembled, however, every other place where communist architects and contractors had done their worst: long rows of identical, drab, concrete tower blocks, lined up in ranks like soldiers – a symbol of the party's absolute power and constant efforts to make people look small, he thought, as the car drove at top speed towards the city centre. Actually, Toftlund had no real feelings about Budapest one way or the other, or Hungary for that matter. He had never been to the country before, and although as a member of the Warsaw Pact it had been on the enemy side during the cold war, Hungary had not come under Denmark's area of responsibility. Unlike Poland. To Poland had been allotted the task of landing troops along the Zealand coastline. Poland was a near neighbour. From Poland had come the agents who recruited Danish fifth-columnists and buried military equipment and radio receivers in the woods in preparation for the day of the planned invasion. Sitting there in the back of the blue BMW he remembered the chill that had run down his spine the first time he saw the invasion plans in their entirety, after the collapse of communism. Detailed plans which dictated that the first and most important task for the special-forces units from Poland and East Germany set ashore from submarines or dropped by parachute, was to liquidate all of Denmark's highest-ranking officers and members of the government, thereby paralysing the country. If the invasion failed, the plan was to use tactical nuclear weapons for the first time. He might have come to think of this because he had been pondering Gelbert's words about history and Danish naivety. How the Danes somehow always expected to get off lightly, as they had done in the First and Second World Wars. And always assumed that someone else would foot the bill. Yet again it had turned out alright. But it could have been a disaster.

The meeting took place in a modern office building overlooking the Danube and the imposing Parliament building. Two armed guards were stationed at the entrance to the office block where he was dropped off; he was then led past another guard and up to the tenth floor, where he was shown into an empty office. Through the small windows he could see the muddy grey river running past down below. A barge flying the Russian flag slipped slowly past. A woman was hanging out washing in front of the small wheelhouse. Sailing towards the Russian vessel was another barge with the Romanian flag fluttering from the stern. He was offered coffee and mineral water by a middle-aged secretary with a peroxide beehive who smelled heavily of jasmine. She apologised in German for the fact that he was being kept waiting, but Herr Direktor was in a meeting which had run on a little. *'Der Krieg, wissen Sie, mein Herr.'* She gave him that day's edition of the *Herald Tribune* to help pass the time. The big story in the paper was, of course, the NATO bombings. Everything was going according to plan, a NATO spokesman said. Each day new targets were designated and hit. The weather was giving some problems. But there could be no talk of sending in ground troops. They were doing all they could to avoid allied losses. This was a high-tech war, waged from afar. Civilian losses were minimal, NATO said. He read the words: *Minimum collateral damage.* Other articles painted a less rosy picture. They told of hundreds of thousands of Kosovo Albanian refugees. Fleeing from what? The intensive ethnic cleansing of the Serbs? Or NATO's bombs? They sought refuge in Macedonia and Albania, both of which were almost collapsing under the weight of refugees. In the parliaments of the wealthy European countries they debated whether they should accept a thousand, or maybe two thousand, refugees. The world was all upside-down, he thought to himself as two men entered the room and introduced themselves.

'Colonel Karoly Karancsi, head of the Intelligence Service. An honour to meet you. May we speak German?'

'By all means,' Toftlund said, thanking his stars that he had grown up in Tønder, near the German border. 'Detective Inspector Per Toftlund.'

Karoly Karancsi was a short, stout man with a narrow moustache. He looked a little like Chaplin in his later years, but his hair was black, possibly dyed, his cheeks were round and smooth as a baby's and slightly reddened by his close morning shave, his eyes close set under a low brow. His handshake was firm and dry. His well-fitting suit looked tailor-made. With it he wore a pale-blue shirt and and a dark, self-coloured tie. A bureaucrat with dress sense.

'Laszlo Krozsel, criminal investigation department,' the other man said and offered his hand. He was dressed in a crumpled suit, his tie loosened at the neck. He looked to be in his mid-thirties, but was already bald. His face was lined, his eyes grey and beady and his fingers stained with nicotine. He looked like a cop with too many cases on his desk and more landing on it every single day. It was also he who was carrying the case files. In his hand the colonel had just one grey folder. There was something stamped on it in Hungarian – Toftlund guessed it might stand for 'Strictly Confidential' or 'Top Secret' or something of the sort.

'Shall we sit down?' Karancsi said. 'My apologies for keeping you waiting. But only days after becoming members of NATO Hungary now finds itself at war with one of its neighbours. The situation is anything but simple. There is a large Hungarian minority in Vojvodina. The war has generated a lot of uncertainty in Hungary. The people may not altogether understand NATO's decision. I'm sure I don't have to tell you how complicated the security situation could become if we permit bombing raids to be made from Hungarian territory, or the passage of military supplies through our country. You were regrettably kept waiting because I had been asked to brief the cabinet on this matter.'

'I understand,' Toftlund said. 'These are difficult times we're living in.'

'You're very kind, Inspector. Thank you,' the colonel said. 'We are allies now, after all. Fighting on the same side. Danish pilots actively, at that. Such a drastic step would be too much for the Hungarian people – the idea that Hungarian pilots might have to drop bombs on their own countrymen, people who, simply due to the vagaries of history, have ended up living in Yugoslavia. But we civil servants have to leave such decisions to the politicans.'

The two men sat down across from Toftlund at the gleaming wooden table. He could not help feeling that they were about to haggle over fish or butter quotas. The colonel nodded to the policeman, who opened one of the files. First, though, Karancsi said:

'We have studied the material we received from Denmark and from Poland. We would, of course, like to help you, but to be honest I don't think there is much we can do for you. You may, however, be able to do something for us. We'll come back to that. First, though, might I suggest that Inspector Krozsel gives you a rundown of that side of the matter pertaining to the murder of the Danish citizen. Herr Krozsel?'

Kroszel's German was slow, but easy to understand. He presented a factual report, outlining all the facts of the case, and these Toftlund carefully jotted down in his notebook. He could almost have been sitting at the station in Middelfart, listening to a Danish colleague bringing him up to date on an ongoing case.

Police detectives worked in pretty much the same way everywhere in Europe, so it seemed. At any rate they all spoke the same dry, dispassionate language. There was nothing they didn't know about the follies of mankind. Few facets of human nature were beyond their ken. Their remit was clear, in one case after another: find enough evidence to make it stand up in court, then it was on to the next one. Because there was always another case waiting to be dealt with.

The Danish citizen Niels Lassen had been found in the morning, after his daughter had begun to wonder why he had not come down for breakfast and did not answer the phone when she called his room. He had been killed by repeated blows to the back of the head with a blunt instrument. The first blow had killed him instantly. With a face void of expression Krozsel handed Toftlund the pictures taken by the forensic photographer. The back of Lassen's head was a tangled mass of blood and hair. The body lay curled up beside the window in a foetal position. The eyes were wide open. He was wearing only underpants. Next to him lay the white bathrobe provided by the hotel as part of their service. Other photographs showed the room. It was a perfectly ordinary, decent hotel room containing a bed, a television, a table and two chairs. It had been ransacked: clothes, newspapers, books were scattered everywhere. The chair had been tipped over. The duvet and sheet had been pulled off the bed, the mattress slit. Two empty suitcases had also been ripped open.

Toftlund handed back the pictures.

'How did the killer or killers get in?' he asked.

'Well the door doesn't appear to have been forced,' Krozsel said. 'Although that doesn't mean much, I'm afraid. Hotel guests are not as careful as they ought to be. Most of them will open the door if someone knocks. Also, it's very easy to get hold of the – what do you call it – the master key. Cleaners, room service – you know. Will I go on?'

Toftlund nodded and Krozsel continued. Per could tell that

he was desperate for a cigarette, but the colonel did not smell of smoke so he was obviously not going to allow that. Which suited Toftlund fine.

The Hungarian CID had interviewed the hotel staff and residents, paying particular attention to those from Denmark. Niels Lassen's movements were easily reconstructed. He had attended the opera with the Danish delegation. They had got back to the hotel around eleven and had a drink in the bar. Lassen had gone to bed around midnight, as had most of the Danish party, only a few had hung on in the bar for another hour, among them Lassen's daughter. She had passed the door of her father's room on her way to her own, but had not heard anything. The investigation had been complicated slightly right from the start by the fact that Lassen's room was registered in the name of Theodor Nikolaj Pedersen, Danish citizen, and Niels's daughter had, naturally enough, been in a bit of a state. The leader of the delegation, Klaus Brandt, had cleared up the misunderstanding. The hotel had been reprimanded for not keeping its register properly updated. The pathologist estimated time of death to be around four a.m. The hour when the hotel was at its quietest. There were no signs of the victim having put up a fight. No traces of skin under the fingernails. It was their belief that Lassen had opened the door, taken two steps back or been pushed and then hit hard on the back of the head. The only fingerprints found in the room were those of the deceased and another set which had been identified as belonging to one of the cleaners. The deceased's daughter had observed that traveller's cheques, his Visa card, some cash, a CD player, mobile phone and a laptop computer – make: Compaq Presario – were all missing. The police had come to the conclusion that it was a case of a robbery which had gone wrong, but they had no suspects. Inquiries among the criminal fraternity had not turned up anything new.

Krozsel raised his eyes and closed the file. A wasted life lay within those covers, Toftlund thought to himself. What he said was:

'What about the hotel's security cameras?'

'We've looked at the tapes covering the lobby, the main entrance, the casino and the car park. There are a lot of comings and goings, as you might imagine, but no known faces. Or any suspicious looking individuals, for that matter. Sorry.'

'Not even this woman?' Toftlund asked, placing the photograph of Maria on the table in front of Krozsel, who glanced first at it then at the colonel, who nodded imperceptibly.

'If it's alright with you, Colonel Karancsi would like to come back to this woman a little later, but I am authorised to say that she does not appear on the videotapes, nor do we have any witnesses placing her anywhere near the hotel or in Budapest at all, come to that. We will of course let you know if we catch the person or persons who did this. But the odds are not great, I'm afraid. That is the downside of freedom. The great gulf between rich and poor. The soaring rise in crime. We have a lot of gypsies in Budapest. We lie on the outskirts of the Balkans. We attract a lot of shady characters.'

Krozsel sat back. As if that was the end of the matter. Or at least, that's how it seemed to Toftlund. While it might not officially be shelved, the case would now be added to the steadily growing pile of paperwork which the overworked and underpaid police officers of this new era had to wade through every day.

'Is there any way of getting into the hotel without being caught on film?' Toftlund asked.

'It's possible, yes.'

'How?'

'Unfortunately the camera covering the service entrance was out of order. The security manager felt it was safe to wait until the next day to get it fixed.'

'Had it been out of order long?'

'It had been tampered with.'

'When did you discover this?'

'Not until yesterday, I'm afraid.'

'So it looks like there's been some planning behind it, after all.'

'That was our conclusion too. Unfortunately, Chief Inspector. Our gangs are both professional and ruthless. We have a lot of hotel robberies. But for the sake of our tourist trade we tend not to publicise the fact.'

Toftlund thought for a moment, then he said:

'Last question: were any other rooms burgled that night?'

'No.'

'Doesn't it make you wonder – to go to so much trouble, all for just one room? I mean, come on – a handful of traveller's cheques and a computer!'

'That's not such a bad haul, Inspector. Not in our part of the world, where the standard pension is less than a hundred Deutschmarks a week. But we do not believe the killing of this Danish man was premeditated. Whoever did it panicked and fled. Maybe Mr Lassen refused to hand over his valuables? Maybe he screamed.'

'And no one heard anything?'

'The room on one side was empty. The German gentleman on the other side had a young lady in his room. He did not hear anything. He had other things to think about, you might say. Or as he put it, not without a hint of pride: "My own companion was screaming like a stuck pig".'

Toftlund could not help smiling. And Krozsel smiled back. One cop to another. Sorry pal, you know how it is, that smile seemed to say to Toftlund. And with that the Hungarian detective gathered up his papers, rose, shook Per's hand and left. Clearly the next part of the proceedings was closed to a common DI. Now it was the colonel's turn.

Karancsi leaned forward, rested his elbows on the table and clasped his hands under his chin. A ludicrous pose, clearly meant to convey an air of importance, Toftlund thought. He had the suspicion, albeit unfounded, that the colonel was a political appointee and not a professional intelligence officer. Like Gelbert in Poland, but with one crucial difference: sincerity. On the one hand the opportunist who stuck his finger in the air to check which way the wind was blowing, on the other the idealist who believed that he could make a difference.

Slowly and solemnly Colonel Karancsi said:

'It is a complex situation, Chief Inspector. Extremely complex. I have been given the honourable task of endeavouring to protect our country's security interests. In that capacity I am, of course, prepared to cooperate at all levels with an allied service, but very recently I was also assigned another role, one which is not necessarily so *transnational* in nature, if you get my drift?'

'No, I don't, not at all.'

'No. Well, as I say, it's complex. Have a look at this picture.'

He handed Toftlund a colour photograph which he had produced, almost conjuror-like, from the slim folder. A picture of a woman. It was obviously Maria Bujic, but she looked totally different. Her hair was blonde, falling in curls over her collar and she was wearing a pair of ordinary spectacles. She was pictured standing next to a car, regarding the photographer through narrowed eyes, as if she sensed that she was being watched. She was dressed in blue jeans and what looked like an expensive leather jacket.

'That's her, the woman we know as Maria,' Toftlund said.

'Yes and no.'

'Now you really have lost me.'

Karancsi cleared his throat and again pressed his fingertips together affectedly before going on in his halting German:

'We know her as Svetlana Kreisler, Russian citizen, but of German origin. Dating back to Catherine the Great, you know? A Volga German. And as such automatically a German citizen. She also travels on a German passport. She has been coming here for the past four or five years, as far as we know. We believe her to have links not with any national intelligence agency, but with the Russian and Hungarian mafia. This is where I come in, in my other capacity.'

Again he paused for effect. Toflund waited. Sometimes, during an interrogation or similar situation, it was better to keep one's mouth shut. To let the silence drag on for so long that one's interlocutor felt compelled to speak. Toftlund glanced out of the window. The river flowed broad and slow outside. Barges passed endlessly up and down, along with the occasional sightseeing boat. Karancsi cleared his throat again:

'I have been made head of a new department here. One which corresponds, more or less, to the Americans' Department of Internal Affairs. It has been set up on the instructions of the government and parliament to investigate possible instances of corruption within the national police force. I will therefore have to ask you to regard what I am about to tell you as absolutely confidential. As a private briefing of a representative of a friendly nation. Agreed?'

'Of course.'

'Good. Svetlana appears to have been the go-between in what we refer to as the oil fraud. Possibly even the brains behind it. A con so simple it was almost banal. We have high import taxes on diesel oil in this country and low taxes on heating oil. That's pretty common in the free world, I believe. These people bought diesel oil abroad, coloured it red so it could be sent through customs as heating oil and then sold it here in Hungary as diesel. Saving millions of dollars in tax and making millions of dollars in profit. It was every con man's dream. Five years later we still have no clear idea of how much money the Treasury was cheated out of.'

'But what does all this have to do with your Internal Affairs department?'

'Well, let me put it another way: all that money led to a – how do you say – an upgrading of organised crime in this country. It enabled our really rather primitive gangs to organise themselves and expand. Into the classic areas with which you are familiar: prostitution, drugs, stolen cars and money laundering. But they also infiltrated the legitimate business world. We guess – although we've no way of knowing for sure – that this fraud has cost the Hungarian state something like four hundred million dollars.

That's four hundred million straight into the pockets of what one could call the mafia.'

'And such a fraud was only possible if the police and customs people were looking the other way?' Toftlund said.

'Exactly. It is up to me to investigate the extent of the bribery. Even if it means going all the way to the top. It is not only a question of whether an officer or an ordinary policeman has accepted bribes. It is also a matter of checking to see whether it can actually be true, as is claimed, that out of the ten honest, hard-working police detectives in this country who have tried, over the years, to get to the bottom of this case, six committed suicide.' He cleared his throat, coughed discreetly. 'We suspect that pathology reports were falsified. Our government employees are not the best paid, you know. It doesn't take much, I'm afraid. It's all part of life in our post-communist world. And even if Hungary does have one of the highest suicide rates in the world, there do seem to be rather too many coincidences, wouldn't you say?'

'Yes, but I still don't see any connection between this and a Danish citizen by the name of Niels Lassen. Do you?'

'Not a direct connection, no. But an indirect one. Because, sad to say, Chief Inspector, all of that money which was suddenly put into circulation gave a boost, so to speak, to crime of every shape and form.'

'I see.'

'I'm glad. Then I hope you will also understand that we cannot offer you any direct assistance. But if you should succeed in apprehending the woman whom you call Maria Bujic we would be extremely grateful to you and to Denmark if you could let us know. I would like a word or two with her.'

Everybody would like a word or two with that woman, so it seems, Toftlund thought to himself later. He was at the airport, waiting for his plane to Bratislava. He had trout for lunch and drank water with it. The water tasted good. He read through his notes, but could discern no real connection. He still could not shake off the feeling, though, that she was central to the whole thing. At any rate he could well understand the Hungarian colonel. Toftlund was also keen to have a word with the mysterious woman of many faces. He slipped his notebook back into his bag and ordered coffee. Then, for the first time since leaving home he switched on his mobile.

Toftlund did not trust mobile phones. He did not mind using them to make quick calls during operations in Denmark. At such times he preferred to use a mobile phone rather than a walkie-talkie, which any reporter or amateur detective could tune in to. But when it came to confidential conversations he did not trust mobiles. Intelligence organisations all over the world scanned the airwaves, monitoring calls made on these things. There were computers programmed to react to certain code words. Echelon, some people called this system. Toftlund could not really have cared less what they called it. He simply took it for granted that such a system existed. If he had had the resources, he would have made use of it himself.

His mobile beeped furiously. There were several messages for him. He called the answering service number. There were two messages from Lise. The first was warm and tender: Hope you're okay. The other was considerably cooler: Could he possibly find a minute to phone home? He sat for a moment, holding the phone. This was an unwonted situation for him. Never before in his career had he had cause to call home from work. At Customs and Immigration there had been no reason to: you could have set your clock by his shifts. And before that, when he was with PET, he had been single. Toftlund was not, by nature, a great one for analysing things. He had the ability to focus completely on a job, but not for looking inside himself. From his time as a Royal Navy frogman he had learned that if you were to survive the tough demands made on you and the impossible tasks with which you were faced, first during training and then on manoeuvres, you simply had to concentrate on the job in hand and block out everything else. If you allowed thoughts on unrelated or personal matters to hinder the completion of your mission then sooner or later you would come to grief. Instinct, reinforced by his military training told him that for the sake of his sanity it was best to compartmentalise things in his mind. And deal with one thing at a time. So he was surprised, sitting there at the airport, to feel a twinge of guilt. More than a twinge, in fact. Maybe he should have called. But what would have been the point? He was getting on with his work. If Lise didn't hear from him it was because he was busy with the case and because things were going as they should. No news was good news.

He sipped his coffee and considered his little phone. A blessing and a curse. Then he glanced at his watch and keyed in their home number. He waited until he heard the answering machine click in, then he hung up. He sat for a moment. Then he called Lise's direct number at the newspaper office. This early in the afternoon she would normally be getting on with her work on the arts page of *Politiken*, and even though she was now on maternity leave it would not have surprised him to find that she had popped into the office. He could hear her telling him that he did actually have her mobile number. There it was again. A blessing and a curse. You were never completely out of touch these days. But the mobile phone had one drawback: it could be traced, wherever it happened to be. The closest radio mast would always betray its location and he did not like that idea at all.

He was a little taken aback, nonetheless, to discover that she was at the office.

'Lise Carlsen,' she said. The sound of her voice made him feel warm all over, and to his amazement he suddenly realised that he missed her terribly. It came as something of a shock to him that such feelings could strike him when he was at work. It was as though a breach had been made in the dykes between his different compartments.

'Hi, Lise, sweetheart. It's me. I miss you. How are you doing?'

'Per. Where are you?'

'In Budapest.'

'Oh, *that's* nice,' she said tartly.

'Well, I haven't seen anything but airports and offices, so I wouldn't know.'

'It's nice of you to call,' she said in the same crisp, correct tone. As if he were a contact who had been good enough to call her back.

'I thought you were on leave. What are you doing at work?'

'Ganløse got a bit lonely. I wanted to see if my chair still fitted me. And Pernille asked me out for a bite to eat. She felt sorry for me, vegetating out there in the sticks while my husband was gallivanting all over Central Europe and seemed to have forgotten all about his wife.'

Pernille was a fellow journalist and friend. She was probably finishing off an article before they went out to eat.

'For Christ's sake, Lise. I've been busy. It's very complicated,' he said, sounding more annoyed than he really meant to.

'Oh, I'm sure you have. When are you coming home?'

'In a day or so.'

'That sounds very precise.'

'Look, I can't discuss this on an open line.'

'No, of course you can't.'

'You're upset, Lise.'

'I'm tired and I'm big as a house and my back aches; I'm sweating like a pig, I'm sick of being pregnant and I'm sick of my husband just running off and not even bothering to call home to ask if his pregant wife is okay. And whether she's maybe gone into labour early.'

His heart began to pound. As if he had run a long way very fast.

'Have you? What are you trying to say. Is there something wrong?'

She laughed and her laughter warmed his heart. Now he recognised her again.

'Ooh, the daring detective was worried there for a moment, eh?'

'Is something the matter, Lise?'

'No, Per, you stupid old fool. I'm fine. I went for a check-up yesterday. Everything is just as it should be. If we didn't know it was a girl I would swear we were having a boy. She's got a kick like David Beckham. She can't come out quick enough as far as I'm concerned. And I would really like to hear from my husband, even if he is racing all over the world, playing at being James Bond.'

'Okay.'

'You and your "okay". You're not on your own now, you know. What if I had gone into labour? You wouldn't have known.'

'Yes, but you didn't.'

'Ah, but what if,' she said again, but he could tell that she was no longer mad at him.

'Then I would have flown home in my private, supersonic James Bond jet. You know – the one with the caviar and champagne and the three big blondes.'

'Just you try …'

'I love you, Lise,' he said, the words coming as a surprise even to him, uttered as they were without any ulterior motive.

'I love you, too. Even if you *have* been very naughty. Just call me now and again, will you? Or at least keep your mobile switched on. Babies have been known to come early, you know. Alright?'

'Will do.'

'Alright, honey. Take care.'

'See you in a day or two,' he said. 'I'll call you from the hotel this evening.'

'And where might that be?'

He paused. He could hear the hiss of the link from mast, to satellite, to mast and from there to the *Politiken* offices. There were so many ways of picking up words as they travelled through the ether, but that was neither here nor there. The fact was that it went against the grain for him to say any more than was absolutely necessary. There was no reason to disclose unnecessary information. Again it was a matter of training. If you stuck to the basic principle of saying as little as possible rather than as much as possible, then you were less liable to slip up when it came to the crunch.

'Bratislava,' he said nonetheless.

'Ooh, that hurt, huh, Per!'

She laughed and he could not help laughing with her. They chatted briefly about the garden which was soon going to be laid out as agreed with the contractors, and about the baby she was carrying. Afterwards he sat at the airport, clutching his mobile and experiencing the same surge of happiness which welled up inside him every morning when he woke up beside Lise. It was odd, because it made him feel happy in a strangely unfamiliar way, but at the same time it scared the shit out of him.

12

PER STAYED AT THE SAME HOTEL as Teddy had done some days earlier, the Hotel Forum on the fringes of the Old Town. By now though he was finding it hard to tell one Central European city from the next. There were differences, of course, but in each one you found the same beggars, the same trilling mobile phones, the same cigarette ads, McDonald's outlets and faux Irish pubs. The wretchedly drab and dreary communist system might be dead and buried, but the blatant capitalism which had taken its place seemed to him more vulgar than free. The whole place had a sort of bargain-basement air about it, from the food and the beggars to the country's politicians. He could not have explained what made him think this, but that was how it struck him. Maybe he was simply missing Lise. Maybe he was just tired of all these meetings. Maybe he was just angry and annoyed that there had been no one to meet him at the airport.

He took a taxi to the hotel. It surprised him with its Western-style efficiency and international standard. It was like a business executive's oasis in the poverty-stricken Central European desert. The roads to the hotel had been ridged and rutted. He called the number he had been given in Denmark and asked for Eduard Finca. There was a lot of crackling and hissing on the line. He had the feeling that his call was transferred several times. He heard distinct clicks and at one point a woman's voice said something incomprehensible, in Slovakian he supposed. At long last a young man came on the crackly line and said in heavily accented English:

'Chief Inspector Toftlund. I'm so sorry. Mr Finca is away on business.'

'But we had an appointment.'

'I'm sorry. It was quite unavoidable. The war, you know.'

'Is there someone else I could speak to?'

'It is difficult. Maybe tomorrow. You call back tomorrow, okay?'

'When will your boss be back?'

'Very hard to say. The war, you know.'

'But you're not even members of NATO.'

'Slovakia lies where Slovakia lies.'

'That's very true.'

'Goodbye, Chief Inspector.'

'Up yours,' Toftlund muttered. And hung up.

He sat for a moment, then called Vuldom. Again he used the hotel phone. Not because he felt it was any more secure, but rather a landline than a mobile, which the really big ears with their expensive, sophisticated equipment could listen in to if so inclined.

'Vuldom,' she said in her dry, pleasant voice. She seemed to drag out that first vowel slightly, giving it a musical lilt.

'Toftlund,' he responded and proceeded to brief her. He kept it short and to the point, naming no names. He knew Vuldom was not one for small talk, certainly not on the phone. He gave her the gist of his various meetings without going into particulars and wound up by saying:

'Our friend is a strange, multi-faceted character. I don't quite know what to make of her, but I've a feeling she has some bearing on the case. I'll pop over to Prague on the way home. Looks like we might have a pretty good contact there. I'm not so sure about here in Slovakia.'

The line was excellent. Vuldom's voice came over loud and clear:

'Fair enough, but get back as soon as you can. Our Polish friend called. He guessed you would check in. He says hello. You made a good impression on him. He said you'd be as well to move on. The people there won't talk to you anyway. And if I put any pressure on them they'll just spin you some line.'

'Okay,' Toftlund said.

'Our Polish chum does think, however, that you should get in touch with our mutual friend. Watch your back, though. Okay?'

'Okay,' Toftlund said.

'And Per? Come home soon. Things are hotting up.'

'How d'you mean?'

'Eastern Europe just joined the modern world. Tune into CNN and take care.'

'See you,' he said, but she had already hung up.

He found the remote control and switched on the large Japanese-made television. Changed days indeed. He could zap through a whole bunch of channels, including CNN of course. He switched on in the middle of the story, but even without having caught the beginning he had no trouble following what was going on. *Breaking News* the banner running across the screen proclaimed proudly. CNN was broadcasting live, its correspondents reporting in from Brussels to Washington and the Italian air base from which NATO dispatched its fighter bombers to Kosovo and Yugoslavia. Toftlund could not believe his eyes. A Yugoslavian air-defence unit had managed to shoot down a Stealth bomber. That simply should not be possible. The aircraft's contruction was supposed to make it undetectable to radar. The Americans had used Stealths with great success in the Gulf War, where even Saddam Hussein's highly developed missile-defence system had not downed any of them. How the hell had the Yugoslavs managed to hit this one? Listening to the experts on CNN left him none the wiser. It was always the same, whenever there was a crisis of one sort or another. Whether on Danish, German or American TV. A whole load of talking heads, waffling on and speculating like mad. Television was such an accommodating medium. You could say anything on it. And people might take it seriously, or it might be forgotten the next day. And then you could speculate all over again. He did not know how they could bring themselves to do it. They spouted the same extravagant verbiage every time. Everything was a crisis, a catastrophe, a confrontation, a dead end. The most common question posed by reporters the world over was: 'What if …?' Thus leaving one free to speculate to one's heart's content.

There were shots of the wreckage of the black plane. The pilot had apparently been lifted to safety by a rescue helicopter. CNN made it sound like a great victory. Toftlund shook his head. NATO was conducting air strikes in which it was imperative that it did not suffer any losses. Meanwhile, the Serbs pursued their appalling campaign of ethnic cleansing, the refugees poured into Albania and Macedonia, and now a Stealth bomber had bitten the dust. You could be sure the Russians were already on the spot, eager to get their mitts on the aircraft's advanced electronic equipment and pieces of the fuselage, in order to analyse and replicate the radar-deflecting coating. How in hell's name had it been shot down?

Toftlund fetched a bottle of mineral water from the minibar and drank from this as he followed the stream of news updates. Darkness fell outside and he could tell by the sound of the traffic that it had started to rain. He got up and looked out. There was a small palace on the opposite side of the busy square. Outside the hotel a handful of people shuddered and took shelter under the broad concrete roof canopy. Several buses and a few taxis were parked out front. In the rainswept twilight he could see a large statue rearing up into the dark sky. Some piece of social-realist gung-ho crap, he thought to himself. He was in a bad mood and he did not know why.

Per felt his innate loathing of self-analysis and negative thinking rise to the surface. That got you nowhere, though. When faced with a problem, more often than not he found that physical exercise was the answer. He stripped down to his underpants and did press-ups until he almost blacked-out, his stomach, arm and shoulder muscles were aching and he was gasping for breath. Then he showered and called Lise, but there was no answer. He slammed down the receiver, even more annoyed with himself. Why should he expect her to sit at home and wait for him? She was probably out somewhere with Pernille.

To keep his growing mental turmoil at bay he sat down and looked at his notes, but they did not make much sense either. He was hungry, and yet not hungry. He decided to call the number which Gelbert had given him in Warsaw. A woman's voice answered in Slovakian. Toftlund asked in English if he could speak to Pavel Samson. He heard the woman call to someone. He could hear the babble of a television and children's voices in the background. Nice homey sounds on a cold, rainy evening in Bratislava. He felt very envious and far from home, but shrugged off such childish feelings.

'Samson,' a faint voice said.

'Do you speak English?' Toftlund asked.

'I do.'

'My name is …'

'I know who you are.'

'Can we meet?'

'Not tonight.'

'Tomorrow?'

'Go through the gate into the Old Town, keep walking straight ahead. There's a statue, it looks like a man climbing out of a sewer. Wait next to it. Around ten a.m.'

'I just wanted …' Toftlund started, but Pavel Samson had hung up.

Per wrote down Samson's instructions. Then he went downstairs to the hotel restaurant. He had a pork chop with thick potato cakes and red cabbage; it tasted neither good nor bad, but it was food. He washed it down with the better part of a bottle of heavy red wine then returned to his room and called home again. Still no reply. This time he left a message on the answering machine. Lise's soft, sexy voice made him feel sick at heart. That was the phrase that came to mind. Sick at heart. Real women's mag codswallop, that was, but with the rain battering off the windowpanes it described exactly how he felt. He switched on the television and picked a film from the hotel's selection of in-room movies.

Die Hard 2, just what he needed. It finished around midnight. He called home again, and again he got the answering machine. He started to worry. What if she's been taken into hospital. But then he told himself that she was probably staying with Pernille at her flat in town. He went to bed and, as always, fell asleep straight away.

Per woke feeling rested. Normally he did not remember his dreams. But just before he surfaced from sleep, before the first flicker of consciousness, he had dreamed briefly that he and Lise were standing on the banks of a smooth, grey lake, watching their child. Already a little girl of three she was wearing a white dress and she was walking across the water towards them with a paper aeroplane in her hand. Even once he was fully awake he could still remember her happy face and her laughter skimming over the mirror-like surface. Outside the sun was shining, and this gave his spirits an added lift. Small, fluffy white clouds drifted across a clear blue sky, as if lightly daubed on by a painter. The hideous war memorial stood out clearly in the morning light.

He ate a big breakfast of bacon, scrambled eggs, sausages, bread and cheese along with men who could only be international business executives: the itinerants of the global economy, always on the move, more often abroad than at home. They were like modern-day pilgrims, dedicated solely to the gods of cash and contracts. They all had the same blank, jaded eyes and their snowy white shirts and discreet, elegant ties did nothing to disguise how sick they were of travelling and how wearied by the thought of yet another breakfast in an anonymous hotel restaurant.

Toftlund left the hotel at ten minutes to ten. He had checked the map and could see that it was only a few minutes' walk from there to what the receptionist called 'the new sculptures'. He turned a corner and stepped through an old city gate into an area of narrow, cobbled streets. There were not too many people about. The moment he stepped through the gate and into this warren of lanes and alleyways the noise of the traffic disappeared. The hush of the Old Town wrapped itself around him. Any noise he did hear was muffled: brisk footsteps on cobbles, a voice rising an octave, a woman's bright laugh in the sunshine. Only when a mobile-phone jingle rang out did the sound seem to reverberate off the grimy walls. He glowered so forbiddingly at a bunch of raggedy gypsy kids that they scurried away from him like scared chickens. He walked on past two beggars and an old man in a shabby black coat playing a plaintive, off-key fiddle. At the scruffy musician's feet lay a greasy cap. Two humble coins gleamed dully in the sunlight. A new day in the new world order for Europe's youngest nation.

Seeing it from a distance, Toftlund thought at first that the statue, or sculpture, was a real person. It was so lifelike. Only its silver-grey colour betrayed the fact, when he got a bit closer, that it was a naturalistic work of art depicting a workman in a helmet clambering out of a manhole from a sewer or tunnel. As if he had just been fixing a faulty telephone cable. Toftlund positioned himself next to the sculpture, which sat at a crossroads. There were quite a lot of people on the street now. The young people eating ice cream or talking on their mobiles, or both at the same time. They were all quite stylishly dressed, he thought. Then suddenly another world walked past him: an old granny with a shawl wrapped round her hunched shoulders and a mouth full of gold teeth. She was wrapped up as if it was mid-winter and not an astonishingly lovely spring day. His eye was caught by two young men in the classic garb of the Eastern European mafia: blue jeans and leather jackets, crew-cut hair and pudgy bull-necks. One of them had the crooked nose of a boxer and a gold ring in his ear. They walked past him, eyeing him as they did so, stopped on the corner and lit up cigarettes from their red Marlboro packs.

Toftlund waited fifteen minutes. Wandered back and forth a bit. Looked in the window of a shop selling radios, televisions and mobile phones, another selling musical instruments and a bookshop, though he could not even read the titles of the books on display. Each time he would stroll no further than fifty or seventy-five metres before returning to the silent statue. Capitalism had won the day – he could tell just by looking at people. The kids' taste in clothes was dictated by the big international brands, the young women's especially. But still there was something distinctly Eastern European about them as they click-clacked along on their spindly legs and vertiginously high platform shoes. There was a time when there would have been signs hailing some long-forgotten Five Year Plan. But the old posters urging the people to follow the party on the road to socialism were now supplanted by a sign advertising an international insurance concern. The hammer and sickle by the Sony logo. The proud working girl by an erotic ad for a new mobile phone. Once, the communist slogans had promised eternal happiness if one simply toed the party line. Now Ericsson promised you sex if you bought their tiny new mobile and called the love of your life.

A gypsy boy approached him. He wore tattered jeans and a crumpled shirt under a grubby windcheater. His bare feet were stuck into a pair of trainers that looked way too big for him. Toftlund prepared to give him his forbidding glare. With those cold, cop eyes, as Lise had once described them, when he had got mad at her and then regretted it five minutes later. But something stopped him from dismissing the boy out of hand. Two of his front teeth were missing. He put out his right hand beseechingly and said something in Slovakian. Like a conjuror he flashed his left hand open and closed, allowing Toftlund a glimpse of a slip of white paper folded between his fingers. Per stuck his hand in his pocket and pulled out a dollar bill. While he was doing this the boy must have moved the slip from his left hand to his right with a sleight of hand so slick and quick that it defied the naked eye. Because when Toftlund placed the ten-dollar bill in his hand he felt the boy press the tiny, folded piece of paper into his palm without meeting his gaze. Then he turned and left, stepping out with a nimble, almost dancer-like gait. Toftlund shoved the piece of paper into his pocket and kept his hand there. He saw one of the two mafia heavies he had spotted earlier hurry off after the boy. But he was too slow. The boy broke into a smooth, easy lope and headed up one side-street, down another and out of sight before the big bruiser could build up any speed.

Toftlund sauntered off, like any other sightseer strolling back to his hotel. The leather-jacketed thug with the gold ring in his ear stepped out deliberately into the middle of the narrow street. He had a small scar above his left eye. Per removed his hand from his pocket, let his arms swing loosely. He shifted his weight onto the balls of his feet, found his balance. The uniformed policeman who had been patrolling the spot earlier was nowhere to be seen. Maybe someone had slipped him a couple of bills to go and get himself a coffee. Preferably somewhere well away from here.

'Was that gypsy bothering you?' Leather Jacket asked. He spoke English like a B-movie baddie. Toftlund tried to go round him, but with a little chassé he blocked the way again. Per's heart was beating faster now. He measured the guy. He was big, but he looked slow. It had to be done before his mate got back.

'No,' Per said.

'You shouldn't give anything to beggars.'

'Excuse me,' Toftlund said, taking a step to the side, but Leather Jacket moved with him, as if they were dancing.

'Or not without getting something in return, anyway.'

'You're in my way.'

'Maybe he gave you something you should give to me.'

Toftlund could hear people on the street, but they were obviously steering well clear. There did not appear to be anyone close by. The citizens of Bratislava seemed to know that there were certain things it was better not to witness. Per felt he ought to let the other man make the first move, lay a hand on him first. But it was time to drop the pretence, stop playing games. There was no doubt that Leather Jacket knew who he was.

'Fuck you!' Toftlund said.

That did it. Leather Jacket was so sure of himself that he took a

| 184 |

step closer, puffed out his chest, raised his right hand and clamped it over Toftlund's left arm just above the elbow. Leather Jacket was used to intimidating folk; used to getting his way. The boss would take care of the formalities with the authorities later. But his cockiness made him careless and stupid. Toftlund's right hand shot up and with one quick flick he grabbed hold of the earring and tore it off. Blood gushed from the thug's ear, it must have hurt because he let go of Toftlund's arm and pressed his hand to his lobeless appendage. Toftlund belted him in the chest with his left fist, sending him reeling into the side of the building behind them, threw the little earring in his face and strode off quickly towards the Old Town gate. An elderly couple shrank back against a wall. Two young girls stared at him in alarm, but made no attempt to accost him and when he glanced backed he saw Leather Jacket standing with one hand over his ear while trying to key in a number on his mobile with the other.

Per's heart was pounding, but he was not afraid. Nonetheless, he felt happier once he was back inside the cosmopolitan hotel lobby. He walked into the bar and ordered a cup of coffee. Through the bar's panorama windows he could see the other heavy standing outside on the pavement, looking, but he did not come in. He too made a call on his mobile and shortly afterwards a black BMW arrived and picked him up. Toftlund removed the slip of paper from his pocket. It was neatly folded, like a love letter sent from the back row in class to the front. On it in bold capitals was written: 'You were followed. Same time tomorrow. But in Prague. On Charles Bridge.'

He went up to the travel agent's desk, which lay next to Reception and the usual Business Centre equipped with fax machine, phones, computers and Internet connection and handed the woman behind it his sheaf of plane tickets.

'I'd like to take the next plane to Prague. Are there any more flights today?'

'Lots. When would you like to leave?'

'As soon as possible.'

'If you go ahead and check out, sir, I'll see to that for you.'

'I'm not booked into a hotel in Prague until tomorrow.'

She smiled at him. Only now did he notice how attractive she was, and would have been even more so if she wore less make-up. She had dark wavy hair, big brown eyes, a sensual little mouth and a cute up-turned nose.

'If you would be so good as to let me have the confirmation of your reservation I'll see to that too,' she said, almost flirtatiously.

'Now that's what I call service!'

'Oh, we try, we try,' she said, glancing at his ticket. 'We do our best, Mr Toftlund. We do so want to be a part of Europe.'

'You'll get there, don't worry.'

She picked up the phone to make the necessary arrangements, gave him a little smile and said, almost hopelessly – as if he, who had it so good, had no idea of the obstacles she could see along the way to that Europe from which her parents' generation had barred her for so long:

'Maybe. If we work for it. But as a Slovak you learn not to take anything for granted. There is always someone who has other ideas.'

13

PER TOFTLUND HAD TO BE ONE of the few people from Denmark who had never been to Prague. Since the collapse of the communist system thousands of Danes, spearheaded by beer-thirsty high-school students, had made the trip to the Czech capital. Prague was inexpensive. And the Danes are great ones for going places where the food and drink are cheap. Not only that but, to begin with at least, Prague was a bit more exotic than Majorca. Toftlund was not greatly impressed by the city, though. Not that the buildings weren't beautiful, but everything seemed to be geared towards the tourists. On every other corner of the narrow streets in the city centre stood young people in production-line folk costumes, handing out fliers. You were never allowed to forget that Mozart had once lived here, what with all these pushy, costumed kids waving yellow handbills under your nose, every one promising Mozart's music as it was played in Mozart's day. Toftlund could not have cared less. He had no interest in Mozart's music, or any other classical music. He had never outgrown rock. Although in actual fact he rarely listened to anything but whatever happened to be on the car radio and simply could not see how Lise could put on a CD in the living room at home and just sit and listen. Without doing anything else. What a waste of time. It looked like those kids were wasting their time too. People did take their fliers, but with scores of them being blown about the street it seemed clear that most were dropped, unread, onto the cobbles. They made a hell of a mess. One of the odd things about walking around the city was that he heard so many languages being spoken: Danish, German, Swedish, Norwegian, American, Japanese – just about everything, in fact, except Czech. At one point he passed a group of fifteen or so young men in hideous trousers and identical down jackets. Under the down jackets beer bellies strained over white T-shirts printed with the legend *Danske ølbamser* – Danish ale-heads. Pathetic! Prague was a magnet for gullible Mozart lovers and the citizens of heavily taxed countries who monitored the beer prices the way a speculator keeps an eye on the share index. There was nobody in this city but tourists, Per thought to himself, as he walked down to Charles Bridge, which he had located on his map. The crowds milling about on this cold, windy early spring day suited him just fine. He nipped into a shop and out again. Cut across a courtyard encircled by newly renovated restaurants and up a long avenue lined with trees on which tender new buds were all set to burst into leaf. Here, ten years after the breakdown of the Soviet Union, one was continually struck by the contrasts in the buildings: a lovely, freshly painted mansion abutting onto an old house with the plaster and paint peeling off its walls. He was constantly being confronted with evidence of the communists' appalling taste and ineptitude. There was rain in the air, but as yet it had come to nothing. He studied the bizarre equipment in a porn shop, stopped to look into the gleaming window of an elegant jeweller's. Churches towered over his head. By the time he reached the Old Town Square he was certain that no one was following him. Or if there was, then they really knew their job. A crowd of sightseers was standing gazing up at a clock surrounded by painted wooden figures. He thought they looked a bit like garden gnomes. But this had to be something special, what with all these people peering up at it as if waiting for a miracle to occur. He made his way through the crowd. A number of horse-drawn carriages were lined up in the square. In the pavement cafés tourists sat under awnings and heat lamps. With colourful guidebooks lying next to their coffee cups, they surveyed the square as if not knowing quite what to do with themselves. You had to travel, but when you reached your destination and saw all the other people who had had the same idea, you could not help wondering what exactly you were doing in Prague.

Toftlund stood for a moment and pretended to be looking up at the chiming clock and the figures revolving around it. He noticed nothing and nobody suspicious. No one among the down-jacketed tourists and importunate pushers of local musical offerings stood out or seemed out of place. He had memorised the map so now he turned left onto the street leading down to Charles Bridge. The time was nine forty-five a.m. when he caught his first sight of the bridge, lined with tall statues, extending from a huge tower. He chose to ignore the outstretched hands proffering fliers. This was not like India, where they begged for money. Here they did their begging with advertisements. What did they get for every one they gave away – a *krone*? Just before the busy road which ran past the bridge he spied a young girl in an old jacket. She was listening to music on her Walkman and smoking a cigarette with half-shut eyes. She carried a sign advertising a museum of torture and an Internet café. Toftlund stopped next to her. He waited until the lumbering red tramcar was almost level with him then strode smartly across to the other side and into the huddle of pedestrians waiting patiently for the lights to change. Behind him he heard the angry clang of the tram bell and the tooting of horns as he made a quick left turn and bore towards what looked like a church or a concert hall. He pulled up behind two big men in black folk costumes who were waving the eternal fliers for concerts and purportedly historic musical experiences. The tramcar moved on and still he noticed nothing untoward. No one scanning the street for him. And, more importantly, no one forging their way through the slow-moving lines of traffic. Now he was absolutely sure: he was not being followed. He walked onto the bridge at a leisurely saunter to make it easy for Pavel Samson to spot him and, when ready, make contact. Toftlund glanced up and around. From the mass of people on the bridge even this early in the day back to the massive bridge tower and from there to the buildings on the other side of the river: Samson could be hiding anywhere, equipped with a pair of binoculars. Through the slight haze he could see the Castle, which he knew to be the Czech president's official residence – known locally as 'the palace on the hill'. The river, brown and muddy, flowed sluggishly past. Some sort of excursion boat was turning lazily at the bridge. Along the riverside, too, the buds on the trees seemed simply to be waiting for a sign from God to spring open.

Toftlund was not much of a one for art, but he was intrigued by the statues on the bridge: a grotesque mix of demons and Christ figures. Bizarre black ghouls with leering faces. Kings and slaves. Traitors and heroes. There seemed to be no rhyme nor reason to them. But their expressions were all either agonised or baleful. The only things they had in common were those fascinating faces and the pigeon droppings. They seemed to lean in over the bridge, while at the same time having a kind of laid-back look about them. Charles Bridge was a pedestrian bridge, he noted. It was also a con artists' bridge! One big tourist trap. A place where the crafty ripped off the less crafty. A place where tourists were tempted by fake antiques, dashed-off watercolours of the Castle, tacky postcards and other weird tat, and risked having their portraits painted or caricatures sketched by youthful art students, or being taken to the cleaners by the ancient, but apparently undying scam which involved hapless suckers trying to guess under which of three egg cups a pea was hidden. How could people let themselves be taken in like that? And then there was Per's pet hate: the buskers. Every twenty yards or so there was another musician, or a group of them, with their hats on the ground, screeching out some song or other. Prague might be Mozart's city, but Charles Bridge would have given Mozart a heart attack. That much even someone as tone-deaf as Per could tell as he sauntered across to the far side then turned to walk back. This music would have driven Lise up the wall. One wrong note, even on the car radio, was all it took for her to switch off or change station. It actually made her feel physically ill. He felt a pang of guilt. He had not got round to calling her this morning and he had his mobile switched off. Where could she have been yesterday evening? He shook off the thought the way he shook off the pest of a beggar who kept bothering him, and slowly proceeded to stroll back across Charles Bridge.

He knew the rules of the game. He was the wooer, but in this game it was up to the wooed to make himself known. If he was at all interested in the proposal, that was.

He stopped in the middle of the bridge. There was a box set up against the parapet at the foot of one of the statues, painted black and decorated with primitive stars. Inside it was a tiny microphone on a stand. At about the height of an overgrown Barbie doll. Next to the microphone stand was a miniature black grand piano. Also in the box was a skeleton – about half a metre tall and made of plastic, but a very lifelike skeleton nonetheless, with a hat on its head. Per Toftlund watched, mesmerised, as the skeleton began to move. A young man dressed in what Per would have described as hippie gear, had picked up the microphone and switched on a ghetto blaster. With his long, lank hair and straggly beard he looked like something out of a black-and-white photo from the early seventies. Toftlund could not make out the strings connecting the skeleton to the man. But, of course – puppet shows were a big thing in Prague. Among the fliers handed out by all those kids there had also been lots advertising different marionette theatres. He seemed to remember learning at school that the Czechs had practically invented puppet shows. These days, at any rate, they were pushing marionettes as doggedly as a drug dealer touting his wares. And going by the number of handbills these touts tried to stick into his hand, they must assume that this was what the tourists wanted. Puppet shows and Mozart. That was what Prague was famous for. And for Kafka, Toftlund suddenly remembered. One of Lise's favourite writers. He had written a novel which she had told him he had to read. It might help him to comprehend what he himself had gone through after the Flakfortet business, with its depiction of how an individual can be rendered utterly helpless, like a fly caught in a spider's web, when unseen powers make accusations which cannot possibly be answered. When, simply by responding to the charges and thus acknowledging them, one confirms one's guilt, even though one never, in fact, knows what exactly one stands accused of. This novel, the title of which had slipped his mind, was still lying on the bedside table with a bookmark at page four. But that in itself was a start.

The hippie had finished his technical preparations and the skeleton began to speak. The hippie pulled the strings, making the mouth with its big, yellowish teeth open and shut realistically, but it was the tape in the ghetto blaster which actually provided the soundtrack.

'Hello,' said the skeleton in the black top hat. 'How are you all today?' It spoke English with an American accent. It bobbed back and forth in the box, working to catch the attention of the tourists. With some success. People stopped to look at this curious apparition, so obviously plastic and yet so alive. It was like something out of a second-rate horror movie, but it also had a sinister air to it that was both exciting and compelling. There was something eerie, too, about the deep bass voice emanating from the tape recorder, its words as perfectly in synch with the movements of the skeleton's mouth as the careful dubbing of a film on some awful German TV channel.

'Ladies and gentlemen,' it said, as its long, knobbly fingers sketched the air in front of it. 'This is how we all look in death. And death is waiting just around the corner. Death is the shadowy companion who walks by your side. Turn around and try to catch sight of it and it is gone, moving faster than your own shadow. But do not fool yourselves. It is there. So live your life while you have it. Your time on this earth is short compared to the time you will spend with me.'

The skeleton gave a guttural laugh, sat down on the piano stool and proceeded, in the same sinister vein, to mime to the strains of Leonard Cohen's 'First We Take Manhattan', now hissing from concealed speakers. *'They sentenced me to twenty years of boredom, for trying to change the system from within ...'* The skeleton's singing and playing were so well synchronised that a ripple of uneasy laughter ran through the crowd now standing in a semi-circle around the puppet show. *'First we take Manhatten. Then we take Berlin.'* When it came to the chorus the puppet master gave a quick jerk of his left hand and three more skeletons, clad in minuscule bikinis, sprang up from the floor of the box and began to sing the backing vocals with their grotesque red-painted lips.

A spontaneous burst of applause broke out and the clapping grew even louder as the number reached its climax, with the male skeleton on his feet, pounding the keys, and the bony backing singers trilling and jigging about like can-can dancers in gay Paree. All to the accompaniment of Cohen's deep, seductive voice and the mellow light over the grey bridge. Still, though, most of the tourists drifted off without dropping any money into the hat in front of the black box. Toftlund placed some Czech notes in it as he watched the puppeteer laying the skeleton on its sleeping bench in the corner, ready for the next performance.

'One of the better street acts, wouldn't you say, Chief Inspector?' a light voice behind him said. Toftlund turned round. Pavel Samson in no way lived up to his surname. He was a short, tubby middle-aged man clad in a hideously patterned jacket and a green shirt which bulged paunchily over his grey flannels. His face was almost perfectly round and pocked with acne scars; small grey eyes looked out from under a low forehead. A few thin strands of hair looked as though they had been planted across his pallid scalp by an attentive gardener. His face was a ruddy brown. Not the skin tone which, this early in the year, Czechs and Slovaks could acquire in one of the new tanning salons, but that deriving from a close acquaintance with the excellent Czech beer, vodka and spicy, cinnamon flavoured Becherovka.

'Mr Samson,' Toftlund said and gave him his hand. Samson's grip was limp and rather clammy, but there was a keen light in the alert grey eyes.

'Do you mind if we speak German?' Samson asked.

'Fine by me.'

'Good, then let's take a little stroll,' he said in almost flawless German.

They walked for a while in silence, Toftlund allowing Samson to lead the way. They crossed the bridge to the Castle side. Once over, Samson turned right and they strolled along the riverbank. A barge slid past and the sightseeing boat from before was turning in the stream again.

'I noticed you took your precautions,' Samson said. His voice was light and soft, almost feminine. 'They were excellent, and you were not followed.'

'Who could be following me – exactly?' Toftlund asked.

Samson laughed. A high-pitched little laugh:

'Everybody and anybody. Prague, Bratislava, Budapest. This part of the world is a real hotbed of spies. Like something out of a novel by Eric Ambler. There's a real feel of the thirties about Central Europe today. What with the war, they're falling over one another: spies, traitors, lost souls, those who missed the boat first time round. They're all here: the British, the Germans, the Russians, our own people, the Yugoslavians, not to mention the Croats. This is the inflamed flashpoint of Europe, where loyalties and information are bought and sold. Everybody is out to make a killing, but a lot of them want to get out of the game before it's too late. Ten years after the Wall came down we still have people with one foot in the old camp and the other in NATO and the EU. We have old agents and torturers who are worried that the files will spit out the truth. We've got it all here. Cut-price capitalism and anarchic liberty mingled with a burgeoning authoritarianism. Post-communism they call it. The legacy of Lenin's failed experiment is not that easily expunged.'

Quite a little speech, Toftlund thought to himself. Interesting, though. It held the promise of more to come. The wind caught at Samson's wispy hair and sent the neatly arranged strands flying up from his white pate. He looked like a badly-paid office worker, but behind the unprepossing exterior Toflund sensed a shrewd and formidable personality.

'Now then. Our friend in Poland believed you had something to tell me? Your counterparts in Bratislava were not particularly helpful.'

The little man blew down his nose in something approaching a snort:

'No. They want nothing to do with anything. They're scared. As you may know, Slovakia is without a president at the moment. They are hoping that Meciar will win the forthcoming election. In which case they'll be safe for a while yet. If one of the other candidates wins, who knows what will happen. It could be that a new president and the new government might actually mean what they say. That intelligence and counter-intelligence agencies are actually there to serve the people and not working against the people.'

'That's what you believe?'

'Perhaps. There's not much I believe in. But I have two daughters in their early teens, Chief Inspector. When you have children you can no longer allow yourself to be misanthropic. You have to believe in the future. Believe that there are honest people in the world. Do you have children, Mr Toftlund?'

'I have a daughter on the way. Due in a couple of weeks.'

'Congratulations. And you already know it's a girl. How advanced.'

'Well, that's modern technology for you.'

'Ah, but it should not rob us of our surprises.'

'Well, we wanted to know that everything was alright,' Toftlund said, against his will really. He was not a person given to discussing his private life with strangers. And suddenly he lost his focus and found himself thinking about Lise instead of the job in hand. Thrown slightly by this he did not catch what Samson said next. The little Slovak smiled, as if he could see right through Toftlund and had found his weak spot.

'There's no shame in showing that one misses one's loved ones,' he said.

Toftlund felt annoyance and anger well up inside him.

'That's not what we're here to talk about, though, is it,' he said, but Samson continued to pursue his own train of thought:

'Take me, for instance. Why should I help a Pole and a Dane? Some time ago I was transferred to the vice squad. A department in which even the most stalwart officer can be corrupted. Sex, drugs, money. It's a potent cocktail, one which can break the strongest will.'

'I see. Why?'

'My wife, my daughters. To get a little revenge on those who had me removed from the service. To be able to look myself in the eye in the mornings. Because I'm a fool.'

Samson had misunderstood his question, but Toftlund pursued the thread, saying instead:

'Now that I don't believe.'

They came to another bridge, Samson walked on to it and they began to stroll back to the other side. This bridge was open to traffic and Toftlund noted the mixture of old Eastern European cars and shiny new Mercedes, Audis and BMWs on the road. The contrasts leapt out at you everywhere here. In the buildings, the cars, the people, the air, the light, the city and the times.

They walked on again in silence, side by side. Samson took short, brisk strides and Toftlund frequently had to do a little skip to keep up with him. Samson's German was rapid, precise and grammatically correct, rather like that spoken in the old GDR, and yet not quite.

'Your German is excellent,' Toftlund said.

'I did part of my training with our beloved allies in the former GDR, may they rot in hell.'

'Why did you do that?'

'That is a typical Western question. As if I had a choice.'

'Everyone has a choice.'

'That's easy to say for someone who has been brought up to take freedom for granted. The choice was harder to make than you think. I also have a son from a previous marriage. My courage did not extend to becoming a non-person and seeing him and my then wife treated as outcasts. Communism was as good at ostracising people as those fundamentalist Christian sects in the United States. I tried to do my little bit in other ways.'

Suddenly Toftlund understood. He stopped, put a hand on Samson's arm. The latter turned and looked up into his face.

'You were a double agent,' Toftlund said. 'You worked for the Americans.'

'Well, the British actually, but yes, you're right.'

'But you ought to be a hero now. And have been paid compensation.'

Samson laughed his high, shrill laugh:

'Life isn't that simple. No one likes a traitor, not even the winning side. And certainly not the losers. If you've betrayed your country once you could do it again. You see before you, Chief Inspector, one of the cold war's countless punch-drunk sluggers.'

'That's not how I see you,' Toftlund said, and meant it. A double agent's life was a hell on earth. Constantly saying one thing and thinking something else. Never knowing whether your cover might be blown by the other side's willing helpers or a renegade in the long corridors of the spy chief's office. Knowing that you are not the only one who can betray secrets. That you are a piece of merchandise which can be swapped or traded. That you always have a corner deep inside you to which not even those closest to you can gain access. That your name is secreted in a file somewhere. And that name and the reference number attached to it are like a tumour, only waiting to grow and spread. Per's respect for the little Slovak grew. Behind the bland clerkish façade was a tough little character.

Samson halted outside a café.

'There's no one on our tail. Can I buy you a cup of coffee?'

'That would be great, thanks.'

The café was small and dim with a short wooden bar and a score of tables and chairs. Three young men sat at a table with large glasses of beer in front of them. Samson and Toftlund seated themselves at a table by the window. They were tucked well into the corner and the curtain hanging over the café window hid their faces from anyone who might have felt like peering through the window.

'You're Slovakian …'

'Czechoslovakian, actually,' Samson said with a smile and lit a long filter cigarette. 'The term doesn't exist any more, I know, but I really do feel Czechoslovakian. My mother was a Czech, and a Sudeten German – just to make things even more complicated. My father was a Slovak. My wife is the daughter of a Czech father and a Slovakian mother. Today we – and hence our children too – are Slovakian citizens. Things tend to get a bit mixed up in this part of the world. Our history is in itself a pretty complex affair. Are you familiar with it at all?

'Not really.'

'No, why should you be?' he said, and continued: 'But during the Second World War Slovakia was a Nazi vassal state, although officially independent. The Czech part of the republic was occupied. After the war the Czechs either deported or imprisoned the surviving Sudeten Germans. That was a very dark chapter. In '48 came the communist coup. By some miracle my father and mother lived through it all and by the sixties when I was about to start at university, that part of our history had been forgiven. Normally, forgiveness is hard to come by. But there was a need for new cadres. And with the communists, opportunism and cynicism often outweighed their desire to punish generation after generation of the same family. Which was lucky for me.'

The plump waitress came over with their coffee and placed it on the table in front of them. It was good and strong.

Pavel Samson leaned across the table and said:

'You're interested in the woman from Bratislava.'

'Yes, the Serbian spy.'

'Spy, yes. But not Serbian. She worked for Tito for many years. Since 1990 she has been a Croatian spy, all unknown to Belgrade. They thought she was working for Milosevic. When they found out, her life was not worth a handful of devalued Serbian dinars. And what does an agent do when things get too hot for her? She sells what she has. Either to the highest bidder, or to whoever she thinks is likely to come out on top. Which is to say: NATO. How? With Serbian agents breathing down her neck. Tailing her, most likely. Who can she trust? What if she's turned away at the door? How to find a way in? She turns her history to her advantage, Chief Inspector. Her knowledge that she has a Danish father and Danish half-siblings. She knows that one of her half-brothers is in the area, because, like the fox, a canny agent always makes a point of having at least one exit unknown to any of her employers.'

'And the half-sister?' Toftlund asked.

'May have been in the files. Or may have been discovered in the files.'

'How do you know that?'

'I don't need to tell you that intelligence work is an equal mix of hard work and luck. Maybe someone got lucky when on the hunt for some potential form of insurance.'

'Any proof?'

'Of course not,' the little man retorted irritably.

Toftlund thought for a moment, then he said:

'The woman from Bratislava – why do you have so much on her?'

'We've had our eye on her for years.'

'You and everyone else apparently.'

'Yes, because who actually owned her soul? The price of loyalty fell drastically when the communists gave up trying to hang on to power.'

Samson sipped his coffee and lit another cigarette.

| 199 |

'Have you any idea what she has to sell?'

'No, but I know it was big enough for the Serbs or the Croats to try and get their hands on it in Budapest. With fatal consequences for an innocent man. But then, there are casualties in every war, or so they would say, if they had any moral scruples at all.'

'So it has to be something to do with the war?' Toftlund said.

'Obviously.'

'Something valuable?'

'Obviously.'

'Do you know what it is?'

'No. It was in your countryman's suitcase, which went missing at Bratislava Airport.'

'But that went missing in transit, it happens all the time.'

'No, it was lifted at the airport. Another suitcase was sent off on an endless world tour.'

'You're sure about this?'

'Positive. I know the man who lifted it. He owed me a favour.'

'And the woman?'

Samson shrugged and drank the last of his coffee:

'Gone to ground. Word is the Serbs have a contract out on her. I don't know how much they are offering, but it's in Deutschmarks, and in today's Yugoslavia they go a long way, so there are bound to be plenty of bidders. She has approached the British and the Americans. They don't trust her. They showed her the door. So now she has her heart set on the Danes. You're a small nation. A bit sentimental. And, she hopes, might feel a little flattered. And you have nothing to lose. And then there are the old ties. She has her hopes pinned on those.'

Toftlund sat for a moment. Then he looked into the Slovak's cool, steady grey eyes:

'Might she perhaps know a name that has some special significance for Denmark?'

Samson said nothing, but he held Toftlund's gaze.

'A Danish spy, whose code name we may have from Stasi, but

not their real name. A Danish spy, a person so highly-placed that someone would be prepared to kill to protect them. What do you say to that, Mr Samson?'

Samson beckoned to the waitress and said:

'In our world anything is possible. All the signs are, at any rate, that the trail points to Denmark. That it may have its beginnings in this part of the world, but that it points to Denmark. If you would care to buy me lunch around the corner I will fill you in on the background. Like everything else in this country it is bound up with the past and is quite fascinating.'

'You're on,' Toftlund said, feeling pretty damn good.

14

IT WAS AN ODD PLACE Pavel Samson had chosen for them to have lunch, Toftlund thought. They might just as well have been in Copenhagen or Hamburg, or even Beijing. It was a thoroughly American concept: from the young man in the white shirt, tie with a single knot, sharp creases and badge saying 'Shift Manager' and the nippy little waitresses, not all of whom had the legs for their short skirts, to the menu with its endless variations on the hamburgers, steak and fries theme. The restaurant was big, with a long bar at which what appeared to be three expat Brits were idly discussing golf handicaps. The tablecloths were the red-and-white check of the pizzeria. For caps the waitresses had stupid-looking bunny ears; they were ordered about by the short-tempered shift manager. At one table a party of suits was gabbling animatedly in Czech about complicated business matters. At any rate Toftlund caught the words 'stock market' every now and again. So brokers maybe – four burly men whose suits might have been tailor-made, but somehow still did not sit quite right on them. As if they would have been more at home in tight jeans and leather jackets. With them was a young blonde with her breasts amply exposed. She sat with a drink in her hand and the food in front of her untouched, taking bored puffs of her cigarette. The men paid her no heed. The place smelled faintly of cleaning fluids and deep-fat frying. Mainly the latter. But the big, red beef steaks and the hamburgers with mounds of potato chips actually looked very tempting. The prices quoted on the menu were high even by Copenhagen standards, but the restaurant was almost full.

Samson and Toftlund were shown to a table not far from the bar. Or rather: a booth. It was all very American. Samson slid onto the bench, Toftlund took a seat across from him. The menu arrived straight away, along with glasses of iced water and a 'How are you all today' delivered with a Czech accent. It was all so artificial that Toftlund could not help remarking:

'Very Czech, Mr Samson.'

Pavel gave his high-pitched laugh:

'Bloody expensive. Exotic for me. That's why.'

'Fair enough.'

'But this place is also a part of our recent history. A marker on our route from communism to the golden promise of capitalism. On this spot there used to be a good old traditional Czech restaurant serving pork chops, red cabbage, potato dumplings, bread dumplings ... Decent food at decent prices, even under the communists. Big glasses of draught beer. Then it was privatised. But during that process there arose, how shall I put it, certain differences of opinion between business partners, a disagreement which was settled by simply bombing the restaurant.'

'Interesting,' Toftlund said and waited for him to go on.

But instead: 'I think I'm going to go for a gin and tonic and some potato soup, followed by steak and mushrooms,' Samson said, and glanced up at Toftlund.

'The same for me.'

'And a good bottle of wine. For me that would be a whole month's wages gone. Anyway – for months this building was nothing but a shell. No one wanted to touch it after the mafia had displayed such a clear interest in it, but then a man came riding into town from the great US of A. Third generation Czechoslovak with papers stating that his family had owned the building until it was nationalised by the communists in 1948. So it was given back to him free of charge, and here you see the result.'

'What about the mafia?'

Samson shrugged:

'Who knows. Maybe he paid them off, or bought himself some protection? Money's what counts these days, after all. Ideals and Utopias have, dare I say it, failed miserably.'

'And he was able to get his building back, just like that?'

'As long as he promised to rebuild it. That's the law. The Czech president and all the world's blue-eyed boy, Havel, is a very wealthy man. His family estate was restored to him. There are lots of similar cases. And the people who have lived in these houses for the past fifty years have to pack up all their worldly goods and move out. Or pay the going market rate for them, and very few can afford to do that. That's capitalism for you,' he said, and Toftlund was reminded of an old, forgotten song from his childhood the lyrics of which had said exactly the same thing.

'You must also have been living in stolen property then.'

'Maybe, Chief Inspector. Maybe. Shall we order?'

Their drinks and dishes arrived promptly, the food attractively served. It was alright; nothing special, but it tasted fresh, in much the same way that the restaurant interior was fresh, brassily efficient and strangely foreign. A young man with a crew-cut came in and took a seat at the bar. He wore a black leather jacket and had a little ring in his ear. He ordered a Czech Budweiser and ran an eye around the room. It lingered fleetingly on Samson's semi-profile and on Toftlund, before passing nonchalantly on. He lit a cigarette and casually pulled a mobile phone from his jacket pocket. Another Czech thug, Toftlund thought to himself as he waited impatiently for the story he was paying for with this meal. But Samson began by telling him about the men at the table with the blonde. They were all well-known denizens of the local underworld: mobsters now on their way to becoming respectable businessmen. They too were a part of the new Czech Republic. Characters like these operated all over the former Soviet bloc. They were in their element in this weird hybrid of plan economy and market economy, in which rules were made to be bent. The new knights of dollars and deals, as Samson put it in the midst of his flow of perfect German.

'You had another story for me though, didn't you,' Toftlund said when they were almost finished their main course. They had both eaten well. Samson had clearly enjoyed his meal. Toftlund was almost always hungry and would eat whatever was put in front of him. As long as it involved meat and potatoes. He had never been much for French *haute cuisine*. You always seemed to leave the table wanting more.

'I think I would like a large ice cream and some coffee,' Samson announced, like a child on a trip to town with his dad. But then he got down to it. Toftlund removed his little notebook and a pen from his jacket pocket and glanced expectantly at Samson, who merely nodded. It was a fascinating story and one which he told so well that Toftlund rarely needed to break in with a question.

'I'm afraid I will have to bore you with a little history lesson. Hitler's Germany occupied Yugoslavia early in 1941. A quite spectacular parachute attack. The Serbs put up a fight. Most Croats supported the occupation forces. They were members of the Ustashi, a fascist, nationalist movement which was fiercely anti-Serb. But not all Croats were of the same mind. Tito was a Croat too, remember, and it was Tito who organised the resistance movement. Something which he did both skilfully and brutally. But the German occupation force was every bit as brutal, surpassed only by its Ustashi sidekicks. An eye for an eye, a tooth for a tooth, that was their motto. Caught in the middle were the Italian troops, who were involved in the occupation much against their will. But believe you me, Mr Toftlund, the war in the Balkans was a bitter and bloody partisan affair. Seeds of hate were sown which, as you well know, have lain there waiting to send up shoots now in the nineties.'

He paused while the little waitress with the podgy, mini-skirted legs removed their plates and took the order for Samson's ice cream and coffee for them both. Toftlund had been expecting the worst sort of dishwater, but the coffee placed in front of them was an excellent espresso, hot and strong with the delicious aroma of good beans.

Samson continued:

'It was hell on earth: killings, executions, incarceration, torture, ambushes, torched villages, traitors, double agents. Into this hell, one day in 1943 came a group of Danes. Soldiers in the Waffen SS.'

'Danes in Yugolsavia during World War II. I hadn't heard about that. Or at least – not until recently.'

'No. The majority of people choose only to hang onto the heroic side of their history. The victors' version. Most folk prefer legend to truth. There are certain things which most nations would rather suppress, either that or stash them away in the dusty libraries of academia.'

'Who were these people?'

'Perfectly ordinary Danes. Who also just happened to be officers, non-coms and common soldiers in Himmler's storm-trooper regiment. Some had gone from Denmark to basic training in Germany and from there straight to Croatia; others had had their baptism of fire on the Eastern Front. In 1943 the Waffen SS was reorganised and the small national units were absorbed into larger regiments. These Danes had been with the Danish Legion.'

'Okay, now I'm with you,' Toftlund said, although prior to this his only knowledge of the Danish legionnaires had been gleaned from his father's stories about these bewildered halfwits and social misfits, and from a popular Danish television serial.

'They were now incorporated into the Danish Regiment, which formed part of the Nordland Division. They had been sent to Yugoslavia for a bit of R&R, to put some meat on their bones and train with the other national units in the Division before being sent back to the Eastern Front to fight the Soviets. To begin with they loved Croatia. Well, no wonder – it was warm and sunny and there was masses of food. They had come from the cold north or from the ice-bound hell of the Eastern Front, and in Croatia they found palm trees, exotic fruit, nuts, wine, the excellent slivovitz and beautiful women. To these front-liners it was paradise!'

Samson paused for a moment. Toftlund considered him. His face had grown even ruddier thanks to the gin and the wine. Toftlund did not want brandy, but waited patiently while the little Slovak ordered a large French cognac. The babble of voices in a variety of tongues drifted up to the white-painted ceiling and coiled itself around the apparently random assortment of advertisements for American cars which adorned the beige walls. The young crew-cut guy in the leather jacket paid for his beer and sauntered out of the door as if time was the one thing he had plenty of. The four mafiosi with the blonde had reached the cigar stage. They sat with their heads together across a table strewn with the leavings from their meal. Engrossed in conversation – but about what. The blonde lit another cigarette and gazed blankly at her surroundings through her thick layer of make-up. Samson went on:

'The young Danes arrived in August 1943 and were billetted in villages such as Sisak, Glina and Petrinja, south of Zagreb. Some of them right down by the Adriatic Sea, near Dubrovnik. In September the Italian forces capitulated and the Danes' first assignment was to assist with the disarming of the Italians, to save them going over to Tito's communist partisans, or the partisans getting hold of their weapons. The Italians didn't really care, all most of them wanted was to go home. Tito managed to get his hands on a lot of equipment and rapidly stepped up the partisan war. With ambushes and so on, but also with actual offensives against the German troops and their Croatian auxiliaries. They showed no mercy. And took few prisoners.' Samson took a big slug of his cognac before proceeding:

'Among the young Danes was one *Sturmbannführer* Jørgen Pedersen. A fine-looking man with dark-blonde hair and green eyes. A true Aryan and confirmed Nazi and SS man. Volunteered in 1941. Awarded the Iron Cross for the previous year's Russian Campaign. Proud to be fighting under the Danish flag – the *Dannebrog* – and the Swastika. In that order ...'

'You're good at names,' Toftlund could not help interrupting. '*Dannebrog, Jørgen*. Your pronunciation is almost perfect.'

'It's a story that interests me.'

'Sorry for interrupting.'

'A cognac. No? The Danish flag on Pedersen's epaulette meant more to him than the SS insignia on his collar. Like the rest of them he hated Jews and Bolsheviks. They were to blame for the slump of the thirties, for poverty and unemployment. The democratic nations had failed. It was pretty much the same argument that was used for becoming a communist. Communism and Nazism have always been the diabolical mirror-images of one another. Which is why they hated one another so much. They looked in the mirror and really did not like what they saw. Sorry, I'm digressing. But this is part of my heritage. These two grim ideals. Anyway – Hitler wanted to create a new world. Pedersen wanted to help him do it. Croatia changed his life. Two diametrically opposed forces were at work here: evil and love. On the beach where the young soldiers went on their days off he met a young woman, a twenty-year-old with glossy black hair, lovely brown eyes and silky olive skin – his rough hands had never felt anything so beautifully soft and smooth. They met on the beach and then again at a dance, because she lived only ten kilometres from the village further inland at which the Danes were stationed. Her father was the chairman of the local political wing of the Ustashi. They fell head over heels in love. They did their best to be together day and night. They tried to forget the war. To forget that the tide of war was turning on the terrible Eastern Front. One day when Pedersen was on patrol with his squad they came upon another unit which had been caught in an ambush. They found their comrades laid out side by side on a grassy slope. Most of them were Danes, with a couple of Norwegians and their Croatian guide. They were all in the same position, on their backs. Every one of them had had his dick cut off and stuck in his mouths by the partisans. There they lay, neatly ranged up, as if on parade.'

Samson broke off.

'I think I'll have that cognac now,' Toftlund said. He could picture that scene all too clearly.

'Certainly.' Samson signalled to the waitress, pointed to his glass and raised two fingers. The restaurant was starting to empty. Only four or five tables were still occupied, among them that occupied by the four men in suits and the listless, jaded blonde. One of the men was talking on his mobile. The other guys were listening in, but the blonde concentrated on the last of her drink and another cigarette. Toftlund took a big and appreciative gulp of his brandy and almost choked when the fiery liquor went down the wrong way.

'It was not an unusual sight,' Samson went on unfazed. 'Revenge was a powerful driving force on both sides. Through their spies, Pedersen and the rest of the regiment learned that the band of partisans responsible for the ambush and the massacre hid out in a village fifteen kilometres away. They sneaked into it at night and left again in the morning. The Danish SS troops set out for this village and were there, ready and waiting at daybreak, but no partisans were seen leaving the village, which lay quiet and peaceful on a bend in the river. So the Danes moved in and searched the houses, but found no weapons. Nonetheless, they then began systematically to hang all the men and boys in the village – one after another. Just as the slaves were crucified after the rebellion in Capua. There they dangled in rows. Each time, the Danish *Sturmbannführer* asked: Where are the terrorists? The women, who had been herded into the village square, wept and begged and pleaded and denied that they had ever sheltered partisans. Then another man or boy was hung by the neck.'

'But it was a Croatian village, wasn't it?'

'Not all Croats sided with the Germans. As I say, Tito was a Croat. In the Balkans, Chief Inspector, nothing is straightforward.'

'Then what happened?'

Samson took another sip of his brandy and dabbed his lips almost primly with his crumpled, red-checked napkin, before saying:

'Once all the men and boys had been hung, they drove the women and children into the church, set fire to it and to the other

| 209 |

buildings in the village and burned the whole lot to the ground. One massacre among many, then as now. Afterwards, when the blood-lust had left them the SS soldiers felt sickened by what they had done. They drank to forget, but some could not get those images out of their minds – among them Pedersen. He never got over it. He had lost his faith in the cause. It was one thing to have an image of himself fighting the Bolsheviks and seeing the Jews being taken away, but now the atrocities had struck at the countrymen of the girl he loved. Love and evil fought it out in his heart, and the battle continued when, in the December, they returned to the Eastern Front, far fewer in number than when they first came to Croatia.'

Samson drained his glass. Toftlund left his where it was for a moment, then slid it across to the Slovak, who lifted it and swirled the dark liquid around the glass, as if it was his first cognac and and he wanted to release the full aroma.

'There's not much more to tell, really,' Samson said at length. 'Obviously there are some gaps in the story. The Nordland Division and with it the Danish Regiment and *Sturmbannführer* Pedersen, was sent to Oranienburg, not far from Leningrad. That was in December 1943, and it was the beginning of the end. We know that Pedersen took part in the retreat to Narva, that he came home to Denmark once on leave, but that he then deserted. In the early spring he turned up in his sweetheart's village, where the baker was dead and his daughter had switched her allegiance to Tito. How he managed to get from the front, or Denmark, to Yugoslavia we do not know. He never said. Only that he had walked through Poland, down through Slovakia, from there into Hungary and south to Croatia. He had travelled by night. Occasionally he had been helped by people who thought he was one of the partisans. Or because they realised he was a deserter. Or possibly because there are good people everywhere. In any case, on a spring day in 1945 he walked into the village and sat down in a café. As if he had merely been out for a little stroll. He looked like a toilworn farm labourer. He was nothing but skin and bone and he had lost two teeth. Word of his coming must have reached his sweetheart, because she found him. She was eager to find him, so that he could see his baby daughter. Why wasn't he shot? Who knows. Maybe she shielded him. Maybe everyone was simply tired of all the killing. Maybe his life was spared for the simple reason that he was a baker: the village lacked a baker and there he was. He stayed for six months, the war came to an end, and then he vanished again, as suddenly as he had appeared. Then, in the early fifties he returned and remained there until his death. Everyone knew him as the baker. Not as anything else. Unless it was as the baker with the beautiful daughter who worked for the nameless ones in Belgrade. No one was interested in the past. Everyone had a past.'

'What an amazing story,' Toftlund said. 'How come you know it in such detail?'

'Because one of the volunteers in Pedersen's company was my father. A Sudeten German. My father told me this story six years ago, before he died. He made me promise that I would help Pedersen's daughter, if she ever needed it. Because the Dane had saved his life more than once on the Eastern Front. Because they had deserted together, although they soon became separated. Because he felt he owed the Dane something. Because they shared the dreadful secret of those Croatian women and children in that burning church.'

'How did they get in touch again after the war?'

'These people know one another, Toftlund.'

'An old Nazi network!'

Samson laughed out loud, almost a little too loudly. Two of the guys in suits turned to stare at their table and the blonde crossed one nylon-clad leg languidly over the other.

'No, Chief Inspector. Nothing could be farther from the truth. They are not Nazis. Nazism is dead and buried, thank God. And the so-called neo-Nazis are nothing but a bunch of frustrated racists, men with no knowledge of history who, inferior as they are, imagine that they are living by a historic ideal. The others are old comrades who help one another because they have a common history, one which they cannot share with others.'

'Most of them must be dead by now anyway.'

'Yes, they are, but their children are alive, and that is why I am asking you to help this woman. You don't have to do it for nothing. She has something for you, something you could use. She doesn't come empty-handed.'

'What does she want?'

'Asylum, a residence permit, to blank out the past, enjoy peace of mind in her old age.'

Toftlund said nothing for a moment. Then:

'Such things are not up to me.'

'Denmark is a liberal, open-minded country.'

'Not any more, it isn't,' Toftlund said. 'Nonetheless, I think it's safe to say that something can be arranged. If what she has to offer is of sufficient interest, I should be able to bend the rules. We've done it before. More than that I can't promise right now.'

'Well, for now that will have to do.'

'Where is she? And what's her name?'

'I don't know where she is. She's on the run. I may be able to find out, though. She goes by many names, but her real name is Maria Borija Pedersen. Although naturally she has never used that last name.'

'And what would she give in payment?' Toftlund asked, although he already knew the answer. Samson did not reply, but his eyes narrowed. The door had swung open. Toftlund was sitting side on to it, Samson more with his back to it, but he had looked round. Two men in black leather jackets walked in. Their faces were covered by motorbike helmets with smoked visors. Samson and Toftlund both caught sight of them at the same moment: the Russian-made Markarov pistols held straight down alongside their trouser legs, almost merging with the black jeans, but becoming hideously distinct as the arms of the two black-clad men came up in perfect sync, almost as if their strings were being pulled by the puppet master on Charles Bridge. Toftlund and Samson both saw what was happening, but only Toftlund was quick enough to react. He threw himself sideways out of the booth and onto the floor, instinctively reaching, as he did so, for the gun that was normally stuck into his belt. Per rolled over and slid under the neighbouring table as the first shots rang out. He saw half of Samson's face disappear as the heavy dum-dum bullet hit him at close range. He kept on rolling across the floor, with the screams of the waitresses in his ears; he looked up into the astounded face of the blonde, who was staring at the red blotch now spreading between her breasts. The man sitting next to her clutched at his shoulder and fell on top of her. Toftlund tried to crawl away. One of the visored men took two steps forward and drew a bead on Per, straight-armed with a two-handed grip on his gun. Nothing happened. Toftlund was conscious of the gunman trying again, but again the pistol misfired. It was jamming somehow. Toftlund grabbed the leg of the nearest chair and hurled it with all his might at the knees of the gunman, who staggered back a few paces. He shouted something above the screams, his partner took his eye off the room and brought his pistol round to point at Toftlund, moving, so it seemed to the Dane, in slow motion. He made another effort to scramble away, but he appeared to have no command over his limbs, he lay there as if riveted to the floor. Then he heard more shots. These had a different sound to them. As if they came from a revolver: the short, sharp crack of a Smith & Wesson. One of the visored men spun round and keeled over, hitting the bar where the three Englishmen had been having their peaceable chat about golf. The other whipped his gun arm and his face round to confront two of the men in suits. One of them had a snub-nosed revolver in his hand. His face was contorted with shock and fear. His companion clutched the edge of the table as if it were a lifebelt which could render him immune to the bullets which were bound to be coming his way. His face was white as a sheet and drool ran from the corner of his mouth. The revolver barked again, but a tinkle from the mirror behind the bar told Toftlund that the bullet had missed the assassin. The latter froze for a second, as if he had felt the rush of air from the projectile and was surprised to find himself still alive; then, with a quick glance at the still form of his partner he turned on his heel and ran out. The smell of cordite smothered that of fried food and cigarette smoke. And the only sounds in the restaurant were of sniffling somewhere out back and the steady drip-drip of Pavel Samson's blood trickling onto the new, nicely polished parquet floor.

Part 3

IRMA'S SECRET LIFE

'It sounds like a thriller, doesn't it, but the thrillers are like life –
more like life than you are.'
Graham Greene, *The Ministry of Fear*

15

Dearest sister,

I write to you knowing full well that you are unlikely ever to receive my letter, but you are the only one I can talk to. They have given me my computer, having first copied every single little document, of course. I can't help laughing at the stupid, uneducated cops who are at this very moment poring over my dissertation on 'The new role of women in the globalised, late-capitalist economy – a literary perspective'. Other than that there's not much to laugh at. I am writing in our common language, German; using a code to hide my words. Might they be able to break it? Not that I care, because I might as well be writing in soap or in sand. Once I am finished I will erase my thoughts.

I am sitting in a cell: seven metres square by my calculations, containing a cot, a washbasin and a small table. The walls are an ugly yellow. It is night. I can sense more than see the moon out there beyond the little window high above my head – just under the ceiling, about three metres up, I would guess. An impression of a golden light shining down on the Western Prison, a light which would like to break through the walls and caress me if it could. I am a political prisoner in a country that boasts of being civilised and democratic while, in all its hypocrisy, practising the worse possible form of torture: that of cutting a person off from their fellow human beings.

I am allowed to speak to one member of my family for an hour once a week, strictly supervised of course. Fritz was here the other day, sat there in the interview room, heavy and silent as always, uncomfortable with the policeman who was monitoring our conversation. All he could talk about was his bread and buns. He looks like Dad. As Dad could have looked had he been permitted to lead a normal life. With none of Dad's charm, but with his nose for business. Fritz may seem a bit dense, but he's smarter than he looks. I can't talk to him about serious personal matters, though. He sees everything in terms of buns and French loaves. As long as he can make a decent living, go hunting, enjoy life with his wife, ensure that the factory is doing well and his pension savings multiplying nicely, and know that his children continue to thrive, Fritz is a happy man. Teddy has not been to see me yet. He was out travelling when I was arrested. But he got me a lawyer so he must be back. I am expecting to see my shrewd and intelligent, if somewhat superficial, little brother very soon.

Otherwise, it's just one interrogation after another. I can tell from their questions that they have spoken to everyone I know, but they have nothing; nor do they realise that the world has changed. They are like sheep, they follow the herd, and unlike you and me they have never understood that the world is an unjust place which only the chosen can change, to assure a better life for all. They are marionettes in the grim puppet show of capitalism, in which the people are seduced with Coca-Cola and TV. And in which a company director in the US earns as much as 479,000 farmworkers in Zimbabwe, as I read in one of the newspapers which they do, at least, allow me to read. That we, the affluent ten per cent of the world's population, control eighty-six per cent of its resources – I don't need to ask you: is that the justice of liberalism, because you know the answer as well as I do. We believed in another kind of society. Our dreams were shattered by the folly of mankind, but does that mean we have to throw the baby out with the bathwater? Would Christians deny Jesus Christ simply because the church has for centuries committed indescribable atrocities in his name? Should we deny our fundamental principles because of the rape by a handful of individuals of the great socialist and communist ideals. Something tells me, too, that a new generation of young people is waking up to these facts. They have cast off the trauma of socialism's downfall and are starting to protest – in word and action – against global injustice.

But I did not mean to rant on about politics to you, sister. I simply wanted to while away the night by talking to you. I cannot sleep anyway, and the time goes so slowly. I know they'll be back again tomorrow, asking the same – albeit courteous, but at the same time accusatory – questions. They think they actually know the answers and merely want me to confirm their misapprehensions, but I won't.

It has grown darker outside, the moon has disappeared and I can hear the rain pattering against the wall and the little window. The sound of the cold spring rain takes me back to the day that marked the end of my childhood. Then as now, there was a sense that the rain could turn to sleet and thereafter to snow even. In the sort of false winter that can sometimes strike in the Danish autumn: the soft snow rendering the whole world hushed and white. It doesn't seem quite right, though, for it to fall when we are looking forward to spring.

May I share that day with you?

It was not a spring day, but a day in autumn. Very early in the morning. I was twelve at the time, riding with a bunch of other twelve- to sixteen-year-olds in a wagon pulled by a dark-grey tractor, one of the new Fergusons which were starting to appear in the country. Even then, in 1952, they were something of a sensation in a land which, in many ways, still bore the scars of the war and where horses still supplied the main pulling power on the land. The tractor was driven by Niels Ejnar. We could see the back of his neck under his greasy cap and every now and again the breeze would blow the smell of his pipe tobacco back to us in the wagon. The scent of Virginia tobacco, which still seemed strange, but rich and sensual after the peculiar weed the grown-ups had smoked during the war. The tractor's big wheels ploughed along the muddy cart-tracks and the wagon rocked and rolled as if we were on a ship. We were all dressed in warm trousers and sweaters, with thick socks inside our high rubber boots. It was a chilly morning, but with that crispness to the air which makes you feel good to be alive. It was still dark, but there was a lovely, slender band of light on the horizon against which I could see the bare-branched trees taking shape and coming to life. Rain lurked in the domed clouds.

Niels Ejnar was a big, beefy man in his early thirties with a high bald head and little blue eyes. He and his brother had a smallholding out on the fen, not far from the marsh that bordered on the beach, down where the meadows gave way to old grass-covered dykes. He was a friend of Dad's, or at least they were somehow connected: they had a certain way of looking at one another sometimes. He never said much, but people didn't in those days. He minded his own business and toiled for his bread, as they said. Along with his wife, a tall thin woman with a narrow, pockmarked faced of whom we were terrified as kids, because we thought she looked like the witch in *Hansel and Gretel*.

It was a chilly morning, but fraught with anticipation. My little brother Fritz was sitting across from me, next to Peter, the lawyer's son who only had eyes for Bente, who was ages with himself. Fritz was only nine, but he had been allowed to join the beaters on the first big autumn shoot to be hosted by the Count. Hence the reason we kids were in that wagon, on our way to the first beat, with the promise of a *daler* at the end of the day and lemonade and pastries in the course of it. It made me all warm and fluttery and happy inside to think of my father being there with the other fine men of the district and the guests whom the Count had invited all the way from Copenhagen. The Count was a tall gaunt man with a little goatee beard, which was quite unusual back then. He was a curiously aloof man who lived on his estate a little way outside the town. As with so many others there was some mystery surrounding his wartime activities. Like the other farmers he had apparently made good money out of supplying produce to the Germans, but in 1944 the Count had had a change of heart. Still, though, when liberation came he managed to escape repercussions only because he had given shelter to two British airmen, or so my father and mother said. After the war he had gone on living in the area, on his estate. We had moved from South Zealand to the clement island of Fünen and taken over the bakery, which had been going cheap. 'The comrades helped us,' my parents said. It was best that no one knew about our past. The photograph of my father in his black uniform had been hidden away as far back as 1944, though he was not even home at that point. They never mentioned the war, or where he had been. Why he had suddenly vanished after being home on leave in 1943. Fritz stemmed from that visit. And why he had suddenly shown up again towards the end of 1947. My little brother Teddy was the product of that homecoming.

I don't remember much about the war. Only, in the early days, a feeling of happiness, uniforms, songs and speeches, the aroma of tobacco, the women's heavy perfumes and my mother and father at the hub of elevated conversation in Danish and in German, that strange language that was both hard and soft. My lovely mother was the object of much attention from the handsome men. But I loved my Dad best. He was tall and slim and carried himself with dignity. It seemed perfectly natural when he said that some people were chosen to lead and that the Nordic race was superior to all the others. These words sounded so true, coming from the fine lips under his straight nose. Although maybe I don't really remember this at all? Maybe it's just something I read. My knowledge of that time is, after all, a product of my reading. But I do remember that good feeling inside. Or did I simply pick that up from the letters I found years later when my mother moved into a nursing home and I, as the oldest and the daughter, had the job of clearing out the house? I was only four when he came home from the front. All I remember is that he was very thin, his face grey, and his hands shook. That and the voices from my parents' bedroom in the house where we were living at the time. They were loud and shrill; I remember my mother's tears and my father's hacking cough.

Before, when he'd been home on leave, neighbours and friends had flocked to the house to sing songs and listen to speeches. But on this last furlough hardly anyone came to see us. Life went on just the same, though. Everyone carried on as normal. Did business with the Germans, got on with their work, listened to the government's urgings to stay calm. But it was as if we had contracted a disease. As if the good times were over. Even though Dad and the others had gone off to war with the government's support and blessing. With brass bands and parades and speeches on the radio. Later I learned the whole story, of course, but as a child I only sensed, more with my heart than my mind, how everything changed, slowly and imperceptibly, and treachery and hypocrisy became the order of the day. How the big men knew how to look out for themselves, offering up the small fry to satisfy the mob's thirst for revenge at the end of the war.

But on that morning in 1952, riding in that wagon, the war seemed a million miles away. The country might have been poor and battle-scarred, but there was something in the air. We had moved to a new place where no one knew us, and the Danes seemed mainly concerned with making a better life for themselves. Most political prisoners had been released and if anyone was acquainted with my family's past then they kept quiet about it, because they were a part of that same past. We lived in a big white house with lots and lots of rooms. It sat right next to the bakery, in which two time-served bakers and an apprentice were employed. We had a driver who delivered bread to all the farms. We also had a cold store to which people consigned their sides of pork or whole pigs. Come Christmas the house was filled with the smell of roast pork and roast duck. Not just from Mum's kitchen, but also from the bakery to which the locals brought their Yuletide joints and birds for roasting in the big oven. In Europe, cities – not to mention whole countries – still lay in ruins, but once again Denmark had emerged more or less unscathed: the Danes are highly adaptable and know how to make the best of things.

That was a happy time. My mother began to dress up nice again, she smelled of perfume once more, and mysterious sounds, both ominous and deliciously intriguing, issued from the big bedroom. The summer before that autumn shoot my father hired a photographer to take an aerial picture of the house and the bakery. It was a really hot summer's day, the air heavy with scent and a-hum with insects, when the small single-engined plane swooped over my childhood home, skimming over the red tiled roof and the elm trees I remember so clearly from our huge garden. We were lined up in front of the house; Mum and Dad had put Fritz into baker's togs just like Dad's, because even at that point it was more or less understood that Fritz would be a baker like Dad.

The wagon jounced along and I looked across at Fritz. He might have been three years younger than me, but he was already a big lad with his father's wide mouth and hefty shoulders. Under the raincoat his sweater strained across his chest. Beneath the rough cap which he had pulled down low over his forehead as always, he was grinning. My other little brother, Theodor, was at home, of course. At the age of four he was still a baby as far as we were concerned. While Fritz and I took after Dad, Teddy, with his blonde curls, beautiful eyes and sunny smile looked more like Mum. And like Mum he cried easily. Even for a little kid it didn't take much for him to burst into tears. And not just if he happened to hurt himself: at the thought of someone dying, the sight of a mouse caught in a trap in the bakery or taken by the cat, or a dead ladybird on the sun-warmed stone of the front step, he was liable to start howling heartrendingly. It seemed only natural to call him Teddy, because he was exactly like a soft, cuddly little teddy bear. He was the family pet, as late babies often are. My father thought him a bit of a namby-pamby, but my mother defended him and coddled and cossetted him. Then my father would eye me proudly, remove the pipe from his mouth and say: 'Irma, my lass. You're a damn fine chap. The sort one can rely on. A true comrade. And you should always be able to rely on a comrade. Through thick and thin. Remember that! Never fail a comrade!' My whole world revolved around my father and I loved him with all my heart.

He was there with the other men when we drove up. Niels Ejnar stopped the tractor – its enormous, brand-new rear tyres now caked with thick, black mud – clambered down from the driving seat and touched his cap to the gentlemen, but like us beaters he kept his distance from them. They were standing in a group, all drinking from steaming mugs of real coffee laced with aquavit to take the edge off the morning chill. 'To warm the bones,' Dad said as he passed the hip-flask round. The members of the shooting party were all burly men in heavy coats and green plus-fours which stopped just below the knee, leaving a length of thick knitted sock showing between them and the top of their rubber boots. They were all wearing caps and smoking pipes, cigarettes or cheroots. They reeked of masculinity, standing there discussing the forthcoming shoot. We kids were also offered coffee or lemonade, proper coffee with creamy milk and sugar, and bread rolls from Dad's bakery with real butter, spread so thickly in honour of the occasion that it tickled the roof of the mouth when you bit into it. As the baker's family we had no shortage of butter, but we had margarine scraped on our sandwiches at home, just like everyone else. Because that was what one did. Dad smiled at Fritz and me, but stayed with the other men, naturally. The colour had come back into his cheeks, he had filled out again too, and he stood there chatting away easily to the Count – so I noted out of the corner of my eye, while Fritz was fooling about with Niels Ole who was his best chum, even though his father was a vicar and didn't take part in the shoot, and we never went to church. 'The church has made people soft,' Dad always said. We had been christened, though, and would be confirmed, because that was all part of being Danish, Mum felt – and Dad too really, I'm sure. We shivered in the cold air, but were proud to be on the shoot.

It was quite normal for us to be given the day off a couple of times a year, when the Count held one of his big shooting parties for friends and business acquaintances. Among the guns were local farmers whom I knew, because I was often allowed to go with Kaj on his bread rounds. Sometimes they would give me a piece of rock candy or a glass of squash. Others were gentry from the local market town. A few of the guns came from much further afield: the Count was a well-known and highly respected man. Mum said that just after peace was declared there had been rumours that he had done rather too well for himself during the early war years, but that he had been careful to break with all dubious associates before it was too late. The people at the top always looked after number one. Such insinuations from the grown-ups were often lost on me, although I was always a very observant child. But what I remembered most clearly about our home was that those who were constantly being hailed as heroes were regarded, in our family, as villains who had not understood the necessity of shaping a new Europe under the leadership of Germany. Hadn't former prime minister Stauning himself said that Denmark would have to fall in with the German plan economy, which would also act as a shield against the dreaded capitalism. But no one mentioned that now. The general feeling seemed to be that it was best to put all of that behind one and make a fresh start. And although we were never told this in so many words, Fritz and I knew not to talk about the war to anyone else. Nothing good could come of that. But Teddy did not know anything, nor was he ever told anything. 'There's no need for anyone born after the war to be burdened with all that,' my mother would later say to Fritz and me.

One of the Count's gamekeepers came over to us and kindly inquired whether we had had coffee and rolls. Because, if so, the Count would like to get started at first light. 'Drive them over to the Vesterås boundary, Niels Ejnar Jensen,' he said, tipping a finger to his green cap. Like the other men he had his shotgun open and resting in the crook of his arm and his cartridges in the bag slung over his green coat. Guffaws of laughter sounded from the group of guns, backs were thumped and thighs slapped in that noisy, all-boys-together way which, later in life, would drive me mad. Such masculine arrogance – as if they really believe that they are the stronger sex and the world belongs to them.

On that morning, however, it seemed perfectly natural to me. We climbed back into the wagon and Niels Ejnar drove us north to the boundary of a field. Two other tractors and wagons from the next parish were already drawn up there. Ahead of us lay stubble-fields dotted with narrow furrows and occasional pools – little more than puddles really – left by the autumn rain. The Count always left little clumps of bush and scrub standing in the fields – for the game – and in some spots even delayed the autumn ploughing until after the first shoot. Further off, past the first little ash grove, the meadows stretched out, damp and steaming. On the horizon lay the forest and beyond it more fields. Way out on the edge of the area we hoped to cover that day, the marshes began.

The keepers had organised the beats in consultation with the Count, in such a way as to ensure that they were drawn as efficiently and thoroughly as possible. They would be shooting both hare and pheasant and if anyone happened to bag a fox into the bargain then so much the better. I knew that a dead fox caused the men to swagger even more when they surveyed the bag laid out on display at the end of the day. We were strung out in a long line with a keeper in the middle and one at either end, their job being to keep the beaters in line so that the game would have no chance to break through their ranks. The keepers' liver-coloured hunting dogs were whining and straining at their leashes, quivering with excitement. Much as we were, I suppose, although I winced every time I saw a bird or an animal hit. Not that I would ever have admitted that – to myself or to Dad.

The keepers had us ranged up like soldiers in an old-style war. In the cold, grey morning light we saw the guns forming a line down at the other end of the field, well spaced-out, with their shotguns over their arms. And far away though they were, I could see their breath swirling around their faces. I could just make out

Dad, way out on the right. Then a hunting horn keened, high and mournful in the distance. As the sound died away over the flat fields the keepers' whistles trilled. We moved forward, clapping our hands. A few of the boys thwacked pieces of wood together, but the line of beaters made so much noise as it swished through the wet stubble that that in itself was enough to flush out the game. The keepers yelled at us to hold the line. The dogs strained at their long leashes. It could not have been more than a few seconds before the first pheasant flew up, wings clattering, to be followed by partridge and more bright-feathered pheasant cocks, and even before I heard the shots I saw the grey plumes of smoke issuing from the barrel mouths when the guns, as if on command, raised their twin barrels to the sky, from which the beautiful birds, checked in their flight, plummeted groundwards, suddenly and without warning, like hard, alien fruit, and sundered feathers fluttered in the breeze and blew over our heads. Two hares also sprang up, right at my feet. They zigzagged down the beaters' line; we whooped and hollered and one of them bolted, ears flattened, straight towards the guns – only to be hit and sent rolling across the ground like a football that had just been kicked. The other hare stopped in mid-spring, turned, spotted a gap in the beaters' ranks, darted through it and sped off across the field in a series of mighty bounds.

'Hold the bloody line, young 'uns!' the keepers bellowed, all shouting at once. It sounded worse than it was. As if they were angry or annoyed, but they weren't really. That was just how they spoke to children. But it was early in the morning, the first drive had produced a fine bag and spirits were high. The keepers gathered up the game and piled it into the wagon which Niels Ejnar on the tractor pulled round after each drive, while the guns carried on down the lane. Dad strode out alongside the Count and a farmer whom I knew because he had once paid his bill with a side of pork instead of cash. The odd spit of rain fell from the grey sky, moving some of the men to get out their hip-flasks and take a swig as they made their way to the next beat, where they spread out as before and the whole performance was repeated.

At the third beat we were ranged just in front of a ditch lined by stunted willows. There was water in the bottom of the ditch. We could see all the way across the flat meadows to the dyke which ran out to the shallow channel. We had to drive the game down the side of the dyke towards the row of guns who appeared, by now, to be looking forward to the light mid-morning refreshment which the Count laid on. The maids would bring out coffee and schnapps and sandwiches for the shooting party. For us there would be boiled sausages and soft drinks. The girls carried the sausages out in a big pot, from which clouds of steam and the most glorious smell escaped when they lifted off the heavy lid. We ate the red-skinned frankfurters wrapped in greaseproof paper out there in the fields. They were delicious, and smelled faintly of vinegar and onions from the cooking water. But if the gentlemen looked forward to their elevenses, this was as nothing compared to the eagerness with which they anticipated the lunch which would bring the shoot to a halt for a couple of hours. We beaters were looking forward to that too. There would be rye-bread sandwiches with salami, liver paste, rolled-lamb sausage and cheese, and all the lemon or orange squash we could drink. And it would be a bit warmer in the big garage where we children were usually fed, while the gentlemen sat down to table in the Count's banqueting hall. Ploughs, harrows and other farming implements were moved outside to make room for us, the keepers and Niels Ejnar. The morning was beginning to tell on our legs. It was heavy going in the damp soil which clogged the soles of our rubber boots. But I could tell from Fritz's face that he was still keyed-up and rather exhilarated by the shoot. Possibly by the blood from the dead creatures. He did not appear to have been upset by the sight of those lovely birds stopping in mid-flight and dropping like stones when hit by the lead shot. Or the hares, cartwheeling pathetically across the ground when their lithe progress was cut short in mid-leap. He seemed quite comfortable with the smell of blood and gunpowder. One could tell just by looking at him that he could not wait for the day when he could stand next to Dad, alongside the other guns, peering at the line of beaters with his shotgun at the ready.

The only little fly in the ointment was Peter, who was always sucking up to the keepers and showing off, because he had already turned sixteen. Peter's Dad was a lawyer in the town. He had been on the right side during the war and Peter was always boasting about how his father had met Montgomery and chucked a whole load of Nazi swine into jail on May 4th and 5th, the days of liberation. I didn't know if this was true. Folk were always bragging about what they had done during the occupation. You would have thought the whole country had been united against the Germans, when the truth was, in fact, that most people had stayed out of it, minded their own business. Or collaborated. But when Peter or anyone else started holding forth I either had to keep my mouth shut or try to talk about something else. Not that he was interested in talking to a twelve-year-old girl anyway, but sometimes you'd be standing on the fringes of a group in the playground, talking about this and that, and you heard things. Peter's father hadn't yet joined the shooting party. He had gone to pick up another man in Odense, some bigwig all the way from Copenhagen. This was Peter's way of rubbing in the fact that his Dad had a private car with black registration plates, as opposed to the yellow commercial ones which Dad, for example, had. Luckily Peter was way down at the the other end of the line when the keepers blew their whistles and we started moving down towards the bottom of the field where the guns were waiting impatiently.

Again we flushed out both pheasant and partridge. And two hares that bounded away, running for all they were worth. Dad brought down one of them, the other was smarter; it darted sideways, down the line of beaters and disappeared over the dyke. A few of the guns appeared to have been hitting their hip-flasks again: they were starting to shoot wild now, or merely winging their quarry; the keepers had to send the dogs out to find the downed creatures. Yet another hare leapt from cover. It was a mystery to me how they managed to hide in the virtually bare, reaped field. But they stayed very still, blending into the earth. Then all at once they would spring up and run for their lives – first dashing towards the beaters, then leaping round on themselves. More often than not they made the wrong decision and ended up running straight to their deaths. This particular hare was a big beast which looked as though it had been in this same situation before. It raced straight for me, I clapped my hands furiously and shouted and yelled. One of its ears appeared to have taken a shot at some point. It was smaller than the other and flopped at an odd angle, as if dragged down by the weight of an old lead pellet, but it had powerful legs and a thick coat. The hare stopped right in front of me, looked at me for a split-second, and I was filled with a burning desire to step aside and let him through; then he turned round – I'm pretty certain it was a buck – and ran, in long, graceful bounds that caused the wind to ruffle his fur, towards the guns. And, typically, there was one gun who simply could not wait for the hare to come properly within range. I saw him take aim, saw the puff of gunsmoke and, a moment later heard the two sharp cracks from the double-barrelled shotgun. The hare tumbled head over heels, but it got back onto its feet. It was limping now, though, trailing one of its forelegs which was stained red with its blood. It hopped back and forth between the guns and the beaters. Our own line was so close to that of the shooting party that no one dared shoot. I saw one of the keepers raise his gun to put the creature out of its misery, but I think he was afraid some stray shot might hit one of the gentlemen. It looked as though the wounded animal might get away. We beaters stood stock-still – almost as if ordered to do so, although no one had said a word – and followed the hare's lurching course. We knew enough about shooting to comprehend that it was wounded and ought to die, nonetheless I could not help hoping – a hope shared, I felt sure, by some of the other beaters – that he would run away, over the dyke to freedom, if only to find himself a place to hide and die there peacefully and alone.

The keeper on our line's outermost flank released his dog. It was a big Danish pointer with a beautiful shaded dark-brown coat. It sprang away, its stubby docked tail quivering with excitement. It bounded across the clayey stubble-field with great, powerful strides, running diagonal to the hare. The hare seemed to sense this new threat. It hopped even faster, but I could see that it was in pain from its wounded foot. It changed direction. Everything happened very fast, and yet so slowly. I kept my eyes on the dog, counting the seconds and praying inwardly to God to save the hare, to give it the strength to run faster than the wind. But the Lord was not listening to me then either. The pointer caught up with the hare, but did not manage to bring it down right off. The hare stumbled and fell, got up again, somewhat unsteadily; the dog wheeled around, so excited by the chase that it almost lost its footing. But before the grey hare had time to build up any speed the dog had it by the throat and bit down. Until that morning I had not known that hares had voices. But this one uttered a heart-rending cry, like the squeal of a scalded baby. The scream faded to a whimpering sigh and then there was silence.

The keeper stood for a moment. Everyone stood for a moment. Possibly no more than a couple of seconds, but it felt like an eternity. Then the keeper put his whistle to his lips and called his dog back. When one thinks of the changes in our lives that were set in motion on that day, the incident with the hare is really neither here nor there. Since then, though, it has occurred to me that my twelve-year-old self might unconsciously have felt that the hare's agony foreshadowed my own. I am a rationalist, but one should never underestimate the subconscious. In that scream lay the germ of my own outward and inner pain, as well as relief from them through the insight the years would bring.

Because I remember it as if it was yesterday. The low, grey

clouds, the withered grass on the dyke, the black, wet, cold earth, the raindrops mingling with the tears on my cheeks, the beaters and the guns, facing each other like two armies, and the echo of the hare's plaintive, agonised, stricken squeal, hanging like a shrill false note in the bitter autumn air.

16

ON THE NEXT DRIVE we were quieter. The hare's scream was still in our ears. The dog alone seemed pleased and happy after the praise given to it by the keeper when it brought him the mangled quarry. Were the guns, too, a little rattled perhaps? At any rate they showed more patience, waited for the game to come closer before shooting. I did not want to appear soppy or girly so I stepped out again, clapping my hands, like the boys on either side of me, but a couple of the bigger teenage girls were struggling to hold back the tears. It was odd, really. I don't know why the dog's kill affected us more than those made by the men. Could it be that we, in fact, ascribe to animals a rationality and goodness – a sort of inverse humanity – which they do not possess?

The last beat yielded only a single pheasant and a hare, then came our sausages and soft drinks. It cheered us up to reach the end and see the two maids from the big house standing beside the cart with the huge, steaming soup pot and baskets full of little hot-dog rolls with big jars of mustard alongside, as well as home-made ketchup in old white milk bottles. The guns stood in their own little group, some way apart from us in a clearing in the forest, where they were served sandwiches and beer and coffee laced with schnapps. They missed out on the firm, red frankfurters and the golden orange squash, which tasted wonderful in the keen, grey autumn air. Everything looked and smelled of autumn. The odour of rotting leaves mingled with the salty scent of the sea beyond the dyke. The clouds drifted in two layers over those yellow leaves which still clung to the trees. The big hardwoods in the forest were only waiting now for the first proper autumn storm. It had been threatening to rain all day, but only a few drops had fallen. Then suddenly the sun broke through the clouds, the thick layer parting as though the Almighty had sliced through it with a bread-knife. Dad came over to Fritz and me and asked how we were doing. Were we warm and dry? Then he gave my arm a little squeeze, as if he understood that I was upset but knew that *I* knew that I could not let him or anyone else see it. Fritz was the younger of us two, but his cheeks were flushed and his eyes were shining. He was as tall as me and it was easy to see that he took after Dad. The keepers came over to tell us to finish off and get back into the wagon: it would be good if we could get in a couple more drives before lunch at one. We climbed aboard and Niels Ejnar drove us out to our new positions. We were happy as larks again by now and sang all the songs we could remember from morning assembly at school as we trundled along the rutted country lane. And so things continued until lunch.

We were in the lofty barn, sitting or standing around, eating our sandwiches and drinking lemonade, when Peter's father arrived with the guest from Copenhagen. The barn smelled of oil and hay; all of the farm machinery had been hauled out apart from the old combine harvester which sat in a corner swathed in cobwebs and looking as though it had been wrapped in silk by some storybook fairy. Peter suddenly drew himself up tall and it was all he could do not to point. He was just about bursting with pride when, as if on cue, we kids all dashed out of the barn to admire the car. It was a long, low blue Buick with huge tail fins and a sweeping bonnet. Peter's father drove slowly past the barn and us pop-eyed kids and up to the big house. The big, broad white-walled tyres scrunched over the gravel as it glided past an ancient oak tree and pulled up in front of the broad steps leading up to the big front door. The Count came out together with his wife, a skinny woman with jingling bracelets and red hair. The Count's face was flushed from schnapps and the indoor warmth. He had taken off his jacket and stood there in his shirtsleeves. Broad braces held his trousers up over his narrow hips and small backside. Out of Peter's Dad's car stepped the guest. He was a middle-aged, dried-out husk of a man with grey hair and wrinkled cheeks. He was in hunting garb: dark-green plus-fours and boots, three-quarter-length jacket and cap. The Count walked down a couple of steps and met him halfway. They shook hands and although I could not hear what the Count said it was clear that the newcomer was being warmly welcomed. Peter's father stood a step or two below them, looking like a conjuror who had magicked this grand guest out of thin air. We children stood there gawping, awestruck by the whole scenario. Because here was a genuine celebrity. We had seen pictures of him in the paper, read about him and heard him on the radio. He was one of our country's true heroes, a member of the Danish Freedom Council who had fought valiantly throughout those five dark years. He was also said to have shot several traitors personally. The liquidation of informers they called it on the radio. He did not look like a hero. He looked more like a rather timid bank clerk, or a schoolteacher. The sort that taught bible studies or geography and could deliver the odd clip round the ear without it mattering too much, because he did not hit very hard. You could not have told from looking at him that he had actually killed people – in cold blood, at that. Somehow I had thought that this would leave a mark, physically too, on a person, that they would be surrounded by a special aura of death and mutilation, but that was not the case. And at that point, of course, I did not know that Dad had probably witnessed more death and misery than all of the others present put together, and in all likelihood had also taken more lives. A thought which I still find hard to come to terms with: he seemed so normal. A perfectly normal baker dressed in white and enveloped in the scent of flour and pipe smoke.

The three gentlemen and the lady disappeared into the big house, the white double doors were closed behind them and we went back for a last piece of rye bread, a last drink of lemonade and the tea that had now been poured for us. The Count took pride in always doing well by his servants and his beaters. There was to be no scrimping on the first big shoot of the year, as he said. We finished eating. We girls were chattering and larking about and the boys, desperate to show off, had just started playing freedom fighters and Germans in the big barn, when I saw Dad come down the steps from the house. His face was white as a sheet and his hands were shaking. He marched straight into the barn, grabbed me roughly by the arm and, in a cold and distant voice, asked me where Fritz was.

'He's playing, Dad,' I said.

'Get him!'

'What is it, Dad?'

'Just get him.'

'You're squeezing my arm. It hurts, Dad,' I said.

He let go of my arm. For a moment I saw a strange look of confusion in his eyes, then his face became a pallid grey mask again. I raced off to the far end of the barn, where Fritz, armed with a stick for a Sten gun, was fighting a bunch of Germans into submission. The boys were making rat-a-tat-tat machine-gun noises and yelling at their adversaries that they were dead and ought to fall down. The Germans were dug in behind the combine harvester, which was doing duty as a bunker like the ones we had seen on the west coast of Jutland.

'Fritz, come here.'

He made some shooting noises, threw an imaginary hand grenade at the Germans, then emitted a nasal whistle to imitate the swoosh of the grenade's flight, followed by a boom.

I grabbed hold of him.

'Dad says you've got to come!'

'But I'm playing.'

'Right now, he said!'

He could tell from my expression that I was upset. He lowered his stick and slouched after me. Dad was standing at the barn door, paying no heed to the other men or the other children. His mind seemed to be somewhere else. Most of the kids noticed nothing,

| 236 |

but I could see the keepers giving him looks. What was one of the gentlemen doing in the barn in the middle of the shooting party lunch? That was not the done thing at all. And why was he so pale? It was a pallor against which the black stubble of his beard stood out sharp and clear, despite the fact that he had given himself an extra close shave that morning before we left. I knew, because I had been allowed to whip up his shaving foam in the little bowl he kept for this purpose, before he scraped the bristles off his face, using a brand-new razor in honour of the occasion.

'Come on,' was all he said when I came back with Fritz in tow. He walked off ahead of us, taking such long, quick strides that Fritz and I had to half run to keep up with him as he headed towards the bread van. We climbed in beside him. He reversed and drove away. I could see now that Fritz was as shaken up as I was. We knew that grown-ups could often be unpredictable and that they were liable to sudden swings in mood, but we were not used to seeing a father with such a blank, white face and trembling hands. He drew hard on his cigarette and drove far too fast down the narrow roads, and I felt the tears welling up.

'What's the matter, Dad?' I asked in a small voice.

'Nothing. Now shut up!' he shouted, and my tears began to fall.

'Stop that snivelling!' he snapped, so roughly that Fritz began to cry too because he, like me, had no idea what was going on. One minute we were part of the gang, with food and lemonade in our stomachs, while Dad was having a rare old time with the shooting party. The next we had been dragged away without any explanation. Dad had gone into lunch windswept and rosy-cheeked, with a wink at us and a remark that made the other gentlemen laugh. He had emerged again white as a sheet, his hands shaking.

'Stop that snivelling, both of you!' he shouted again, with real anger in his voice. The anger we knew from the rows he gave us if we did something wrong, or didn't do as we were told, or were driving Mum up the wall with our rough-and-tumble games. He had never hit us, but we were scared of his wrath, which could be so icy and fierce once he was provoked. So Fritz and I fought back the tears. As well as we could. We wiped the tears from our eyes and the snot from our noses and tried not to sniff any more than we could help, but he didn't even seem to be aware of us any more, as long we stayed quiet. He just kept driving, with his white, stony face, smoking one cigarette after another. He smelled of beer and schnapps and very faintly of shaving lotion, but he was not drunk. He was simply in another world. When we pulled up outside the bakery Mum came out of the house with Teddy by the hand. They stood at the top of the broad flight of steps leading up to the front door. It was lovely to sit on those steps in the summer with my dolls when the sun was blazing down on the bakery and the village. At first Mum merely stared at Dad in surprise, but then she too turned pale.

'What is it, Jørgen? Has something happened to the children?' Mum asked.

But then she caught sight of us and breathed more easily. She noticed our red eyes, though, and I could tell that she was relieved and yet troubled.

'Go up to your rooms!' Dad said. 'And take Teddy with you.'

'Jørgen ...' my mother said. 'What's happened?'

'Do as I say, dammit!'

I took Fritz by one hand and a howling Teddy, who did not want to let go of Mum, by the other and dashed up the stairs and into my room on the first floor, with a huge lump in my throat. I plonked my little brother on the bed, found a book and proceeded to read aloud to him. Teddy's sobs soon subsided: he was quick to cry, but just as quick to smile again. Even though I was reading out loud I could still hear my parents' voices down in the living room. First quiet, then louder, then shouting angrily and, eventually, my mother's weeping and my father's voice, sounding both angry and confused. As if he could have cried too, but that was not what men did. I don't think I have ever – before or since – been so afraid. I was convinced that one of my parents was about to die. I have no idea why. But that is what I thought. I read and read, oblivious to the words and their content. The reading kept the tears at bay. Not the fear, though. Deep in the pit of my stomach it gnawed away at me like a poisonous parasite.

After a while my mother appeared. We could see that she had been crying, but she had put on more make-up in an attempt to conceal this. Her eyes were swollen. She looked at us for a moment from the doorway and I stopped reading. We were huddled together on the bed, all three. Fritz and I were still in our beaters' clothes, thick jumpers and all, but we were not sweating. If anything I was freezing. The only things we had taken off, automatically in the hall, were our boots. Wordlessly my mother came over and put her arms around us. She gave way to tears again, they streamed quietly down her cheeks. This prompted Teddy to utter a loud wail and at long last Fritz and I could let go and cry on Mum's shoulder and into her nice apron, clinging tightly to her.

'What's wrong with Dad?' I hiccupped after some time.

'Later, Irma dear. Later!'

'But what is it?'

'Later. Everything's going to be alright, Irma pet,' she said in a strangely watery voice. At that my weeping subsided. I was well aware that to the grown-ups I was still just a silly little girl who did not have eyes in her head. But I felt let down: neither my mother nor my father thought it necessary to tell me why our lives should suddenly be turned upside down. Not until years later did I hear the whole story from Mum. But in the days following the shoot, what with the veiled remarks made by my mother and father and the changes at the bakery I was able to piece together most of the puzzle and gain a pretty clear picture of what had happened before we moved.

17

THE NEXT DAY it was as if nothing had happened, and for a brief moment I hoped it had all been just a dream. I woke up, as usual, at the sound of Dad's step on the stairs. He always rose very early and went down to start baking the rolls and French loaves. But that morning after the shoot something was different. I could tell right away. He wasn't whistling. Dad always whistled on his way down the stairs, just after I heard him pull the chain in the bathroom, which was right next to my room. I usually dropped off again after I heard his whistle, but that morning I could not go back to sleep. I lay in bed with my heart pounding so hard I was afraid it was about to leap right out of my chest. But I did not want to worry my mother, so I stayed in bed until she came in at seven, as usual, to get me up for school. I lay with my eyes shut, listening to her footsteps in the hall and opened them only when she said, as she normally did: 'Morning, dear. Did you sleep well? Time to get up.' Her voice was almost the same as always, but only almost. It had a cut-glass quality to it, a brittleness that had not been there before.

And it soon became clear to me, and to Fritz, that something was up. It may not have happened from one day to the next, but gradually the customers stopped coming to the shop and I noticed that when the driver loaded up the bread van for his daily rounds he was sliding fewer and fewer trays of French loaves, rye loaves, cakes and pastries onto the racks in the back. He did not whistle either, as he usually did, when he drove out of the yard. The word round about was that it was better to steer clear of Pedersen's bakery. Not that anybody actually said that, of course. Danes are not given to saying things straight out. Not when it is a matter of

| 240 |

something unpleasant. But there was a lot of whispering in corners in the little community, on the farms, in tradesmen's homes and labourers' cottages. The implicit understanding was that decent people did not shop there. Because it appeared that he had fought on the wrong side. Well, he was not alone in that, but if the attention was on the baker then it was not being directed at anyone else. And if perhaps one had not realised until it was too late that the new Europe was not going to come to anything, after all, then there was even more reason to give Pedersen's shop a wide berth and frequent one of the bakers in town instead – for the time being at least. Some customers did, however, stay loyal, mainly the well-to-do or folk who did not listen to, or were not interested in, rumours and possibly had not heard about the incident at the Count's shooting party: people who lost no sleep over the past. Because no matter what anybody said, there was no better bread baked in all the area than that which Pedersen took from his oven. Let bygones be bygones. So said those who could not have cared less what folk said or thought about this, that or the other. But, as always, only the minority dared to go against the stream.

Things were not helped by the fact that the law was quick to put in an appearance. Not Karlsen, the local constable, but two police officers all the way from Odense. Although they wore plain clothes and were friendly and polite, they still helped to fan the rumours. I do not know what they and Dad spoke about, but they drove off again after an hour. Later Mum told me that they said they had had to come and have a word with him. Someone had reported him. But although his name was on file and he was known to have fought on the Eastern Front, he had committed no criminal act on Danish soil. His breach with society was a closed chapter. His comrades had been jailed for a couple of years, but had all long since been released. Those who had not been found guilty of breaking the law in Denmark. And as far as *that* went they had nothing on Dad. So the CID men had left, saying that it was a pretty old case and times had changed since '45. And anyway, a lot of people had been on the wrong side. As a child I did not understand much of all this. Grown-ups were always so mysterious.

Both my father and my mother grew thinner that winter. The November was exceptionally warm and the weather over Christmas was very odd indeed, with rain and temperatures in December rising as high as fifteen degrees celsius. Christmas was normally a busy time for us, but that year only one goose, four ducks and six loins of pork went into the big bakery oven. And of those one duck and one pork loin were for ourselves. Because Christmas would be celebrated, no matter what, Mum said. The shop had hardly any customers. Both the bakers had been sacked. Dad could manage everything on his own with just the apprentice, whose name was Kurt and who was thick as two short planks and had no clue about anything. Besides, Fritz had started helping out in the bakery, and I also lent a hand whenever I could, although it was more or less understood that it was more important for me to stick in at school. Of the two of us I was definitely the more academic and this my parents simply accepted. Mum and Dad did not say much to one another during the day, but in the evenings I would often slip out of bed and sit at the top of the stairs, listening to their serious voices down below in the living room. I could not make out what they said, but sometimes Mum would burst into tears and once I heard her shouting that they couldn't go on like this, that the bills just kept on piling up and soon there would be no more deliveries of flour, sugar and butter.

My father had always had a kind welcome for the gentlemen of the road who came to the door, begging for a bit of stale bread, or maybe a beer or a dram, and sometimes even permission to bed down for the night in the flour store. It was as if he had always understood their longing to be on the move, their pain and their restlessness. The tramps had special signs that they carved into our front gate to tell other vagabonds that this was a hospitable house. A shifting succession of knife-grinders were also allowed to sharpen knives and scissors for a few coins, even though we had a big hand-driven whetstone in the backyard. But now he had taken to hanging out behind the bakehouse in the more or less empty flour store, drinking beer and schnapps with these raggedy, bearded characters who stank of pee and tobacco. I would hear Mum going on at him about it, but it made no difference. All Dad wanted to do was to stand out back, bleary-eyed, chewing the fat with these dirty, smelly men. Fritz and I were scared of them, while baby brother Teddy, in all his usual innocent naivety, loved their cheery banter and the boiled sweets they always slipped him.

Soon there was trouble at school too. Not so much for me as for Fritz, who had to stand up for himself, me and Dad when Peter and some of the others called him a Nazi brat or said that Dad had been involved in killing freedom fighters and murdering millions of Jews and Russians. He regularly came home with a bloody nose or a black eye, but always refused to tell Mum what the other kids were saying. Although she knew, of course. Dad either said nothing or came out with stupid tough-guy remarks about boys having to be able to defend themselves, it was all part of growing up. He did not really seem to care that much, though, as long as he could hang around out back, drinking beer with his friends the tramps.

The teachers pretended not to notice, but I could tell that they felt more and more sorry for me. They knew it was not my fault. Besides which, I was a good student who learned my lessons and was never any trouble.

One day in history class we were reading about the occupation and the teacher, Mr Hansen, was waxing lyrical about Kaj Munk, the vicar and dramatist who was murdered by the Nazis. Munk was a good Christian Dane who had bravely spoken out against the occupying power. He had looked his enemies straight in the eye and had not hidden his face. He should stand as a shining example to us of how a healthy Christian spirit and a patriotic heart would carry us through the trials and tribulations of life straightbacked and undaunted. Mr Hansen spoke about the resistance movement and how the Danish people had shown their worth by standing shoulder to shoulder against the German oppression throughout those five accursed years. The people of Denmark had fought for their freedom; that was why we put lit candles in our windows on May 4th, he said. It was a fine custom and one which we should pass on to our own children when we had them, to ensure that the memory of the fallen and the regaining of our liberty would never die, but testify always to the strength of the Danish nation and Danish values.

My parents put candles in the windows too. It was grotesque, really, but they did their best not to stand out from the crowd. From all of those Danish opportunists, every one of whom now had a resistance armband tucked away in a drawer as a treasured memento. Mr Hansen said that we, the rising generation, could learn from the fight which the Danes had put up. *Kæmp for alt, hvad du har kært. Dø om så det gælder* as we had sung so beautifully at assembly that morning: Fight for all that you hold dear. Die if die you must. Words which we should take with us when we went out into the world.

I did not stop to consider. Although normally I always did. I tried to keep everyone happy, to be the good girl who did not call too much attention to herself. I tried to be like all the others, and never betray the fact that my family had a secret; that I knew there was a secret, although my parents had never really said anything to me, not even now that I was older.

Nonetheless, I stupidly put up my hand and said:

'But Mr Hansen, I don't understand. If that's true, then how come the Danish government called the resistance people criminals for so many years? And why were they arrested by the police?'

His face blanched, he grabbed me by the ear, slapped my face and hissed at me not to be so impertinent, asking the sort of questions that could only come from one quarter. I should think myself lucky that I lived in a free country where even the likes of me were allowed to go to school along with decent Danish children!

I felt my eyes fill with tears, but I refused to cry. My cheek stung from the slap, the first I had ever received at school. Fritz, like other boys, had had plenty, of course. But I did not cry, and I never told my parents what had happened in school that day. They had enough to worry about.

The cheery tinkle of the shop bell sounded less and less often to announce a customer. At the start of the new year, Dad dismissed Mrs Sørensen, who helped out in the shop on Sundays and often in the afternoons too. Mum could easily keep house, look after us kids and serve the bakery's dwindling clientele. The only person who did not really seem to have grasped that our life had changed was little Teddy, who was as petted and pampered as ever. But then he *was* only five, and used to toddling about the house at Mum's heels, sitting on a little chair in the corner of the shop, running over to Dad or playing with Lene from next door. All of which he continued to do. Several of my friends and Fritz's chums stopped coming to see us or playing with us, having been forbidden to do so, but they did not act any differently towards Teddy. Even so, I think he must have sensed that something was wrong. He lost weight and was even more readily given to tears than before. He also became more clingy, hanging onto Mum's apron like a little baby.

I eventually figured out that the villain of the piece was the grand visitor from Copenhagen. Referred to by my parents when they thought I was not listening simply as the Jew. As if in their minds, this term covered everything and everyone that was against them, everything they hated. But the idea that they were not only anti-Zionist – that being, after all, a sound political persuasion – but positively regarded the Jewish race as a plague on the earth – this I find very hard to accept. Like us they were, however, a product of the society in which they had grown up and in which they lived. A product of circumstances and the capitalistic chaos which prevailed (and prevails) in the world. They grew up seeing the world as an unjust, exploitative place, but unfortunately they did not have genuine insight or the schooling necessary for them to make the right choices. Instead, choices were made for them by powers beyond their ken. Sadly, they were not sufficiently enlightened as to the class system which shaped their lives and their thoughts. And so they called everyone who hurt our family Jews, although the honoured guest from Copenhagen was every bit as Danish as we were.

I'm sorry, sister. I promised not to rant on about politics.

Slowly I pieced together the story and formed a picture of that lunch – one which, years later, my mother reluctantly confirmed.

The Jew had been ushered in to the laden lunch table and the gentlemen sitting around it, their faces rosy from the warmth and the schnapps; quite a few of them had already undone the top button of their trousers to accommodate all the plump herring, the excellent brawn, the liver pâté and salami, the warm roast pork, home-made rolled-lamb sausage, game terrines and the host of other rich delicacies which the Count served up at his famous shooting-party lunches. My father had been allocated a very prestigious place at the long table, only two seats down from the Count's own place at the head of the table and next to the managing director of the engine works. The gentlemen were looking forward to the cheese, another little glass of schnapps, coffee and cigars before returning to the field, well fired-up. The keepers were *not* looking forward to that. The afternoon shoot was always a dicier affair than the morning shoot.

The Jew inclined his head to the assembled company as the Count introduced him and led him up to the empty place on his right-hand side. With an air of great self-importance he nodded affably to the other guests. His lateness was a mark of his high standing: he was a member of so many important committees. He viewed his work as a moral calling. It was his duty to see to it that traitors received their just deserts, in the press if nothing else, and that heroes were not forgotten. He was forced, much against his will, to associate with politicians, now back in power, who endeavoured to make out that their collaboration with the Germans during the early years of the war had been purely accidental, or at any rate merely a pragmatic and very Danish ploy which had spared the country a great deal of misery.

The Jew shook hands with a couple of men whom he knew and was just about to take his seat at the place reserved for him when he caught sight of my father and my father caught sight of him. Their eyes were like blades clashing in the smoke-filled air between them. Dad's face turned white. The Jew's face turned red and the hand which he had out of habit and politeness extended to greet those of the Count's guests closest to him checked in mid-air and hovered there as if it did not know what to do with itself. The Jew took a step forward and said loudly and clearly, in a voice that cut through the room and made everyone look up at him and Dad:

'One is not in the habit of sitting at table with Nazis and Jew killers. One has no desire to eat with men who donned enemy uniform. One is quite prepared to leave. If you gentlemen would rather break Danish bread with the SS.'

There is a saying in Danish. I don't know whether you have a similar expression in German. We say: an angel passed through the room. It is used to describe a moment when time stands still and everyone knows that something significant has just occurred, but no one yet knows exactly what. That statement was the angel in the room. It hung in the air and could not be called back. The lunch guests were discomfited by this turn of events. Just when they had been having such a nice, convivial time of it, with no women or children around. But such a statement was not to be ignored. This was a serious accusation; it gave rise to some unease among certain people at the table, a fear that attention might also be directed at them and their own sympathies back in the days when one faithfully followed the government's recommendations until one deemed it wise to retreat from those positions as the tide of war began to turn at the front.

Hardly any time elapsed between the words being uttered and

their effect being seen, but it felt like an age. Dad had risen from his chair and put out his hand. It dropped to his side again and he had to steady himself against the table, as if he were drunk, or had had a momentary dizzy turn. The Count stood at the head of the table with his hand on the back of the chair which he had been about to pull out in order to sit down and merrily resume this most agreeable lunch. He looked from the Jew to my father and back again. Then his eyes flicked back and forth again. Clearly he, like the other men, was waiting for a response from my father or further clarification from the Jew. The two men squared up to one another like a couple of he-dogs, but Dad was the one with his tail between his legs. The Jew overpowered him with his gaze. Dad said nothing. That may have been a mistake, but it would have been unlikely to change anything. The Count, as host, felt bound to resolve the situation. With his first words he made it quite plain where he stood. He did not refute the Jew's accusation, instead he simply said:

'Perhaps you owe us an explanation, Mr Pedersen ...'

Dad stared at him. He was still white as a sheet. But, shaken and mortified though he was, he was also seething with rage. What angered him most was the fact that the Count, their host, could permit someone who had just walked in to insult one of his guests. A respectable citizen and substantial pillar of the local community, a man who always paid his dues.

So: 'I don't owe anyone anything,' my father said in a voice not much above a whisper, or like the hiss of a snake, the words uttered with so much venom and defiance. The Jew said nothing, only stared at Dad as if recognising the man before him from pictures in the files he pored over every day for the government, intent on digging up the weeds and keeping the torch of freedom burning, as he had written in the resistance movement's newspaper, *Information*. He took a pace to the right, a tiny, imperceptible turn of the head indicating that he was all set to return to Copenhagen, when the Count said:

'Perhaps it would be best if you were to leave my house, Mr Pedersen.'

Dad gazed at him as if not really understanding what he had said. Did not understand that he was being banished from the table and from the local community because of some stranger from Copenhagen who had suddenly shown up armed with accusations from a past which everyone at that table had tacitly agreed to put behind them, now that new times were so obviously on the way.

And it was after that, of course, that I had seen him come out, looking as though he had just set eyes on the Devil himself, and maybe he had.

By the early spring the patience of my father's creditors had run out and on a day in March a removal van came to pick up the few bits and pieces of furniture and household utensils which we had been allowed to keep in order to pursue a modest, if very meagre existence. The car, most of the furniture, the paintings, Dad's shotguns, his trophies, most of our books, the Royal Copenhagen porcelain figurines and everything else that had formed the framework of our lives was left behind to be sold at auction. I did not want to look back and see the white house retreating into the distance. I looked straight ahead. Oddly enough, I do not remember the removal man, only that he had a wooden figure of a naked African woman hanging from his rear-view mirror. It was a dull day with rain in the air and a stiff west wind blowing. Fritz sat stony-faced next to me on the front seat of the removal van. He did not look to right or left. There was only just enough room for the two of us in the new lorry. Dad and Mum had to take the bus to Odense with Teddy and the train from there to our new home in Jutland. The last I heard of them was Teddy's howls and Dad's deep voice rebuking him for being such a cry-baby.

Fritz and I had received a hug from Mum and a handshake from Dad. My father's face was pale, but his eyes were red and bloodshot. I did not want to say goodbye to the house. Nor did

I want to cry. I was not going to give those hateful people that satisfaction. While Fritz made a round of the half-empty rooms I sat on the steps, gazing across at the vicar's enormous beech tree. The curtains were drawn over there and the village was deserted. Strangest of all, no sound emanated from the bakehouse, and no smell. The fragrant odour of sugar and flour, and the distinctive clunk made by the biggest of the mixers as it kneaded the dough for the rye bread and a slight bump in the rotor shaft knocked against the bowl at every turn. The creditors had had a padlock put on the bakehouse door. A man known as the 'Royal Bailiff' had taken care of this matter. What a fitting name for a person representing the nameless denizens of a pseudo-democracy who wield power for international capitalism.

No neighbours came out to say goodbye to us. I did not realise that this was the last time I would see the father I knew, and that not until years later would I see his ghost when, thanks to you, we held hands across the decades, before death took him for good and all.

18

SOME DAYS HAVE PASSED. They keep asking me questions about my life and my contacts. But they have nothing. They may think that Stasi's Edelweiss and I are one and the same person. But they do not know for sure. It is hard to believe that they would waste so much money and manpower on a past which died along with Soviet communism. What does any of that matter today? And yet it is like something straight out of Kafka: they cannot prove my guilt, so it's up to me to prove my innocence. They are interviewing everyone I have ever known. The prospect of punishment does not worry me. By delving into my life and revealing its most intimate details to friends, family and colleagues they have already punished me. They have branded me, and that mark will never wash off. In this they have been ably supported by the conservative press, which swallows police statements raw. But that's not hard to understand, is it? You and I know that the conservative press is as easily bought as a Hamburg whore.

They keep going back to an incident in the Baltic states. A case which, since it dates from 1987, they feel is still recent enough to be prosecuted. Possibly even so serious that the statute of limitations has never run out on it. Because it involved the loss of lives, in some of the Soviet Union's last executions for treason. The victims had apparently been denounced by a Western spy. It's insane, really. As if that could be of interest to anyone today. But that is just how it is. The one side's spies are the other side's traitors. And the final verdict rests always with the victors. That is how it has always been. And that is how it was for my father.

I tell them I don't know what they are talking about. That I do not know who Edelweiss is. They've got the wrong person. I am a scholar and a woman and I have never had access to confidential information. That is their weak spot. They can find no link between what I'm supposed to have done and my work as an academic and exposer of late capitalism's oppression of women. They keep harking back to the fact that for two years in the mid-sixties I had a student job with the Ministry of Foreign Affairs. Good God! That's such a long time ago! Such an awfully long time ago – I was only a young girl, photocopying freely available information for men who thought themselves very important. That is not enough. Even one of capitalism's own judges would not agree to me being imprisoned for something that happened so many years ago. Then they say that I might have recruited others back then. And I have to laugh. They have no proof of that either. But they keep going on about that time because it is the only period in my life during which I have had access to anything other than public information. They're getting desperate, because my remand warrant is about to run out and I know that they know they'll have a hard job getting yet another extension. My lawyer says the same. He is full of contempt for them. They have no case. And yet they go through the masquerade because they feel compelled to come up with a scapegoat, with the right wing now baying for blood in the conservative press – which, in Denmark today, means the media as a whole.

They weren't all that interested ten years ago, when the Wall came down. Well, why would they be? I look around me in this country: all of my old friends and allies, my comrades from the meetings, groups, collectives, consciousness-raising groups, party schools and pioneer camps are now firmly in control of government, business and the media. They have put the past behind them. It is time to move on. It was all just an innocent bit of fun. I am not like them. Mistakes were made, but no amount of trendy make-up can disguise the evils of capitalism. Look over the welfare walls of Europe and America and the poverty and misery will hurt your eyes. The objective course of history will not be denied. Scholars of the future will look back on the time around the turn of the century as a somewhat inexplicable setback before the peoples of the Third World set out to take back what imperialism had stolen from them.

So maybe I will soon be released from this inhuman solitary confinement, in which I have actually got to the point of looking forward to seeing my tormentors at those interminable interrogations. That is what happens to people when they are cut off from their fellow human beings. They become attached to their persecutors, driven mad as they are by loneliness and the lack of social contact. Even such a thorn in the side as that witless stud Toftlund is welcome. He has just shown up again, can barely move for testosterone, struts around as if he were God's gift to women. But rather this atavistic macho man than that searing solitude in which time stands still and every day is the same. I have regular talks with my lawyer, but always on a strictly professional footing. Usually he is also with me when I am questioned, but not always. Sometimes I agree to being interviewed without my lawyer being present.

The fact is, you see, that occasionally I am surprised to find these sessions intellectually stimulating. It is like sitting an exam, and I have a lifetime's experience of exams, whether sitting or setting them. During the interrogation sessions, as in the examination room, assertions are made and one tries to make sense of the argumentation, dissect the hypotheses, find the weak points and expose the examinee's ignorance or the gaps in the examiner's own fund of knowledge by analysing the substance of the questions.

Toftlund does not know anything either. Like an angler he casts his line haphazardly. Thinks he is digging up bait from old yellowing files from Berlin. I cannot help but smile at their naivety. They believe that the Stasi files contain an objective truth. As if they were historical documents which would be of use to serious scholars. But Stasi did not write the truth. Stasi wrote what is, still, a work of fiction in which agents and informers, spies and controllers, guilty and innocent, were all – wittingly or unwittingly – figures in a bizarre serial. It was not about reporting the truth. It was about making oneself seem important and impressing one's superiors. An innocent exchange of opinions over lunch would, in a report, become a revealing conversation concerning the strategic considerations of the other side. An article in a newspaper on a forthcoming defence agreement became a classified summary of NATO's plans for the Baltic region. No one ever expected these reports to be read. No one imagined there would ever come a time when these exaggerations, distortions, half-truths and downright lies would be studied for the purposes of research. No historian would ever do that. A historian deals in historical facts, not interpretations. But the intelligence service is not interested in the objective truth. It is only interested in finding a scapegoat. And I am it.

Toftlund has been away for a couple of days, but he came back armed with questions about my father. I told him that was none of his business. It was a personal matter. Private. His questions worried me, though. He also asked about you. He shouldn't have known anything about you. As always, it hurt to have that part of my past raked up again. He said that everything was his business. When one was accused of a serious crime, there was no such thing as privacy. Not for the accused, nor for that person's close family and friends. A crime did not only involve the perpetrator and the victim. The secrets and mental blocks of their nearest and dearest were no longer sacrosanct. Even casual acquaintances could be called in, their statements taken down, secrets revealed. A police investigation lays a person's life bare in much the same way as a surgeon lays bare a growth, in order to cut away the diseased tissue. That was the image he used. Even his metaphors are rotten, they reek of male chauvinism.

I told him I had nothing to say. My father had left us in 1953, shortly before my thirteenth birthday and was declared dead the following year. That was the expression the authorities used:

declared dead. And it was that same wording which nurtured my hopes of his return. My mother remarried in 1955. My step-father adopted Teddy, but Fritz and I would have none of that, we wept as if our hearts would break and my mother bowed to our wishes.

Naturally the police have interviewed my mother, but her senility is so far advanced that nothing she says is of any use to them. That much was plain to me from Toftlund's manner. She keeps contradicting herself and cannot remember whether she is ninety years old or twelve. One minute she says that Dad has gone for a walk, or is over in the bakehouse. The next, that she has never known a man by that name and that her husband died five years ago. It does not help, of course, that both her husbands bore the same good Danish surname: Pedersen. Teddy alone adopted the middle-name of Nikolaj, from my step-father. My mother's memory is like one of those play pits full of little coloured plastic balls which kids happily hop about in while their parents are shopping or having lunch. In the same way, the balls of her memories bounce willy-nilly around her calcified brain.

Teddy came to see me today. He gave me a hug and held my hand across the table at which we are allowed to sit and talk. This was the one weekly private visit granted me in my solitary confinement. A prison guard seated on a high-backed chair monitored our conversation, which I am sure was also recorded. There are limits to how deep a conversation one can have under such conditions, but it's better than nothing. Other than that all I have to distract me are the sessions with my tormentors and the couple of times each day when I am allowed to stretch my legs in the enclosed prison yard – though always alone. I consider myself a law-abiding citizen and yet I dream of being able to stroll around the yard along with the other inmates. To take the morning air with murderers, rapists and thieves would be like receiving an unexpected gift. To eat my meals with others would be a sheer delight, even if my companions were serious felons of the first water. That is how much I yearn for human company.

Teddy was looking a bit rough. He said he had both backache and toothache; it was part of the price you had to pay for growing older. I found that quite funny. Typical male whinging. I am eight years older than Teddy and sound as a bell, mentally and physically. I don't feel my age, but I do take care of myself. That Teddy has never done, and all his good living is starting to show on his face and body, but he is still his old, charming self. He gave me all the gossip from the academic world: who had won what grants, who was about to deliver their thesis, who could bask in the reflected glory of their clever Ph.D. students' success and get their name into the academic journals, whose name was in the papers, who had been interviewed on TV, which of my fellow lecturers had attempted to put a stop to NATO's crazy war, who was sleeping with whom. The wonderful stuff of the everyday to which you never give a second thought until you are deprived of it. He made me laugh out loud several times. And it was so nice to hear him call me 'sis' and 'Irma, my lass' as he always did, and still does even though I'm pushing sixty. He was always the apple of our eyes. I wonder if maybe Fritz and I compensated for our bitterness and disappointment by projecting all the love we felt we had lost onto little Theodor with his golden curls – they didn't turn brown until he was well up in years.

Obviously we could not talk about what was really on our minds. Teddy asked how I was, of course, and I shrugged, and then he said I looked thinner, but I was still his lovely Irma with the stunning eyes. That's my baby brother, always ready with a compliment and a little white lie, but stupid he is not and he knew it was best to leave certain things unsaid.

The hour went all too quickly. As it was drawing to a close he could not resist asking:

'What really happened to your father?'

I noticed he said *your* father. Teddy regarded our mother's second husband as his dad. He didn't remember anything else, and our step-father had spoiled little Teddy rotten. There was never any talk of a wicked step-parent in Teddy's case. I thought for a moment. He was holding my hand across the table, but he let it go and lit a cigarette, and even though I gave up smoking years ago I took a cig from his pack and lit it. It tasted strange, I felt my head swim for a second. It brought back memories of my youth. One single, sublime drag and I was transported back to a time of smoke-filled bars, loud voices, long hair and twanging guitars. Night-long philosophical discussions about the need for revolution and the liberating, consciousness-raising process of feminism. Into my mind, too, came a picture of a long-forgotten lover and a morning in a bed with the light streaming through the window along with the May birdsong. All of that in a couple of drags, then I stubbed out the cigarette in the ashtray and took Teddy's hand again.

'I thought he died in Hamburg,' I said, leaning across the table, so that we looked like a couple of lovebirds in a café. 'That was what the police told us. Found in the harbour. The body had almost disintegrated, it had been in the water for weeks. There were some signs of foul play, though. A contusion on the head. Dad's passport was in the jacket pocket, it too had almost fallen apart completely, but was still barely legible. End of story.'

He considered me:

'Ah, but is it? I met a woman in Bratislava, Irma.'

'We don't need to go into that right now.'

'She said she was my half-sister, and that our father died less than a year ago.'

I looked at him. He looked back at me. There was a look of desperation in his eyes. A frantic longing to know the whole story and since it sounded from Toftlund's questions as if they must know something of it, I decided that I might as well confirm Teddy's suspicions.

'It's true,' I said.

'What is?'

'That Dad died just under a year ago and you have a half-sister.'

| 257 |

'Jesus Christ. Why the hell did no one ever tell me? Does Fritz know?'

'Fritz has known for some years.'

'But not little brother?'

'Would it have mattered to you?'

He sat for a moment, puffed on his cigarette and said quietly:

'No, sis. To be honest, no, it wouldn't.'

'There you are then.'

'She showed me a picture of him in SS uniform. Fucking disgusting.'

'Don't be so childish. You're a historian. You know how it was.'

'Was he there on the Eastern Front. Did he lock up and torture decent Danish men and women?'

'Yes to the first. A definite no to the second. But I think we should save this until I'm released.'

'Will you be?'

'Yes. They have nothing on me.'

'They've been questioning me too, and other people. About your revolutionary past.'

'I never did anything illegal.'

'What about all your lot's talk of revolution and bombs. Christ, you even had your own little newspapers. You were all so flaming high-minded that you wouldn't give house room to any opinions but your own.'

That angered me, he saw it in my eyes and drew in his horns.

'Sorry, sis. That sounded worse than it meant to. But Christ, the seventies was a weird time.'

'Could I have another cigarette?' I asked, and he lit one for me. This time it only tasted of smoke. It would be easy to start smoking again, it takes the edge off and gives you something to do with your hands. Like being a baby again, stuffing something in your mouth and being soothed by it.

I said: 'Having such high principles probably did engender a certain lack of sensitivity. The aim justified the means. I freely

| 258 |

admit it. Some people remember the late-sixties as a dream, a time of hope, of euphoria. My own memories are actually tinged with bitterness at the implacability of the men in particular. My good memories are associated with the solidarity of the women's movement. I do miss that sometimes. But the male revolutionaries? No thanks. I also admit that the ghost of totalitarianism hovered over our ranks, but the revolution never came to anything. Our principles were not put to the test, as Dad's were. For the large majority of us theorising was as far as it went. The Danes did not want revolution. We did not have to choose which side to fight on in a war.'

'Thank God for that.'

'You're an old social democrat, Teddy.'

'Oh, no – I'm not anything, really. Slightly to the left, tending towards the centre, Danish wishy-washy, that's my style.'

I smiled at him, my unprincipled little brother:

'There was no actual risk attached to any of it, for me or the others. We took it very seriously, of course, all the time knowing, perhaps, that it was only a phase. And if you really want to know, I changed my outlook in the early nineties, after the Wall came down. I don't suppose there is any way round the reforms. Totalitarianism is not the answer. The cost is too high. I have laid the totalitarian ghost, Teddy. Besides, I've always been a good girl, dutifully attending to my studies, my lectureship, my students and, eventually, my professorship.'

'Better late than never,' he said, and I felt a surge of resentment at his implicit disdain. He had never had any principles to speak of and like most people with no principles he found it easy to judge.

'Oh, well,' he said. 'They can't do you for that, anyway. If they did, they'd have to collar a whole load of the nation's finest sons and daughters along with you, haul them out of Parliament and Danmarks Radio and managing editors' offices and wherever else the revolution's somewhat ageing advance guard now spends its respectable, market-oriented time. They'd have trouble fitting them all in here, I tell you. But it's like I've always said: words are cheap in this country. They have no consequences.'

'I'm sure you're right, Teddy. But don't worry. They have nothing on me. This is just the last shock wave from the front line of the cold war. I'll be out soon.'

'I'm glad to hear it, sis. I mean, what would we do without you? You're what holds the family together.'

I could tell there were a lot of private questions he wanted to ask, but he could see from my face that this would not be wise, not with so many ears – both human and electronic – listening in. We sat for a moment or two, holding hands, and then, unable to resist, he said:

'What's her name, this dear sister I've suddenly acquired?'

'Mira. Mira Majola.'

'Very pretty sounding, I must say, but she told me her name was Maria.'

'Some other time, brother mine.'

The prison guard coughed and announced that our time was up, we would have to say our goodbyes. Sorry, he said, quite kindly really, but those were the rules. I could picture Toftlund with the headphones over his ears, cursing this stickler for cutting us off just as the conversation was getting interesting. I would have loved to spend the whole afternoon with Teddy anywhere else but the Western Prison, but I was also happy that the time was up. I was in no mood for sharing family secrets with the intelligence service's great, hearkening ear.

We both stood up, hugged, and Teddy whispered in my ear:

'So what's your feeling about our real father, sis?'

'How do you mean?'

'Nazi, bigamist, traitor to his country and his family. A murderer too, for all we know. Whose was that body in Hamburg harbour with his passport on it? Have you ever wondered about that? Because that's one hell of a note.'

I felt anger well up inside me, but I did not want to part from my little brother on bad terms, so I did not rise to the bait. Instead I simply said:

'You don't understand, Teddy. But one day it will all be explained to you. And then you'll understand. But not now and not here.'

'Alright, sis,' he said and gave me a squeeze, although I could tell that it hurt his back. 'Take care. We can't wait to see you out of here.'

'Neither can I. Say hi to Fritz for me.'

'Right-oh.'

'And give Mum a call.'

'She doesn't understand a word you say.'

'She recognises your voice. Talk about the weather. It doesn't matter what you say. She just likes to hear our voices.'

'How can you tell. The inside of her head's like a chalk pit.'

I took a step backwards, laughed at him. He could always make me laugh.

'Teddy. Behave yourself.'

'Come home soon, sis. We miss you.'

'It won't be long now. Say hello to Janne too.'

'Will do, sis. Will do.'

He left and I was taken back to my cell, but not, strangely enough, to interrogation. Maybe they had to decipher and analyse my conversation with my little brother before coming back to plague me with questions which, more and more, seemed to go round in circles.

So I paced up and down my seven square metres, staring at the yellow walls and the tiny window. The light outside my cell had a blue cast to it today, as if the April sun was beginning to gain the upper hand. Easter can't be that far away. I sat down on my cot then got up again, my thoughts going back in time, as I tried yet again to remember.

The truth is that I can recall very little of the time after we trundled off in the removal van, leaving the village on the island of Fünen like thieves in the night. There are a couple of years which are shrouded in twilight in my memory. A darkness relieved only by a few fragmented recollections, but otherwise consisting of nothing but a dull, constant ache and a sense of loss.

19

THE FACT WAS that I felt betrayed, but I also missed my father as badly as only my adolescent heart could. I could not accept that he would willingly have left us. There had to be more to it than that: some deep, dark conspiracy which the grown-ups were keeping from me. My mind seemed to be caught in an eternal twilight. I do not think my mother was particularly aware of how I was feeling. I don't think she realised how unhappy I was. If she did then she certainly did not do anything about it. She wanted no hysterics, as she put it. In any case she had more than enough on her plate, getting us installed in a small three-room flat in a sedate provincial town in Jutland and creating a decent life for us in the thrifty fifties when times were still lean. Money was tight. Being a single mother with three young children was no picnic then either.

Mum was intelligent, she had taken her school-leavers' certificate. This gained her a job in a solicitor's office as a sort of general dogsbody. But it was not long before her sunny smile and quick wit made her indispensable to Mr Kelstrup the solicitor. He was a stout, rubicund widower in his early sixties, with a penchant for partaking of lengthy and substantial lunches at the town's quality restaurant in the Chamber of Commerce building, while a trainee took care of the most pressing business. Mr Kelstrup was an easygoing sort of man who did not worry too much about expensive academic qualifications. So in no time Mum was acting as secretary, personal assistant and even something of a sparring partner, whom her employer could bounce ideas off. There were not that many of them in the office, it was not a big practice. It dealt mainly with conveyancing, a bit of debt-collecting from lowlier members of the community, the execution of wills and the occasional court case, providing legal aid for petty criminals. Only later did I discover that he too had been on the wrong side in the war and had even spent six months at Faarhus Prison Camp for collaboration. His sentence had been suspended, though, and his licence to practise law restored to him. The last German refugees had been sent home long ago, or chased out like cattle, the last executions for treason carried out and most people in the town felt that, well, they had always known Mr Kelstrup the solicitor, and he was only a little fish. And besides, he was cheaper than the other solicitors in town, so for goodness sake. There was really no more to it than that. And anyway, plenty of folk had been taken with the thought of a *Neueuropa* in the days when everything had looked very different. As long as he remembered to put a light in the window on May 4th then he was no different from anyone else.

Mum was given some help getting started. By people who remained nameless, but also by Kelstrup. It was no accident that he should have given her a job at a time when his practice was not doing enough business to merit taking on another member of staff. But Mum was good for business. She was well-liked, she inspired confidence and she organised Mr Kelstrup's diary, thus ensuring that he kept all of his appointments – something which, due to his weakness for the delights of the table, he had not always been so good at doing. As a teenager I did not understand the set-up. This was something I only discovered later: how people discreetly tried to help one another, even when they had long since forsaken their old ideals. A small favour here and there. That was how it worked all over Denmark. And that, I suppose, is how it still works in my native land.

So my mother found her feet. Teddy was looked after by a nice lady known to us simply as Mrs Hansen, found through Mr Kelstrup, and Fritz had made a good pal with whom he spent all his time. The whole family quickly fell into a routine that did not differ from anyone else's. The essential thing was not to stand out. To have the same furniture and curtains as other Danes. To keep one's house and children neat and clean. To adhere to the bourgeois norms of the silent majority. Not to imagine one was anything special. Not to push oneself forward or show off.

At school we simply said that our father was dead, hinting that he had fallen in the battle for the Freedom of Denmark. When the boys played their war games Fritz was a resistance fighter as often as he was a German. You had to take turns. More and more often, though, they would play cowboys and Indians instead, inspired by the Westerns they saw at the cinema on Sunday afternoons. But in any event our Mum and Dad were not divorced. That we made very clear.

Pretty soon people ceased to take any great interest in why we had moved to the town. Society was changing. Maybe not so as you would notice yet, in the latter half of the fifties, but the old world was on its last legs and a new one was knocking at the door. When Fritz turned fourteen and, to his great relief, could finally leave school at the end of seventh grade, Mr Kelstrup secured him an apprenticeship to one of the local baker's. Fritz was happy at his simple, straightforward work – his main concern was whether his greased-back quiff made him look like James Dean.

Teddy was too young to understand. The one time Mum mentioned Dad's name was on the day after she got the job at Mr Kelstrup's office. She sat us down around the tile-topped coffee table and told us that now we were going to make a life for ourselves here. We had been granted a fresh start and starting afresh was never easy, but it was all going to be alright. We were not to say anything to anyone about our past, where we came from, or about Dad. The war was in the past now and the man in the street no longer gave it much thought. Only the newspapers still wrote about the resistance movement and those five accursed years. Ordinary people had other things to think about and we were now decent folk like all the rest. Which was good, and we should be happy about that. As usual, Fritz said nothing, but I asked about Dad. Mum took my hand and said:

'I'll be honest with you, pet. I don't know. He's been gone before, but he always came back.'

'Is he going to come back this time, Mum?' I asked, tears filling my eyes.

'I don't think you should count on that, Irma dear. I think you should consider your Dad dead.'

'He's not dead. He'll come back to us!' I had screamed, not surprisingly, and ran from the table to my bed, where I wept into my pillow and railed at Mum for letting Dad down until she came in to comfort me. She stroked my hair, which both pleased and infuriated me. She made soothing noises, but said nothing. I think she felt just as confused as I did, but as a woman her first instinct was to comply with the ways of a man's world, bow her head and accept the situation.

I appeared to be the only one with an aching heart, a hollow sense of longing and betrayal mingled with the hope of once more hearing my father whistling as he came up the stairs, this time to ring the bell on our nice, brown front door. It may sound as if I remember a lot, but I don't really. In actual fact, I only remember the feeling of loss and the terrible loneliness, because I did not form any close ties. I made no friends, had no school pals. I was not part of any of the giggling, whispering groups of girls who sauntered around the playground, arm in arm, pretending not to see the boys. But I was never bullied either. It was simply accepted that I was a bit of a weirdo, who did not play with the others or, later, talk to the boys, but just read books and was boring. I don't even remember my mother's marriage, at the town hall, to our head teacher and have only the vaguest memory of moving into his spacious headmaster's residence. I remember my room there, but I was sixteen by then and starting to emerge from the gloom. It is the years from thirteen to eighteen that are like a dark tunnel containing only brief flashes of recollection and I am not even sure whether these are things I remember or only heard about. Mum told me much later, when I was grown up, that she had been very, very worried about me. I wore away to a shadow, grew so thin that she had been seriously concerned for my health. And the onset of my periods was long overdue, or so both my mother and the doctor felt. The doctor recommended that I drink double cream and have regular phototherapy sessions at the hospital. You could have talked to me about Dad, I told my mother later when I was a grown woman, but she had looked hurt and replied that she had not wanted to waste any more of her life on that man. And anyway, she had had more than enough to do, providing food and clothing for three young children. Then later she had found a new husband who had been good to her and the children, so there had been no reason to go raking up the past. No good could come of that. She would never talk about him. It was almost as if she denied his very existence. She insisted on us calling the headmaster Dad. Fritz went along with it for the sake of peace and Teddy because he loved our step-father, but I absolutely refused, even though this earned me the only slap in the face my mother has ever given me. However, once she understood that I had no intention of relenting, she let it go. Possibly also because my step-father did not seem to have any problem with me calling him by his first name. Although, looking back on it, I think he was hurt. He had married late and felt that he had accepted his wife's family as his own. They had no children together. I don't know whether it was too late, or Mum didn't want to, or maybe my step-father couldn't have chldren.

I don't know why my mother married the headmaster. He was very much in love with her though. Anybody could see that. He adored her and would have done anything for her. Mum liked him for his patience and kindness and selfless love, but she was not the slightest bit in love with him. That much was obvious to me. She may have grown to love him eventually, but their's was not a passionate relationship. Mum went on working after she got married, which was still not all that common then. She already had the same surname as him, but she took a certain satisfaction now in introducing herself as Mrs Pedersen, the headmaster's wife. Perhaps she married him because he promised to be faithful to her and because he gave her financial security. In those days the headmaster was one of the leading lights of the community, a solid figure of authority who commanded respect. Perhaps she married him because he was dull and predictable and would never surprise her, positively or negatively, as Dad had continually done throughout their stormy, passionate years together.

By the time I learned Dad's secret it was too late to talk to her about it properly. Because by then my mother's brain could no longer distinguish between reality and fantasy. She inhabited her own imaginary world and I could not get through to her. Or was her ability to repress things so highly developed that even in her dementia she upheld the pretence of a happy marriage to just one man, my step-father?

Mum never knew that I lived a double life. That as a double agent I had one face which I presented to the world and another belonging to my secret life, into which no one was allowed entry. I was known as a quiet girl, with a reputation for being moody, but I worked hard at school. Because I had realised very early on that education was my ticket out of the prison in which I felt myself confined; that if I was to hold my own in the rough, tough, suppressive world of men then I would have to be smarter and better qualified than them. It had not taken me long to figure out that even the dumbest, most poorly educated man believed he had a right to lord it over women purely by virtue of his sex.

It was taken for granted that I would go to high school, even though at that time it was still not a matter of course for girls to do so. But my step-father, my mother and my teachers were all agreed that I was a very bright child and that, even if I was a little too withdrawn and did not show enough initiative in class, I was definitely high school material. My marks were always excellent. And I was never any trouble, which in those days was the ultimate seal of approval.

If only they had known how I felt inside. I hated them with all my heart. I hated their bourgeois way of life, their double standards, their concealment of the truth, their hypocrisy and their ability to shape the past to fit their present life. I saw the people around me as insects trapped in a bottle, fluttering about, beating their heads off the glass which, in their blind stupidity, they could not see. These people did not know they were imprisoned. That for all their surface gloss, they could not hide how haplessly they were formed by the spirit of the times. Their notion that the more they bought they happier they would be, that the good times were here and could only get better, made me sick. I was sure that my father would have seen right through them. He could not stand the complacency of Danish provincial life and had left us, not because he did not love us, but because our two-facedness made him sick at heart. Although obviously I knew nothing of it back then I intuitively perceived the repressive tolerance of capitalism and its exploitation of the individual. Although I could not have put it into words, my eyes were opened to the petit-bourgeois shackles of society.

I sought refuge in the world of books, read every book in the library. To read was to be alone. To read was to be left in peace. To read was to be free. And reading held at bay, at least for a while, the urge to kill every last one of them. The only thing I liked about my step-father was that his income made it possible for us to live in a house where I had my own room. With a door which I could shut and lock. Which no one could enter. A room of my own. Nothing unusual in that today, but in those days it was no more than a dream for most women. Because it was not just the four walls themselves that mattered, but the fact of having a place that was totally your own domain. Where you could be a free woman.

It was in this room that I endeavoured to understand what Denmark had been like under the German occupation. The local library was not a great help in this respect: most of its new acquisitions tended to be about the valiant freedom fighters and the

Danish resistance during those five dark years when the people had stood shoulder to shoulder. Shelves and shelves on that subject. But about the other side, about the collaborators and those who fought on the German side, there was next to nothing. But reading between the lines, in all the touched-up accounts and the things left unsaid, I divined the hypocrisy of it all, the misrepresentation of those years from 1940 to 1945. I realised it was a case of a collective memory lapse and a general consensus to stick to the myth. The truth was suppressed, only myths were created. Victims were unearthed and scapegoats appointed, my father being one of the latter. I instinctively understood in my head and in my heart that Nazism was a heinous ideology, and I wished I could have asked my father how he could serve such a system, but I could not. I never disputed the killing of the six million Jews, but I understood all the Nazi talk of a super-race. The idea that some people were born to lead the masses, who did not know any better and needed, therefore, to be moulded. And I saw also that even worse than Nazism were the double standards of the bourgeois, so-called democratic society and its cynical exploitation of the naivety of ordinary human beings. I am not sure if I was capable of expressing myself in such terms at that time, but that is how I felt. I had been betrayed by my father, who had been betrayed by the society in which he lived and had therefore been forced to act as he did. They said he had acted of his own free will. They wanted us to believe that people are free to choose. The truth, as I saw it, was that like a puppet he had been manoeuvred towards his inevitable fate.

So I was ripe for the picking when I met the man who initiated my awakening as a woman and as a human being. I was in third year at high school. It was early spring, with the time for some serious exam revision fast approaching. As so often before I was in the library, trying to find a book on the occupation which I had read about in the paper. Strictly speaking I had no time for reading novels, with so much studying to do for my exams, but I had not been able to resist this one. It had been published the year before and had at last found its way into the library.

I spotted him right away, stole glances at him out of the corner of my eye. He was young, early twenties. He looked different from other young men. His hair was long and fair, not slicked back with Brylcreme, but falling over his ears. It looked all soft and lovely. He wore brown corduroys and a thick sweater. He was tall and slim with limpid blue eyes and a high forehead. He looked a little like Jens August Schade, the poet, whom I had seen pictures of in the paper. They both had the same strong nose, but E–'s chin was more masculine, with a cleft in it. Almost like a film star's. I could make out the cleft through his closely trimmed beard. It was also unusual to see a man with a beard. He actually bore a slight resemblance to Frederik of Nina and Frederik. He had a strangely charismatic air about him, I felt. The sort of sexual magnetism which some people possess without even knowing it. I was a virgin, knew nothing of sex apart from the heat and longing that flared up between my legs at the most inconvenient moments. That was definitely not the sort of thing which respectable people talked about at home or at school. It felt somehow dirty and wrong, like the silly, sniggering remarks of schoolboys or the rude drawings which young men from the lower classes found amusing. I was familiar with my body's yearnings, even if I did not understand them and was even alarmed by them, but I could not imagine an attractive man ever seeing anything in me. I was short and skinny and I felt plain and awkward. E– said later that nothing could have been more wrong. I had the most beautiful, gentle, sad, yet striking eyes, small, well-formed breasts and skin as luminous and delicate as Thai silk. My well-turned, harmonious features were set off perfectly by the long hair which I pulled back into a ponytail. He told me he fell in love with me the minute he laid eyes on me. Both because my sex appeal, latent though it was, was so powerful, and because he instinctively felt that our destinies were linked, sensing as he did that I harboured a secret in my shattered heart. Even as a young man E– had a way with words.

He came over to me. I felt myself blush, but he took the book I was looking at out of my hand, as if we knew one another, and looked at the title page.

'Tage Skou-Hansen, *The Naked Trees*,' he read. His voice was husky, it almost seemed to crackle. 'This is a good novel actually, even if it does represent the official picture. But it's more realistic than all the other rubbish written about those years. You can safely read this. You won't be any stupider for it.'

I was flabbergasted by his words. It was unheard-of for anyone to speak of those years in such terms. Not with such detachment, showing no respect for the freedom fighters.

'What do you mean?' I asked stupidly.

'That it's time we took a more realistic look at that period. It was not so much a time of heroes and villains, as of victims.'

Those were the most remarkable words I had ever heard in my life. I did not know how to reply, or whether I even wanted to reply to this strange young man. But before I could say anything:

'Can I buy you a cup of coffee,' he said, taking my arm. 'You must have exams coming up soon, you can read all the novels you want after that.'

'How do you know I have exams coming up?'

'Well, you're obviously a student. You have that hunted look in your eyes that they all get at this time of year. But just bear in mind that this is the last lovely spring you'll have to miss out on. And besides, there's something else you really ought to read. I've got this collection of poetry by a new Danish writer – his name's Klaus Rifbjerg. You're going to be hearing a lot more of him. He is part of the future. The old guard can stuff their stupid conservativism.'

As he talked he was steering me towards the exit.

'I've no money to buy books,' was all I said. 'Do they have this guy Rifbjerg in the library?'

'I told you, I'll lend you the book. Or give you it. If you would like?'

'You can't just go giving your books away like that.'

'Of course I can. We should not be slaves to material possessions. The only things worth holding on to are the knowledge and insight we have between our ears.'

'What an odd thing to say.'

'The truth is sometimes odd, but that doesn't make it any the less true. Don't listen to all the garbage your teachers fill your poor student heads with. But get your degree, whatever you do, and then your life can begin. You still have to have the piece of paper, but you can forget everything you've learned.'

He was just making small talk really, but it was so new to me that I could not help laughing, something I rarely did. Nobody talked like that.

'What do you do when you're not spouting weird statements?' I asked, as if it was the most normal thing in the world for me to be walking with a young man in the lovely early spring light, which was lending the first touch of warmth to the keen wind blowing down the main street.

'I'm at Århus University, I'm writing a novel.'

He said it so matter-of-factly. As if it was perfectly natural for a person who was walking beside me to be writing a novel. To me, bookworm that I was, writers were like some sort of divine race who would never dream of mixing with ordinary mortals. But here I was, walking next to a man who said he was writing a novel, said it as casually as he might have said he was just running down to the baker's.

'Oh, and what's it about, this novel?'

'The truth.'

I laughed again. I do not know why. It's not as if it was not funny. Just unusual. We went down to Brodersen's pastry shop. He ordered coffee and pastries for us both. He was not to know that it was a totally new experience for me to eat a pastry with relish, but this I did, while we talked. I cannot remember the details of our conversation, only that it simply flowed. We chatted about books, about the approaching spring, about my teachers, whom I described with a wit I would never have believed I possessed, and about my forthcoming exams. A perfectly normal conversation of a sort which I had never had with a young man before. He ordered more coffee and then he walked me home. At the garden gate he asked:

'Would you like to go to the pictures with me?'

'Yes, please.'

'How about this evening?'

'I'll have to ask my parents.'

'Okay, why don't we ask them now.'

'They're not home.'

'Of course you can go, dear,' he said, making his voice deeper, and I laughed again and felt myself blush.

'I don't even know your name.'

He told me his name then asked:

'What's your name?'

'Irma.'

'It suits you.'

And with that we were friends. He shook my hand and walked off and I watched him go with a pounding heart. He was going to call for me at half past six.

To my great surprise I had no trouble obtaining permission to go to the cinema. Obviously they asked who this young man was and I told them he was a student I had met at the library a few times. My mother and step-father actually looked relieved and my step-father even gave me a whole five-kroner note, saying it was high time such a pretty girl had a boyfriend. Mum shook her head at him, but she looked pleased, for all her warnings not to be late home, I needed my sleep, had to be fresh for school the next day. I could tell it reassured them to see me acting like a normal girl, getting invited to the pictures, like all the others.

They were at the living-room window, watching, when E– came

to pick me up for the early evening showing. He had changed his clothes, was now wearing a pair of smart grey flannels, a tweed jacket and even a tie. I had put on a floral print dress with a broad belt, like the ones starlet Ghita Nørby wore, and had my hair in a ponytail. E– nodded to my mother and step-father through the window, offered me his arm and off we went to the pictures, for all the world as if this were not a first date, but simply the latest of many – it felt so natural, being with him. I was walking on air, but I was also absolutely terrified. I could not help wondering whether it was all a dream from which, at any moment, I would wake to the same old emptiness and loneliness.

I do not remember which film we saw. All I remember is his hand, soft, warm and dry, taking mine as the lights went down in the packed cinema. Afterwards we walked back along dark streets wet with rain which glistened so poetically in the glow of the street lamps that I found myself thinking that only a great writer could have described the magic of that evening. I was certain that a poet like Frank Jæger would have captured the mood of it perfectly.

We halted in the darkness between two street lamps and he turned me to face him. I had to stand on tiptoe to reach his lips. He kissed me, lightly at first, then probingly with his tongue, and I felt a flicker of heat between my legs. I had never kissed a boy before. I thought it was something you had to learn, but there was nothing difficult about it. He knew all about kissing so it was just a matter of following his lead. We kissed many, many times before we reached my house. It was one of the most unsettling experiences I had ever had. There was a light on in the living room, of course. The headmaster and my mother were silhouetted against the blind. E– played his cards well right from the start. Made sure that those in authority would never suspect a thing. He got me home on time and merely pecked me on the cheek when we said goodbye at the white garden gate in the light of the street lamp, but he knew that I took the taste of his tongue and lips into the house with me. That I could feel his hand on my breast.

From the very beginning he was an adept double agent who knew never to reveal his true identity to the enemy. Outwardly leading a life which accorded with the establishment's outmoded ideas of propriety and order, while at the same time pursuing another, secret, existence of which other people knew nothing, and of which they could never be a part. I lay in bed and thought about him and about that wonderful day, with my pillow squeezed tightly between my legs, and felt almost happy for the first time since my father had left me.

20

WHAT MORE IS THERE to tell you, sister? Only, perhaps, about the final, decisive chain of events. In which two people lay bare their lives, openly and honestly. It is night again. There is no moon tonight, only a dark chill from the tiny window, as if it were winter out there in the free air. I count the days until the next court hearing. They have to let me go, but with this system you can never be sure of anything. They will do anything they can to cover themselves, although they will of course dress up their coercive methods in legal jargon. The bourgeois, capitalist society in a nutshell, wouldn't you say: hypocrisy is its mainstay, dissemblance the key to understanding it, and, at its core, lies and self-deception? But they will not break me. I will be strong, as I have been all my life. As I needed to be, in order to survive in the cold, harsh, materialistic world of men.

This I learned from E– during the first, wonderful summer after I met him. The summer of 1958, when the weather went haywire, with frost in June and rain, rain, rain all summer through. But I didn't care if the sun didn't shine. I was eighteen and a high-school graduate. The legal age of majority was still twenty-one then, but I had already gained my independence. My step-father and my mother accepted that I should be able to live my own life now. They had no real worries about me either. I was a good, sensible girl, after all. I had graduated with flying colours, praised by all my teachers. They too had noticed how I had blossomed, and how I spoke up more in class. Besides which, my fiancé from Århus was such a nice, polite young man. In his tweed sports jacket and tie and neatly pressed slacks he could look like every mother-in-law's dream when he wanted to. He had also chosen to study a subject with excellent prospects. He was so good to Irma and so well-spoken. You really could not complain, not when you saw the sorts of characters other parents' daughters brought home these days. They had not met his parents. But there was time enough for that. Irma was possibly a bit on the young side, but it certainly looked as if these two young people planned to get married once the young man had got a bit further with his studies. And his father was something with the State Railways over on Zealand. So he came from a good, solid background. A respectable family. Well, you could see that – his manners were excellent. The only thing that struck them as rather odd was that Irma wanted to go to university in Copenhagen, and not in Århus, but teenagers nowadays were so restless and independent. Life was good in little Denmark. The younger generation already appeared to have forgotten those five terrible years. They took their nice, secure life for granted. They never gave a thought to what we went through. No, the young did not always appreciate what their parents' generation had endured, but Irma was a good girl who knew how to say 'Thank you'. She would have to find herself a job now, though: a university education cost money and they couldn't afford to do more than help out every now and again. Well, it was the least they could do. And of course Copenhagen was a long way off, but there was work to be had there. And it was true that if you wanted to study literature, then the University of Copenhagen, with its long and illustrious history, was the place to be. If nothing else, at least they had helped her to find a room. Not big, but neat and clean and with a nice family.

So my mother went on, all summer long, pleased as punch with her clever and now – so everyone said – pretty daughter. Fritz was doing well too, a big, strong lad with his journeyman's papers within reach and, thereafter, a job with a big bakery in Odense obtained for him by Mr Kelstrup the solicitor. And Theodor was still just sweet little Teddy whom everyone spoiled. My mother's gratitude that life had worked out so well for her despite the dark years, as she called her life with my father, was almost palpable.

Had they but known. As it was, they had no idea that I had stepped out of my darkness and into a secret life to which only E– and I were privy. In any case, my mother and step-father were only interested in material things. They no longer listened reverently to the radio, or read books. Instead they sat in front of the monstrosity of a television they had purchased. Sat there staring at the test card or the black-and-white clock with the hands that ticked round, marking the time until the programmes started. The new household altar had made its entry into the small Danish homes. My mother and step-father also bought a little car. A green Volkswagen Beetle, only slightly used. Like all other middle-class Danes they took to going on Sunday drives, equipped with a thermos of coffee and camping stools. Fritz had no desire to go with them. All he was interested in was his bored-out moped – that and girls. I, too, always found excuses, but young Teddy thought it was great fun to go for a drive on a Sunday. There they would sit at the side of the road, the little nuclear family – letting everyone get a good look at their *nice* car while they drank coffee, ate their sandwiches and had such a *nice* time. God, how I hate *nice*! Later they also went on their first package tour, travelling by bus to Harzen in Germany and from there all the way to the Mediterranean with Spies, Denmark's first package tour operator. The good times were finally here, they sighed with typical Danish smugness.

All of this suited me down to the ground. It left me free to live my own life, and have my other life with E–. To be honest, it was a miracle that I did so well in my high-school finals: I had no thought for anything but E–. One look at his picture and my stomach would start to flutter. Even when reading one of my favourite authors I would suddenly fall to daydreaming about the world we shared, and miss having him near. I felt I knew every inch of his body and yet it continued to surprise me. But three years of hard work and conscientious study at high school paid off. I knew my stuff. Not only that, but E– insisted that I study properly for my exams. Whatever opportunities the future might have to offer would go to those with a good academic education. We would be the new ruling class. The coming aristocracy, but born of the people, whom we would guide and liberate. He also had to study for an exam, so until the summer holidays we only saw one another from Saturday to Sunday.

He rented a room in Århus and I would visit him there whenever I could scrape together the train fare. He came to my house when we knew that the headmaster and Mum were going for a drive. We sent Fritz off into town. We went to bed together for the first time only a week after our first date. I was nervous and scared, as one might expect, but he was gentle and experienced, with warm, soft fingers and patient, persuasive lips, so it only hurt a little. And very soon I could not get enough of it. How odd and wrong it seemed that sex had not figured in my life before. An erotic being had apparently been slumbering inside me. E– woke that being, and the discovery and exploration of my sexuality was like an unexpected, unguessed-at gift: a side of being a woman which no one had told me about. It would take the future women's movement to find words to describe female sexuality and its age-long suppression, but E– understood, accepted and enjoyed the fact that the female libido is every bit as great and legitimate as the male. This may seem obvious today, but in 1958 it wasn't. Although we did not know it, in the permissiveness of our relationship we were actually part of a consciousness-raising process which sowed the seeds of the rebellion against the established, hypocritical society. All unwittingly, we were in at the conception of what would grow into the student revolt of the late sixties and the massive left-wing revivalist movement in the seventies. We were pioneers. In our discussions and our reading too: Camus, Sartre, the banned Henry Miller, the exciting new Danish writer Klaus Rifbjerg, Erik Knudsen, and later Marx. But most of all in the music which we played on his new record player: jazz and rock, the music of this new age. E– taught me about the ways of the world; thanks to him I matured early, as a woman and as an intellectual.

It was E– who arranged for me to be fitted with a diaphragm before we went on a cycling holiday that summer, which did have its warm, sunny moments, but was for the most part wet and stormy. We did not mind the rain, though. We put up our little tent, crawled into our sleeping bag and made love with the rain hammering off the canvas. At the end of July E– got a student job with one of the ministries in Copenhagen and it was only logical for him to switch university. He helped me move in to my little room. We could not live together without being married, and although I am sure I would have said yes had he proposed, there was never any thought of this. There was a tacit understanding that marriage would hinder our development as free individuals. Besides which, E–, and I, felt it was vital that I should take my degree. I would be the family's first academic. Education was synonymous with freedom. We were going to be part of a new movement, one which would cast off the bourgeois norms. We might even move to Paris, live with the other existentialists on the Left Bank and, like Sartre and Simone de Beauvoir, be lovers, discussion partners and comrades.

I loved Copenhagen from the word go. I loved the anonymity of the big city, the dense traffic, the life and the sounds of the night and my classes at university, because I found most of the professors interesting, even if they were like gods, preaching to us little students from on high. I rarely went home to Jutland. In my first year I possibly went back only once or twice. I think my mother was hurt, but I had my own life to live. And so what if we never seemed to have any money? Looking back on it I don't really know what we lived on. But almost everybody was hard up, so it did not matter. It was all part of being young and at university. The only person I missed was Teddy. Mum told me later that he asked for me almost every day.

But my new life outweighed even my love for my little brother.

It was also E– who first suggested we test our sexual boundaries. I still remember the first time he tied me down and told me to say the word if I felt violated or frightened, but that the pain would take me to new heights of desire and pleasure. That pain and desire were two sides of the same coin. That through these forbidden games we would attain an undreamt-of sense of unity, so deep that it would bind us to one another for ever. And he was right. We were never wholly separated. There was always a bond tying us to the past and the other life we shared alongside our everyday existences. It goes without saying that we could not stay together in the traditional sense. Or remain faithful only to one another, as the Danish establishment preached, once the waves of change began to wash over our lives, bringing ban-the-bomb marches, the pill, the student revolt, free love, travel, Women's Lib and the revolutionary awareness that came as a natural consequence of our development.

So, as I say, marriage was never on the cards. That was only a line we fed the grown-ups when we were very young, so that we could be together in the narrow-minded, bourgeois Danish society. We wanted to be free, original individuals, untrammelled by the ties of convention. This was not as easy as it may sound, but it was a necessary progression if the shackles of the old order were to be broken.

Throughout our lives we were, however, true to each other on another, much higher plane. True to our innermost convictions and, in spite of the setbacks, true to our realisation that only a new social order could fundamentally alter the state of global injustice which keeps the majority of the world's population in abject poverty while the rest of us, led by the United States, live high on the hog thanks to this inhuman exploitation.

And then there was our own private secret, which E– shared with me at Christmastime in 1960, when I had come home for the holidays, knowing I would have the house to myself. Fritz and Teddy had gone with the headmaster and Mum to spend Christmas with our step-father's brother in Tønder. They had left on the 22nd. The weather was wet, but mild. Even so, we spent most of our time indoors. We made food together, talked, drank schnapps and lemonade, listened to music, danced, experimented and enjoyed not having to worry about the neighbours as we did in Copenhagen, where only the thin walls of our rooms separated us from other people. There was such physical and mental satisfaction in using our bodies, conscious of how naturally in accord they were, like two finely tuned instruments. The heavy curtains were drawn, the door locked. We had the radiators turned full on, wore as little clothing as possible and I was gloriously happy. I never asked him what he did when he wasn't with me, or whether he had anyone else. Nor did he ask me, but I knew that he was less readily prey to the green-eyed monster than I was. I tried to fight off this feeling, but it hurt to think I might be sharing him with other girls. He did not lose his temper on those occasions when, nonetheless, I hinted that I felt jealous. He only laughed, showing his strong, white teeth and said that right here and now we were together and nothing else existed. I was hopelessly in love with him, but I knew – and this was what really hurt – that if I were to express this love in standard, conventional terms, I would lose him. I would rather have him to myself completely every now and again, than lose him completely. That was what my heart said. My mind was in unconditional agreement with his revolutionary talk of sexual freedom as a logical consequence of personal and political liberation. But, then as now, a person does not simply throw away all their historical baggage and everything that has made them who they are without some cost and emotional upheaval.

It was on Christmas Eve that he told me another of his secrets, when he confessed that he had not simply happened to run into me in the library, but had come there looking for me. We were lying in bed, smoking. The bedroom was in semi-darkness, lit only by candles, their flickering light tracing patterns on our sweat-soaked naked bodies. He lay on his back. There were red welts across his chest from the whip, I caressed them lightly with my lips. I had removed the handcuffs from his wrists and we were both sated and content. While everyone else in Denmark was dancing around the Christmas tree we had been acting out our fantasies. We felt so superior to all those common little slaves to convention. There was more cheap wine on the table next door and in a little while we would go through to the kitchen and rustle up something to eat. It was the best Christmas I had had since I was a girl during the war. We had entered upon a new decade. In the October E– and I had marched the sixty kilometres from Holbæk in the west of Zealand to Copenhagen along with eight hundred other pioneers from the new left wing, in protest against the A-bomb, that appalling weapon. I remember the stiff wind and the rain pelting down on all those hundreds of young people. But the weather was nothing to us because we were all part of a new phenomenon, unlike anything the world had ever seen. We did not know the term – it had not yet entered the Danish language – but we represented Denmark's first grassroots movement. The radio and television stations boycotted the march and made no mention of it whatsoever. As so often before we felt the tide of history sweeping across the country. Although I could not know it that Christmas in 1960, come Easter we would march again. Despite the snow and sleet our ranks would swell from less than two thousand marchers when we raised our placards in Holbæk to over ten thousand by the time we reached Copenhagen. The Campaign for Nuclear Disarmament was the first big step forward. Lying in bed on that Christmas Eve I knew that we had entered a decade which, I was sure, would change Denmark and the rest of the world for ever.

E– cleared his throat and said:

'Irma, I love you.'

Those banal little words made me feel faint with happiness.

'I love you too.'

'Merry Christmas, Irma.'

'Merry Christmas to you too.'

'And because I love you I'm going to tell you something. But you have to promise not to be mad at me.'

'Why should I be mad at you?'

'I know who your father is.'

He knew me. I got mad. He was trespassing on emotional territory where not even he was allowed to tread. Invading the private, locked room to which only I held the key. I lifted my lips off his chest and dug a fingernail into one of the red welts.

'Ow! Je-sus!' he yelled and shot up in bed, so suddenly that I almost rolled off it.

'That hurt,' he said.

'I thought you liked that.'

'You promised me you wouldn't be mad.'

He regarded me with eyes which, while they shone with indignation, were also playful and calculating. As if in everything he did there lay the germ of an experiment, a way of testing other people, a study of transience and the lack of control. Even in those days he was extremely charismatic, a great seducer and manipulator, but probably also, in truth, cold and callous. This was a side of his character with which I never came to terms. I can see now that I may not fully have understood the way his mind worked, and I never penetrated his most secret recesses. Then, as now, it was hard for me to understand how he could be so well-balanced, articulate and in control in his outward, everyday life, yet in the dimness and intimacy of the bedoom liked to be dominated and totally defenceless. Because that became the pattern after our first experiments. In bed, as a rule, we swapped roles. Not always, though. I too had come to know and to appreciate the link between pain and desire. But we only indulged in these forbidden pursuits every now and again. As if fearing that it could be a very slippery slope. We had no formal knowledge about what we did. Such things were not spoken of, or written about. More often than not we simply made love in the normal way, passionately and joyously, seemingly unable to get enough of one another.

I stubbed out my cigarette, lit another and smoked it, with E– eyeing me searchingly: he knew I would calm down once his

| 285 |

words had sunk in. He leaned back against the bed-head, then swung his legs out of bed, got up and fetched two glasses of red wine. He handed me one, still without saying a word. I drained my glass in three big gulps and placed it on the floor. He sipped his own wine and set his glass down on the other side of the bed. I looked at him and was filled with love for him. We sat cross-legged, facing one another, like a couple of Red Indians, and he began gently to stroke my breasts and my face.

'Little Irma. You and I have no secrets from one another, but there's a time for everything.'

'You surprised me, that's all,' I said, and heard the faint tremor in my voice.

'That's because you're ashamed.'

I felt my temper rise:

'What would you know about that?'

'I just know, that's all. Because your shame is a reflection of the shame I once felt. Because in the eyes of society we're branded. We're bound to inherit the sins of our fathers. Society demands it of us.'

'I'm not with you,' I said, hearing myself how thick my voice sounded.

He lifted my hand and kissed it, leaned forwards, took my cigarette, put it out, kissed me on the lips and eased me down onto my back with my head on the pillow; then he began to talk, while his warm, gentle hands stroked my body, as if he were giving me some new sort of healing massage.

'My uncle and your father fought together on the Eastern Front. I don't know exactly what happened to your father, but I've seen a picture of him with your mother, you and Fritz. Your father's in uniform in it. I found this picture in the attic at home among a lot of other old stuff left by my father and my uncle. It wasn't hard to see Irma the child in Irma the teenager, and your mother was easily recognisable. I knew who you were the first time I saw you on the street. You must have been about fifteen, you came walking

| 286 |

towards me with your mother. A chance meeting, but such things don't really happen by chance. You and I were always meant to meet. I'm convinced of it. The fact that my aunt lives where she does was no coincidence. So I found out who you were. And tied up whatever information I was able to unearth with the things my father and uncle had told me when I was a little boy. When I felt you were old enough, and could no longer fight my longing for you I made contact with you. The happiest contact I have ever made. What I know about that time I learned from my uncle and father. And from what I read. Like you I tried to piece together the forgotten, hidden story.'

He paused, took a swig of his wine, put the glass back on the floor, lit a cigarette and let me take a couple of drags. I did not raise my head from the pillow, merely gazed at him, captivated by the beginning of his story, his gentle hands, which I longed to have running over me again, the strangely suggestive tone of his voice and the sense, beyond the heavy curtains, of a dark and rainy Christmas night cloaked in the strange hush that hangs over Denmark on Christmas Eve, when everyone is indoors.

We took turns smoking the cigarette. There was no one in the world but us and we had all the time in the world. Then he went on:

'My father did not fight at the Front. We'll come back to him. My uncle's name was Karl Viggo. In 1940, after Denmark was occupied, he and my father went to Germany to work like so many thousands of others. They had no choice. They either took the work or lost their unemployment benefits. They were impressed with the Germans' sense for order and discipline and the fact that jobs were found for everyone. Prime Minister Stauning was actually a social democrat, but once even he had spoken of the inevitability of the new order, it was only a short step to national socialism. It was easy for them to accept that the Jews were the root of all evil. Because the Jews were the symbol of capitalism. Weren't pawn-brokers always Jewish? Even in the works of Shakespeare. And hadn't Johannes V. Jensen said that the Nordic race was special? Didn't rational men on national radio talk about the Germans' new order? And had the government not called on everyone to cooperate? My father was not a clever man. He was a simple smith who took care of his wife and their baby – that was me – and kept himself to himself. Karl Viggo joined the Danish Legion, but my father was rejected as unfit: the hard physical labour he had been doing since the age of twelve had already taken its toll on his back. But in 1942 he started attending party meetings, he distributed newspapers and spoke on the radio, urging all good Danish men to enlist in the Danish Legion. By the end of 1943, however, he had lost faith in the party, although he remained a member, not least because Karl Viggo was still fighting for God and Denmark on the Eastern Front. He did not want to let his older brother down. Karl Viggo came home on leave for the last time in May 1944. They had a simple lunch together. Karl Viggo was in uniform. In the restaurant they sat in a corner by themselves. The Danes knew now that the Germans had lost the war, and were starting to distance themselves from them and forget all the talk of cooperation and adjustment. Then, too, the Danes were an opportunistic little nation. Two days after Karl Viggo returned to the front my father was killed in Aalborg in broad daylight. He was waylaid by two men who shot him seven times in the back and once in the head as he lay on the pavement in a pool of blood.'

There was total silence in the bedroom. Not a sound came from the Christmas-quiet street. I looked at E–, saw the pain in his eyes. I got up, got us some more red wine to go with the fresh cigarettes which we lit.

'After the war they called it the liquidation of a collaborator, but it was cold-blooded murder,' E– said in a voice full of pent-up bitterness. 'My mother and I were branded as a German whore and a traitor's brat. We moved to Århus and later across to Zealand with my step-father, who knew nothing of my parents' past. But that's another story. I've looked at the files. Four hundred people were liquidated in the same way as my father. Every case filed and forgotten about. We have been condemned for good and all by respectable society. The killers were regarded as heroes. The victims as butchers. Justice went by the board along with the truth, smothered by hypocrisy.'

I stroked his face hesitantly.

'You lost your Dad, just like I did. That's why you understand me so well,' I said.

'That's not the only reason, my love. But it's part of the explanation. We can never get our fathers back. They're lost to us for ever, but we can hope that someday they may be vindicated. Not because they were good men, but because they were unfairly treated, and we have had to pay the price for the crimes which society claims they committed.'

'You know what it means to feel betrayed. To feel so black and empty inside that it's like being made of glass and surrounded by spiteful, staring eyes.'

'Yes, I know what it's like.'

'Thank you.'

He smiled. I took his face in my hands and covered it with little kisses until at last I found his mouth with its greedy tongue and he laid me back and we made love quietly and yet so passionately that it seemed we would never let each other go.

On Christmas Day E– took me out to the woods north of the town. It was late in the morning and very quiet, the winter mist mantling the bare trees as if wrapping them in cotton wool. We biked out there in silence. There were only a few people on the streets, but we heard the church bells ringing for the Christmas service as we cycled out of the town and into the woods. The ground was damp and spongy and we had to wheel our bikes over the muddiest patches. I was tired and had a bit of a hangover, but I also felt totally lucid and almost euphoric. We parked our bikes on the edge of a thicket of pines and E– led me in among the trees. Water dripped from the green needles onto my coat and hat. There were signs of animals in the layer of needles underfoot and clearer tracks around the edges of the rain-filled puddles along the path we took. Even without snow it was a beautiful, cold, Danish winter forest, with the white mist and the quiet, moist drip-drip from bare branches and green needles. E– held my hand, almost dragging me through the pines and out into a clearing which looked as if it were man-made. We were deep inside the woods. It was very, very quiet, the silence seeming to be intensified by the winter mist.

In the clearing stood a man in an old black overcoat and a battered grey cap. He was tall, with rugged, fine-drawn features. He was standing, shoulders slightly bowed, beside a small grey stone set in the middle of the clearing: discreet and yet forming a natural focal point. A single red poinsettia sat next to the stone. The man regarded us. He looked to be in his forties and had clear grey eyes, not unlike E–'s.

'Irma, this is my uncle,' E– said.

I removed my glove and shook his hand. It was firm, dry and cold.

'How do you do,' I said politely, yet feeling oddly heartened. Here was a man who had known my father in a quite different way from me.

'I'm delighted to meet the daughter of such a brave man,' Karl Viggo said. His voice was deep and rasping, it sounded as though he smoked way too many strong cigarettes.

'Could you tell me about him?'

'Whatever I know I will certainly tell you. We'll have lunch together today. Then you shall hear.'

I stepped forward to look at the stone. The inscription on it said simply: They fell for Denmark.

'This is just the start,' he said. 'One day we'll erect a proper stone, here and in the place out east where our comrades are buried. One day they'll be vindicated and justice will triumph.'

'Uncle was jailed for three years after the war,' E– said. 'He spent some months in Frøslev prison camp with your father. They had changed its name to Faarhus by then. Both Karl Viggo and your dad were released once the worst of the anger and the recriminations had died down. But they were marked men nonetheless. Why were they convicted? In the case of many, including Karl Viggo and your dad, for joining up, and yet they had done so with the government's blessing. There lies the injustice.'

'Yes, I see that,' I said.

'Today that camp is just a plain, ordinary army barracks. No one wants to be reminded of that injustice. They commemorate the members of the Danish resistance who were interned there during the last years of the war under excellent conditions. But the fact that Frøslev became Faarhus, the biggest concentration camp for political prisoners in so-called free Denmark – this they don't want anyone to know. It doesn't fit with the nation's image of itself.'

I understood what E– was saying, but in my mind I could also see those awful pictures of the gas chambers and the walking skeletons from the concentration camps. That appalling massacre of millions of people. As if E– read my mind he said:

'Irma, Nazism is dead, but that doesn't make it right for society to lie about the past and tailor the truth to suit the myths which the powers that be want the people to believe in. This we can learn from.'

I touched the stone. It felt cold and rough. But there was something magical about it too. As if it were possessed of some power, a link with the past. When I touched it I felt a line running from me to my father, a faint but distinct connection which brought me peace at heart, because I was no longer alone in the world with my loss and my pain.

E–'s uncle stood with his head lowered and his eyes half-shut, as if he were praying. And the place did have a religious air about it, I thought. But, as always, E– maintained his cool, analytical overview, wherein emotions were never allowed to gain the upper hand. And as usual he knew just what to say:

'Our fathers' analysis of society was correct, but they drew the wrong conclusion. They had their guns pointed in the wrong direction. But the hypocritical society which bred them must not be allowed to blacken their memories and penalise them and us in the belief that by doing so it can conceal its own shame. That is what their story teaches us. You shouldn't feel guilty, Irma. It's the others who should be ashamed.'

I looked at him. That may have been the moment when my life acquired meaning. At any rate, when he took me in his arms and held me I burst into tears. There in the bare, hushed clearing in the woods I knew that I would never let this man down.

Part 4

FOR THE GLORY OF DENMARK

'Misery acquaints a man with strange bed-fellows.'
William Shakespeare, *The Tempest*

21

PER TOFTLUND WOKE before the alarm went off and lay in the morning gloom listening to Lise's slow, laboured breathing. She was lying on her back, her enormous stomach swelling like a great hump under the duvet. Her face was faintly blotched and covered with a fine layer of sweat which plastered her thick hair to her temples. He did not know why, but he felt very tired and a little off-colour, almost as if he were coming down with a spring cold. Or maybe he did know. There had been small signs at work: how the time seemed suddenly to disappear; someone would say something to him and he would not catch it. Little lapses of memory which disturbed him. Maybe it had been like this ever since he made a mess of the assignment at Flakfortet, or maybe he was simply afraid that he was not up to the job to which he had returned? During the working day he would also find himself worrying about becoming a father. He felt bad for not looking forward to it wholeheartedly. That, after all, was how it was supposed to be. Maybe it was just that he did not know what he was getting himself in to. There was no denying it, he was over forty now, and he could feel it. That alone ought to be a clear sign that, from a purely biological point of view, tying the knot had been the right thing to do. But tying the knot meant being tied down and maybe that was what made him nervous. There was no doubt in his mind that he loved Lise, but marriage was also a daunting business and coming home this time had not been easy. The image of the blood slowly running onto the floor of the restaurant kept coming back to him, awake and in his dreams. Sometimes it was vividly realistic. Other times the blood was bright orange, almost fluorescent. And on a couple of occasions he had been the man on the floor, with another version of himself looking down on him, notebook in hand. Lise had been angry and hurt. At first he had thought she was mad at him for not calling home to ask how things were with her and the baby, but then it had dawned on him that she felt let down. She felt he was selfish, thinking only about himself and what she called his bloody work. 'Talk to me, damn you!' she had screamed and then burst into tears. He had stood in the kitchen, staring out at the bare, loamy garden like a fool, instead of going to her and putting his arms round her. He loved her so much, so why was he so emotionally inept? They had had a couple of weird days when they had circled around one another like two strangers. They had still not had a proper talk about his trip or his failure to keep in touch while he was away but the air appeared to have been cleared by the unborn baby when she kicked one evening while they were watching the news and they saw the contours of a tiny foot under the smooth stretched skin of Lise's stomach. They had both started to laugh and Lise's great belly had bounced up and down like a huge basketball. The mood had changed, they had kissed and his penis had swelled hard and tight. There was nothing to be done about that, though.

Lise sighed and made little snoring sounds. She lay with her mouth half-open in the faint, grey April light and he was overcome by a great sense of love and a rush of old-fashioned protectiveness. He knew himself well enough, though, not to lie there in the semi-darkness making promises he could not keep, either to Lise or to himself. He was the way he was. From Lise's point of view he could probably shape up a bit, but deep down there was no changing him. Or so he felt, at any rate, although he was certain that women always believed they could alter a man to fit their image of him. Make him the man they wanted him to be. There was something missionary-like about this constant urge women had to transform and improve upon their men. Was the same true of Lise?

Toftlund did what he always did whenever he found himself thinking too much. He resorted to physical activity. He stroked

Lise's stomach gently and kissed her on the cheek, making her sigh luxuriously. He went for his morning run in the misty dawn which, with its light and its delicate tones held the promise of spring. After his shower he went through to the kitchen and gave Lise a nice, big morning kiss. She was standing with one hand in the small of her back, her big belly bulging under her blue dressing gown. In her other hand she held a mug of tea, resting it on the flat top of the hump under her heavy breasts.

'Won't be long now,' he said.

'Oh, I can't wait. Everything's ready.'

'You've been a proper little nest-builder.'

'Who would have thought it – a career woman like me,' she said with laughter in her voice, and he was happy because she was in a good mood this morning. The house smelled fresh and clean. The baby clothes – those they had bought and those passed on by friends and family – were all freshly washed and ironed and arranged in neat piles in cupboards and drawers; the crib was made up, the linen and the lovely little duvet smelling faintly of soap. And out in the carport the pram waited as eagerly as them. Lise had spent the past eight days cleaning and making everything ready, as if driven by her biological clock. The cleaner had been asked to come in for an extra day and the two women had scrubbed the house from top to bottom, until there was not a speck of dust or fluff to be found even in the remotest corner. Women were in so many ways a mystery to Toftlund.

They had breakfast together, read the paper, listened to the radio news. NATO was still conducting daily bombing raids, weather permitting, on Yugoslavia and Kosovo, both of which were still sending thousands of refugees to the neighbouring countries of Macedonia and Albania. The refugees arrived there wet, cold and hungry with appalling tales of murder, arson, torture and mass rape. The newsreader announced that despite being the poorest country in Europe, Albania had now taken in over half a million refugees. The situation there was chaotic. Meanwhile, in Denmark, there was fierce debate concerning the government's proposal to grant asylum to two thousand Kosovo Albanian refugees. Per noticed the old light of battle flicker in Lise's eyes, but instead she asked:

'How's it actually going with that case of yours?'

He looked up. She rarely asked him about his work. She knew there were so many things he could not talk about.

'So-so.'

'It says here that you've got nothing on this woman you've arrested. That you'll have to let her go.'

'That's not altogether untrue.'

'And what then?'

'She'll get a nice fat sum in compensation.'

'That's fair enough, don't you think.'

'Yeah, but she's mixed up in it somehow. I'm sure of it'

'But you can't prove it?'

'Not as things stand at the moment. The lead isn't strong enough.'

'Well, then it's only fair that she should be released. I mean, as far as I know in this country one is still innocent until proven otherwise.'

'Of course.'

'And that being so it's only fair that she should receive compensation, right?'

He looked up again:

'Are you trying to pick a fight?'

'Not at all. I'm just asking.'

'It doesn't matter what I think. By law she has a right to compensation. That's just how it is.'

'Fine,' she said a mite snippily and turned back to her newspaper.

'There's something about her. I know it. She's betrayed her country. She's indirectly responsible for the deaths of a lot of people. She should be behind bars,' he said.

She glanced up from the paper. She had simply pulled her hair back into an elastic band, but he thought he had never seen her look lovelier, even if her eyes did look dull and a little tired. She wasn't getting enough sleep, he told himself.

'So what's the next move, Per?'

'Well, we'll just have to see what else this line of inquiry turns up. But I haven't given up yet.'

'More overtime?'

'It's all part of the job. That's what you get for marrying a policeman.'

'Bullshit. I know all about irregular working hours. I used to be a journalist – remember?'

'You're still a journalist.'

'I'm a pregnant cow,' she said and went back to the article she had been reading, although he had a feeling her mind was not really on it. She looked up again.

'You promised, Per …'

'I'll be there, don't worry.'

'It's due in less than a fortnight.'

'I'll be there, Lise. Trust me!'

'It's our baby, Per. Our own little miracle. It's ours. Ours. I didn't think I could have children. But I could. With you. It's ours, Per.'

Now he saw the tears in the corners of her eyes, he got up, went round behind her chair and wrapped his arms round her, kissed her on the back of the neck, little pecks, while gently stroking her breast and her stomach. He felt movement and kicking feet beneath the skin, as if the unborn baby was playing football with his hand. Lise winced, both laughing and crying.

'She's got a helluva kick,' she said. 'Per, for God's sake. Hand me a Kleenex. I can't bear to see myself like this.'

He let go of her and fetched her a tissue. She dried her eyes and blew her nose. He handed her a fresh tissue and she repeated this sniffling process. Her eyes were red and puffy, her face a little swollen too.

'I love you, Lise,' he said.

'How can you possibly love me when I look like this and act like a stupid cow.'

'Goose.'

'Cow!'

'Moo.'

'Oh, Per, you big idiot. Or no, it's me – I'm an even bigger idiot. I'm looking forward to it so much, but obviously I'm dreading it too.'

'I'm here for you, Lise.'

'It's okay. I'm okay now. It's just these mornings, with you running out the door and being gone all day. But I know – it's your job. So off you go and catch your spies.'

'My paternity leave is all arranged. I've told Vuldom about it.'

'Even if you have to let her go? Because then you're really going to be kept busy, aren't you?'

'Yes. That's probably true.'

Lise pointed to the newspaper.

'This mate of mine says you've got fuck all.'

'It says that in the paper?' he said, genuinely surprised, although very little of what appeared in the papers surprised him any more.

'Not in so many words, but that's the drift of it.'

But those were exactly the words Jytte Vuldom used an hour later, announcing through a blue haze of cigarette smoke:

'The newspapers are right. You've got fuck all, Toftlund. I doubt very much if we'll get an extension. And our Irma is a sly little devil. She's spelled it out for you loud and clear: she won't talk. She knew we couldn't prove anything, and the fact that we can't establish that she had access, means – DCI Toftlund – that we have a very flimsy case. But do, please, give me a rundown and we'll take it from there.'

Vuldom had been sympathetic when he got back from Prague with his terrible story, but she had not got where she was on the strength of her maternal instincts. After he refused to take a couple of days off to digest the experience and laughed off her only half-serious offer of counselling, Vuldom wasted no more time on what she referred to as the 'personal aspects'. The information from Prague was written up in a report and added to the steadily growing case file in which Irma's outward and secret lives were charted and uncovered. Search warrants enabled them to delve into the most private and intimate sides of a person's life with the full blessing of the court, in order to find the proof, or a body of circumstantial evidence, which would lead first to an extension of the isolation warrant and later to a conviction. That was pretty much the whole point of the exercise. Society's reckoning. Society's revenge. Often in the course of an inquiry innocent individuals would also disclose aspects of their lives which they would have preferred to remain secret until the day they died. But in a criminal investigation there are always other victims besides those directly involved. In this case, however, it looked as if the perpetrator was going to cheat society of its revenge, even though, by detaining her in custody for so long the state had already let the general public know, through the offices of the press, that this particular citizen was, in all probability, guilty as sin.

The core investigation team had gathered for a status meeting in Vuldom's spacious office. Outside the sun was providing more assurance that spring was just around the corner, and Toftlund found himself looking forward to the holidays he still had coming to him and the paternity leave for which he had applied, even though his older male colleagues had sniggered at the notion. The younger men simply took it for granted. He rose, stepped up to the front and looked around him. He could not sit still when he had to speak. Present in the room, besides Vuldom and her trusty secretary Lene Nielsen, were the middle-aged Bjergager, who coordinated and collected their reports, and Toftlund's second-in-command Charlotte Bastrup, whom he had come to respect and, he feared, to fancy. She was small and slim: at the time when she applied to join the force she must only just have managed to fulfil the then height requirement of 165 centimetres.

She had very short, sleek, black hair and took great care over her appearance, from her discreet make-up and little pierced earrings to the practical, but stylish clothes she always wore. Her face was on the round side, her lips straight, narrow and unexceptional, but her eyes were fabulous: a bright, subtly shifting greyish-brown. Her Polish forebears had settled down south in the flatlands of Lolland, where she hailed from. She carried herself with seductive self-assurance, confident of her sexual allure and the analytical gifts which had helped take her well up the career ladder. Most of the others from her year had been left far behind. She lived alone. Somewhere in Østerbro. She cycled to work, that much he knew, but she never said much about her private life. He also knew that she was thirty-two and a hell of a good detective, conscientious and thorough, and it was a privilege to work with her. Toftlund had not the slightest thing against female police officers. But he did not like the thought that he might have fallen for one of them. He tried to concentrate and keep his eyes off her. He was afraid that Vuldom would see through him. She had a knack for reading people's minds. He was a married man, for Christ's sake, with a heavily pregnant wife. But he was also a normal man and it was weeks since sex had been possible for Lise and him. The last time they had done it she had bled afterwards. It had stopped by the time they got to the casualty department, frantic with worry, but the doctor had advised them against having intercourse. There was no point in taking any chances. It had sounded so simple and straightforward, but they both missed the physical closeness. There it was again. That sudden, fleeting state in which he was lost to the world, his surroundings seeming to fade away until some outside element roused him and brought him slap-bang back to reality.

In this instance, Vuldom's wry tones:

'Toftlund …? Shall we get on with it? Or do you need more time to think?'

'No, I'm ready now.'

'Excellent. The rest of us have been ready for some time.'

Toftlund collected his thoughts and began, trying as he did so to find his way to that nucleus of self-confidence which he knew he possessed:

'We've made the link between the various individuals concerned, and everything points in the same direction. Their stories tie up all the way down the line. Irma was born in 1940, her parents were Nazis – they're both listed in the Bovrup Files. Her father was among the first to enlist when the Danish Legion was formed in '41. He served on the Russian Front, then in Yugoslavia and, later, in Russia again. He appears to have deserted, but we now know that he was living illegally in Yugoslavia. Fritz was born in 1943, nine months after his father had been home in Denmark on furlough. He's led a pretty undramatic life: trained as a baker, national service, married, children, comfortably off, runs a big business, solid citizen. The only slightly unusual thing about him is that he's a regular donor to the Danish Legion Veterans' Association. But that's because of his father, obviously. Fritz himself has been a member of the Conservative Party since 1982. Teddy was born in 1948. A somewhat erratic career, finances in a terrible mess, more wives and girlfriends that I can count, but nothing criminal on record. Adopted by his step-father. I'm sure it came as a complete surprise to him to hear that he had a half-sister and that his father didn't die when he was a baby. Both Teddy and Fritz have been extremely cooperative. Same goes for Irma's friends and other family members. The mother has forgotten her past. She's in a nursing home on Fünen. Advanced Alzheimer's. Impossible to get any sense out of her.'

Toftlund crossed to the table and took a swig of his mineral water before continuing:

'The Nazi father returned home after the worst of the Danes' thirst for revenge had been satisfied. After a couple of months in Faarhus prison camp his sentence was suspended. No public mention of this. No one seems to have paid much attention to

| 303 |

him until 1952, when he was recognised at a shooting party. He ran off back to Yugoslavia. We think he appropriated the papers of a Norwegian sailor who was reported missing around then by the Norwegian Seamen's Mission. Later, a badly decomposed body was found in the harbour with the father's papers on it. The German police believe the Norwegian was murdered. But they didn't pursue the case at the time and now it's just some yellowing papers in a file. Then there's Mira, or Maria. Born around 1944 in what is now Croatia. The joker in the pack, if you like. Definitely an intelligence agent. According to my Slovakian contact possibly a double or even triple agent. All in all a woman of many talents.'

He paused again.

'It began during the war. The Second World War and the occupation, but forget all thought of neo-Nazi conspiracies. It's got nothing to do with that. Charlotte has been following up that line of inquiry ...'

'Keep it brief, Charlotte,' Vuldom said.

Charlotte Bastrup drew herself up in her chair. Her grey blouse suited her slim form, Toftlund thought, and forced himself to concentrate on anything other than her lips, her eyes, her little ears and the body under the thin fabric, through which he could just discern her bra. Bastrup kept it short and to the point:

'Twelve thousand young men joined the Waffen SS between 1940 and 1945. Six thousand of these served with the Danish Legion on the Eastern Front, and later with various SS units. Around three thousand of them were killed. The figures are a bit vague. These troops were dispatched with the blessing of the Danish government. Officers were allowed to keep their pension entitlements and so on. Their commander-in-chief made recruitment speeches on national radio. They were given a rousing send-off with a parade, brass band and all. When their great hero, a Commander von Schalburg, was killed on the Eastern Front, members of the royal family and the government attended the memorial service for him. After the war, most of the survivors were sentenced to between two and four years in prison for having joined the other side. None of them were convicted of war crimes on the Eastern Front, even though the SS as a whole was condemned by the Nuremberg Tribunal for crimes against humanity. While some veterans of the Eastern Front were executed by the Danish police, this was for crimes committed on Danish soil. After the war people tried to forget that most of the Danes who fell during those 'five black years', as they are called, died fighting for the Germans. Not against the occupying power. Few, if any, history books mention that fact. And I certainly didn't learn about it at school.'

'No, we're good at sweeping the muck under the carpet,' Vuldom put in. 'As a nation we're good at suppressing the darker chapters of our common history.'

'That's what Huey, Dewey and Uni said too,' Bastrup said.

'Who?'

Charlotte's ear lobes reddened slightly, Toflund noted, but her voice was steady enough when she went on:

'The three researchers at Roskilde University whom I've spoken to about this. Like just about every young person nowadays they all have these awfully long names – you know the sort of thing: Oliver Munck-Halle Ebbesen or whatever, so for simplicity's sake I've christened them Huey, Dewey and Uni. They have a book about the whole affair coming out soon. Their research project. They also tell me that there's a network of old front-liners and their descendants which is quietly working to have the Legion volunteers rehabilitated, bearing in mind that they went off to war with the government's blessing – in other words were almost encouraged to go. They were only acting in the spirit of collaboration. So they say.'

Charlotte shrugged, as if to say that this was all history, part of the background, but not necessarily a line that would lead them anywhere. In any case this had all happened long before she was born and in many ways she found it hard to understand why it should be of such interest.

Vuldom looked at her:

'There is a difference, Charlotte. Between looking the other way, and picking up a shovel to build earthworks on the west coast; between taking a job in Germany rather than lose your unemployment benefits, and taking up a rifle to fight for the Nazis. It was their choice. Just as other Danes, among them my father, chose, thank God, to put up a fight, enabling us to make it through by the skin of our teeth. Because in Papa Stalin's eyes we were all collaborators. German-lovers. The Misty Shores. The model protectorate. They made their choices. Whether to keep their mouths shut. Or collaborate. Or go off to fight on the Eastern Front. Or to make a stand. It was their own, free, personal decision, and there was a price to pay. And no post-modern historian can change that, no matter how much they may revise Danish history.'

Vuldom's voice was stern, reprimanding. The other four stared at her in some surprise, each of them absorbing the new little nugget of information about this very private person, Jytte Vuldom: that her father had been a member of the resistance.

Charlotte Bastrup cleared her throat once and only the slender fingers fiddling with her pen betrayed that she had just been given a small taste of the notorious Vuldom wrath which was liable to come pouring down on anyone who acted unprofessionally, was not serious enough about their work or simply stepped on her toes and said things which went against her ideas of justice and fairness.

Toftlund came to Charlotte's aid:

'I think Charlotte, like me, was unaware of what a touchy and controversial issue this is, even today. It can still ruffle the feathers of old front-liners and resistance fighters, their descendants and the historians, who can't agree on anything. Incidentally, it's interesting to note that these three researchers knew nothing of Irma's association with the SS veterans' movement. Or her father's story. She has kept that under her hat, even though she is in many ways their mentor. Their guidance counsellor I think they call it down there. In their research project she has steered them in the direction that accords with her view of events.'

Vuldom lit a cigarette. She was still upset, Toftlund could tell. Angry about something which seemed a small thing to him – unless, that was, it could help to get Irma convicted of the acts of treason which he was positive she had committed.

'Interesting,' Vuldom said. 'Our little Irma is a consummate manipulator of others. She has learned from a great teacher, our dear Irma-Edelweiss.' The sentence was left hanging in the air as if asking to be expanded upon, but no more came. Toftlund was standing out front, when she did not go on he picked up the thread:

'Born, as I say, in 1940. Very attached to her father. Difficult adolescence in Silkeborg, to which they moved after the scandal broke. No one can remember the young man, E–. And the mother's brain is too far gone. Irma and E– were never married. Not on paper anyway. In 1989 Irma married a fellow lecturer, he died of cancer three years ago. They had no children. She studied literature and history at the University of Copenhagen and went on to win a professorship at the University of Roskilde with a thesis in which she argued that depictions of female characters in classic Danish literature were false, inasmuch as they were based upon the capitalist, male-chauvinist society's repressive image of women. She chucked, you might say, the whole body of Danish literature written by men on the midden of history.'

Toftlund sounded as though he was quoting one of the academics he had interviewed, and this did not escape Vuldom's notice:

'That was some mouthful,' she said jokingly, as if she knew he was not quite himself today. 'Something you read?'

'Nope. Anyway, that's neither here nor there. So much for Irma's public life. But she has also had another life. We have a big, fat file on her. She was extremely politically active. Officially in the women's movement, but she was also involved with several revolutionary factions operating within and around the far left and the

Communist Workers' Party. She wrote articles about the necessity of violent action. Supported the Baader-Meinhof Gang. Knew people close to the terrorist bankrobbers in the Blekingegade gang. As a very young girl she was a Nazi, but appears to have had no trouble making the shift from there to revolutionary Marxism. From one form of totalitarianism to another. There's possibly not that much difference between them anyway. One thing they certainly have in common is their hatred of middle-class society. Like Fritz she has kept in touch with her father's old comrades.'

'War makes for strange bedfellows,' Vuldom remarked.

'Sorry?'

'I think it was Churchill who said that,' she offered.

Bjergager gave a little cough. They turned to him in surprise. He generally did not say much during these sessions. He noted everything down and remembered everything, but he was not a hasty man, he preferred not to make any comment until he had had the chance to turn over in his mind the points discussed and the evidence presented.

'Yes, Bjergager?' Vuldom said.

Bjergager leaned a little way across the table:

'Churchill did say something to that effect,' he said in his deep, dry voice. 'But that was because he was a well-read man. The original quote comes from Shakespeare's *The Tempest*: 'Misery makes for strange bedfellows' or something like that. Churchill just changed the wording slightly – to explain his unholy alliance with Stalin against Hitler.'

'Thanks for the lecture, Bjergager,' Vuldom said and nodded to Toftlund who took a sip of water and glanced at Charlotte before continuing:

'I think we'll find the explanation for her treason ...'

'Which we cannot prove,' Vuldom broke in.

'... for her treason in her revolutionary youth. She's no longer active. But then we haven't had her under observation for some time. She's never been convicted of anything.'

'She's just like all the rest,' Vuldom said. 'The Danes never started a revolution. There was no war. Their theories remained just that. Their cold talk of terrorism was never anything but talk. Their apocalyptic visions never amounted to any more than visions. They were lucky that all their revolutionary spoutings didn't have serious consequences for the liberal society they hated so much.'

Toftlund did not know what apocalyptic meant, and was actually expecting to be enlightened, but Vuldom simply stubbed out her cigarette and glanced first at him, then at Charlotte Bastrup who was sitting with a pile of reports and her own notebook in front of her. Toftlund felt a shudder run through him, as if someone had opened a window, letting a chill draught into the warm, modern office. Vuldom's gift for reading both situations and people was legendary, but she wasn't a fucking mind-reader, surely?

'Does Irma know you're reading her account?' was all she asked.

'No.'

'Do you mean to confront her with it?'

'Yes. There are things there I can use. To which she'll have to provide answers.'

'How did you hack into it?'

'That was Charlotte.'

Vuldom glanced inquiringly at Bastrup who raised her head and looked her straight in the eye:

'It's a standard Word programme. She had devised a code. Most people are pretty unimaginative. I started with her own name, forwards then backwards, then her brothers' names, her father's and so on. It turned out to be Teddy spelled backwards. I transferred the document from her computer when she was being interviewed or in the exercise yard.'

'Teddy spelled backwards – not very original,' Vuldom said.

'People rarely are.'

'There is another possibility, of course. That she wanted us to read it. That she assumed we were smart enough to break her simple code. Have you considered that? Have you considered that our dear Irma might have wanted us to read her little memoir?'

Toftlund and Bastrup nodded and waited for their boss's next words:

'So she's sendng you a message, Toftlund, loud and clear.' Vuldom picked up the printout of Irma's diary and read aloud: '"I looked at him. That may have been the moment when my life acquired meaning. At any rate, when he took me in his arms and held me I burst into tears. There in that bare, hushed clearing in the woods I knew that I would never let this man down."'

Vuldom looked up, put the paper down and repeated:

'"I knew that I would never let this man down." I'm right, aren't I. A heavy hint.'

'And a confession,' Toflund added.

'That too, but not one that would stand up in court. So who's E–?'

'Our spy. The one passing secrets to the Serbs. Or to the Russians, who pass it on to the Serbs. It may well have been E– who provided the details of the Stealth's flight path, thus enabling them to hit it. It shouldn't have been possible to shoot that thing down. It was invisible, for God's sake. Irma doesn't have access, but E– does.'

Toftlund paced up and down. Vuldom followed him with her eyes before saying:

'If he has worked with NATO's armed forces, or the Foreign Department, or within the EU organisation, and if we're to believe Irma, then he must be nearing retirement age, or already retired. He's a relic from the cold war. He thought he was safe because Stasi managed to destroy the tape containing the names of its foreign agents. Or most of them, at least. If he himself does not have access then maybe he recruited someone who has. Then suddenly one day there's a knock at the door and there's some Russian, say, who knows him by his Stasi cover name and wants to reactivate him. He has to get hold of the flight coordinates of NATO planes over Yugoslavia and Kosovo or else …?'

Vuldom let the sentence hang.

Bastrup cleared her throat and said:

'I know the Russians are against the war and are, to some extent, on the Serbs' side in this matter, but it's not like them to go so far as to risk compromising their own agents and – more importantly – letting the rest of us know that they actually have a complete list of Stasi's old network of moles and undercover agents and, hence, a potential bargaining tool and possible blackmail material. Although they could, of course, also find themselves called upon to make such a list public. Is that what you're saying, boss?'

Vuldom smiled and nodded, like a teacher receiving an answer from a good student:

'Exactly. So the reward for revealing to the rest of us that they have a copy of the details of Wolf's old network would have to be very big. And it was. Access for Russian engineers to America's top-secret Stealth technology is a reward beyond price. The cold war and all that may be over, but Russia is still keen to possess this technology. And if the Yugoslavian air defence knew the flight coordinates, the odds of them shooting down a Stealth bomber would suddenly be greatly improved, and with them the chances of Russia building its own Stealth aircraft, which they could hawk to the Iranians or the Chinese, or whoever else buys arms from the Russians these days. It would be worth it, even if it meant giving away information or compromising an agent.'

Toftlund said:

'But who is E–?'

'Yes, who is E–?' Vuldom repeated. 'What do the files say? About the liquidations during the war? Have you found anything?'

Toftlund walked over to Bastrup, who handed him a sheet of paper. He ran a quick eye over it then said:

'The resistance carried out somewhere in the region of four hundred liquidations in '44 and '45. After the war, representatives from the resistance movement looked at all the unsolved killings and if there was any mention of an informer liquidation the case was shelved. And since the occupation no one, not the press, nor the historians nor any other researchers have had any inclination to delve into that matter. It's still very much a taboo subject. No one has tried to find eyewitnesses or surviving relatives. Both those who did the killing and the families who were hit bear the scars to this day. The majority of those who were directly involved are dead. Many of the surviving spouses changed their names, remarried and so on. There are a lot of faded old case files. But they got us nowhere. We can find no trace of any young man fitting Irma's description of E–. It's like this blank spot in Danish history. We've been able to track down hardly any survivors, in fact. Or locate any relative now occupying a post which offers access to classified information. But E–'s mother could have remarried and taken her secret with her to the grave. That's what usually happened.'

Toftlund regarded Vuldom regretfully.

'Okay,' she said. 'Let's rephrase the question then: who knows who E– is?'

'Irma does. But she's not telling. I'm convinced that, while Irma may well be Edelweiss, she is not the actual spy, only the spy's carrier pigeon. E– has survived this long only because he has had plenty of filters between himself and the recipients of his reports – be it the KGB, or Stasi, or both. Irma was one of these filters. E–'s identity was not even known to the normal spy chiefs within Stasi or, earlier, the KGB. Apart, perhaps, from the director himself. He was a vital asset, and as such was closely protected. He delivered his reports through human carrier pigeons like Irma. But there was more than one Irma in his life.'

Toftlund glanced at Vuldom, who nodded:

'I've reached the same conclusion,' she said. 'E– is our man. He thought he was home and dry, but there's always just one more job. Always one last job when you've pledged your soul to the Devil.'

'And the other sister? The secret one?'

Toftlund was anxious to hear whether, here too, Vuldom had reached the same conclusion as himself. She had:

'I see where you're going, Per. E–'s real name may have been the currency which Mira Majola or Maria Bujic, or whatever this good sister calls herself, brought to Teddy, thus ensuring that it went into his suitcase. And what she wanted to buy – having burned all her bridges – was, of course, a new name and a new identity in peaceful little Denmark.'

'Exactly,' Toftlund said.

'So if we're to get any further with Irma, then we'll have to establish a link between them. Not in the past, but in the present. Between all three of them, if possible.'

'And how are we to do that?'

Charlotte looked up, a smile on her sensual red lips as she held aloft a sheet of paper. Laughter lines appeared at the corners of her eyes, so fine as to be almost invisible, and Toftlund had a most unprofessional urge to kiss the smooth bare nape of her neck below her cropped hair.

'I think I may have managed it last night,' Charlotte Bastrup said with a self-confidence which Toftlund found both attractive and annoying, reminding him as it did of the invulnerability he too had felt at that age, before life became so bloody complicated.

22

TOFTLUND AND BASTRUP drove down towards the Storebælt Bridge. It was still the same day, but the springlike weather of the morning had been seen off by grey clouds which had just sent a shower of sleet sweeping across the motorway. The road glistened dull-grey and made the tyres hum faintly; then suddenly they were running over dry tarmac again. Toftlund was in the driver's seat with Charlotte sitting, legs crossed, next to him. They were listening to Radio 2, its smooth stream of hit tunes running in one ear and out the other, unbroken by the incessant chatter that pervaded Danmarks Radio's programmes. Toftlund was acutely aware of Charlotte's scent and if he glanced sideways and down he could see her slim thigh and rounded knee showing below the hem of her skirt. He could not help thinking he should really have been the one to arrive at the deduction which Charlotte had made. By reasoning. By deduction. By inference. The holy trinity of every investigation. But his experiences in Prague had hit him harder than he cared to admit. It was like being a bodyguard again. Which he wasn't. So why these shadows of doubt in his mind? Maybe he should talk to Lise. Try to explain how he felt. But that just wasn't in his nature. He was not like Irma, who could write about the most intimate details of her life. He did not understand the current penchant for putting oneself on display, for baring one's soul in public. He just did not get it: how could television make people say and do the things they did? Exposing the most private sides of themselves. And why this great need to talk about oneself and one's feelings? Lise too believed that you could get to the root of any problem by discussing it. Even Vuldom had deemed it only natural, although she herself would never have

| 314 |

done it. 'It's a form of self-therapy which works for a lot of people,' she had said. 'It's no crime to be unhappy, to have suffered. It's a far greater crime not to face the fact that one is merely human.' He had not been altogether sure what she meant. As far as he was concerned, opening up was a sign of weakness. His personal problems and inner doubts were nobody else's concern. You had to fight these things on your own. There – now his mind was wandering again. Running off at a tangent, where it had no business going. In an effort to thrust aside what he could not bear to think about he forced himself to concentrate on and consider the discovery which Charlotte had made and presented. It was actually very simple, but then breakthroughs often were – if, that is, this was a breakthrough. Or at the very least a piece of evidence with which he could confront Irma and thereafter persuade the prosecutor to submit in court.

Charlotte Bastrup had made yet another study of the extensive surveillance material they had procured. This included Irma's bank statements and records of phone calls made and faxes sent from her work, from her home phone and her mobile. This last was especially important. Not only could they check whom she had called and at which numbers, they could also pinpoint the physical location of a recipient phone to within a radius of a few metres. Bastrup had obtained the last piece of the puzzle through the unofficial channels commonly referred to in the media as 'Echelon'. Major intelligence gathering stations in the UK and other parts of Europe as well as Greenland and the US traced, intercepted and recorded the mass of electronic traffic travelling along the wireless motorways of cyberspace, via the Internet and email. Rows of dry numbers, lined up like soldiers on parade, traced the electronic life of a modern-day individual – here disclosed, laid out, courtesy of the huge hearkening ears and all-seeing eyes which dog a person's every step along the global highway.

Bastrup's search had paid off. She had noticed that, according to Irma's bank statements, in the weeks prior to her arrest she had made regular trips across the Storebælt Bridge, paid for with her bank debit card. A clear pattern began to emerge. These trips usually followed a call from abroad – from a call box to Irma's mobile. Not always, but often enough for it to be more than a coincidence. Between the brief call to her mobile and the debiting of the bridge toll from her account she received an email, sent via a public domain such as Hotmail or Yahoo mail from a computer in some library or Internet café. In each instance the sender address, set up for this express purpose, was used only once, thus ensuring that the sender could not be traced.

Leaning over the long printouts spread out on Vuldom's white conference table, Bastrup explained how these regular meetings had been arranged. She had chosen to circle four groups of numbers which closely predated Irma's arrest.

The first three read: 1302 /54, 2402/ 47 and 0303/ 65/15. The fourth circle was drawn around a double set of figures: 1203/30/13 and 1203/68/16. This was all that appeared in the emails. Sent via Hotmail, each time using a new, randomly selected sender name. In this universe people could invent both names and identities for themselves when chatting with others or sending messages. You could reinvent yourself again and again. Become the person you dreamed of being, or highlight those sides of yourself which were normally kept under wraps.

What Charlotte detected in these random numerical sequences were coded messages – setting up meetings or telling Irma to pick up a document, a roll of microfilm or a package, possibly from E–. From what, in the trade, was known as a dead letter drop or dead letter box. The first part of the sequence, she explained, gave the date. In the first set of numbers she had circled this would, therefore, be February 13th. The second part denoted the closest motorway lay-by – in that first set the Kildebjerg lay-by on Fünen, off exit number 54. So: on February 13th, Irma could pick up a message from her controller or from E– at the Kildebjerg lay-by. They must have agreed in advance whether the drop would be made on the southbound or the northbound side since the coded message did not say. What had struck Bastrup was that each trip tied in with an e-mail. She had checked the other sets of numbers. She pointed to the fourth, longer, sequence and explained that the numbers thirteen and sixteen referred to times. This too she had concluded after comparing the emails and the record of the bridge-toll payments with the driving distance from Copenhagen or Roskilde. In each case the dates and times fitted. And each time Irma had received a brief call, or had made a call herself at the lay-by. Or close enough to it to confirm the pattern.

So on March 12th it appeared that Irma had met someone at one p.m. at the closest lay-by to exit 30. Which would be the Karslunde Vest services, south of Copenhagen. There she had picked up the person in question and driven on. Almost an hour later she had used her debit card at Halsskov. The travelling time – driving at normal speed, observing the speed limit – corresponded with the closest lay-by to exit 68: Ulstrup services, south of Haderselv, not far from the German border. At any rate, Irma had made a call from there around five p.m., a seemingly routine call to the university. Which accorded with her having rung to say that she was unwell and would have to cancel her lecture for the following morning. On March 12th the war drums had started thundering and NATO had prepared to initiate its bombing raids. On March 12th the Czech Republic, Hungary and Poland had become members of NATO. This move on NATO's part was regarded in Moscow as an unnecessary and alarming measure which could only result in a crisis-hit Russia turning inwards and electing a hawkish, nationalistic president. The doom and gloom merchants had not minced their words. By then E– must have been well and truly active again. Things were, it appeared, coming to a head – or so Charlotte Bastrup reckoned.

Vuldom eyed her approvingly:

'Very good,' she said. 'But exactly how does all of this help us?'

Toftlund could tell from Charlotte's face that she had saved her trump card till last. That she had been looking forward to revealing it to him, to Bjergager, the silent secretary and Vuldom who, fair though she was, made no secret of the fact that if she had to choose between two equally good candidates for a job, one male, one female, she would choose the woman.

With a smile on her thin red lips Charlotte said:

'Everyone who pays by credit or debit card at the Storebælt toll plaza is photographed, and these pictures are kept on computer file for at least three months. We know the dates and times of Irma's payments. I thought maybe the people down at the bridge might be able to dig up her picture. We might be able to see her passenger.'

'Excellent. Well, what are you waiting for?'

'The Storebælt guys say they're happy to help the police, but that we'll need a warrant. We're talking confidential information here.'

'So we'll get one. I'll fax it down to them. Now off you go. Go get a picture of little Irma with the big, bad wolf who's hiding behind the initial E–. And thinks he can play games with us.'

The massive pylons of the bridge loomed into view, then disappeared again as yet another shower of sleet burst from a low, black cloud, then gradually turned to lashing rain which stopped as abruptly as it had begun.

'Spring in Denmark,' Charlotte said. She had a light, but very pleasant voice.

'Yeah, I know.'

'When this is over I'm heading south. I've got about a million hours of overtime owing to me.'

'On your own?'

She turned to look at him and he held that amazingly clear gaze for a second before concentrating on the road again. There was not much traffic. Mainly heavy trucks which he overtook without any trouble. Muddy water spraying the windscreen every time.

'That depends on whether there's anyone who fancies coming with me,' she said.

'A boyfriend, maybe?'

'Not at the moment,' she said. 'Or, not anyone I'd want to go on holiday with anyway.'

'How do you mean?'

'You're wearing a ring.'

'Yes, I am,' he said, and was saved by a sign informing them that they were approaching the toll plaza. Toftlund indicated to leave the motorway, drove up to the roundabout and past a petrol station, heading for the Storebælt Bridge administration building. They passed the defunct ferry terminal where yellow grass had forced cracks in the grey cement of the old marshalling lanes, although it was less than a year since the cars had last queued up here to board the ferries. It all looked so derelict and forsaken, as if no one knew quite what to do with it now. It might have been years since it had been in use. Dilapidated pipes ran down to the water and the snack bar was dark and deserted. It was a long time since its opening hours had accorded with reality. The wind whipped up the water in the empty ferry berth. The gulls hovered almost motionless on the wind as if waiting for a boat to leave, not knowing that the age of the ferries was long past.

'God, many's the time I've sat here waiting for the ferry,' Toftlund said, nodding towards the abandoned marshalling lanes. To their right the cars were driving in under the toll plaza canopy which extended from the administration building to hang suspended, like a flying carpet of glass and steel, over the driving lanes. They could see the small cameras directed at each booth and even with the windows closed they could hear the squeal of the trucks' brakes as they pulled up to them.

'I do miss the ferries sometimes,' Charlotte said. 'They were kind of part of being Danish. Of being a kid, in fact. Going on summer holiday, racing up the stairs to grab a table in the cafeteria, have a hotdog. And a lemonade. Don't you miss that?'

'Not one bit,' came the curt reply. 'Load of romantic claptrap.'

'Well, pardon me.'

'No, I didn't mean it like that. But that bridge is a blessing. It's made life so much easier. It feels as if it's always been there. No one ever regretted a bridge being built.'

'Well, there was plenty of opposition to the idea of this one being built.'

'The Danes are a conservative lot. They're like children. They want everything to stay the same as it's always been. We're a nation of romantics, dreaming of a Denmark straight out of some corny old Morten Korch film – all country lasses and jolly vagabonds breaking into song. A Denmark which we imagine once existed, but which never did. Come up with a suggestion for any new venture in this country, from EU membership to a bridge, and right away someone will form an action group to protest against it. Because we don't want change.'

'How perceptive,' she said wryly, but with a smile, as he parked the car. 'I had no idea you were such a thoughtful man.'

'I'm not,' he said, pulling on the handbrake. There were only two other cars in the car park. The wind buffeted the trees and they could hear the sea as they stood there shivering in the bitter cold. The concrete and steel administration building stood square and solid in the grey light which played across its big windows.

'What's the name of the guy you've arranged to meet?'

The wind made her short, black hair flutter around her neat rounded head and her cheeks were already pink. Her skin was very delicate, almost transparent despite the faint olive teint. Her nose was straight, but there was a little white scar over one nostril where she must have cut herself at some time. It was very attractive, the tiny flaw in that pure complexion.

'Peter Svendsen. He's the operations and security manager.'

Svendsen, a tall thin man in an open-necked blue shirt, came down a spiral staircase to meet them in reception. He was around forty, with close-cropped hair and a friendly smile on his fine-featured face. He shook hands and asked to see their ID: 'Purely as a matter of form,' then he led them up the spiral staircase to his office. Upstairs the corridor walls were painted grey, the pale parquet flooring was new and scrupulously clean. Svendsen's office was large and bright; there was a desk with a computer on it and a conference table strewn with papers. Pleasant, unremarkable Danish prints on the walls. A view of cars driving onto Zealand. Others on their way across the bridge.

'Have a seat,' Peter Svendsen said. 'I've just received the warrant, so that's okay. As I said, we're more than happy to help the police, but I'm not sure how much we can do.'

Svendsen had a military air about him. Toftlund recognised it from himself: the way former professional soldiers carried themselves, a certain self-assurance teamed with a clipped, precise way of speaking.

'Just tell us what you keep on file here,' Toftlund said.

'Okay. And afterwards we'll go up to the Ops room.' He crossed his arms and explained, as if he had given this spiel a hundred times: 'The system isn't designed to record who crosses the bridge. The video cameras are there only to enable us to monitor the toll payments. We're linked up online to the PBS direct debit system and can match up a credit or debit card transaction with a registration number, but not the driver. We hold onto the video footage for three to four months. With almost twenty thousand cars a day that's an awful lot of photographs. So if you've come here with just a name or a registration number then I'm sorry to say there's no way we could trace the car owner without some very time-consuming computer searches.'

'Is every car photographed and filed?' Toftlund asked.

'Not if the driver pays cash. As I say: the system is designed to check credit and debit card payments, because we don't operate with pin codes. So if someone pays in cash no photograph is taken.' He paused for effect, his eye going to Charlotte who had her notebook out. 'Unfortunately the crooks have caught on to this,' he went on. 'They pay cash, that way they know we have no record of them.'

'So what's the point then?' Charlotte asked.

He looked her straight in the eye and clasped his hands on the table:

'If, for example, someone pays with a stolen card, we have the vehicle's registration number and can pass that on to PBS or to you if you need it. Or it could be a matter of insufficient funds or whatever. Although there's surprisingly little of that, considering the volume of traffic we handle.' There was a note of pride in his voice: 'When the ferries were running they carried between eight and nine thousand cars a day. On any normal day now an average of nineteen thousand vehicles pass through here,' he said, as if every car was a victory for the bridge.

Toftlund leaned forward:

'If we have a date for a transaction, and a time, what can you do?'

'With that I can locate a picture of the car. That's for sure. But that's not to say there will be a clear shot of the driver. These aren't speed cameras. You have a warrant granting you access to the suspect's bank accounts, I expect, and you have a warrant authorising me to let you see the photographs, so that takes care of the formalities. If that's what you're after I can help you.'

Toftlund pointed to the computer on Svendsen's desk.

'Can you do it from here?'

'Yes. But let's go up to the Ops room first, to give you an idea of how the system works.'

The operations room reminded Toftlund of the bridge of a modern cargo vessel. The large panorama windows offered an excellent overview of the toll plaza beneath the canopy which arched over the driving lanes in both directions. On a large monitor suspended from the ceiling Toftlund could see the traffic passing smoothly and steadily through the toll lanes and up onto the beautiful, curving sweep of the high section of the bridge. The monitor showed the traffic on both the low and high sections. There were four people on duty, three men and a woman. They nodded and smiled when Svendsen briefly introduced Toftlund and Bastrup, but otherwise kept their eyes on their computer screens. One screen showed different angled shots of the red and white barriers on Sprogø, there to prevent some motorist from driving off for a look around the little island which everyone drove over, but on which no one stopped. Another monitor showed the wind and weather conditions, the current wind strength and the surface temperature on the bridge. At the moment conditions were normal, Toftlund could see, but it was from here, in the Ops room that the speed limit would be lowered in the case of high winds, or the bridge be closed completely should a real storm blow up.

Toftlund and Bastrup watched the stream of trucks and cars driving into the toll lanes, their drivers either paying cash or sticking a card into the narrow slit in the machine, pressing a button and driving on. They could follow the flow of traffic with the naked eye, but each transaction also flashed up onto another of the computer screens, along with a wide shot and a semi-wide of the vehicle and a close-up of the number plate. Thus tying together the card transaction and the car registration. Toftlund glanced up at the underside of the canopy. Three video cameras sat above each lane: one which apparently took a wide shot of the vehicle, one which zoomed in a little closer, and one focusing solely on the number plate. Toftlund also noticed that unfortunately only every now and again was it possible to make out the faces of drivers or passengers in the various vehicles before the three pictures, now stored on the server's massive hard disk, disappeared and were replaced by a fresh set. He was duly impressed by the efficiency and the simplicity of the whole process. Nineteen thousand cars on such a capricious April day. And yet there had been a campaign in protest against this bridge! The Danes were crazy!

'Impressive,' he said.

'It is, isn't it,' Svendsen agreed, proudly surveying his work. 'Shall we go back down ...?'

Svendsen seated himself at his computer and logged in, using a password. The warrant lay next to the keyboard on his desk. 'Okay, now I'm into the database,' he said. 'What have you got there?'

Charlotte Bastrup referred to her notebook and read out the details she had copied from the PBS payment advice: 'Date: March 12th, 1999, Time: 13.59. There are some terminal reference numbers. Do you need those?'

'Not to start with, no,' Svendsen said. He keyed in the date and the time. A moment later a whole series of transaction reports flashed up onto the screen, row upon row of them. Thirteen vehicles had passed through the toll plaza and paid by card at 13.59 on March 12th, 1999.

'Card number?' Svendsen asked.

Bastrup read it out:

'Dankort no. 4573 3002, four times x, 8652. 220.00 kroner. Terminal 9006015–07699. Ref. No. 7799, no. 234801. Lane no. 15. Cat. 2.'

'Okay, okay. That's more than enough, thanks,' Svendsen said. He typed again and a picture of a vehicle appeared on the screen. It was a digital still from a video camera and not particularly sharp, but what they were looking at was quite clearly a blue Toyota Corolla, not quite new, seen from above.

'Irma's car,' Bastrup said, although the shot of the number plate had not yet come up on the screen.

Svendsen pressed some more buttons. The wide shot gave way to a closer shot of the car taken from a sharper downward angle. By camera two. They were in luck. They recognised Irma's face, but only because they knew it had to be her. Again the image was not very clear, nonetheless they thought they glimpsed someone else in the passenger seat.

'The picture quality's not great,' Svendsen said. 'We keep it low on purpose to save space on the hard disk. Do you want to see the last shot?'

Toftlund felt his heart pounding. Svendsen pressd the keys. Up came a clear shot of the number plate, taken by camera three. But neither the passenger's face nor Irma's was visible. Irma's hands could be seen on the steering wheel, and barely discernible was another hand which seemed to be resting on top of the dashboard. It was a slender hand with long, well-shaped nails. They could also see the back of a head covered in short, black curls – it looked as though this person was bending down. Possibly to pick up something that had fallen onto the floor of the car – a lighter or a cigarette maybe?

'A woman,' Toftlund and Bastrup burst out at the same time.

'Would you like a print of those?'

'Yes, please.'

Svendsen printed out the three pictures and then repeated the process for the return journey which Irma had also paid for with her Dankort debit card. The record of the transaction showed that she had driven back across the bridge to Zealand the following day, March 13th. Her face was not visible on this set of video images, but unless someone was deliberately hiding in the car then she was alone. She had passed through the toll plaza at 20.32. With the aid of Bastrup's notes Svendsen was able to retrieve other pictures, all of which showed Irma alone in the car. Or at least, it was not possible to say for sure whether she was carrying a passenger. But that accorded with the other card transactions they had accessed. Irma had bought petrol and paid with a fuel card just south of the Danish-German border. That too had been on March 12th. The following morning she had used her Eurocard to withdraw 300 Deutschmarks from an ATM at Hamburg Airport. Who had that money been for? There had been no receipt in her purse. She had filled up again in Kolding in Jutland on March 13th on the way to Copenhagen. On March 14th she had purchased an air ticket to Zurich, an expensive Business Class seat on a flight departing two days later, returning via Brussels. She had made the booking by phone and given her Eurocard number. She had flown back to

Denmark on March 27th. There were no electronic traces from her visit to Zurich. By March 20th they had had her under scrutiny. They had come up with her name a week earlier and linked her to Edelweiss. She was arrested on landing at Copenhagen Airport. Since then Irma had, by and large, invoked her statutory right to remain silent and had either refused to answer their questions or dismissed their accusations with a scornful laugh. But her spell in solitary was starting to get to her. She was slowly cracking. You could tell by looking at her. And by reading what she wrote. She wouldn't be human if it didn't, Toftlund thought to himself as they headed back to Copenhagen.

They drove in silence for the first five minutes, then Charlotte said: 'It's frightening to think what the authorities can find out about you.' 'We think no one knows our movements and all the while we're leaving one electronic trace after another. We think that because there are so many of us we are just lost in the crowd. When in fact the exact opposite is the case. Although, of course, people like us should be glad of that.'

'That was a fine piece of detective work,' Toftlund said. 'You remind me of Hawkeye.'

'Thanks for the compliment,' came the dry retort.

'Do you know who Hawkeye was?'

'I have an older brother, you know. A trapper in some Western, wasn't he.'

Toftlund laughed.

'Close. A pathfinder. A tracker. He could read the forest floor and tell you how many animals or people had gone along a path and when. Run his fingers over a piece of charred wood and say when a fire had been put out. Tell from the sap from a leaf when a man's shoulder had brushed against it. You're a modern-day pathfinder. Only you use your computer. That was an excellent piece of work.'

'Well, thank you,' she said with a smile of satisfaction. Knowing full well that he was right. She could tell that he understood her:

obviously the whole point was to obtain the proof necessary to convict the guilty party, but it was the hunt that was the truly exciting thing about the job – the actual solving of a case was really just a bonus. Wisely, though, she kept such thoughts to herself.

Just after Slagelse Toftlund pulled onto the hard shoulder and switched on the hazard warning lights.

'Would you mind driving?' he said, getting out and walking round to the passenger side. He took out his mobile – he wasn't happy about using it, but he didn't intend to mention any names. Vuldom answered right away and Toftlund filled her in on what they could see in the pictures and what they could not see, and told her it was unlikely that their technicians could improve much on the quality of them. They'd drawn a blank. There was certainly little chance of them being able to identify the woman in them.

'Not a complete blank,' Vuldom said. 'Something tells me the woman in the passenger seat is her step-sister, and that she arrived in Copenhagen on a plane landing somewhere between eleven a.m. and noon on March 12th. I'll have that checked. She's then taken a taxi to the Karslunde lay-by. That's a fair drive. The sort a taxi driver would remember. I'll have that checked too. Irma has picked her up at the lay-by and taken her to meet E– at the Haderselv services. My feeling is that whatever these three had to talk about was so important that the woman from Bratislava insisted on doing it face to face. This was the big one, for E– and for her. In some way. It was very big. And the only person who could orchestrate and arrange such a meeting was Irma, who knew Mira Majola had something to sell, or was willing to buy something.'

'I don't quite follow,' Toftlund said.

'This is an open line, so we'll discuss it later. But we've been looking at it all back to front,' Vuldom said. 'We thought it was E– who was doing the wooing, but it was Mira. Mira, or Maria, holds the key. And Irma, of course. She knows everything, but that doesn't help us.'

'Right.'

'Exactly. So do me a favour, Toftlund – find the mysterious Mira for me. We know from Teddy that she was spotted in Albania. I had pretty much decided that it wasn't worth the bother, but we'll have to give it a try. You could do that, couldn't you?'

'Of course,' he said, with no great conviction. Because he knew this would mean leaving the country again and he did not know how he was going to explain to Lise that he had to go.

23

TOFTLUND PRESSED THE RECORD BUTTON on the cassette player and said: 'April 21st, 1999. The time is 16.32. Interview with Irma Pedersen. Conducted by myself, DCI Per Toftlund. Also present, DI Charlotte Bastrup.'

It was warm in the bare little room. Bastrup was leaning against the painted wall. She was wearing a pair of tight, black trousers and a white shirt beneath which he could see the edging of the bra covering her small, round breasts. She stood there watching with her cool, clear eyes, had not greeted Irma. Unlike Toftlund who, as usual, had thanked the accused for coming – as if she had any choice – and explained that there were a couple of minor details which needed clarification. This was the usual opening gambit used by Toftlund and countless other investigators. In her hand Bastrup held a manila folder, unopened. Toftlund sat opposite Irma in the same sort of rigid, straight-backed chair as she. Before him lay another manila folder. The only other items on the laminated table were a blue plastic disposable lighter and a freshly opened pack of filter cigarettes lying next to a heavy ceramic ashtray, its base grey and greasy, smeared by countless fidgety arrestees. Toftlund hated cigarette smoke but he was as pleased to see that Irma was smoking as he was that Lise had given it up. It was yet another sign that she was not quite as calm and self-assured as those green eyes, the faint smile and the straight back would have it. Today she was dressed in a workmanlike shirt and a pair of light-blue denims – a young person's attire, but then her generation had never outgrown jeans and that whole functional style of dress. She had made an effort, applied a light coating of discreet pink lipstick and accentuated her eyes with black liner and a touch of green shadow that brought out the colour of her irises and went well with her pale skin. The lines on her face were actually very becoming to her well-shaped, almost classical features. She was undeniably an attractive woman, even if she was pushing sixty, Toftlund thought. She was naturally slim, which may have been why her figure had retained a certain litheness in its curves which rendered it still sensual and appealing. Nonetheless, her complexion was starting to acquire a greyish pallor. Prison did that to people. And behind those cool, intelligent eyes he sensed an uncertainty and a tiredness. As if she was not getting enough sleep. As if solitary was finally starting to get to her. Denmark's widespread practice of holding detainees in solitary confinement was often criticised in the media and by other countries, but Toftlund found it an effective means of breaking down an individual's defence mechanisms. Luckily they were not expected to beat confessions out of suspects and for that Toftlund was thankful. He had nothing but contempt for those of his colleagues who occasionally resorted to the wet towel approach. But the aim was, of course, the same: if a criminal was not prepared to own up right away, thus saving everyone a lot of time, then you had to make use of whatever methods the law allowed. Because he did not doubt for one second that Irma was guilty.

She looked up as she lit her cigarette, deliberately blew the smoke in his face. It might be that he was gradually learning to read her, but she knew just how to get his back up.

'Well, well. I'm being honoured by both Donald *and* Daisy today,' she said and drew on her cig with her eyes half-shut. Her voice was light and melodious.

'Why don't we just cut the crap, Irma,' Toftlund replied. 'Let's save ourselves a lot of trouble, put our cards on the table. Why bother going over the same old ground again and again?'

'I thought that's what you were paid to do.'

'I'm paid to work on society's behalf to bring people like you to court, to receive the sentence that society sees fit to pass on them.'

'They can't be paying you much then.'

'Look, we've been through all this. We've established that you have passed top-secret information to foreign powers. We've shown that you have harmed your country. We've linked you with your cover name in the Stasi files. We've presented you with the proof, set down in black and white, of how it all fits together. As I said, you could save a lot of time by filling in the few remaining gaps. I know you see it differently, and I know your lawyer says differently, but there's no denying the facts.'

'You've got nothing.'

'Okay – you're obviously still not prepared to see sense, so maybe I should show you something,' he said, undaunted, although she had elicited a wry little grin from him for that comment about his low pay. It was going to be a long afternoon. She knew she had to appear in the High Court within eight days, and if they had no new and significant evidence to present at that point then she would go free. That, certainly, was the prospect outlined to her by her lawyer. Or at least, that was what he had told the press. Among the left-wing parties at Christiansborg, and even within the government, more and more voices were being raised, protesting that the state was going too far. Either the authorities had to show their hand, present whatever evidence they had, or they had to release the accused, who was referred to only as Edelweiss. The whole affair was starting to become rather embarrassing. The media knew nothing of the Serbian lead: that relating to the NATO aircraft flight paths. They thought it was simply a matter of crimes committed more than ten years ago during the cold war in the name of a country known by the acronym GDR – which the majority of young people today would probably think was the name of a new TV channel rather than a communist state which died as abruptly as it came into being. Most people felt that the whole business was something of an anachronism. Let all that old rubbish rest in peace, as one paper had put it.

Toftlund produced the printout of the three pictures from the Storebælt Bridge.

| 331 |

'Is this your car?'

'It could be,' she said. 'It's certainly blue and it's Japanese.'

'Do you know where and when these photographs were taken?'

'No.'

'At Storebælt on March 12th this year, around one p.m.'

'If you say so.'

'I do. And you're not alone in the car, Irma.'

'Dear me, that must be worth at least ten years in the clink. Illegal presence of passenger while crossing the new bridge over Storebælt. And here was I thinking the toll fee covered the car, the driver and any eventual passengers.'

'You're a right pain in the ass, Irma, do you know that?'

'Ah, so the feeling's mutual, then.'

'Who's your passenger?'

'I've no idea. A colleague maybe. Or a hitchhiker. I really can't remember, but something tells me you have your own ideas about this too.'

'It was your dear little sister,' Toftlund said, fixing his eyes on her. Behind him he was conscious of Bastrup pulling away from the wall slightly so that she too could study Irma's expression. She surprised them by laughing out loud:

'God, you're as easy to read as some hyped-up children's book,' she sighed as she stubbed out her cigarette, lit another and puffed the smoke in Toftlund's face. This time he instinctively, and much against his will, wafted away the acrid grey cloud.

'I don't know who it is. I'm back and forth across the bridge all the time. I have a brother and a mother living on the other side of Storebælt. I don't know what you're trying to achieve with this, but it sounds to me as if you're getting a bit desperate. Am I right?'

She looked Toftlund in the eye:

'I am right,' was all she said.

Toftlund leaned right across the table, holding her gaze:

'You wrote a long letter to your dear sister.'

'It's not polite to read other people's letters or diaries.'

She puffed indignantly on her cigarette, but he could tell that she was not the slightest bit surprised. Vuldom had been right. She had written that account assuming that they would read it. She had thrown them some clues, but they might just as easily be fiction as recollections. Everything she did was done with manipulation in mind. Toftlund suddenly remembered someone saying once – he could not remember where – that the world of espionage was like a hall of mirrors: what you saw was not what was actually there.

'As far as you're concerned I can do whatever I like. Leave no stone in your life unturned. For someone in your situation there's no longer any such thing as a private life.'

'Are we about to start the third degree?'

'That I'm not allowed to do.'

'Do I detect an unspoken "unfortunately"?'

'No. The systems you worked for are the ones who use such methods. That's only one of many differences between them and us. Who's this sister you've been writing to, Irma?'

Irma glanced over at Charlotte, who idly opened the file she was holding. Then she said:

'A sister is a sister. It could be Daisy there. It's all women. The other half of the population. The downtrodden half of the population. Right? That's what we called one another in the women's movement. Sister. Do you see.'

Charlotte said:

'You sound every bit as pathetic as my mother. Don't try to lecture me. Or drag me into it. You're the one who wrote, and I quote: "In the Peasant and Worker State of the GDR they have succeeded, despite the machinations of Imperialism, in producing both an industrial miracle and an equality between the sexes and the classes which does not exist in late-capitalist West Germany." Let's just think about that for a moment.'

Irma said nothing. They waited, then Charlotte continued:

'Here's another little titbit from your totalitarian past: "Although the armed conflict being waged by the Baader-Meinhof group may not be readily defensible within a Danish context it is not the function of the new left to blindly join in the bourgeois press's hue-and-cry against the righteous struggle of the anti-Imperialist powers, a struggle to which they have been driven by the repressive tolerance of late-capitalist society." How in hell's name does a woman like you get to be a university professor with responsibility for educating future generations?'

Irma still said nothing, merely stubbed out her cigarette and promptly lit another.

Charlotte stepped up to the table, waving the documents in her hand:

'There's a whole lot more in the same vein. Going all the way back to your teens. Your smooth and apparently effortless progress through totalitarianism from the fifties to the eighties ended well and at no time entailed any real risk for you, although of course you were never caught – unlike your German comrades.'

'Or your father,' Toftlund added, and finally he got a response:

'You keep him out of this,' she all but shouted, her neck flushing an angry red. 'He's dead. This has nothing to do with him.'

'It has everything to do with him, Irma,' Toftlund rejoined. 'He is your pain, his fate is what drives you, his betrayal the burden you feel you must bear. Because his betrayal hurt you, you felt bound to hurt the democratic society which hounded him.'

'Why does every cop fancy himself as a psychologist?' Her voice was steady again, but the hectic flush spread from her throat down to the opening of her shirt.

'Your father was a son of a bitch.'

'That's enough.'

'A traitor, in the pay of the Germans, a war criminal like the rest of those dirty SS bastards, a Nazi ...'

'Are you about finished?'

'A bad father, a bad husband, an imposter, a liar, a bigamist. A whoremaster. Your sister is a bastard, your mother's present marriage invalid. And all because of that son of a bitch you call your father!'

Toftlund managed to duck and barely missed being hit by the ashtray which Irma had picked up and hurled at him with an astonishingly powerful underhand throw – but only because he had been expecting her to erupt. Charlotte Bastrup was not so lucky. The heavy ashtray sailed past her nose, but some of the ash and one butt flew up in her face. She started coughing and rubbing one of her eyes. Irma got to her feet and pushed back her chair. Toftlund sat where he was, ignoring Charlotte's coughing. Irma moved back to the far wall and pressed herself against it, as if she could break down the wall by sheer physical force. Her fists were clenched, her face strained and chalk-white. She was having trouble breathing. A sidelong glance told Toftlund that Charlotte was still rubbing her eye. She ought to stop that, but it was her funeral. Toftlund kept his eyes pinned on Irma. The tape turned steadily. Her lawyer was going to give them grief. Especially if, as it seemed, she was starting to hyperventilate. The lawyer would definitely be of the opinion that he had overstepped the mark, but Toftlund didn't care. A big crack had finally appeared in her defences. She had sat there coolly and calmly while he had presented her with a whole stack of documents testifying to the fact that Irma was Edelweiss and Edelweiss was Irma. Not even when he informed her that her acts of treachery had led to lives being lost in the Baltic region had she made any response. Except to say the same things over and over again: secret files are works of fiction written by insignificant little men who always wanted to make themselves seem more important than they were. A newspaper article was made out to be a confidential report. An innocent lunch became a rendezvous with an informant. As a researcher she wouldn't trust those so-called intelligence files any further than she could throw them. You could not believe a word of them. That had been her constant mantra, but now a chink had appeared and so he kept up the pressure :

'Face it, Irma. Your Dad was an out-and-out bastard, with no thought for anybody but himself. You don't owe him a thing. You owe yourself something, though. You owe it to yourself to ease your conscience, to lay down this burden you're carrying.'

Irma was still standing with her back to the wall. Her face was pale, but her breathing was becoming more controlled. There were tears in her green eyes, but he was sorry to see that the old coldness was also starting to steal back into them. Charlotte was still trying to quell her coughing fit. Her mind was not on the job in hand and that annoyed him, but at the same time he felt the urge to comfort her.

'Who is E–?' Toftlund asked.

'A better man than you'll ever be.'

'So he does exist?'

'Unlike you he is a decent human being. A man of principle.'

'What is E–'s real name?'

She stared at him, crossed her arms over her chest.

'I would like to go back to my cell.'

'Soon, Irma. What is E–'s name and where can we find him?'

'I don't know.'

'Irma!'

'I don't know. I refuse to say any more on the grounds that it might incriminate me.'

'Where is your sister?'

'I don't know.'

'But she is your sister?'

'Yes. She is my sister.' She was almost yelling at him now.

'What is her real name?'

'Mira Majola.'

'Where is she?'

'I don't know, I tell you.'

'Was your sister in Denmark on March 12th this year?'

'You know very well she was.'

'What was she doing here?'

'Visiting me.'

'So that you could pass top-secret information to her?'

'Are you really that stupid, Toftlund? Where would I get my hands on top-secret information?'

'So you could introduce her to E–, then?'

'Perhaps.'

'Why, Irma?'

She stepped away from the wall and waggled her hands as if they were wet and she was trying to shake water or some nasty, sticky fluid off them.

'Because I wanted the two people who mean most to me to meet.'

'I don't believe that, Irma.'

'You can believe what you like. I'm saying no more. I want to speak to my lawyer. This is psychological torture.'

'Did Mira work for the Serbs?'

'If you say so then she must have.'

'Did she double-cross them? Are they after her?'

'Perhaps.'

'We can help her.'

'I'm not saying any more. You're exerting undue pressure on me.'

'So you and E– were going to help her?'

'I have nothing more to say.'

'But that seems reasonable enough. The world is a different place now, after all.'

'Leave me alone.'

'Or was it one last deal?'

'Can't you get it into your head – I have nothing more to say.'

'These two were to meet because this was to be the last deal, and it was a big one, with a lot of money riding on it.'

'I have nothing more to say.'

'A nice retirement pension, so to speak, for both E– and little sister.'

'I have nothing more to say.'

'A pension for little sister Mira because time is running out for Milosevic and his gang. He's up against NATO now, not unarmed women and children. He's about to lose his fourth war. It's going to be one war too many. Time is running out for the butcher. Little sister meant to cash in on his downfall. And E– wanted a piece of the cake because he has had his day too and he's worried about what might be in the Stasi or old KGB files. I'm right, aren't I, Irma? It's not cheap living underground and there aren't very many places left in the world that are still willing to give house room to the spies of the past.'

She sniffed, and sighed as if giving in, and Toftlund's hopes rose as she lifted her toppled chair, sat down again and lit a cigarette. Charlotte Bastrup stood with her back to the wall. She was glaring at Irma. Her left eye was red and slightly swollen and wet, as if she had been crying.

'You don't understand the first thing about it,' Irma said softly. 'You see life as being black and white. You see life and existence as things that can be explained rationally. You see life as being linear, but it isn't. It's convoluted and inexplicable. You forget our dreams, and you forget hope. You think life is a crossword puzzle. That people will find the solution and get it to work out. You don't understand a thing.'

'Who is E–?'

She considered him.

'Figure it out for yourself. Ah, but you can't, can you?'

'Irma. You've admitted that E– exists. That Mira Majola is your sister. And we know from your brothers that your father lived the life he lived. That you consort with members of the SS vet-erans' association. That you were once a revolutionary because you hate bourgeois society. We know that you are Edelweiss. We know that you introduced Mira, a Serbian agent, to E–. Basically, all we need is a name, and for you to tell us that our information is correct. Then you can go free. You'll be released from solitary confinement. You can pick up the pieces of your life again. Where does E– work? Within NATO? Within the EU? Is he a Danish ambassador? Working with the Ministry of Foreign Affairs?'

'Who said he was Danish?' she rejoined. That cool, mocking look was, unfortunately, back in her eyes.

'You – you wrote that he was.'

'Maybe I'm writing a novel. To pass the time.'

'That I don't believe.'

'Does Simone de Beauvoir write novels or memoirs?'

'I've never read anything by her. As a matter of fact I've no idea who she is.'

'Well, you should read her, it would do you good.'

'That's not what we're talking about.'

'It's exactly what we're talking about. Because what we're talking about is liberation.'

'Who is he?'

She leaned across the table:

'That, Per Toftlund, you will never learn from me. My secrets are my own. And I'll take them with me to my grave. And now I have nothing more to say. I would like to go back to my cell.'

Toftlund sighed:

'Okay,' he said. 'But you don't get off that easily. I'll be seeing you.'

'Tell that to the judge in a week's time.'

Toftlund glanced at his watch, stated the time and switched off the cassette recorder. Charlotte walked quietly up to the table and leaned over Irma. Then she clenched a hand round the face of the other woman, who sat perfectly still, though with fear now showing in those lovely green eyes.

'Bitch!' Charlotte hissed and Toftlund could see her hand squeezing tighter and tighter. 'How can you live with yourself?'

'For God's sake, Charlotte,' Toftlund broke in.

Charlotte let go of Irma's face and straightened up.

'Bitch,' she repeated in the same icy tone.

| 339 |

'It takes one to know one,' Irma snapped. Bastrup, already moving away from the table, froze in mid-step.

'Charlotte!' was all Toftlund said.

'I'm okay,' she said.

She said it again after Irma had been led away and they were back in Toftlund's office. He had dampened a piece of cotton wool and was holding her face up to the light while he tried to remove the last of the tiny specks of ash from her eye. She had tried, unsuccessfully, to do it herself. With his left hand cupped lightly round her face he dabbed the red, inflamed eye, then very gently tried to winkle out the three specks which he could clearly see, lodged under her lower lid. She smelled faintly of tobacco, but mostly of some delicate perfume. Her lips were moist. He had no luck at the first attempt, but the second time he managed to catch all three specks on the edge of the damp cotton wool and ease them out. He kept his hand curled around her face, in much the same way as Charlotte had held Irma's, only Toftlund's grip was gentle and his fingers began to stroke her cheek. Her skin was soft and warm. She blinked the irritated eye a few times and peered up at him. He ran his hand down the back of her head, over the cropped hair. His other arm slipped round her waist and when she turned her whole face up to him, he kissed her. He could feel the pent-up desire when she pressed herself against him and slid her tongue between his lips. He ran his hand down her back and over her little rump and felt her tugging at his shirt to pull it free of his trousers so that she could get at his bare skin. His own hand glided from her buttocks and under her shirt. The skin there was moist and warm as his fingers stroked her back before moving downwards, under her waistband, as far as he could reach, to her tailbone. Her breath was coming in quick, short pants, it felt hot against his cheek and he felt his own desire growing, his penis almost aching from the nudging of her pelvis and the play of their tongues. But in the midst of the longing and the aching the voice in his head said: Let her go. You have to let go of her. This is a workmate. You can't do this to Lise. Let go of her.

He would never know whether he would have had the strength or the moral fibre to stop there, because he was saved by the telephone on the desk. He could see from the display when he removed his lips from Charlotte's that the call was from Vuldom. He took a quick step backwards. She stayed where she was, her lips moist and slightly swollen, her shirt hanging loose over her trousers and her breasts rising with each breath. Did he look the same? She gave him a look that was both lustful and taunting. It seemed to say: It's up to you. But you won't get another chance. If you pick up that phone the spell is broken and it can never be recaptured.

He picked up the phone.

'Toftlund,' he said, his eyes still on Charlotte, who was idly trying to tuck her shirt back into her waistband. She gave up, undid her narrow, black belt and he caught a glimpse of her thin white panties as her trousers slid down, she slowly arranged her shirt and with languorous sensuality buckled her belt again, still with those bright, intense, provocative eyes fixed on him. Give me a sign, they said. A smile, a gesture, telling me to lock the door, or to say that very soon we're going to go back to my place. Put a hand over the phone and blow me a kiss. Let me know that something earth-shattering just happened between us, and that you want it to continue. He turned his face away and proceeded to give Vuldom an account of the day's interview. He was surprised to find how steady his voice was. He heard the click as Charlotte shut the door behind her, while he was agreeing with Vuldom that they had made some progress, but that it would still be hard to get it to stand up in court.

'There's nothing else for it – you'll have to leave for Albania tomorrow,' Vuldom concluded. 'I'll get someone onto booking the tickets right away. You'll have to ask for assistance from NATO, or the Emergency Management Agency or one of our guys with the UN peacekeeping force down there. Take Teddy with you.'

'What if he doesn't want to go?'

'He has no choice. I'll call him shortly. I'll hire him as an interpreter. Threaten him with something or other. Appeal to his sense of duty, if he has any such thing. You need him with you. He knows what she looks like.'

'There are half a million refugees down there, scattered all over a country in total upheaval.'

'She's the key, Toftlund.'

'Right.'

'You're thinking about the baby, aren't you.'

'Yes, actually I was,' he said, surprised that she should think of it.

'When's it due?'

'A week's time.'

'We have to be in court eight days from now. So you'll have to be home by then. For one reason and another.'

'What about Bastrup?'

'What about her?'

'Is she coming too?' he asked and waited, not knowing which answer he wanted Vuldom to give him.

'That would probably be helpful in some ways, but you can manage on your own. She'll have to carry on with the investigation at this end. In any case I think she's better at the computer than out in the field. From what I hear Albania's no picnic.'

'Right you are, ma'am,' he said, feeling more relieved than anything else.

He called home. Lise sounded happy.

'Hi, sweetheart,' she said.

'I'm on my way home now. Have you eaten?'

'Nope, and I'm in the mood for something really tasty.'

'How's about I pick up some takeaway Sticks'n'Sushi?'

'You read my mind, honey. Hurry home.'

'I'll be home in about forty-five minutes.'

'We can't wait to see you.'

He drove home in a strange mood, ridden with guilt, but at the same time relieved that things had not gone any further – although he was shocked by the ease with which he could be tempted and seduced, by the frailty of human resolve. He was quite sure that it would never happen again. But could he have kept that promise if Charlotte had been coming to Albania with him? He did not know how he would tell Lise that he was flying out the next day, or the day after that at the very latest. He could not expect her to have any faith in his promises now. On the other hand, she could not expect him to tell his boss that he wasn't going? He tried to put his thoughts in order, but his mind was like a big boxful of Lego tipped out onto the floor all higgledy-piggledy by a child who cannot understand why the instructions for building the fabulous constructions pictured on the box no longer seem to make any sense.

It was still light when he pulled up outside their little red-brick house. It was not even particularly cold. The wind had died down and the sky was bright, only the last vestiges of the heavy grey clouds visible far down on the horizon. He called a friendly hello to their neighbour, his heart lifting at the thought that he had a home and a wife whom he loved waiting for him inside it, while at the same time cursing his own hypocrisy.

Lise was curled up on the sofa, watching television. He set the bag containing the sushi on the table and gave her a long, lingering kiss. Her lips tasted good from the white wine in the glass in front of her.

'Hm, lovely. I think a little glass of wine is good for the baby and this is just perfect for sushi,' she said.

'What are you watching?'

'It's supposed to be a news programme, but really just another example of the prevailing ideology of the nineties: self-promotion, the cult of narcissism.'

'God, what a lot of big words you know, Lise.'

She laughed. She knew his own vocabulary was a great deal more extensive than he let on. He stroked her neck, his eyes too on the TV screen. It was obviously news of a sort, although you would hardly have known it: some young twenty-something guy had been voted the hottest man in Denmark. He was well-built in the standard, vapid body-building fashion which Toftlund despised. There was a clip of him standing on a stage along with other muscular young men in minuscule underpants. He was being presented with a bottle of champagne and was beaming so ecstatically that anyone would have thought he had won some really distinguished award. The other guys clapped half-heartedly and tried to smile, jealous that it was him in the spotlight and not them. Then it was back to the studio, where the young female presenter asked kittenishly:

'And how do you feel about posing in your underwear?'

The young man tilted his head to one side and smiled coyly:

'I don't really mind it,' he replied.

'But why do you do it?'

'Well, it's really important to be seen, you know. I just love it. There's nothing else like it, as far as I'm concerned. I'd like to work in television.'

'So isn't it brilliant to be voted the hottest guy in Denmark?' the presenter asked, smiling at the country's sexiest man.

His grin grew even broader, so delighted was he to be under the television lights:

'Yeah, well, obviously it's kind of brilliant if people think you're hot.'

Per and Lise both hooted with laughter.

'There, what did I tell you,' Lise chuckled. 'What a wonderful country we live in, eh?'

The girl presenter thanked her guest, as if the hottest guy in the country had done every single Dane an enormous favour by coming into the studio, then her expression turned to one of studied gravity, she lowered her voice half an octave just as the voice coach had taught her and announced: 'Again today thousands of Kosovo Albanians streamed into the poorest country in Europe, fleeing from the NATO bombings and the Serbian campaign of terror and violence. Our correspondent in the region sent us this report from Albania ...'

'I have to go down there tomorrow or the day after, Lise. I'm sorry,' Per said.

She turned her face up to his, causing his hand to slip from the back of her neck:

'I'll bet you are,' she muttered tonelessly.

'It's only for a couple of days.'

'Please yourself. You will do anyway.'

'It's my job.'

'This is our life.'

He stood for a moment – all of a sudden he simply could not be bothered saying any more or explaining any further.

'I'd better see to the sushi.'

'Actually, I think I just lost the notion for sushi, Per,' she said, picking up the remote control and demonstratively turning up the sound.

24

TEDDY AND PER were on the plane to Frankfurt, and after only an hour together with Pedersen at the airport and fifteen minutes in the air, Toftlund was already sick of this infuriating, opinionated motormouth of a man who seemed to imagine that the whole world was interested in his views on everything under the sun. Toftlund had nothing against a bit of conversation, but for his own part he was careful not to express his opinions on any topic. If he had any fault to find with Lise it was that she could not watch the news or read an article in the paper without instantly feeling moved to say what she thought. As if you were not really living unless you were expressing an opinion, preferably in the media. Toftlund held, as he saw it, to a few basic convictions, but it was also his belief that there was more than one answer to most questions, that nothing was black and white, but that more often than not life was made up of shades of grey, with each answer giving rise to fresh questions. He was, in his own eyes, the down-to-earth sort. He was not particularly interested in abstracts. It was a waste of time. He was interested in practicalities: how to carry out a specific task, be it buying a carton of milk, getting a suspect to confess, or eliminating him or her from his inquiries. That was more than enough for him. Not so Teddy Pedersen. With him everything had to be considered from every angle and duly commented upon. That, so it seemed, was intellectuals for you. Or academics rather. They could never accept anything at face value, always had to be picking holes in an argument or twisting something simple and straightforward so that it suddenly became complex and obscure. Life was difficult enough as it was without making it even more complicated with these eternal 'what-ifs'. This same trend was becoming more and more prevalent in television journalism too. What if the government resigned? What if a fire broke out in the tunnel under Storebælt? What if you were to drink four litres of chlorine a day – would you get cancer? Why couldn't one just take things as they came. When you got right down to it, though, it probably just went to show how astonishingly little actually happened in Denmark. They had to make simple things seem complicated or make up stories to fill air time and newspaper columns.

Toftlund sighed. He missed Lise, he was fed up with his job and sorry about the way they had parted. Lise with her big belly and a polite, but cool: 'Have a good trip.' The words had sounded right, but the tone had been all wrong. As if he were going off on a well-deserved holiday. 'It's only for a few days,' he had muttered, feeling angry and resentful and upset. She had closed the door when the taxi appeared, nosing its way uncertainly down the road, the estate they lived on being so new that it probably had not yet made it into the latest street map.

He did not feel like eating the cold snack which was SAS's idea of a breakfast or early lunch. Instead he shut his eyes, fell asleep and did not wake until he felt the plane beginning its descent to Frankfurt Airport. In the window seat, Teddy was gazing out at the clouds that seemed almost to wrap the aircraft in grey cotton wool. He reeked of free red wine and an early brandy, but he held his peace, and Toftlund felt actually better for his nap and decided to be a little more tolerant. It was April 23rd; they emerged from the layer of low, grey cloud to see green fields below them. Spring – the real thing and not the prolonged, half-hearted forerunner to it – was just around the corner, he would go home and very soon there would be three of them, all set to embark on a new life together, because this baby would change things for ever.

It was not easy to maintain this buoyant mood once inside Frankfurt's grubby, chaotic airport, which accorded so badly with the German reputation for cleanliness and order.

'Frankfurt is sheer hell. I'd swear it was designed by a mad

Russian with Italian blood in his veins,' Teddy moaned as they lugged their bags towards the escalators leading to Gate B41. Toftlund could not help laughing. The description was so apt: the crowds of travellers trailing over the grimy floors, the acrid smoke rising from a group gathered, as if for a prayer meeting, around a foul-smelling ashtray with a sign above it saying: 'Raucher'.

'I just need to join the cortège of sinners over there,' Teddy said. 'We've got loads of time.'

He strode across to the huddle of smokers, lit a cigarette and inhaled it greedily. Toftlund waited patiently, surveying the scene: the hordes of people, like lost souls struggling to find their way through the jungle of signs: C20–98, A20–90, B20–41 – it was more like an intricate code devised by some crazy cryptologist. The only orderly elements were the white trains on the elevated railway which shuttled back and forth, picking up passengers. He realised he had a hollow feeling in his stomach. He had never been to Albania before. That was part of it. He knew it was a country in turmoil, swamped by the greatest refugee disaster in living memory. It was poverty-stricken and falling apart and, like the other former Soviet bloc countries, still laboured under the heavy legacy of communism. And in Albania, what is more, a distinct and very weird Chinese-Albanian brand of communism cooked up by that megalomaniac Enver Hoxha. He had sealed the country off from the rest of Europe, consigning it to a paranoid, self-sufficient dictatorship which left it destitute, despised and degraded. Now it styled itself a democracy with a market economy, but as far as Toftlund could gather from the short briefing document from the Ministry of Foreign Affairs which had been handed to him by a tight-lipped, coolly correct Charlotte, said democracy was a pretty abstract quantity and the so-called market economy a madman's version of raw capitalism in which mafia-style organisations controlled both the grey and the black markets, which were far bigger than the white.

But the other reason for that sinking sensation in his stomach was the nature of the assignment. Finding Mira Majola, who could be operating under any name, in a chaotic country containing over half a million unregistered refugees, seemed like an impossible task, but he gathered from the Emergency Service Agency that some form of registration was always carried out when exhausted, hungry, thirsty refugees turned for help to the UN or one of the many private relief organisations already working in Albania. He had sent copies of the material which they at PET possessed to the Danish office at Durrës, which was responsible for coordinating the efforts of the UN and the Danish Refugee Council.

This was the Albania he was describing to Teddy when the two of them finally succeeded in negotiating the airport's bewildering maze of corridors and reached the departure lounge. They stood at the back of the queue, surrounded by dark-haired people, most of them young men. Flights to Albania were as unreliable as the Danish April weather. They had been lucky even to get a connecting flight from Frankfurt with Slovenia Air to Ljubljana and from there to Tirana. At least that way they were spared a long, slow flight on one of the air force's Hercules troop carriers.

'All perfectly correct, Toftlund,' Teddy declared in his distinctive, melodious and slightly drawling voice. 'But to that you can add clan wars and blood feuds dating back three generations. First Hoxha's lunatic brand of communism, then rampant capitalism, with everybody investing like mad in pyramid schemes which, of course, came tumbling down with a bang. Bandits and muggers at every turn. Every man has his Kalashnikov, stolen when the shit hit the fan in '96. Albania is one fucked-up country, I'm telling you.'

'Have you been there before?'

Teddy laughed and took a long draw on his cigarette – the signs said No Smoking, but the dark-skinned, long-haired youths around them didn't give a toss about that. There was one young man who stood out from the rest. He looked like a Serb with his fair, crew-cut hair. He had soldier written all over him, and there

| 349 |

was a menacing litheness about his muscular frame which the discreet suit, button-down shirt and subtly patterned tie could not disguise. He had square-cut features and small close-set eyes. What looked like a knife scar ran across his cheek from his nose. Like Pedersen and Toftlund he took it easy and let everybody else push and shove their way towards the two buses they could see parked outside the departure lounge. Wherever there was war you found the merchants of death, the vultures of want and the crafts-men of espionage, Toftlund thought to himself, as he listened to Teddy's constant chatter, which continued as they hung on to the straps in the bus on the way out to Slovenian Air's big Airbus – the proud sign that Slovenia was a new, free European country, now first in the queue to join the good guys in the NATO and EU clubs:

'I was in Albania in the seventies, as a young tourist. It wasn't really my area, but I tagged along on a Danish Albanian Friend-ship Assocation trip. It was the weirdest, most surreal experience. The delegation was led by a Danish rock band. They were crazy about Albania. It was exactly like a piece of absurd theatre. You weren't allowed to utter one word of criticism, if you did you were banished to your hotel room. What I remember most is the quiet-ness and these little toadstool-shaped bunkers scattered all over the place, from which each and every Albanian was supposed to pick off invading troops with his own little rifle. It was a ghastly place, but the others couldn't see that. There was nothing to eat, nothing to read, just lies upon lies and an endless succession of kindergartens and factories with robots parrotting whatever the great leader said. Brezhnev's Russia was a liberalistic paradise compared to Albania back then. I said as much in an article I wrote when I got back. That was the end of the invitations from that particular quarter, and since the place went bust I've had no desire to go back.'

'What possessed well-educated Danes to support such a regime?'

'Don't ask me. Why do people seek Utopias? I've no idea. My

| 350 |

own sister has always been that way inclined. They want to be con-firmed in their belief that everything is for a purpose. They want to believe there is a higher cause which is worth serving. If there's no God then you have to come up with a replacement religion.'

'But Hoxha! Albania!'

'In their eyes it was original, pure, anti-materialistic. You know – merry peasants and singing milkmaids all alone in the cruel world, forsaken by the Soviet Union and China, threatened by the US and Italy. It beats me. Lenin's useful idiots came in many shapes and forms, but it's all water under the bridge and no one wants to hear about it any more.'

Teddy was first out of the bus. Like Toftlund he had on a pair of sensible Goretex boots. They had heard about the mud in which the refugees were almost choking. They slept in open fields, or under plastic sheeting on the small carts they had pulled behind their tractors on their flight from the terror of the Serbs. Other-wise, though, Teddy was clad in what he called his uniform: a pair of creased grey flannels with a tweed jacket over a self-coloured shirt and a thin pullover. Over his arm he carried a coat of an indeterminate beige. Toftlund was in blue jeans, a grey shirt, a blue sweater and a scuffed brown leather jacket. The rest of their things they had in their respective holdalls. Toftlund was pleased and possibly a little surprised to see that Teddy, like himself, trav-elled light. He sometimes forgot that Teddy might, in actual fact, be the more widely travelled of the two of them, particularly as regards those parts of the world which had until ten years ago been sealed off behind the Iron Curtain.

Ljubljana Airport was not very big, but it was packed with people. Again mainly young, swarthy men smoking, drinking and gabbling animatedly in Albanian. In a square box of a room with a bar in the middle Per and Teddy paid nine Deutschmarks each for a beer and a slivovitz. The place reeked of black tobacco. Two women in white uniforms with Red Cross badges stood out like sore thumbs among all the battle-ready youths. Toftlund gazed out at the snow-clad mountains in the distance, their tops blanketed by grey cloud. A thermometer gave the temperature as being fifteen degrees celsius. They were travelling towards spring. The noise and the smell of so many people was appalling. Toftlund wandered over into a corner in search of a little peace and quiet. He managed to get a signal on his mobile and Lise answered right away.

'Hi, sweetheart. It's me,' Toftlund said.

'Per! Where are you?'

'In Ljubljana. It looks like we'll be taking off again shortly. I've missed you.'

'I'm glad you called. We miss you too.'

'I'm not sure if my mobile will work in Albania.'

'Don't worry about that. Just take care of yourself.'

'I will …'

'And Per …?'

'Yes?'

'I'm sorry about the way I said goodbye.'

'Don't worry about it.'

'But I do.'

'I'll be home soon.'

'Just you look after yourself and I'll take care of everything at this end.'

Toftlund could picture her: standing in the kitchen maybe, looking out at the bare trees and shrubs, and a shower of rain perhaps, or the sunshine. But as always, spring felt as if it would never come.

'I'll be home soon,' he said again.

'I know. Take care.'

'I will. And Lise …?'

'Yes.'

'I love you.'

'I love you too. And we're fine. It won't be long now.'

Her voice cracked slightly, but he was happy to hear it, and for once he had managed to say what he felt. It helped to express one's feelings. When he switched off his mobile he realised that Teddy was standing right behind him.

'Aw, isn't that nice,' Teddy said.

'What the hell …! Are you in the habit of listening in to other people's telephone conversations?'

'I was born nosy, old boy. We could call this picture: *Teddy Overhears Policeman's Declaration of Love*. I wasn't being sarcastic. It's great to be in love with your wife. If that was your wife, that is.'

'It was,' Toftlund replied irritably.

'Your first?'

'If you must know, yes.'

'Ah, it'll pass.'

'What the blazes would you know about that?'

'I've had three.'

'A week from now I'll be a father,' Toftlund went on, growing even more annoyed – although as much with himself as with Teddy.

'Is that a first too?'

'Yes, dammit.'

'Me, I'd need to count up how many I have and with whom.'

'God, you're asking for it,' Toftlund seethed.

'Yep, that's Teddy. My wives used to say the same thing. And a lot else besides.'

Toftlund glowered at him then stalked back to the bar to finish his drink before, at long last, their flight was called. Apart from those occupied by Teddy, Per and the two Red Cross nurses or doctors all the seats on the plane were taken up by young, black-haired men.

'Cannon fodder for the UKC, the Kosovo Albanian liberation army,' Teddy muttered as they fastened their seatbelts.

'For once in your life would you shut up,' Toftlund hissed back.

'Off to the mountains to kill Serbs,' Teddy went on, nothing daunted. 'Drummed up from around Europe and the US to serve the great cause of Kosovo and the UCK. They don't know what they're letting themselves in for.'

'Well, that's not our worry. We have to find your half-sister. The rest is none of our business.'

'You'll find, Inspector, that in the Balkans things have a way of becoming your business whether you like it or not.'

The aircraft accelerated. Toftlund looked away from Teddy and stared pointedly out of the window. The Airbus climbed steeply over the mountains. The minute the captain switched off the 'Fasten Seatbelts' sign and with it the 'No Smoking' sign one would have thought a fire had broken out in the cabin as all the Albanian youths lit up as one man. It was an incredible sight. Toftlund could not remember the last time he had flown in a plane in which people were smoking. Teddy chuckled and groped about in his own pockets while Toftlund felt the pungent smoke stinging his eyes and throat. The four flustered Slovenian stewardesses bustled up and down the aisle, pointing to the 'No Smoking' sign, which had come back on and flapping scandalised hands in front of their faces as they endeavoured, with remonstrations in English, to have the fire put out. The young Albanians simply carried on talking and smoking, until an older man – ramrod straight and with a flat, bald head – marched down from the rear of the plane, shouting and bawling in Albanian. The chastened youths tried frantically to put out their cigarettes, stubbing so vigorously that sparks flew up around their hands. Teddy laughed so hard that Toftlund thought he was going to burst a blood vessel.

'Oh dear, oh dear,' he gasped. 'I just love Albania.'

They flew over snow-capped mountains on the long roundabout route to Albania. The usual approach paths were closed to allow the high-flying NATO F-16 fighters to swoop unhindered from their bases in Italy across Serbia, Montenegro and Kosovo with their deadly cargo of laser-controlled precision missiles. As the plane approached Rina Airport, between Tirana and Dürres, Toflund saw rivers like dun-coloured ribbons winding through the mountains, and small villages dotted here and there among green and brown fields. He felt hollow and tense, unsure what awaited them down there, and as usual when he felt a twinge of uncertainty he tried to concentrate on the task ahead of him. They began their descent and Per pointed out to Teddy the long, straight row of American Apache attack helicopters ranged up at the airport. Right next door was the American army camp: regimented khaki tents planked straight down in the mud like soldiers.

'The Apache,' Toftlund said. 'The world's most efficient attack helicopter. Wait till the Serbs get a taste of that.'

'It'll never happen,' Teddy shouted above the din of the braking engines, hanging on for dear life to his armrest as the aircraft made its long descent, wallowing and bucking like a ship in a storm.

'Of course it will. They're here to support the troops on the ground. The infantry will be moving in at some point.'

'Those days are gone. In our part of the world we're not prepared to accept losses. Those helicopters might be efficient, but they're also vulnerable. Neither Uncle Sam nor Mother Denmark wants its boys coming home in body bags. There they sit, and there they will continue to sit. Meanwhile, from high in the air our valiant lads will bomb Milosevic into submission. It's only a matter of time. We bomb TV and radio stations and newspaper offices, power stations, bridges, roads, oil depots, people. We bomb Yugoslavia to the brink of perishment and starvation. That is how we wage war today.'

'At some point in every war they have to send in the infantry. The foot soldiers always have to clear up after the cavalry. That's how it is, that's how it's always been.'

'True. But only after the enemy has laid down his weapons. Then, however, they can expect to be there for years. Because down there on the ground seeds of hate are being sown that will have to be harvested by generations to come.'

'You know it all, don't you?' Toflund said.

'Star Wars, that's our game. We leave the dirty work on the

ground to the UCK. In this war they're the ones who have to look the enemy in the eye. I'm telling you: your modern Westerner want to see no corpses.'

'So you say,' Toftlund retorted, not even trying to conceal his irritation as the plane's wheels hit the bumpy, rutted runway and braked. Beyond the window the host of cargo planes and Hercules troop carriers gradually came into focus at this airport which had never seen so much traffic – not until now, that is, when with awesome efficiency all the world's relief organisations and its most powerful military machines were pumping men, equipment and, not least, money into a society which would otherwise have ground more or less to a halt.

Chaos reigned at passport control, where the cigarette smoke billowed around Toftlund and a solitary, timid sign showing a cigarette with a line through it. There was no system to the queues which were forever forming and breaking up. The military-looking young man from Ljubljana Airport presented an American passport and a slip of paper to a moustachioed, cigarette-smoking man in a blue uniform and was ushered past the control point. The youthful volunteers for the UCK were lined up like soldiers and marched off into the terminal. The weather was warm, the temperature possibly as high as seventeen degrees. But it felt as if there was rain in the air. The airport ground was a sea of mud strewn with deep, swilling puddles; everything was coated in a layer of grime and damp.

Amid the throng Per spotted a middle-aged man who looked rather like a Red Indian who had taken a wrong turn, or a relic from the hippie era. The fringing on his light-coloured leather jacket bobbed up and down along with his long, grizzled ponytail. He wore tight, black jeans and pointed, high-heeled boots, had a gold earring in his right ear and rings on almost every finger. His skin was badly pockmarked. He hadn't been on the plane, had he? He moved with easy familiarity among the innumerable blue uniforms, whose only purpose, apart from their constant smoking, seemed to be to increase the confusion. When the ageing Albanian hippie raised his hand for a second in a gesture that could have meant anything or nothing, Toftlund noticed that he was carrying a gun in a shoulder holster. The guy stuck a hand in his pocket and slipped one of the blue-clad officers some green dollar bills. He made no attempt to conceal this transaction. The officer nodded, the hippie raised his hand again and four young Albanians came round the barrier and picked up two large boxes sitting right next to the battered boom. They carted them off with the customs people paying them no apparent heed.

'Welcome to mafia country,' said a voice in Danish. 'Don't you just love Albania already?!'

The voice belonged to a tall and very skinny man in blue jeans and a blue denim shirt. 'T. Poulsen, UNHCR', the badge on his left breast pocket said. On his right shoulder he bore the UN logo and a tiny Danish flag. He had a friendly, youthful face, intelligent eyes and short, fair hair. At first glance he looked to be in his early twenties, but the fine lines around his eyes revealed that he had to be a good ten years older than that.

Teddy offered his hand:

'Thank God, the cavalry has arrived! Teddy's the name.'

'Torsten Poulsen, Emergency Service Agency. Welcome to Albania.'

Toftlund eyed the newcomer. He had seen him somewhere before, but could not recall where. Poulsen smiled and eyed Toftlund in return.

'You don't remember me, do you, Per?'

'I can't quite ...'

'Langeland, close on fifteen years ago ...'

The penny dropped.

'But, of course, Lieutenant. So this is where you ended up.'

'Here, there, wherever the Agency sends me.'

They shook hands, both grinning from ear to ear like old army chums.

| 357 |

'What's all this about, then?' Teddy asked.

Poulsen lifted Teddy's holdall, saying:

'Let's be on our way, before it gets dark. We don't drive at night in this country. Per blew up a factory that I had been detailed to guard. We had a whole company. There were only three of them. And yet they managed to steal up on us, set their explosives and get away without us knowing they'd even been there.'

'Oh, right, playing at soldiers and all that,' Teddy remarked carelessly.

'Per was a frogman with the Royal Navy in his last life. Didn't you know that?'

'Like the Crown Prince?'

'Before the Crown Prince,' Toftlund put in.

'Well, I suppose somebody has to defend the mother country,' Teddy announced airily and proceeded to make his way up to the actual passport desk, leaving the other two morons to wallow in their stupid, old-soldier reminiscences. Nothing brought out the lad in a grown man like a reunion with an old pal from their army days, a time when everything was manly and uncomplicated. Teddy had served four months with the Civil Defence Corps, so he had got off lightly. Nonetheless he recalled that time as a long and boring waste of his fine gifts. Not only that, but he had had to put up with taking orders from people whom, in civilian life, he would never even have spoken to, never mind listened to what they had to say. He stood patiently while the woman behind the desk took his ten American dollars and meticulously inscribed his name in a large, lined ledger which reminded Teddy of his childhood. There had been a time, so many years ago that he did not care to think about it, when his mother had kept the household accounts in just such a ledger. His gums were beginning to ache again and he could tell that all those hours in an aeroplane seat had not done his back any good.

His backache was not helped by the twenty-kilometre drive in Torsten Poulsen's big, white Toyota Land Cruiser to the port of Dürres. The blue UN logo and the Danish flag were painted on the sides of the four-wheel drive. On its nose waggled a long and powerful radio antenna. Toftlund's mobile was now nothing but a useless electronic gadget with no connection to anything or anyone. The road was narrow, dirty, full of holes and swimming in mud and water. The rusting hulks of old cars lay here, there and everywhere, as if a giant had played with them for a while then tossed them away. Horse-drawn carts crawled along the road which was lined with people selling everything from berries to petrol in clear plastic containers. On every street corner stood lethargic, chain-smoking policemen, each armed with a lollipop with a green circle in the centre. None of them appeared, though, to be doing anything about the chaotic traffic. The countryside was scattered with dingy houses and little concrete bunkers which looked like mushrooms attacked by rot. There they lay, sagging and abandoned, and in the narrow slits through which the revolution's forces were meant to defend their native soil, grass and other weeds had now taken up their positions. Some of the toadstool bunkers lay on their sides with their rusty iron struts sticking out like stiffened entrails into the polluted, blue-grey air. Thus the heroic stand had ended. The abortiveness of socialism, and of raw capitalism, hit you like a slap in the face in Albania. On the banks of a shallow, muddy-brown, noisome river lay what looked like a veritable car cemetery. In their various stages of ruination, decay and rusting, the cars resembled a nightmarish sculpture, or a scene from a film about man's total destruction of his own environment. Not far from the airport they passed a road bridge stretching into nothingness. It had slumped slightly in the middle. It looked like the work of a madman: a bridge to nowhere. Poulsen explained that one of Hoxha's nephews had designed and built it. Not until it was more or less completed did it transpire that he knew absolutely nothing about building bridges: the first car to drive onto it had caused it to fall in on itself. That had been fifteen years ago. Now it just stood there. Albania was like one big rubbish tip, or some futuristic landscape over which a war has swept, leaving everything at a standstill.

Confidently and with care, Poulsen wove his way round cattle, horse-drawn vehicles, noisy little Italian mopeds, pedestrians and craters which could have swallowed up a VW Beetle. The road had clearly been tarmacked at some point. Now there were more holes than tarmac. But what worried Toftlund most were the raggedy little kids who milled barefoot around the white car whenever Poulsen slowed down, as was often necessary, to little more than a snail's pace.

'It's those bloody Italian soldiers,' Poulsen said, tooting furiously at two little boys with dirty faces and hands who were trying to clamber up onto the Toyota's running board, yelling for chocolate. 'When the first of the Italians got here they threw chocolate to the kids. Now they swarm around the cars. It's only a matter of time before we run one of those poor brats down. They flock round the big trucks too. It gives the drivers sleepless nights, I can tell you.'

Dürres hove into view. They caught a glimpse of the sea beyond the tall cranes, but otherwise the scene was the same. Wrecked cars, sunken bunkers, tumbledown houses, unfinished concrete buildings. Old houses with peeling walls. And on every second one a ludicrous modern element: a satellite dish.

'So the poor sods can watch Italian television,' Poulsen said. 'It provides just about the only light relief in the lives of most Albanians.'

They drove past a refugee camp. Army-green tents ranged in neat rows. Over the teeming mass of humanity of the camp – primarily women and children – fluttered the Italian flag. The camp was surrounded by a wire fence and the entrance was guarded. Across from it something like five hundred people lay on the bare ground under large sheets of clear plastic and damp blankets. They were waiting to be registered, or to be allowed in to the overcrowded camp.

Poulsen told them that new batches of refugees turned up at this camp and the too few other camps every day. There would have been a lot more deaths had it not been for the tremendous hospitality of the Albanian people and the fact that spring was not far off. Had this been February he did not dare to think what would have happened.

'Three cheers for the NATO bombings,' Teddy commented wryly.

'So what the hell else were they supposed to do?' Toftlund protested. 'Let Milosevic carry on with his ethnic cleansing? Wait until the last Kosovo Albanian had been driven out or killed?'

'Well, now NATO's doing it for him. What do you think, Poulsen?'

'That it's my job to take in everybody who comes here, no matter why they've come. My list of priorities is very simple, and hence very tricky. It all boils down to basic human needs. I have to provide the refugees with shelter from the weather. I have to supply them with food and clean water. A place in which to take a shit. Security for themselves and, later, some idea of what has become of their nearest and dearest. For the rest, it's all politics and I don't have anything to do with that.'

'That's too bloody easy.'

'Well it's enough to keep me working flat out around the clock. But yes, I know. Let me put it this way. It's Milosevic who's to blame, but it's our responsibility and, hence, our duty. Okay?'

'I won't argue with that,' Teddy said.

Poulsen eased the car over some rusty, buckled lengths of railway track lying across the road like anti-tank obstructions. On the right were more of the redundant one-man bunkers. On the left, beyond the big warehouses clustered under the yellow cranes, they could see the grey-green expanse of the Adriatic. A ferry was docking. The big bow port was lowered and army vehicles rolled ashore. There were both armoured personnel carriers and what Toftlund recognised as self-propelled artillery vehicles. It had all the makings of an invasion. The Toyota's huge, heavy tyres splashed through the muddy puddles.

'We have a convoy up north at the moment,' Poulsen said. 'Which means we have a couple of vacant rooms at the hotel. You'll have to make do with them. Otherwise accommodation is impossible to come by here.'

'That's absolutely fine,' Toftlund told him.

They drove right into the centre of the town. Here, too, the buildings were in a sad state, but there was a bizarre loveliness about their decrepitude: like a once beautiful woman in whose crumbling face traces of that former beauty are still discernible. There were a lot of young people on the streets. They were surprisingly well-dressed, in Italian and French designer gear, especially the young women with their tight jeans and provocative tops, their painted lips and long eyelashes. They went about in pairs, as girl-friends do, smiling and waving voluptuously when they spotted the white UN vehicle. An open Italian jeep came driving towards the Toyota. Three of the soldiers in it whistled and whooped at a couple of particularly pretty girls.

'Well, well,' Teddy cried. 'The young ladies have certainly changed since I was last here.'

Poulsen laughed:

'A lot of them are quite stunning. But I'm going to tell you what I tell my drivers. Every one of those gorgeous young women has at least three brothers, eight uncles and a very touchy father. Get one into trouble and you have two options: either you marry the girl or you wind up in the ocean. Honour, disgrace, revenge – these things are taken very seriously here. So you can look, but please – don't touch.'

They all laughed.

Poulsen steered the Toyota up a narrow, unpaved alley, through the puddles and the mire, between houses with flaking yellow walls. Gaily-coloured washing hung from lines strung between the buildings and a couple of small children waved and gave the

V-sign. Under shuttered windows two satellite dishes were bolted to a wall. Above their heads a tangled skein of electric cables snaked across the alley. Three other white UN vehicles were parked on a piece of waste ground next to a small hotel calling itself The Mediterranean. Poulsen parked the Toyota. Teddy scrambled laboriously out of the back seat and lifted out his bag.

'Just a minute,' Poulsen said to Toftlund, placing a hand on his shoulder. 'I didn't know how much I could say in front of the professor there,' he went on.

'He's in on it,' Toftlund said.

'Fine. We received orders from the very top to help you. As if we didn't bloody well have enough to do as it is. Sorry, no offence. Offhand we can find no trace of your woman in our system. Which doesn't necessarily mean an awful lot. The whole situation is so chaotic, anyway. There is, however, another possibility. The mafia ...'

'What dealings do you have with it?'

'Officially none. But it's like this – the mafia controls the harbour here at Dürres. As a representative of the UN Refugee Agency it's up to me to make sure that the tons of supplies which come into this harbour each day don't end up gathering dust in some warehouse due to problems with customs clearance. Albania is a sovereign nation, it invited NATO and ourselves to come here, but it's very conscious that it is not an occupied land. It is a capitalist country in which shipping agents, customs officers, civil servants and policemen are all out to get rich quick from the boom generated by the war. That's just the way things are. If my supplies don't get through people die of cold or hunger. As long as we don't have enough troops to enable NATO to simply take control of the harbour – always assuming, of course, that the Albanian government in Tirana would grant permission for that – then I have to employ whatever means are necessary – all in a good cause ...'

'You don't have to explain yourself to me.'

'You did ask.'

'Yes, but I didn't mean it like that.'

'Wherever there is need you'll find those who prey on the needy,' Poulsen said and Toftlund observed the weariness in his eyes and the grey tinge to his skin. It was not the easiest job in the world, being at the sharp end of a disaster situation which almost had the wealthy nations of the world beat.

'I didn't mean it like that.'

'That's okay. I've let it be known that you would like to meet with them. Certain contacts have been furnished with the information you sent me. You said it was urgent, so ...'

'That's great.'

'Now we just have to wait and see whether they'll get back to us. But you do realise this does involve an element of risk.'

'I'll need a gun,' Toftlund said, his eyes fixed on Poulsen's.

'I'm a civilian, working for the UN. I did not hear that.'

'Oh, for God's sake, come on.'

Poulsen studied him intently.

'I did not hear that,' he repeated tonelessly. 'But I can't prevent you from meeting another old army mate. Major C. Sørensen, of the Royal Commandos.'

'Christ Almighty, is C. here?'

'The Danish forward division arrived a couple of days ago. They've set up camp not far from here. They're preparing for all-out war, or at any rate the occupation of Kosovo.'

'That's really great, Torsten,' Toftlund assured him.

'Is it? I don't know. But I don't like the idea of you climbing completely naked into bed with the Devil. Because that's what you'll be doing.'

'What would you know about that?'

'I sleep with him all the time, wherever there are people following his commandments, as they're doing right now in this sorely abused corner of Europe. I know him. I see him every day. I clean up after him. And I don't have the time to clean up after you.'

'You won't need to.'

| 364 |

'I hope you're right, and I hope you've brought enough cash with you,' Poulsen said, then he got out of the driver's seat and walked over to Teddy, who stood hunched over a cigarette, his feet solidly planted between two puddles as he contemplated the tumbledown houses with their strangely incongruous satellite dishes, two boys playing football in the mud, the washing lines and a small kiosk from which a toothless old man was grinning inanely and beckoning to Teddy to come closer and see his wares. Teddy looked tired. As if it had suddenly dawned on him that by being here he might be helping to condemn his own sister. Maybe he was simply travel-weary, or shocked to find that Europe could also look like this. Or maybe it was just that his back hurt.

Teddy looked up, tossed his cigarette butt into a dingy grey puddle which was covered by a thin film of oil shot with rainbows. The sky darkened and big, heavy drops began to fall. They could hear the thunder rumbling out across the Adriatic.

'Don't you just adore Albania,' said Teddy, treading on the cigarette butt.

'It's the love of my life,' Poulsen said.

25

A COUPLE OF DAYS WENT BY before they received a message to say that a gentleman respectfully referred to as Don Alberto wished to speak to them, as he had new information regarding a certain woman. This message was delivered to them by a small boy who approached Toftlund down on the promenade in Dürres. Like so many other little ragamuffins he was hustling contraband cigarettes, but there was something in his eyes that stopped Toftlund from shooing him away. The lad looked him straight in the face, handed him a pack of cigarettes and in halting English announced that Don Alberto would like to meet the Danish gentlemen this evening; in the pack, which Toftlund exchanged for a ten-dollar bill, along with a dozen or so cigarettes was a note giving the name of a restaurant and a number, twenty, which Toftlund took to stand for the hour set for this rendezvous. Per knew the restaurant, he had eaten lunch there once. It lay down on the harbourfront, only a few hundred metres from their hotel.

It was about time. The waiting had been driving Toftlund and Teddy crazy. They bickered like an old married couple, snapping and snarling at one another or lapsing into sullen silence in the shoebox of a room they shared. In it were two narrow beds, a small wooden chest-of-drawers and two high-backed chairs which had once been upholstered. Teddy was no longer feeling quite so cooperative. It almost seemed as if he was regretting the whole thing and now felt guilty for helping the police, so Toftlund had had to turn the screws and inform him that he had the choice between cooperating or discovering how it felt to help the police with their inquiries in a rather different way. Teddy spat back that he was stuck here in the arsehole of the world, with no sister, no wife, no money and soon, for all he knew, no job. His back was sore, his gums ached and he fucking well wanted to go home.

'Who the hell's interested in a one-time spy from a long-forgotten cold war,' Pedersen snarled. 'Half the newspaper editors in Denmark – even the director-general of Danmarks Radio, for God's sake – attended party schools in the GDR! So what. It doesn't mean a thing today. You're chasing ghosts, Toftlund. And nobody gives a shit. You're digging up skeletons that no one wants you to find. Let bygones by bygones. Go home, see your baby born. At least there's some meaning to that.'

Toftlund had had no answer to that. He was just as tired of this place as Teddy and missed Lise more than he could have thought possible. It had been a bloody awful spring, as unreal as NATO's unreal war, with all the politicians' Newspeak about it being a humanitarian exercise, despite the fact that people were being killed every day and the stream of refugees was swelling and swelling, while the sleek, grey NATO fighters and lumbering bombers with their cargo of cluster bombs, uranium-tipped warheads and laser-guided missiles circled lazily up above, waiting to dump their loads on dummy Serb military positions or bridges packed with fleeing civilians. And yes. He was chasing a ghost, and he would have to continue the chase. Because those were his orders. Because, against all the odds, Vuldom had succeeded in having Irma's remand warrant extended by another eight days – this she had told him over the Refugee Agency's crackling satellite phone link, but the judge had made it quite clear that this was absolutely the last time – unless, that is, the burden of evidence altered radically in favour of the prosecution.

That call had come yesterday. Afterwards they had repaired to the hotel's bar-cum-restaurant for a large glass of cheap beer. Or at least, Per had stuck to one. Teddy had been on his fourth and growing drunk and argumentative when Toftlund decided to leave him to it and go for another walk. He had strolled down to the harbour and the dirty-grey Adriatic where an oily fringe of scum laced with human excrement, old plastic bottles and all sorts of other imperishable waste was washed up onto the big rocks by the waves rolling in from the civilisation of Italy. From there too came a steady stream of large roll-on, roll-off ferries disgorging men and equipment, including military hardware with the attendant NATO personnel and masses of aid supplies, from blankets to sanitary pads and food, all of which piled up in the port's filthy, dilapidated warehouses. The Serbs had stripped the refugees of all they had: from their homes and their personal papers to the women's right to keep themselves clean.

Torsten Poulsen had to fight harder and harder to keep his weary eyes open as he endeavoured to have the aid supplies moved out of the warehouses and into the country, to the masses of refugees living in makeshift tent cities, disused factories and abandoned schools. He had plenty of drivers and trucks, but getting the inefficient, multicultural UN system to work was a nightmare. Everybody had an opinion on everything. Negotiating the miles of red tape was like trudging through the Albanian mud. The roads were clogged with military traffic and convoys of trucks from private relief organisations, who were also anxious to help, but often ended up delivering the wrong stuff to the wrong places. And around it all, like a swarm of bees, buzzed the press and TV people, getting in the way, elbowing their way to the fore wherever you went, hiring intepreters and expensive fixers who pushed up the prices of everything from petrol to a proficiency in English.

On the other hand, they were a necessary evil. Without their shots of cold, hungry children with beseeching eyes on the evening news, the relief organisations' funds would soon have run out. Torsten knew that the media circus would stay in Albania for only a short time, until the news desks at home tired of their tales of slaughter, rape, murder, terrorism, ethnic cleansing and suffering refugees and turned instead to some other story which would hold their attention for a short while.

'When the journalists and the interest have moved on, I'll still be here,' he had said on the day after Toftlund's arrival, when the latter drove over to the Albanian capital, Tirana, with him to meet C. While Torsten, armed with all of his saintly patience, battled with and against UN bureaucracy, in an effort to get supplies out to his drivers, Toftlund had a brief meeting with Major Carsten Sørensen. They sat down at a pavement café on Tirana's main street. The weather was glorious, the sun shining and the thermometer nudging twenty degrees. Tirana was a bizarre city full of broad, socialist-style avenues, run-down buildings, half-finished glass-and-concrete temples, garish advertisements, market stalls at every turn and cows grazing on the banks of the canal which flowed like an open sewer through the middle of the town. From where they sat they had a view of the Opera House and the imposing Hotel International. Tirana reminded Toftlund of Istanbul, only poorer, with its beggars and cigarette-hustling boys peddling their merchandise from battered old cardboard boxes. Everywhere you looked there were adverts for Marlboro, or for something called Tele-Bingo, in which some lucky contestant could win sixty million Albanian *lek*. As in Dürres there were also an incredibly large number of stylish young people clad in the latest Italian fashions. The traffic was a peculiar mix of horse-drawn carts and ancient, mud-spattered Mercedes saloons – God only knew how they had found their way into the country. The war appeared to have engendered a sudden wave of affluence for the chosen few. Or maybe the more prosperous citizens were simply survivors of Albanian capitalism's big boom? Either that or representatives of the ubiquitous and highly active mafia.

Sørensen and Toftlund ordered coffee and juice. Like everyone else in Albania, C., as he had always been known in the army, had weary eyes. He handed Per a small, cheap sports holdall.

'It's a Beretta 927, standard issue with both the French and the Italian troops. Three spare clips. Shoulder holster. I'd like it back, if possible,' he said.

'Thanks C.,' Toftlund said, placing the holdall between his feet.

'You can't walk around unarmed in this country,' Sørensen went on. 'Tirana is dead after ten o'clock at night. Even we don't go out. There are guns going off all over the shop – mafia showdowns, family feuds. There are shoot-outs and car bombs or bombs in bags. This land is awash with weapons. They all have the same guns and they're not afraid to use them. This restaurant was blown up a year ago during a clash between rival gangs.'

'I didn't know you'd been here before.'

'Weapons inspection for the UN. There are weapons and ammunition in holes and corners all over this country, stored under conditions you just wouldn't believe. The whole idea was that every Albanian had to be able to arm himself if the Italians, or the Russians, or – eventually – the Chinese should come knocking.'

'I'm beginning to think anything is possible here. From the greatest hospitality to the greatest brutality.'

C. lit a cigarette, blew the smoke away from Toftlund.

'That's it in a nutshell. People here are as warm and friendly as they are everywhere else in the Balkans, and as brutal as everywhere else in the Balkans. Their history has made them that way. The worst thing about communism was not really the stupidity of it all, but the fact that it brutalised millions of people, because it had no respect for the individual. The individual was a cog in the great factory of the revolution, I think Stalin said that. Let me give you an example: I was speaking to a woman this morning. She left Kosovo a week ago. Together with seven other women and children. The rest of their village is gone. The Serbian militia came. They separated the men from the women, the old from the children and said to the men: Dig a ditch. So they dug a ditch. Then they said: those of you who have money may go, those who have none must stay, then they took the money, shot those who had given as well as those who had nothing to give and threw them all into the ditch; after that they raped the women and chased them and the children up into the mountains before setting fire to the village. Now all of that is bad enough. But do you know what the worst of it is?'

Toftlund shook his head:

'It's not that there are thousands of similar stories. The worst part is that once we've taken care of Milosevic, the Albanians will return home and pay the Serbs back in their own coin, while we stand by and watch.'

On the drive back to Dürres, Toftlund related this story to Torsten Poulsen. The port was only forty kilometres away, but it took over two hours to get there on the rutted, muddy, busy roads, with the Toyota rocking and rolling like a ship in distress.

'I hear stories like that every day,' Poulsen said. 'I've got another one for you, which might serve to illustrate why we could have our work cut out for us here for many years to come. Enver Hoxha was, of course, a dictator. Everybody knows that. But he was also a raving lunatic, swanning about in that grand palace of his, insisting that everybody around him spoke French – this in a country that could barely afford to feed itself. One day he decided to create a double of himself. His secret police found a little dentist from up north who bore some resemblance to Enver – a man who, at that time, was regarded by some groups in Denmark as a great revolutionary hero. Then Hoxha gathered together the ten or twelve plastic surgeons in Albania and they set about turning the dentist into a perfect double of their glorious leader. With great success. Now the doppelgänger could play the dictator whenever Enver himself feared an assassination attempt, or simply could not be bothered shaking hands or opening a new bunker. With the operation successfully completed, Hoxha summoned all the surgeons and nurses and told them that as a token of his gratitude for their revolutionary efforts he was treating them to a holiday at one of Albania's top luxury hotels. Although I don't even know if they actually had any such thing. Be that as it may, they were all led out to a bus – the swishest, most up-to-date coach in the country. Then they were driven straight into the Adriatic, bus and all, and there they lie to this day, at the bottom of the sea.'

Sitting there with the little holdall on his lap, Toftlund glanced over at Torsten, who was manoeuvering the four-wheel drive round a donkey. It was sitting in the middle of the road, refusing to budge, regardless of the elderly, bearded man laying into its back with a long stick.

'That's a very good story,' Per said. 'But is it true?'

'It's as true as anything else in the Balkans.'

'Where did you get it from?'

'Some guy who was writing a biography of Hoxha.'

'It sounds pretty far out.'

'Albania, the past, the Balkans, this war, Toftlund – it's all so real, with very real problems, and at the same time totally unreal, a nightmare almost, a distorted reflection of the evil we all carry inside us. The only difference is that in our part of the world, thanks to a mixture of luck and skill, we've managed to suppress the beast within for the past fifty years.'

'My, aren't we philosophical,' Toftlund remarked and immediately regretted it. He could tell that he had offended Torsten by making fun of his grave words, but as Lise said, Per always ran for cover the minute there was any talk of emotions or serious ideas.

'I read books, Per. You ought to try it. It's better than what you have in that bag. That solves nothing,' Torsten had said as they trundled into the suburbs of Dürres.

But Toftlund was grateful for the sense of security which the pistol in its shoulder holster gave him as he strolled along the harbourside. At night when he stood at his window looking out at the darkness, he would hear gunfire down here. The shots were always followed by the barking of the dogs, a canine chorus that would strike up in one corner of the district and spread right across the city. One night he had woken up thinking that the war had reached Dürres, but it was only thunder, rolling across the sea, with the lightning illuminating the night sky and the city like an enormous flashbulb. Shortly afterwards the rain had come pouring down and, in his plain, but clean hotel room, he thought of the thousands of refugees still sleeping in the open air, possibly with no more than a blanket or a bit of plastic sheeting for cover. The rain drummed on the roof and sent little rivers rushing down the unpaved streets. Another nightmarish bolt of lightning had ripped through the darkness, throwing the minarets of the nearby mosque into relief, as if etched against the sky for eternity.

That evening when he got back to his hotel room Per checked his gun before going to fetch Teddy, who was shooting crap with three drivers who were moving on the next day. Toftlund admired Teddy's knack of being able to talk to just about anybody. There was no doubt that most of the drivers found this charming little man both easygoing and entertaining. Not at all snobbish, even if he was a university lecturer and all that – this was the general opinion of the taciturn long-distance lorry drivers with eyes which had seen way too much in recent weeks.

'Coming, Teddy?' Toftlund asked.

They walked along the lane in silence, coming out onto Dürres's main street, with the harbour at one end and the mosque at the other. Toftlund had done a bit of reconnaissance, so he was familiar with the area around the little restaurant. Teddy, who had the most amazing fund of knowledge tucked away behind that high brow of his, had also filled him in on the town's history. Dürres was an ancient city, now the second largest in Albania, with a population of eighty-five thousand. It lay in a bay on the Adriatic coast and everywhere one looked one saw signs of Italian influence, from Roman ruins to the present prevailing military presence. In April 1939, Mussolini's troops had been the last in a long succession of armies to invade Dürres, known to the Italians as Durazzo. They had met with fierce opposition. Toftlund and Teddy walked past the memorial to those first martyrs in the national war of liberation. Albania was a country which honoured its dead. Possibly because there had been so many of them. And in 1991 the tide had gone the other way. Thousands of desperate people who had lost all they had in the world attempted to escape across the sea to Italy and the promised land of the EU in just about anything that would float. There had been nothing for it but to send them back and, now, make sure they stayed where they were.

Darkness fell. The air was surprisingly mild, with a hint of rain in it by the time they reached the promenade. There were still people around, but soon they would all retreat indoors and leave the night to the gangsters. Two Italian infantrymen were eating hamburgers and drinking Löwenbräu beer at an open-air restaurant, their storm rifles propped up against the new wooden table. The aroma of barbecued meat drifted up from the open grill. Two French legionnaires walked past with their automatics slung across their chests and waved to their Italian allies.

Toftlund and Teddy walked along the waterside. They saw a ferry leave the harbour and head out to sea. Only every second street lamp was lit, but there were still people to be seen behind the windows of the restaurants. The place where they had arranged to meet lay a little further along the promenade, set back slightly from the road. It was a new Italian restaurant built out of massive logs, as if the owner had wanted it to look like a settler's cabin from the pioneering days of the Old West. The neon had been switched off, but Toftlund could see a faint light burning behind the polka-dot curtains. He turned away from the beach, drew his pistol, cocked it and did not refasten the flap on his shoulder holster. He left his leather jacket hanging open.

'I don't like this,' Teddy muttered.

'You don't have to. Just stay close to me and you'll be fine.'

'Why didn't you get your old army pal to help you? I'm not much bloody good as a bodyguard.'

'They've got their problems. We've got ours.'

'You've got yours, you mean. I'm only along for the ride. Just remember that.'

'Look upon it as an experience,' Toflund said, more nonchalantly than he felt. He could sense the adrenalin pumping through his veins, which was good, as long as it didn't get out of hand. His awareness was heightened and he had the impression that he could hear, see and smell more clearly: the roar of a car in the distance, the incessant barking, yapping mutts up in the town, a pair of heels tapping briskly over the crooked paving stones, the whiff of rotting seaweed and oil from the sea, which lay calm as a millpond in the darkness that had fallen so suddenly, enfolding them in a soft cloak, the air balmy still, though Per knew the temperature would drop fast now.

Toftlund opened the door. Teddy was right behind him. At first they could not see anyone inside, neither staff nor diners. The place was in semi-darkness, lit only by table lamps. They stood for a moment, then Toftlund caught sight of a man sitting at a table at the very back of the restaurant. It looked as though he had just eaten. In front of him was a plate with the last of some fettucine on it. Next to it a bowl of parmesan and a glass half full of red wine. They recognised the pockmarked face and the long, grey ponytail hanging down the back of the leather jacket with the hippie fringing. It was the man from the airport. At a table in the corner sat two blank-faced young men in blue jeans and black leather jackets, each with his cup of espresso.

'Chief Inspector Toftlund, please sit down with your friend and have some wine,' said the man from the airport. His English was clear and fluent with the hint of an American drawl.

They sat down, Toftlund making sure that he had Teddy on his right, between him and the two bodyguards. This could win him a vital few seconds should there be trouble. He hoped there would not be, his heart pounded at the thought of it, but he was banking on the fact that this was business and would be dealt with as such. No more and no less.

The man in the weird Red Indian jacket raised his hand, and for a brief moment all the rings on his fingers glittered in the light. From the gloom of the bar stepped a middle-aged woman in a white shirt and black skirt. Without meeting anyone's eye she placed two glasses and a fresh bottle of red wine on the table and removed the plate. A beringed hand filled their glasses, then their companion lifted his own and nodded. Per and Teddy returned the nod and drank. Teddy sighed blissfully and with a 'Do you mind?' turned the bottle around to read the label.

'Ah, Barolo! Allow me to thank you for this excellent wine,' Teddy said in English. 'Over the past few days I've been forced to betray one of my fundamental principles. So, thank you.'

'What principle has Albania led you to betray?' came the reponse in that mid-Atlantic drawl.

'That life's too short to drink bad wine. That life's too short to drop down a *cru*.'

The almost black eyes in the flat face stared at them. The phrase 'time stood still' flashed across Toftlund's mind. Bullshit, of course, but that was how it felt. Time froze hard as a Siberian river, then all at once the mouth beneath those black eyes opened and uttered a hollow, almost feminine, cackle before their host turned to the two bodyguards as well, perhaps, as the waitress hovering somewhere in the dim regions of the bar, apparently to translate and explain Teddy's remark in Albanian. The bodyguards laughed obligingly, though without much enthusiasm; the mouth in the pockmarked face closed, opened again and said:

'Very good. I must remember that. I beg your pardon, I'm a terrible host. Would you like something to eat?'

'No, thank you,' Toftlund replied. 'That's very kind of you, but we're rather pushed for time.'

'Ah, yes, the curse of modern man, but I sympathise, Inspector Toftlund. I know what it's like, believe me. Being a businessman in these times of war is, how shall I put it – something of a challenge. So let us drink instead to concluding our own little piece of business speedily and to everyone's satisfaction.'

The Albanian raised his glass, Teddy and Per did the same, but Toftlund paused, with the glass to his lips, looked straight into those black eyes and said:

'You know my name. May I have the honour of knowing yours?'

The thin, tight lips permitted themselves the ghost of a smile, before they said:

'Preferico usare un nome italiano. Chiamami Don Alberto.'

Toftlund did not understand, but Teddy surprised him again by saying in English: 'The gentleman would prefer to use an Italian name. He says to call him Don Alberto.'

'I didn't know you spoke Italian,' Toftlund said in Danish, but Teddy continued in English:

'I don't speak much Italian, Don Alberto, but as a young man I did have an Italian girlfriend. A beautiful and talented Neapolitan.'

With a jingle of bracelets Don Alberto raised his slender, heavily ringed hands, smiled again and said:

'You are a connoisseur of Italian wines. You are a connoisseur of Italian women, from whom you have learned the language in the only place where a language is worth learning, in bed, in love-making and in those joyous moments after the embrace, when two people are as close as they can ever be. Before the boredom sets in. May I have the honour of knowing your name?'

'Chiamami Teddy.'

'Teddy?' Don Alberto repeated, rolling this strange name around his tongue. 'It is an honour. To wine and love!'

They drank and Toftlund assumed that, with the ritual dance now over, he might safely open the negotiations, but again it was Teddy who took the lead, astonishing him with his perspicacity. Maybe he was simply worried that Toftlund would let the testosterone get the better of him and charge straight at it like a bull at a gate, rather than employ the acumen which Pedersen obviously felt that he possessed and Toftlund lacked.

'I want to thank you, Don Alberto, for your hospitality and, more importantly, for agreeing to help me find my sister.'

'Your sister! Now that is a surprise. I thought it was merely a matter of assisting our brave allies against that son of a whore Milosevic, may his sons remain impotent for generations and his daughters barren. My pleasure would be as great as Allah himself if I could help reunite a brother and sister.'

'Do you think you can?'

Don Alberto took another swig of the velvety wine. It seemed to Toftlund that the atmosphere had improved. He could not have said why, there had been no physical change, but the tacit air of hostility in the room had abated.

'Your sister …'

'Half-sister actually.'

'The same blood runs in your veins. That is all that counts. Your sister is a popular lady, there are many who are keen to woo her. The Serbian secret service, may the seed of those ungodly barbarians be forever dead, would like a word with her, but the dogs are too busy fighting our gallant allies, may Allah in his greatness watch over them, and Albania's proud sons in the UCK. May Allah protect them and make them strong and lead them to a martyr's death. Your sister is also hiding from godless Albanians who do not understand this heroic struggle in which we must all make sacrifices, and who are collaborating with infidels from Moscow.'

'What do the Serbs want with her?' Toftlund asked, hastily adding, 'Don Alberto.'

'Traitors must die. That is the law of life. She took some papers from a courier and meant to pass them to the enemy. Russian papers which reveal that they are manning the radar station at Pristina and that, as usual, the Russians speak with forked tongues. She was going to sell their agent inside NATO, may Allah defend and strengthen our gallant allies, for vile Mammon. To save her own skin.'

'But she's more Croat then anything else, isn't she?' Teddy put in.

'She was a Yugoslavian, back when that word meant something, and in her heart she is still a Titoist, but that has nothing to do with this. We know Mira Majola. We did not know that she had a brother, or any family, in Denmark, but we were astonished to be presented with her name and her story by our Danish supporters in our great struggle. Allah in his wisdom moves in mysterious ways, but it must have been he who sees all who brought us together. We have done some little bits of business with her, but things have changed. Men of no honour are trying to gain control of our world. Men with no knowledge of our history, no understanding of the bonds of loyalty between families and clans; men with no appreciation of good wine, beautiful women and gentlemen's agreements. Not men of honour as we know them from across the sea.

He put his hands in the air again, as if to emphasise what an unreasonable and immoral place the world had become. Per shot a glance at Teddy. He was definitely not stupid, he knew what the Albanian who called himself Don Alberto was saying. The Russian mafia was also making inroads into this corner of the world, as it was all over Eastern and Central Europe. The old Italian Cosa Nostra was being squeezed by these new, brutal, moneyed counterparts from the disintegrated empire. Mira had sold the famly silver and used her contacts to scrape together enough to be able to leave the sinking ship before it was too late, taking with her the man who was hiding somewhere in the vast bureaucratic maze of NATO or the EU. Either in order to take him down with her or to start a new life with him in some country far from Europe.

Don Alberto poured more wine and lit a cigarette, having first held out the red-and-white pack to the two Danes. Toftlund shook his head, but Teddy's face lit up, of course; he accepted the proffered cigarette, leaned into the lighter flame and added his contribution to the polluted atmosphere. Toftlund also noticed, however, that the two bodyguards had lit their own cancer sticks, which meant that their hands were now occupied. This eased the tension still further.

Don Alberto leaned across the table and began to speak softly. All the theatricality had gone from his speech and with his slightly affected American accent he sounded like any other businessman.

'For the past five years your sister has been living mainly in

Budapest. From there she has organised one of the biggest deals every conceived in this post-communist world. It is known in Hungary as the big oil fraud. Many of us have done well out of it. That is another reason, Signor Teddy, why I am willing to help you. To everything there is a season and that particular deal has run its course, but hey, what the hell – even these days four hundred million dollars profit is a tidy sum, wouldn't you say? And that profit has gone into good investments in new technology, into establishing a working relationship between so-called legal concerns and the more *entrepreneurial*, if I can put it like that.'

'So it all comes down to money?' Teddy asked.

'Most things in this world do, Signor Teddy,' Don Alberto replied.

Almost as if to himself Teddy murmured:

'Maybe, but Irma has never cared about money. So she would never have been driven by that.'

'Who is Irma, Signor Teddy?'

'My other sister.'

'If she is as you say then she is too good for this world,' Don Alberto declared.

'So that is why some of your competitors, shall we say, are looking for Mira?' Toftlund interjected.

'Yes, Signor Toftlund. They are searching for her because they think that if they find her she will be able to point to a spot on the map and tell them that that is where the treasure is buried. All the lovely money which she took with her when things began to get too hot for her and the only thing to do was to secure some sort of life insurance.'

'So how come they haven't been able to find her, if you say that you have, Don Alberto?'

The Albanian smiled, donning his theatrical mask again:

'This is my territory. I am like an old tomcat, I do not allow other tomcats to go pissing all over the ground where I take my evening strolls.'

His face turned cold and his lips narrowed again:

'Mira Majola is in a refugee camp in a disused tobacco factory in Shkodra. She is under my protection, but has agreed to speak to you gentlemen. To speak to her brother and the man from Danish intelligence. But, dear friends – may I call you that, now that we have poured out our hearts to one another? My dear friends, this good sister is under my protection, so in conclusion let us drink to her continued good health.'

The audience was at an end. Per and Teddy groped their way home in the light of the few street lamps still burning. There was hardly a soul around by this time, only on the main street did they see a couple of policemen on the beat and a handful of other pedestrians. The main street was more brightly lit too. They had walked in silence until they stepped into the glow of its street lamps, where Toftlund felt safer than on the dark promenade.

'It makes sense,' he said.

'What does?'

'The mafia, or whatever the hell we're supposed to call them, thought that your sister had given you information concerning the whereabouts of the fortune she stole. They thought it was in those documents that went missing with your suitcase.'

'But there was no money in that envelope. Far less a fortune.'

'That's not how money is hidden these days. It's salted away in secret bank accounts in the Cayman Islands or some such place. You have to have a number and a code word. Once you have those you can move the money elsewhere. That's what she gave you. As security. Concealed among the documents concerning your father. Old, inconsequential documents from the war. As her tools she has had a computer and the Internet. The money is deposited in several different accounts, most likely in different banks. Among the papers she gave you she has concealed numbers, codes and the aliases under which the accounts were opened. Trust me.'

'Smart. If you steal from a thief, to whom is the thief supposed to report the theft?' Teddy said.

They walked on in silence for a while. They could still smell the sea and, as usual, out on the horizon the thunder began to roll. Soon the heavy raindrops would be pelting down. Those crazy dogs were barking in the distance, but near at hand they also heard a growl and a couple of yellow eyes flashed in the dark before disappearing again when Toftlund stamped his foot on the cracked cement.

'What a dump,' Per groaned, shuddering.

'Interesting man,' Teddy said, quite unperturbed. He seemed very relaxed, as if all his fears had vanished after their recent interview. As if he had come to the conclusion that he had landed in a surreal world in which every new piece of information seemed to cancel out or contradict the last, and if you had no choice but to be a participant in an absurd modern tragedy then you might as well accept your fate and not let it get you down. Perhaps he perceived something which Toftlund could not see? Perhaps he was just relieved to have got that meeting out of the way. Or perhaps it was simply that for the first time in days he had had a couple of glasses of excellent red wine.

'Well, obviously he was interesting,' Toftlund retorted irritably. 'But were you thinking of anything in particular?'

'The whole scenario, his choice of words, even his name. None of it was accidental.'

'How do you mean – his name?'

'Don Alberto, not Signor Alberto. The Italians don't use the word *Don*. Only *Signor*, but the Sicilians say *Don*. Don't you see? He was telling you who his friends are. Talk to my sister by all means, Toftlund, but if I were you I wouldn't hurt a hair on her head.'

Teddy began to chuckle, as if he could not keep it in any longer, although as far as Per could see they did not have much to laugh about.

'So you think this is funny, do you?' he snapped, and felt the lassitude that always followed an adrenalin rush starting to wash over him.

Teddy grinned and lit a cigarette before saying:

'You bet I do. It's such a typical post-communist three-ring circus, with no heroes or villains, only crooks and swindlers. It just goes to show that all that talk about a new world order was nothing but pie-in-the-sky. I'd say that's pretty damn funny. And d'you know what, Toftlund?'

'No, Teddy, but I'm sure you're going to tell me.'

'Toftlund, old man – what you have here is a picture of the whole bloody set-up. You could call it *Teddy in Deep Shit in Albania*, but what the hell.'

'Sometimes I have no idea what you're talking about.'

'And – d'you know what else?'

'No, what else.'

'I absolutely love Albania,' Teddy exclaimed and stepped up the pace, shaking his head and chuckling so hard that Per was afraid he was cracking up.

26

THE CONVOY LEFT DÜRRES at first light. It had rained and thundered all night and the puddles lay brimful and brown with silt in the soft morning light. The morning was dull, with low, heavy cloud and a gentle breeze blowing off the rolling Adriatic. There were six trucks and one four-wheel drive in the convoy. One of the articulated lorries had a trailer in tow and it, like all the other vehicles, was painted the UN's signature white. Besides the UNHCR logo three of the trucks also bore the Danish flag; the other three were from the UK, as were their drivers. Toftlund and Teddy had been in luck. The chances of finding transport in Albania were almost as slim as the prospect of peace, but Torsten Poulsen happened to have a convoy travelling to Shkodra with blankets, tents and sanitary pads, and if they did not mind roughing it with the aid agency drivers and possibly having to spend the night in the back of a truck they were welcome to go with it. Most unusually for an officer at his level Poulsen himself would be leading the convoy, quite simply because he had been unable to find anyone else to do it when the UN officials suddenly gave him the word to load up and drive across the mountains to Shkodra, which lay just over a hundred kilometres north of Tirana. Various guidebooks had for years been warning tourists not to visit Shkodra – assuming, that is, that anyone would ever have felt the notion to seek out this bandit's paradise. Now, though, like other poverty-stricken, run-down Albanian towns it was home to thousands of refugees. With road conditions as they were, Poulsen hoped to reach Shkodra within four to five hours, allow a couple of hours for unloading and be back in Dürres before nightfall. This was why he had opted to go himself and leave his Albanian assistant to man the phones. It might be against the rules, but to Poulsen the refugees always came first.

The convoy inched out of Dürres hemmed in by the early-morning buses, big, begrimed Mercedes, the first horse-drawn carts, rusty Chinese bikes and the occasional old woman leading a cow or a sheep or a pig along the hard shoulder in hopes of finding the creature a bit of breakfast.

Toftlund travelled with Poulsen in the Toyota, while Teddy had climbed up into one of the big Volvos with one of his crap game pals who had announced that Teddy was more than welcome to smoke in his truck. Like a long snake the convoy headed over to Tirana, through the greenish-brown countryside with its scattering of little bunkers and oddly gutted or derelict buildings which might have been abandoned, bombed-out factories. It looked as though an invading army had swept across the country, plundering it and leaving only poverty in its wake. The road was pitted with holes and neither animals nor people seemed to know the difference between right and left. Manoeuvring the long, white convoy through the melee was a very slow business. Toftlund could hear the huge trucks behind the Toyota complaining every time they had to gear up or down, and when he turned his head and looked back he saw the lead truck heeling and weaving round the biggest, water-filled craters in the road like an oversize slalom skier. After only a few kilometres the white sides of the trucks were as grey as the low-lying clouds.

'That's Johnny right behind me,' Poulsen said. 'I've worked with him in Iran and in Bosnia. He's the best. He just knows how to read the road and the other guys trust him, they keep their eyes on him and go wherever he goes. The trick is always to maintain the momentum.'

Other than that Per did not have much chance to talk to Poulsen. He hung on to the side-strap and swayed with the Toyota as it crept and crawled along the narrow, winding road which, once they turned north at Tirana, carried on straight through a series of small, ramshackle villages, all of them milling with people, cows, horses, pigs, and sheep. Not to mention the children and teenagers who waved and cheered and made the V-sign when they sighted the white snake. Because Toftlund had very soon realised that Poulsen was the snake's eyes, ears and compass. On the Toyota's nose bobbed the long, powerful antenna which constituted the lifeline of the VHF radios in the trucks behind them, over which Poulsen's steady voice relayed a running commentary on whatever obstacles lay beyond the next corner, house or hole in the road:

'Man with goat on the right, people on the left, watch out for a child, stray cow at next right-turn, traffic coming towards us, four vehicles, the last is a red Mercedes. Johnny, you've got a clear road now, flock of sheep on the left, horse and cart on the right, very uneven road, slow down, almost to a halt, complete halt, moving again, police checkpoint ahead, children on both sides, stray cow on the hard shoulder, very uneven road again, are the Brits through the crossroads?'

Poulsen's commentary was monotonous, but it was fascinating too, Toftlund found: this constant scanning for hazards and hindrances which, Per knew, called for the greatest possible degree of alertness, and it occurred to him that the real heroes in this war as in others, were the civilians in the trucks, forming as they did the only link to other civilians in distress. He very quickly came to sense and to share Poulsen's relief when Johnny's or one of the other drivers' voices squawked over the VHF's loudpeakers to let the leader know that everyone was now through a crossroads, or safely round a turn, or to confirm that the truck towing the trailer was still with them. Time moved as slowly as the convoy, but Toftlund was feeling confident and strangely optimistic. The journey was almost over. If they did not find the woman at Shkodra, there would be nothing more they could do. He tried to push away a thought that kept nagging at him: that when he looked around him at this morass of destitution, knowing that half a million displaced people were scattered across this mud-bound, broken-down country, his own mission seemed absurd and insignificant. And then it was hard to take it seriously. The fact that some twenty or thirty years ago Danes with plenty and to spare should have toyed with the ideas of communism and revolution seemed suddenly so trivial. He ought, somehow, to be able to see Irma's complicity in all this, but he found it difficult to differentiate between cause and effect. Was it the Serbian oppression that had sparked off this horrendous refugee disaster? Or was it the NATO bombings which had provoked this influx of humanity? And what were Irma and her mysterious string-puller or controller but tiny pawns in the game, who had not influenced the situation in the slightest. But it didn't work that way of course. He had to find this woman. Then they could proceed with the case, only then it would be the prosecution's pigeon. And if he didn't find her then he could go home to Denmark, see his child being born and begin a new life, because the High Court would dismiss the case by releasing Irma. And he was forced to admit that it would be a huge relief, because he no longer knew what was right and fair. The weight and the feel of the gun in his shoulder holster was reassuring. The swift and accusing look which Poulsen had shot him as he got into the car and noticed the bulge in his jacket had not been lost on him, but the Beretta made him feel secure and confident.

He sat back as best he could in the comfortable seat and let Torsten's stream of directions play over his ears like background music while he gazed out at the devastated Albanian landscape. Rocky cliffs reared up, green and grey, into the leaden spring sky. The houses were generally small and tumbledown, but occasionally – behind a hedge or a fence – he would be offered an unexpected glimpse of a large house with a new red-tiled roof, surveillance cameras and the inevitable satellite dish. He was amazed to note that many of the wretched little hovels also had brand-new satellite dishes fixed to their walls. On small hilltops he saw the ruins of what might have been medieval castles. They drove past an old factory, a burnt-out shell overgrown with weeds. It seemed to stretch for ever around a bend in the river, looking as if everyone had simply gone home one day with no intention of ever going back. The rusting hulks of cars were strewn all over the place. Toftlund could not think how they ever came to be in Albania in the first place, far less how they had wound up as scrap on the heaps found in every gap in the hills or small field. Poulsen told him that most of the Mercedes they saw were stolen and had arrived there by some pretty shady routes. Tree cover was low on the plain spreading out on either side of the road and on the greenish-brown hills rising up on the horizon. They passed several mosques and, to Toftlund's surprise, a number of brand-new, gilded churches which seemed oddly clean and virginal next to the buildings around them. They drove for some kilometres alongside a rusty railway line overlooking a valley in which smoke rose from little wooden cottages to hang almost motionless in the air. Some sort of market was in progress down there: lots of stalls, lots of grey people and lots of animals. Poulsen slowed down even more, indicated, pulled into the side and switched off the engine.

'Pee break,' he announced, extending his arms above and behind his head to relax the muscles in his shoulders and arms.

Teddy climbed out of his truck and stretched his back, hands kneading the base of his spine. He ambled over to Toftlund, who veered off to the side, but Pedersen stuck with him. On a low hillside lay what looked like an old refinery which someone had abandoned and left to rot. Twisted, rust-covered iron struts encir-cled an old furnace, oil residue floated in waterholes and among the rubble the first weeds of the spring mingled with plants which had survived the winter. The place stank of oil, petrol, tar and piss.

'Robert Jacobsen would have loved this,' Teddy said.

'Who?'

'Danish sculptor – never mind.'

Totftlund and Teddy made their contribution to the stench, standing comfortably side by side.

'Oh, Christ, my back,' Teddy moaned, and then: 'Aah ... relief beyond belief.'

'What is this place?' Per asked.

'Probably some Chinese development project. Hoxha fell out with the Chinese after 1978 when they revised their ideas about Mao's cultural revolution. Almost from one day to the next the Chinese left the country. Whatever they were working on at the time stands in the same state as they left it, or a worse one. Massive factories, railway lines leading nowhere. Albania meant to introduce pure communism, you see. Until as late as 1990 all roads, all factories, all bridges, all schools and anything else you can think of were still dedicated to the memory of Joseph Stalin.'

'Stalin! Even the Russians gave up on him.'

'Papa Stalin. Hoxha came into power in 1944, during the war, and until his death in 1985 he stayed true to Stalin and his principles. The real thing. The other Soviet leaders might have forsaken the pure doctrine but not he. The poor Albanians had their own cultural revolution in the mid-sixties. Every bit as insane as the Chinese. Teachers, professors, intellectuals – out into the fields with them. A ban on all Western literature and newspapers. Religion abolished, forbidden, wiped out. Churches and mosques turned into cinemas or blown sky-high. God was declared dead. Executed, you might say. From 1967 until 1990 Albania was Europe's only officially atheist country. Why the hell do you think the real dyed-in-the wool Danish left-wingers were so crazy about this place? It was the real thing, for God's sake. Here they could salve their Protestant conscience. When all the apparatus of the market-economy spilled into this country in the early nineties the population was totally unprepared for it. It was like putting a virgin in bed with a porn star.'

Toftlund laughed:

'Is this how you teach?'

Teddy's eyes flashed:

'No, I'm a very serious teacher.'

| 389 |

'Well, you know a lot, that's for sure, but I've seen quite a few churches around,' Per said, zipping up.

'Of course. This is primarily a Muslim country, but as you could see from Don Alberto, not everybody here takes the Koran's words about alcohol and other things too seriously. Italy is not far away and the Catholic church is very active here, building churches and schools everywhere. The same goes for the Turks and the Saudis, only in their case they're building mosques. To that you can add ranting American preachers with the Bible in one hand and a bundle of emergency aid in the other. In such chaos as this there are plenty of souls to be fought over and harvested, my friend. And that's what is happening. Would you mind giving me a hand. This picture could be entitled: *Teddy with Bad Back Having Difficulty Descending Albanian Mountain with Old Chinese Factory*.'

Toftlund laughed again, took Teddy's hand and supported him while he half walked, half slid down the slope to the road, where the white snake was parked. The drivers were drinking coffee from their thermoses and both Teddy and Per gratefully accepted a steaming plastic cup. A steady stream of cumbersome old Chinese bikes rolled past them. On their backs little crates from which came the sound of clucking hens. There were also lots of people on foot, poor peasant types with strong, furrowed faces. Some with a goat or a pig on a lead, taking it to market. The more well-to-do had little carts drawn by horses with froth-flecked muzzles and mud up to their knees. Behind them in the cart, besides the driver, there was often a woman, one or two kids and a pig or a couple of sheep. In another, a cow or an old woman holding a basket of spotted apples. In one small waggon with worn rubber tyres, besides the standing driver, there were two young women sitting on the box and a calf and two curly-horned goats in the back. Still more people were walking along the railway line, which did not look as if it had seen a train in a long, long time. This saved them having to run the gauntlet of the muddy puddles. They were all shabbily dressed, but most of them could still manage a smile, a wave or a V-sign as they passed the convoy of white trucks sitting by the side of the road. None of this bore any resemblance to a Europe on the cusp of the millenium; it was more like a scene from some unknown Third World which Toftlund had never imagined could exist so close to the borders of the EU.

Teddy came up beside him and regarded the cavalcade:

'All the talk back home about smoking policies and home-helps and early retirement kind of pales into insignificance when you see this, eh, Per?'

'Anybody would think Albania was at war.'

'It's been at war with itself since 1944.'

'Well, there's certainly nothing picturesque about the poverty in Albania.'

'There never is anything picturesque about poverty, not in the eyes of the poor.'

'The little philosopher again. You just can't help it, can you.'

'That could be the title of this picture: *Teddy the Philosopher Dismayed by the Misery of Albania*.'

'What is it with you and these pictures of yourself?'

'Oh, just a little game. If you stand back and look at yourself from the outside every now and again it's harder to take yourself too seriously.'

'I just don't get you sometimes ...'

'Well, we all have our crosses to bear.'

Toftlund shot him an exasperated look and almost snapped at him; instead he shook his head and wandered over to Poulsen. Teddy called after him:

'Hey, Toftlund, could we swap places for a while? My back's killing me.'

'He won't let you smoke in the car.'

'Ah well, the back before the baccy. That's Teddy's new motto.'

Toftlund travelled the rest of the way in the big front seat of Johnny's Volvo. Now he could listen to Poulsen's voice coming over the loudspeakers, giving the same incessant, precise, monotonous directions. He could see what Teddy had meant when he said to one of the drivers during their rest stop that it was like one of those modern poems with no rhyme – the sort Lise was so fond of. Although Teddy had called it 'broken prose', but that had meant nothing to the driver or to Per. Poulsen had laughed and thanked him for the compliment. Johnny chatted about all the runs he had made over the past few years for the Danish Refugee Council, the UN and Red Cross and how he missed his family back home in Vendsyssel, but couldn't live without the excitement and the challenges of this job. He certainly didn't do it for the money, although the salary was okay, but it got into the blood. Toftlund knew exactly what he meant. He would have felt the same. He knew Johnny was not being cynical – although perhaps a little bit selfish – when he said he was always pleased when the early-morning call came from the Emergency Agency to say his services were required again.

They left the impoverished villages behind them and struck out across a floodplain covered in green meadows. This sight came as a total surprise to Toftlund. The landscape around them was suddenly so beautiful: a majestic, sweeping valley bounded by steep brown-black mountains, their peaks capped with what looked like snowy chef's hats. It appeared to be a fertile valley, but hardly any of the soil was under cultivation. Only in an occasional small garden or vegetable plot had some attempt been made to farm it. There was also something that might have been a rice field. Other than that there was nothing but grass and water, the emptiness broken only by the odd shepherd in the distance with his flock of sheep or a few cows. The river flowed slow and pregnant through the grey-green countryside like a brown ribbon. After another hour the convoy turned off and headed into the suburbs of Shkodra, only to be brought to a halt by a blue-uniformed policeman holding up his lollypop with the green circle on it.

Poulsen got out. Toftlund climbed down after him, stretched and looked to see what was going on. The convoy leader was clearly trying to make himself understood to the policemen. Did they want money? Was he merely asking for directions? They had stopped right next to a brand-new Agia petrol station. Sporting the Italian colours it sat directly across from a completely new church, its cross glinting in the sunlight that was starting to peek through the clouds. Two of the ubiquitous mangy dogs were scurrying timidly about with their tails between their legs. Poulsen was shaking his head, apparently trying to explain something and showing the policemen some documents, but the four officers only shook their heads in return. Ahead of them lay what had to be Shkodra's main street. There were surprisingly many people in the cafés. Drinking coffee or beer. Many of them well-dressed, and once again Toftlund could not help admiring the lovely young women parading about, making eyes at the young men and the outlandish, bearded drivers in the white trucks bearing the Emergency Agency's foreign number plates. After decades of isolation their country was now crawling with foreigners and dangerous – but at the same time beguiling – ideas and influences.

Two mud-streaked Mercedes saloons drove up and six men got out, two of them in black, imitation leather jackets and black or blue jeans, the other four in ill-fitting suits. Five of the men, all with black, greased-back hair, looked to be in their thirties or thereabouts, though it was hard to tell. The sixth was a little older, with grey hair and a bushy moustache. As they climbed out of the cars Toftlund noted that they all carried guns in holsters at their waists. They could have been either plainclothes cops or gangsters and, thought Toftlund, were probably a bit of both. Their seams were pressed, but their shoes were caked with mud. The Albanians walked up to Poulsen. Toftlund could not hear what was said, but it sounded as if they were speaking Albanian. Even when Torsten tried to talk to them in English. Per took a step closer and leaned on the bonnet of Poulsen's Toyota. He saw that the two guys in leather jackets were watching him and it pleased him to see their hands edge towards their belts. It was all to the good if they got the impression that here was a man who might pose a threat. That they might not have it all their own way.

Poulsen walked back to him.

'Does Teddy speak Albanian?' he asked.

'No, Teddy does not,' the man himself replied, stepping out of the Toyota. 'What do these Albanian gentlemen with the lovely manners want?'

'I've no idea. Money most likely. They say they're from the secret service. As far as I can tell. But they could just as easily be from the mafia. Where the hell's the UNHCR rep? I called him an hour ago.'

A white Land Rover with Italian number plates came speeding down the road; it braked, sending muddy water splashing in all directions and pulled up at the petrol station. The driver was a tall, gaunt, sharp-featured man with receding black hair swept back from and accentuating his level brow. There were knife-edge seams in his grey trousers and his tie matched the light-coloured shirt under his expensive tan leather jerkin. His boots were new and spattered with muck. He ignored the six men, walked straight up to Poulsen and shook his hand.

'It's okay, Torsten,' he said. 'I'll deal with this.'

He approached the men and said something to them. They made no protest, but their faces darkened. Then four of them climbed back into one of the Mercedes and drove off. The other two strode across to the other car, but did not leave.

Poulsen muttered tonelessly:

'His name's André. Professor of literature at the University of Pristina in Kosovo. Now a refugee, of course. Acts as coordinator up here for the UNHCR. Brilliant man. His entire family – father, mother, his teacher wife, two young children – is missing. He admires the Albanians' hospitality, but he's also a little shocked by their low level of culture. The Kosovars are rather more advanced than their Albanian neighbours. In fact they are a highly civilised people. Or at least they were until the Serbs embarked on their programme of ethnic cleansing and the eradication of the nation's memory.'

André returned. He had no time to waste on pleasantries and simply ignored Teddy and Toftlund, taking them, perhaps, for reporters.

'They're asking for too much money, but they'll show you the way to the camp. What have you brought?'

'Blankets, tents, toilet paper, sanitary pads, canned goods, water purification tablets, plastic sheeting.'

'How many trucks?'

'Six, one with trailer. That's the tents.'

'I asked for at least twice that much.'

'Talk to Tirana, André.'

'Okay, let's go. The tents and the truck carrying the plastic sheeting follow the Mercedes, the rest of you follow me to the factory.'

It was over ten years since the last cigarette had been rolled at the old tobacco factory. It lay in the mud on the outskirts of the town, surrounded by a fence, like a symbol of the whole situation: bleak and overflowing with people, all with eyes that looked as though they had stared into the heart of evil and would never forget the vision of the beast they had seen there. There was neither order nor disorder. Only a seemingly pointless state of turmoil, like that stirred up by a child on a hot summer day poking at an anthill with a stick, upsetting the normal routine and sending all the inhabitants dashing hither and yon in fear and confusion, trying to discover what powerful forces have invaded their home and smashed up their lives. But the bigger boys in the camp flocked around the trucks and – so rapidly that it was obvious they had done this before – formed a long line down which the cardboard boxes could be passed from hand to hand, from the back of the truck and into one of the old, four-storey factory buildings. Their brick walls had once been a warm red, but now they were fetid and filthy, the glass gone from their windows. From every one of the tall buildings there emanated the curiously dense, clammy fug of unwashed bodies and urine. The earth between the buildings had been stamped into a black, sticky ooze. At one window Toftlund saw an elderly woman with a vacant gaze. From another a small child with its thumb in its mouth stared at him with great brown eyes. There were hardly any grown men to be seen. The few Toftlund did spot were old. One in particular caught his eye, a skinny little manikin with a grey beard and a long stick in his hand. Whenever he felt that the children were clamouring too wildly for chocolate and chewing gum he would scream and shout at them and whack them on the back with his stick. No one paid any mind. Nor was there any logic to the way he meted out punishment. Some kids could beg and laugh and jump up and down and generally make a nuisance of themselves without him doing a thing, while others were clouted if they so much as went near a piece of chocolate or gum. A child who was struck would give a little squeal or a howl, duck and run off. And they were very adept at avoiding the swishing cane. But this needless, petty instance of violence here, in this place – the grim result of large-scale, systematic violence – made Toftlund see red. A tiny lad in a pair of rubber boots several sizes too big for him and trails of snot running from his nose elbowed his way between the bigger boys and up to one of the British drivers who was handing out chocolate. The old man with the stick spotted him and tried several times to hit him, but the little kid was too quick for him. He made it to the front, was given a bar of chocolate and a pack of chewing gum. His face lit up in a big smile. The old guy took a couple of steps forward and raised his cane, and Toftlund snapped. He grabbed hold of the stick on its way down and felt his palm sting as he tore it out of the manikin's hand, broke it across his knee and flung the pieces to the ground. The old man turned and stared at him aghast while the children pulled back into a circle and goggled fearfully at Toftlund's furious face, the icy, alien blue eyes and the clenched fist raised to strike.

'Leave them alone, you arsehole,' Toftlund hissed. 'For God's sake just leave them alone. They only want a bit of chocolate.'

The old man looked at Toftlund, retreated a few steps, picked up the pieces of his stick and fell to mumbling unintelligibly, his head and his whole body shaking. He drew back, out of the crowd, away from the human chain which had ground to a standstill like a conveyor belt suddenly breaking down, and stood up against the wall, trembling, with the tears rolling down his cheeks. Three women gave Toftlund dirty looks as they went over to comfort him.

Toftlund felt a hand on his arm and half-turned, tensing his muscles. He relaxed when he saw André's melancholy face.

'Come, Mr Toftlund. Come with me and leave them alone.'

Per did as he was bid. Teddy was standing a little way off and had seen the whole thing. He smiled wryly. As soon as Toftlund had been pacified the cardboard boxes full of sanitary pads and toilet paper started moving again, the children's cries resumed. And the old man was left with the remains of his stick.

'Why was he hitting them? There was no call to,' Toftlund said. His voice quivered slightly. He did not know why he had reacted like that. Every day people were murdered, burned to death, tortured, robbed, raped and chased from their homes and he had got upset over an old man hitting some half-grown boys.

As if André could read his mind he said:

'At some point it becomes too much for all of us and we feel we have to do something, something that will show an immediate result. Then we can feel good about ourselves. We think that by doing one specific good deed we can make the colossal, abstract evil, which we can do nothing to prevent, disappear. We think that with such an act of exorcism we have absolved ourselves of all responsibility. You have no business here, Inspector Toftlund. I know you are looking for someone. Take a look around you. There are five thousand people here, hundreds more arriving every day, but you're welcome to try. And then go home and let us do our work as best we can. Okay?'

'Okay. But why was he hitting them? Why does he get away with that?'

'He is the only man from his village still alive. All the rest are in a mass grave. He was nothing special in the village, he's a bit of a halfwit really. But now he sees himself as the village elder and, as such, responsible for maintaining decorum, order and discipline. He doesn't hit all of the children. Only the survivors from his own village. He only hits the ones he loves.'

'That makes no sense.'

'Not in your rich world, no. But here it does. Here it makes a lot of sense.'

'But what do the mothers say?' Toftlund ventured desperately.

'Most of the children have been separated from their parents. Most of the men were killed, most of the women were raped and many of them are dead too, others fled up into the hills, still more could be in other refugee camps here or in Macedonia. All of them have lost everything. The old folk are the lucky ones. Some of them. Find your woman, Toftlund, and go back to your rich little country. You have no business here.'

André caught sight of Torsten Poulsen and with a nod to Teddy he walked over to the UN man and they strode off into the camp.

'Your case does seem pretty trivial when you look at all this, doesn't it, Per?' Teddy said.

'Shut up, Teddy.'

'Oops, I hit a nerve there.'

'So?'

'Oh, nothing. First the secret agent shows a glimmer of human feeling, then cracks start to appear in the official armour, a little doubt as to the accepted belief that might is right, the necessity of bringing everything to light. The notion that wrongdoers must be punished.'

'It's not about that.'

'Well, what is it about, Per?'

'It's about justice. Laws are meant to be obeyed.'

'Ah yes. Justice. The laws. Very good. And revenge?'

'There's an element of revenge in all punishment.'

'*Voilà*. But now you're wondering whether it's worth the trouble to go looking for this sister of mine, who was mixed up in some dirty business so long ago that no one is really interested any longer. And the reason you're wondering is that the horrors of today, which you're looking at here, make the sins of the past seem even less important.'

'Oh, I can't discuss this with you.'

'No one's asking you to.'

Teddy slapped Toftlund on the back. Per stared at him in amazement.

'I like you, Toftlund, old man. You're an inarticulate old sod, but somewhere inside that wooden chest beats a good heart. Now what we have here is a picture entitled: *Teddy Shows Affection with Manly Slap on Back.*'

Toftlund shook his head despairingly:

'I'll never understand you. You're absolutely nuts. Try to find your sister. See if she's here, and then we can go home. Because it really doesn't matter much any more. Let's just find out whether she's here.'

Teddy smiled at Per and relished the look of surprise on his face when he said:

'I already know she's here. She was washing clothes over there. She ran off when she spied her darling little brother. Or maybe because she can smell a cop a mile off.'

27

TEDDY TRIED TO EXPLAIN to Per about Dante's *Inferno*, but gave up when it became obvious that the man had no idea what he was talking about. That, though, was how the refugee camp in the old, disused socialist tobacco factory at Shkodra seemed to him. Like an addendum to Dante's description of the seven stages of Hell. It also reminded him of a concentration camp: the big, red-brick, four- and six-storey buildings with their barred windows. All those masses of people in the welter of black mud, and the curiously dead eyes of children peeking from under the plastic sheeting on the trucks that had carried them here from Kosovo's unsown fields and burned-out houses. He had spotted Mira, or Maria, over by the water pump which the UNHCR fed from a long hose. She had been wearing a white jacket and black slacks, and her shorn hair was dyed chestnut-brown. The women were washing the few clothes they had been able to bring with them: as always it was the women who strove to make life as tolerable as possible even under the most intolerable conditions. Children big and small swarmed around them, fussing and whining, being comforted and given a little something to eat. The handful of grown men and youths stood looking on and chain-smoking. It was not cold, nor was it warm, but damp and clammy both outside and in. Per and Teddy stood for a moment, uncertain how to proceed. They heard the clatter of rotor blades and three NATO helicopters came over the mountains and flew across the valley. The children perked up at that. They sprang out into the mud, their hands up above their heads clenched into fists or forming V-signs, yelling in heavily accented English: 'Go! Go! Go! Kill the Serbs. Kill the Serbs!'

'Jesus Christ,' Toftlund murmured.

'I don't think he's anywhere around here,' Teddy responded. 'What do we do now?'

Toftlund thought for a moment:

'We split up. It might be best if you found your sister. Tell her I only want to talk to her. Tell her she has nothing to fear.'

'Okay.'

The helicopters swooped low over the tobacco factory. The children hopped and danced and cheered. The few men raised clenched fists and smiled without removing the cigarettes from their lips. The women bent their heads over their laundry, averting their eyes from the war machines, on which one could clearly see the heavy machine guns and the missiles attached to their undersides. They looked like huge, malevolent insects rattling and roaring their way across the refugee camp and on over Shkodra to the base at Dürres. Outside the fence were two stalls selling fruit, canned goods, chewing gum, chocolate, liquor and beer, but there were no customers because the refugees had no money, so the Albanian stallholders who had been hoping to make a bit extra here also looked up, grinning broadly and revealing mouthfuls of grey metal fillings, and waved at the helicopters until they had dwindled to the size of small hawks in the distance. A white jeep bearing the Red Cross symbol drove past the stalls and up to the main gate. There were two young men in white jackets in the front and through the smoked windows of the roughly painted vehicle the figure of another man could just be made out in the back.

Teddy's heart sank as he wandered around the vast factory grounds, in and around the crumbling red buildings. On every floor people lay or sat in the gloom on the frame bunks which the UN had had installed. Row upon row of them. Beds stacked one on top of another. Men, women and children packed in like factory-farmed cattle. But even in such dire conditions people still tried to create their own little space with the aid of small personal touches: a coloured blanket, a couple of pillows, a picture or two of their missing kin, another blanket hung up in order to screen off a corner and give at least a semblance of privacy, however false. The UN had put in a row of chemical toilets. A heavy reek of urine and excrement rose from them, but the silent, blank-faced individuals in the queue outside the small metal cubicles seemed inured to it. This smell was nothing compared to the sickening stench that hit Teddy when he stepped inside the first building. This had been used as a toilet by the first few thousand refugees, until the chemical toilets had arrived a few days earlier. In a refugee camp he had confirmed the truth of man's most basic need. He felt his stomach turn and hurried out. He scoured building after building, finding them harder and harder to tell apart as he systematically worked his way up and down stairways, looking into identical factory halls filled with identical bunk beds and the smell of unwashed bodies emanating from the huddled figures and the chill, grey, grimy concrete walls. So he could not believe what his nose was telling him when – so suddenly that he was instantly transported back to his earliest childhood – he caught the aroma of fresh-baked bread. Or at any rate the unmistakable smell of bread, making his mouth water and crowding out the stench of shit and piss. His heart began to beat faster and he sniffed the air like a dog, so strong was the memory of his father's bakery, which he had completely forgotten until that scent hit him. All at once he was there again and could plainly see his father's white back as he bent down to the oven and pulled out a long-handled tray of freshly baked French loaves.

Teddy stepped into the room. It was almost completely bare, but along one wall was a long table piled high with loaves of white and brown bread. In front of this was another, equally long table. Between the bread-laden table and the empty one two women were working. A queue of people was inching forwards. Mostly older children and women. A few toddlers. Everyone was given two loaves which they bore off like precious trophies. The scent of the bread drowned out the smell of bodies. A teenage girl in a pair of tight, trendy blue jeans and a sweatshirt printed, quite absurdly, with an advert for the Hard Rock Café in Los Angeles, took the loaves from the piles behind and passed them to another woman who handed them to the next refugee. Teddy regarded her still slim figure in the black slacks, and the narrow, melancholy face framed by the chestnut hair. The whole exercise was carried out quietly and mechanically with no fuss, no hint of unrest, and when the last loaf was gone those still in the queue simply went on standing there, patiently waiting. The teenager said something in Albanian, Teddy assumed she was telling them just to wait, that fresh supplies were on the way. They obviously believed her, because there were no signs of any build-up to the sort of frantic tussles for a single loaf of bread which he had seen on the TV at home in Denmark a month ago. Teddy walked up to the head of the queue. He stopped in front of his half-sister and said:

'Dobryj den, moja sestra.'

She smiled at him and said, also in Russian:

'Hello, Teddy. I had a feeling you would find me. Let's go outside. It's going to be an hour or so anyway before the next shipment of bread arrives and is unloaded.'

They sat down on a couple of small stools with their backs against a white wall and the scent of bread in their nostrils. They were alone, a little apart from everything in a spot where, Teddy assumed, the staff took a break now and again. They sat there smoking their cigarettes and soaking up the sun which had miraculously broken through, as if the Almighty, like a great stage manager, had pulled back the cloud curtains. The sun was warm and they turned up their faces to the light which made the snow on the distant mountaintops sparkle like crystal. They carried on talking in Russian, as if with this language they created their own private little world, assuming as they did that no one else would understand what they were saying to one another. She took a long drag on her cigarette and narrowed her eyes against the dazzling spring light.

'It'll soon be May, and then it will be summer here. It doesn't happen gradually the way it does where you come from. From one moment to the next the season changes,' she said. 'And with the summer will come peace.'

'That's what you believe.'

'It's what I want to believe.'

Teddy swept out a hand, causing the smoke from his cigarette to describe a narrow greyish-white band in the air, like a miniature version of the exhaust trail from one of NATO's high-flying fighters.

'Then they can all go home.'

'Yes. And they will. Home to their burned-out houses, their unsown fields, missing papers, devastated country. Home with all their hate. And another fresh problem for you lot.'

'I thought you were on the Serbs' side.'

'This is my fourth war in ten years, Teddy. I'm not on anyone's side any more. There's no one to side with. It's all over. Everything is in ruins. If I'm on anyone's side then it's that of good people everywhere. Those too you find in Serbia. Maybe they will have a chance now.'

'Was that why you got mixed up in that oil deal?'

'The big oil scam,' she said in English and smiled before switching back to Russian: 'That was what they called it in the headlines. Was that why? I suppose it was. The old alliances no longer seemed to make sense. No one cared about anything but themselves and their pensions. It started as an extension of my work. Well, we were having to finance ourselves more and more. We weren't being paid, either. It was too good an opportunity to miss. When you've lost out on the ideological front there's nothing for it but to try to make a winning on the capitalist side. If you want to judge me, go ahead. It's been years since I could afford to have scruples.'

'Teddy doesn't judge anyone. Teddy doesn't throw stones in his own glasshouse.'

He tried to meet her gaze, but she stared straight ahead:

'What's your real name?' he asked.

She turned to face him, looked him straight in the eye and smiled again. When she smiled she reminded Teddy of Irma. They had the same features and the same sparkling, intelligent green eyes:

'Mira. My name is Mira.'

'And you're my sister?'

'That part of the story is true enough, Teddy. We have the same father.'

Teddy sat quietly for a moment. He tossed away his fag-end and promptly lit another smoke before holding out the pack to her, but Mira shook her head.

Then: 'How did you find Irma?' he asked.

Mira put her arms behind her head and considered the question:

'As a young girl Irma was an all-out revolutionary. She attended a PLO training camp in Lebanon. I spotted her there. According to my own cover story I was a Yugoslavian revolutionary eager to assist our Palestinian comrades in their righteous struggle against Zionism. The kids today would have little clue what I was talking about. I saw her as good raw material, although in some ways she was too radical, too much of a Maoist. But education would fix that.'

'Did you know she was your sister?'

'Not when I first met her in Lebanon. But I soon found out, when we checked her background and Berlin gave me the green light to recruit her. And I asked my father.'

Teddy straightened up, looking flabbergasted:

'Berlin! What the hell does Berlin have to do with all this!'

'Teddy, my boss throughout all those years was Markus Wolf. I worked for the HVA – East German foreign intelligence – within Stasi. That was why I knew I was in trouble when rumours began to circulate that the Americans had cracked the code which protects us. There are at least three hundred of us. We thought we were safe. We knew that Wolf would never reveal our names.'

'The Devil ...' Teddy breathed.

'Yes, it has all the marks of his work, doesn't it,' she commented, still in Russian. Her voice was cool, low and businesslike, but Teddy was in a ferment; he almost stumbled over his words as he said:

'And now you're worried that just about everybody is after you?'

She laughed:

'Just about. Serbs, Croats, NATO, the Russians and now the Danes, not to mention a seriously pissed off division of the mafia. I have betrayed everybody and anybody. I am the absolute, and absolutely the last, double or triple agent. Or no, more: I'm the very last specimen of a race of prehistoric creatures which evolved and died out during the century we're about to leave behind.'

Surprisingly she laughed, as if she found the whole situation very funny:

'It's no wonder that I've been thinking a lot about Australia over the past couple of years. I don't think anyone down there cares – it's so far away from Europe. But it's too dangerous for me to go crossing borders at the moment, what with the war …'

'I don't get it, Mira. How did you wind up in the GDR? And how did Irma wind up there, *if* she wound up there?'

'It's very simple, Teddy. The fact is that personal alliances are everything. After the Second World War the Russians, and later Stasi, took over part of Nazi Germany's Gestapo and SS network. The new enemies were the capitalists and the imperialists. The past ceased to matter so much. If your old enemies now happened to be your new enemy's enemies then that mattered more than some bygone war. It was the same thing in the West. Several of my father's old comrades from the Eastern Front served under the sword and shield of the GDR secret services. They knew the trade. In actual fact there was probably little to choose between the two systems. That was how I was contacted, courted and recruited. That was how I learned about Irma, Fritz and you, although Irma was clearly the most likely to be persuaded that socialism also requires discipline. And that such discipline is found not in small, sectarian left-wing parties, but only in the Communist Party, which knows that at the end of the day Lenin's fatherland must lead the way. I arranged to meet her again at a so-called seminar in Rostock which was attended by a lot of Danes. The rest, as they say, is history.'

Teddy shook his head helplessly, threw away his cigarette butt, lit up again and this time when he held the pack out to Mira she accepted. Around them the clear sounds of the refugee camp had become no more than a backcloth of voices, shouts, cries, sobs, splashing water and boots squelching through the mud. The sun had come out completely and with the sunlight came new smells, carried across the camp fence by the breeze: the scent of damp grass and what might have been budding flowers, a distinct, indefinable sensation of warmth from the crumbling brick which reminded him of summer, and above the voices of the people Teddy thought he could hear birds singing.

'Why did you come to see me in Bratislava?'

She puffed placidly on her cigarette. A faraway look had stolen over her face. She must have been remarkably beautiful as a young woman, Teddy thought to himself. Irma looked good, she always had done, but Mira's Croatian blood had endowed her with a loveliness and a sweetness underneath the tough exterior which Irma lacked.

She looked at him:

'A fox always has two exits. You were to take something out for me.'

'The codes to bank accounts.'

'Something along those lines, but it was more than that.'

'The suitcase is gone,' Teddy said, feeling disappointed that it had not been personal.

'I realise that. I also sent them *poste restante* to myself.'

'But you don't know whether the money has been touched?'

'No, I've no way of knowing.'

She paused as if not entirely sure whether to tell him, but then she went on:

'I gave you notes and things, hidden within our family history. It's a very old method. Written in invisible ink underneath the visible words: details of cash transfers made over the years, the names of agents, of people who now think themselves safe, but whom I know to be what one would term traitors. All sorts of information which I thought might come in handy if I had to make a deal.'

'You crossed borders. Why was I suddenly supposed to be given your life insurance policy?'

'That's a very good name for it, Teddy. An insurance policy. They were after me. A lot of different people, but I wasn't worried about my former colleagues. I was worried about what you call the mafia.'

'What do you call it?'

'The mafia.'

They both giggled. Teddy liked that about her. She had the ability to laugh – at herself too.

'I followed you, but I had the feeling that someone was following me. I don't trust customs officers in this part of the world. They can be bought for a ten-dollar bill, so it occurred to me that it would be better if I could deliver my little hoard of secrets concerning other people and their pasts to a man whom no one has anything on. Namely, you. Had things gone differently I would probably have paid you a visit in Copenhagen. I felt the net closing in on me. I had to get rid of my heaviest piece of baggage.'

'So old Teddy was to be your mule. Like a sort of drug courier.'

She laid a hand on his arm:

'I also wanted to meet my brother. My emotions have been in turmoil for years, after all that has happened. To be perfectly honest I was at my wit's end. I was terrified, Teddy. You don't play games with the Russian mafia. It's active everywhere these days and here in the East or in the Balkans it has a pretty free hand. I was scared, Teddy. I could feel them breathing down my neck and I didn't dare risk carrying that information across yet another border and having some underpaid customs guy give me funny, knowing looks. I watched you for a while first. Not least to see whether anyone else was watching you. I liked what I saw. Maybe I just had a stupid dream that in the family I might find an anchor to cling to amid all the chaos. That as well as everything else.'

'Sounds awfully sentimental.'

'Well, I could never afford to be sentimental, but perhaps that's what I dream of when I dream of a normal life.'

Teddy took her hand:

'Crazy as it may sound, I'm actually happy to have met you.'

'It's nice of you to say so.'

'No doubting the title of this picture: *Teddy Gets All Sloppy in Albania after Reunion with Lost Sister.*'

'I've no idea what you're talking about.'

'We've plenty of time. I'll explain it to you some day.'

Teddy let go of her hand and stood up, stretched his back and massaged his aching lumbar region.'

'Does your back hurt?'

'Ah, it's not too bad.'

'Bend over a little, that's it, now place your hands on the wall,' she instructed and he did as she said, stood with his legs slightly apart and his palms pressed against the rough plaster as if he was about to be searched. Her hands felt good as she massaged his back, first through his jacket, then working their way underneath it.

'You're good at this, Mira,' he said, then asked: 'Why didn't you come to see me again?'

'I had to protect you.'

'From whom?'

'Let's just call them the bad guys. Some of those whom I double-crossed. I had an old friend in Prague and in Bratislava. He created a smokescreen for me, in honour of a youthful love affair and the other bond between us, but they got to him. I think they were afraid he would tell your Danish policeman too much. They didn't know the nature of the relationship which Pavel and I had.'

'You're surrounded by death, Mira.'

She stopped massaging him for a moment, then resumed her gentle stroking of his spine and the small of his back.

'That's why I want to get out. It's over.'

'Is Irma going with you?'

'No, why would she?'

'Because Irma's a spy. Irma is Edelweiss. I realise that now.'

'Yes and no. Irma was a courier. Edelweiss is more than one person. Edelweiss is the best operation we ever ran. Without Irma there would have been no Edelweiss. Without Edelweiss, no Irma. But Edelweiss is also the biggest Danish operation we ever mounted. Several different controllers, several agents. More in Denmark than anywhere else, and Irma was responsible for coordinating their efforts. It wasn't hard to infiltrate Denmark. There were so many like Irma there.'

'So who is he? The mystery man? Irma's secret lover?'

Mira gave another soft laugh and he felt her gentle hands kneading his back.

'I don't know. Maybe he is more than one man. Maybe I know, but don't want to say if Irma is not prepared to say. And she is not. He is Edelweiss, but he is also a dream. Our sister's dream of life-long love, perhaps. Or her dream that it is possible to realise a just society, to create a Utopia. Maybe he's just an illusion. Take your pick. You'll have to finish this story yourself, Teddy. Choose your own ending.'

'It's like Keyser Soze,' Teddy said.

'Who?'

'A guy everyone is terrified of. He crops up everywhere, but nobody has ever seen him. He's a mysterious character in a film called *The Usual Suspects*.'

'Not one I've seen.'

'D'you know what? You will. It's a great film. You'll see it at home with Teddy, with wine in your glass and rain on the window. I've got it on tape. You'll love it. It's a fantastic film.' He paused, then without altering his tone he said: 'The police believe you've met Irma's secret friend.'

Her hands stopped moving. He straightened up and turned to face her smile and her cool eyes.

'Is that what they're saying?'

'They say they can as good as prove it.'

'And perhaps they're right.'

'Why perhaps, Mira?'

She smiled at him again in a way which made him think how lovely she was and what a pity they had not met before. He felt instinctively attracted to her. It was hard to regard her as a half-sister when she was so new to him and so much of a woman.

'Oh, to hell with it,' she said. 'I met him once. Just before I met you. I met him in Denmark along with Irma. She insisted.'

'One last piece of business?'

'No, Teddy. E– has cancer. I don't think he has that long to go. Irma wanted the two people who have meant the most to her to meet before it was too late. We complied with her wishes, each for our own reasons.'

'That was both sentimental and dangerous.'

Unexpectedly she took his hand and held it:

'Teddy, Irma started out as business, but later we became sisters. Very dear sisters. It's many years since we've had any professional dealings with one another, but we exchanged letters, met a couple of times a year in Zurich. It's such a wonderfully anonymous, neutral place. We went walking in the mountains, talked, dreamed, told each other the things sisters tell one another. Irma knows nothing of my links with the underworld. When the Wall collapsed there was no longer anyone to spy for, but that didn't mean that we stopped caring about one another, you know. Quite the opposite.'

'It all sounds so bloody complicated. I don't understand a blind thing.'

'No, and you don't really need to either, Teddy.'

'You make it sound so complex and yet so awfully banal. Like some pop song: I love you and I forgive you and I'll miss you and all that jazz.'

She laughed out loud:

'Well, maybe that's how it is. Love *is* banal, brother mine. Which is why it's also so grand and unpredictable.'

Still holding her hand he eased himself down onto his stool and drew her down beside him.

'Did you see who E– is?'

'I know what he looks like.'

'I'm sure the Danes would like to hear more about that.'

'Forget it. It won't get you anywhere.'

'I'm not so sure the Danes will forget about it.'

'Ah, the Danes,' she sighed. 'They're a little naive. Up in arms one minute, mild as milk the next. All the Danes really want is to have a nice, comfortable life free from too much trouble or conflict. As a nation you're adept at weaving your way through a dangerous world. The Danes would prefer to get off as lightly as possible. That's how it was when our father was a soldier and that's how it is today. No one in Denmark really wants anyone digging up recent history. There was no revolution. No violent action. All those young men and women became worthy pillars of society. That's very Danish. They really didn't mean anything by it. Or at least that's what they say today. So why don't we all just move on.'

'Edelweiss is in the files.'

She laughed again. He liked to hear her laugh and it occurred to him that if she found it so easy to laugh in her current situation then she must be great fun to be with under normal circumstances. Neither Irma nor Fritz had that gift. They both had about as much humour as a doorpost. It would be just like the thing for him finally to meet a relative with a sense of humour only for her to emigrate to Australia or somewhere in Asia, maybe, far from Europe. Well, at any rate, it was good to hear her laugh, feel the warmth of her wrinkled, blue-veined hands in his, hear the mirth in her voice and see it reflected in her eyes, those eyes which he suddenly remembered having likened to a glacial mountain tarn that evening when she visited him in Bratislava.

'Oh, the files! Teddy, you're a historian. You have to believe in the truth of the files. Otherwise what would you have to research? But what will you find in the files of the secret services except the conceited hopes of vain individuals, their attempts to make themselves seem important, their longing to be loved and taken seriously. Intelligence reports consist of ninety per cent bullshit or glaringly obvious facts, ten per cent lies, five per cent truth and possibly the occasional little secret.'

'That's more than a hundred per cent.'

'Deduct as you see fit.'

Teddy beamed happily at her. He was sure the two of them were going to have a lot of fun. She was a sister after his own heart.

She let go of his hand, smiled up at the almost clear blue sky, stretched her arms over her head and tossed her short curls. Teddy was gazing at her with almost lovestruck eyes, so he saw the little red hole appear, heard the dull thud of the bullet driving into her right breast and saw the blood spatter over the wall behind from the much bigger exit wound in her back before he heard the actual shot. It was followed by another and yet another – the last one splintering the plaster only half a metre from his stunned, stricken face – and then, with staring eyes and a gurgling sound in her throat, Mira slid off the stool into the black mud, from which only a few green blades of grass protruded.

Per Toftlund had got there that crucial second too late.

Like Teddy he had roamed around the grim disused factory grounds, doing his best to block out the misery, the hopelessness and the stench as he searched for a woman of whose appearance he had only the vaguest idea. Eventually, down by a building at the very back, he had been stopped by two men in white trousers and jackets with the Red Cross emblem on them. On their left breast pockets they wore a little Norwegian flag.

They had asked him straight out in Norwegian if he was one of the Danes who had come with the convoy from Dürres. They were an odd-looking couple. One was a tall, lanky character with small, fishy, blue eyes and a great bush of hair spilling over his face. The other was a stocky guy with brown hair and eyes to match, little glasses and a smile so dazzlingly white that it seemed the snow of the Norwegian mountains had settled permanently on his teeth. He introduced himself as Dr Per Samuelsen and asked if Toftlund knew the three men who had presented themselves to the Norwegian doctors as members of the Danish health delegation, but had looked blankly at Samuelson when he smiled, and in the spirit of Scandinavian brotherhood, switched to the lovely, lilting Norwegian language.

'It's odd, though,' Samuelsen had said. 'I've never met a Dane who didn't understand at least some Norwegian. They didn't seem like doctors *or* Danes to me so I called the French soldiers.' He patted the neat, new little satellite phone in his hand lovingly, as if it were a precious doctor's bag. Toftlund had simply pointed, and then they had pointed and in their Bergen accent said 'Down at the bread store,' and then Per had started to run, with the mud spurting up over his trouser legs and his heart like a galloping lump in the left side of his chest. Children and women stared at him with horror in their eyes as he whipped his gun out of its shoulder holster, cocked it and hurtled onwards, careless of whether he knocked down any of the startled people in his way. They backed away from him, clutching their loaves of bread or tins of food, because in his face they recognised the violence from which they had fled.

Toftlund rounded the corner of the last building before the bread store, which was housed in the old factory building closest to the fence. Ahead of him was one of the two young men from the restaurant in Dürres, standing like a competition marksman with his legs slightly apart and a two-hand grip on his pistol; at the very second that Toftlund caught sight of him and shouted he fired. Out of the corner of his eye Per saw that he had hit his target, then he instinctively raised his own gun, wrapped both hands round the butt and fired three times in rapid succession. The first bullet embedded itself in the shoulder of the black-haired young man, staining his jacket red. The second hit him above the left eye, causing his head to explode in a cloud of blood and brain matter and the third flew across the fence and burned out somewhere on the way to the suburbs of Shkodra.

As if looking down a tunnel, Toftlund saw the woman start to keel over and slip sideways, saw Teddy screaming and trying to hold onto her; he heard the shrieks of women and children round about him and then he felt a searing pain in his left arm and knew that he had been shot. The bullet bored straight through his left upper-arm, flaying open his jacket and shirt sleeves and taking a large chunk of his triceps with it. The initial burst of pain was like nothing he had ever experienced before, but the shock soon deadened it enough for him to raise his head, go down on his knees and scan his surroundings.

Through a kind of haze, and yet as clearly as if he were spotlit, he saw the other young man from the restaurant. He was standing about twenty metres off, and was clearly in two minds. His gun was pointed at Toftlund, but his eyes were on the woman and Teddy. He turned towards them. The woman had fallen into the mud and Teddy was leaning over her with her face in his hands, yelling in his incomprehensible tongue. Toftlund's arm was on fire; he almost slid right down into the mud, but braced himself with his burning left hand, pushed himself back onto his knees and took aim. It was like a film in slow motion. He saw the young man turn back and discerned the fear in his eyes at the split-second when it dawned on him that he should have kept his attention on Toftlund. He dropped into firing position, both hands gripping his pistol and just managed to raise it before Toftlund shot him three times in the chest and watched him fly backwards as if kicked in the chest by a mad bull.

Toftlund was fghting for air. His throat seemed to have narrowed to nothing and his mouth was full of sand. He simply could not breathe and his heart was about to kill him, hammering at a rate that his system could not take. He knelt there in the mud with the taste of bile in his throat, seeing everything through a fog. But out of the fog came a man in a white jacket with a grizzled ponytail and rings on the fingers curled round yet another gun. An old-style Russian Makarov, Toftlund thought automatically as he struggled to make his arm do what its nerves were commanding it to do: lift his hand, aim and pull the trigger. But it was not listening. He could only watch as the man in the incongruous, white, too-tight jacket, the man who had called himself Don Alberto, stepped closer, shot an indifferent glance at the dying Mira and brought up his gun. And Toftlund told himself: Do something, for God's sake. Raise your gun. Raise your gun, he urged again, but nothing happened. Then Don Alberto's chest was one great splash of scarlet and the white jacket changed colour, looking now as though a mad artist had thrown all he had at it. Toftlund thought he could see the deformed bullets exit Alberto's chest and drop down into the mire at the old gangster's feet before, with an expression of the most profound astonishment, he fell forward into the mud, the blackness of which was slowly covered by red, darkening to brown.

The last thing Toftlund saw was the two French legionnaires in bulletproof vests with their storm rifles in the air. A plume of gunpowder gas issued from the barrel of one of the guns. The faces of both young soldiers were so white that for a moment he was afraid they were ghosts. But then he remembered something from his childhood, a visit to a chalk mine where he had been scared of the same darkness that now engulfed him and filled him with an even greater terror. Because this was the chalk mine all over again. And he was sure that the darkness would never relinquish its grip on him.

28

PER TOFTLUND OBSERVED the Minister of Justice with interest. He looked as young in real life as he did on television, but one should not be fooled by those boyish features, the blonde locks or the soft, benign mouth. Toftlund was well aware that this was a politician who knew his stuff and who had got where he was by dint of a gift for political manoeuvring and a generous dash of brutality. Without such attributes you would not get far in politics. He was not a graduate of the law, but that did not matter. He was in charge of a heavyweight ministry and he had civil servants to take care of the legal side. It was his job to make sure that politics always prevailed over the law and that the Prime Minister was not presented with unnecessary problems.

They were in the minister's office. His secretary had set out three cups and saucers and a coffee jug, along with the cream and sugar which hardly anyone took these days, and then she had left them to it. No minutes would be taken of this meeting. Toftlund was wearing a sling and there were dark circles under his eyes, but his arm did not really hurt that much. The minister sat at the head of the table, Vuldom across from Per. She had been given permission to smoke. The documents of the case lay in front of the minister, both the big fat file and the single sheet of paper which Toftlund took to be the recommendation from the Public Prosecutor. The minister had politely inquired after his health and when Per had replied that he was fine that busy man had prepared to cross this meeting off his schedule.

'We're dropping the case,' the Minister of Justice said, tapping the single sheet of paper in front of him.

'I have here the Public Prosecutor's recommendation. We don't have enough evidence to press charges. And while I must compliment Inspector Toftlund on his report, the Public Prosecutor and I agree that since all we have is hearsay it would never stand up in court.'

Toftlund understood what he was saying, but try as he might he found it hard to pay attention when, more out of duty and routine than conviction, Vuldom proceeded to clarify the more ambiguous aspects of the investigation. As always it was a matter of stressing what massive resources had been used in this case and what massive resources would be required for future investigations. It was all a part of the ritual dance in Denmark today, Toftlund thought fleetingly. And then, in his mind, he was back in Albania. The French helicopter had been quickly on the scene, landing with a bump among horrified adult refugees and awestruck children. On the way to the French field hospital he remembered the rattle of Mira's breathing through the oxygen mask. White coats had been leaning over her, then the doctor had straightened up and shaken his head. Teddy had not kissed her, but he had patted the ageing cheeks as if she were a little child. Toftlund's own arm had been bleeding like blazes and hurt like hell, but the bullet had gone straight through and had not damaged the bone. They had given him a shot of morphine and bound up his arm. A flesh wound was not top priority with a dying Mira on their hands. The Albanians they had left where they were. The local police and the UN could take care of their worthless carcasses. But the one person he really took his hat off to was Teddy. He had drawn himself up to his full and not especially imposing height and declared that if he was not allowed to take his sister home in her coffin to be buried in a place where at least one straight, true person with no hidden agenda could visit her grave then he, Teddy, was not telling anyone what her last words had been. Teddy's lips were sealed as tight as an old maid's twat he had announced so emphatically that even in such tragic circumstances Per and Torsten Poulsen could not help smiling. Torsten had taken care of everything and had been polite enough not to mention that he found himself having to clear up after Toftlund after all. And then they had flown home – a long, lumbering flight in an air force Hercules. The pain in his arm was nothing to the ache in his heart when Torsten informed him that he had received a call from Copenhagen on his satellite phone. Lise had gone into labour and been taken to hospital.

It had preyed on his mind all the way home: here he was, turning up late again. Teddy had not said a word, or at least he had merely sat next to the anonymous body bag patting it and mumbling to himself. To begin with Toftlund could not catch what he was saying for the droning of the engines. Gradually, though, he began to make it out. And he shared Teddy's pain. Because Teddy was right. They had led the Albanian gangsters to Mira. The treacherous, wrathful mafiosi had had a rough idea of where she was hiding, but they did not know exactly how she looked. Teddy and Toftlund had fallen for their ruse, walked straight into the trap and handed Mira on a plate to Don Alberto and his assassins. The Albanian gangsters had played Teddy and Toftlund for the gullible tourists they had turned out to be. They had been chosen as bait. And bait they had been. Don Alberto had put on his courtly Sicilian act, vaunting pledges of honour and links with the classic Cosa Nostra, while in fact he was the hired stooge and paid executioner of the brutal, modern-day Russian mafia. It was not pleasant to know that he had been tricked, conned, and that he had not had the slightest suspicion that he had been walking into a trap. It did not even help to know that he had personally put two of them in the grave. It was not in his nature to kill someone and not feel bad about it or think it wrong. It had, in all ways, been a long trip; throughout it all he had carried a picture of Lise in his mind, but this image had become mixed up with that of Mira sliding sideways into the mud and the sound of her last desperate, gargled breath.

Toftlund was jolted back to the present by the sound of Vuldom asserting in her police chief voice:

'She's guilty! She's guilty as sin.'

'Yes, she is, but you have no proof that she had opportunity,' the Minister of Justice countered. 'Not without – how shall I put it – the *other*, whose identity, unfortunately, remains a mystery. It really is a very complicated affair.'

'So she gets off.'

This was a statement of fact and the minister knew it. He leaned across the table:

'Well, she'll get out of going to jail.'

'Meaning?'

'By law she cannot be named, but we've already made sure the press and TV stations know the court hearing will take place tomorrow. They'll be on the spot with their cameras and microphones when she's released.'

'But the press still can't publish her name,' Vuldom said.

'No, but she'll be free to make a statement and I think she will.'

'And then?'

'Then the Public Prosecutor and I will let the public know, in no uncertain terms, that we consider Edelweiss to be as guilty as sin. But that the case has lapsed and cannot, therefore, be tried. I'll be holding a press conference tomorrow. And the Public Prosecutor will happily make himself available for comment.'

Vuldom stubbed out her cigarette and smiled:

'So – condemned by public opinion. And that she'll have to live with for the rest of her days.'

'The media represent the modern version of the old village stocks,' the Minister of Justice said with satisfaction. 'As for the rest, that will have to be dealt with in the Commission on Cold War Intelligence Activities' report, if it ever gets round to producing one.'

'But you don't think it will?'

'Well, something's bound to come to light. At the moment that's the Danish Institute of Foreign Affairs' problem, but if you ask me it will be up to our children's generation to discover the truth about those who chose the wrong side in the cold war, just as it was left to the post-war generation to look into the darker aspects of the history of the occupation. Every country needs a few good myths about the times in which it lives. And there are too many – how shall I say, living skeletons from the cold war still rattling around in the closet of modern-day Denmark for anyone to be genuinely interested in total disclosure. They're fine where they are, tucked away in the files. In the meantime the journalists can dig all they like, but the articles they write have a very short life. And we can live with that.'

It was almost like a political address, Toftlund thought to himself. Or an attempt to justify himself, or excuse the fact that society was not yet ready to truly confront the recent past. Most people would prefer to forget all about it.

'What about Irma's controller, the mysterious ambassador? Or whatever he is. Because there's no doubt he exists, is there,' Toflund broke in.

They turned to him in surprise. He was present at this meeting because he had been in charge of the investigation and because he deserved to be told how the story ended, but he was not expected to exceed his role and start ad-libbing.

The Minister of Justice sighed and clasped his hands over the closed case.

'Toftlund, you did a good job, and I hope Commissioner Vuldom will reward you with some time off. I also hope that you have been offered the necessary counselling?'

'Toftlund did not want counselling,' Vuldom interposed, as if the minister had just insulted one of her officers.

'Ah – yes, well, I am familiar with your military background. But the offer still stands, of course. It's the least we can do. And congratulations on the new baby. It's great to have children. You've got something to look forward to there. Having kids around – it's such a positive thing. Yes, what about this mysterious ambassador. Does he actually exist? Or is he an illusion, a figment of Mira

Majola's imagination? Has anyone in this story been telling the truth? If he does exist he must be nearing retirement. Or maybe he is dying. Nature or God will punish him for us. We'll win the war in the Balkans. That's a foregone conclusion. It's only a matter of days. Now what we have to do is win the peace.'

He paused, thought for a moment before continuing:

'We'll be holding a referendum on the euro within the year. It's definitely on the cards. And that we have to win. That's our top priority. In a couple of years we'll have the chairmanship of the EU. That is going to be extremely important for Denmark. It will be our first chance in years to put a solid Danish stamp on the future of Europe. Who knows? The chairmanship may never come our way again. What with the expansion of the EU I don't think we can take that for granted.'

'So he'll get away with it, is that what you're saying?' Toftlund persisted.

The Minister of Justice glanced at Vuldom, who took over. In her capacity as the loyal public servant who did not engage in battles she could not win:

'We've looked into it, Toftlund' she said. 'If we do a relatively wide search and draw up a profile based on that, we find at least a dozen candidates who fit that profile. If we include those politicians who have had access to confidential information over the years through their links with the Select Committee on Surveillance Procedures, the Committee for European Affairs or the Foreign Policy Committee, well, the list is a whole lot longer.'

'All with cancer?'

'That is not one of the parameters used in our search. It is deemed neither appropriate nor expedient.'

'At some point there might be an obituary in the paper.'

She regarded him:

'And only a handful of people would read that as anything other than an obituary, right, Toftlund?'

'So those Baltic agents of ours who were executed in '87, they've been sold down the river, is that it?' Toftlund could not keep the note of anger out of his voice, even though he knew he was being given the famous Vuldom look.

The Minister of Justice said:

'Things were different then. It's regrettable, but as responsible politicians we have to put the nation's interests first. That is how we have to think. Denmark is at a critical juncture. Those poor souls were, you might say, the last victims in the cold war. That may sound a little high-flown, but I think we can say that at least they did not die in vain. We have won.'

'Yeah, right – the hell we have,' Toftlund burst out.

'That's enough, Per!' Vuldom snapped and there was a distinctly icy edge to her voice, but the Minister of Justice carried on in the same calm, convincing tone:

'There's nothing to be gained by digging any deeper. Not right now. So we're going to bury the case in the archives and it will be up to future generations to see whether they can learn any lessons from it. Irma will receive a public rap over the knuckles, just to show that we have not forgotten or forgiven the sins of the past, but that we believe it would not be in the country's best interests to instigate a formal inquiry in order to discover whether somewhere in the Foreign Ministry or Military Intelligence or the Defence Staff, or in Parliament, there is a Danish citizen with high security clearance who has betrayed his country at some earlier date or during the first war of aggression Denmark has been involved in since ...'

'1864,' Vuldom prompted.

'As I say, it is not in the nation's best interests. We need to move on,' the Minister of Justice continued.

'Alright,' Vuldom said. 'So neither you nor the Public Prosecutor mean to mention anything about the Serbian angle in your press release?'

'The statue of limitations has run out on the case and hence it is being dropped. Edelweiss's crimes were committed so long ago that they cannot be prosecuted in court. That is the clear conclusion. Anything else will be regarded as speculation.'

'Understood.'

'Bury it, Vuldom.'

'It's as good as gone,' came the dry reply and in spite of everything her sarcasm made Toftlund feel a little better as they all shook hands in best Danish fashion and said their farewells.

Toftlund and Vuldom stood on the street outside the Ministry. The weather was almost summery, with a clear, blue sky and a gentle breeze smelling of salt.

'Well, that was that,' Vuldom said. 'What's she going to do? Do you know?'

'She's going away for a while, or so I gather from Teddy.'

'Where to?'

'It's been planned for some months. She's going to Estonia with some of her father's old army chums. And some sympathisers.'

'Hardly surprising. In the new Estonia they are obviously heroes. They killed Russians.'

'And their new Estonian friends know nothing, of course, of the other story.'

'No. It's dead, Toftlund.'

'It's a strange world.'

'It always has been – but what a weird totalitarian alliance that is, cemented by contempt for untidy, imperfect democracy. You're right about that. What will they be doing in Estonia?'

'Teddy says they're going to erect another memorial to the Danish soldiers who fell on the Eastern Front.'

'Is Teddy going too?'

'Teddy said – and I'm quoting word for word: No way I'm joining them on some sentimental journey to put up a fucking monument to a bunch of hooligans and war criminals.'

'Attaboy, Teddy.'

'Yep, attaboy.'

'How is he?'

'Shocked, upset, tired, ridden with guilt. As I am.'

'It would have happened sooner or later.'

'Even so. Anyway, Teddy is still Teddy, so he says he's okay. He was allowed to bring Mira home. He's going to bury her. And then he wants to get on with his life. That's the way he is. He said, and again I quote: Teddy wants to walk out in the merry, merry May and see whether Nature's turgescent blooming can't inspire some member of the opposite sex to fall for a university lecturer who has been involved in dramatic events out in the wide, wide world. He thinks his appearances in the press and on TV might help. "The title of ths picture, Toftlund," he said, "is obvious: *Teddy the Bold Returns Home from the Fray and the Ladies Swoon in Adulation.*"'

'He's something else.'

'He's okay. He also said that if the swooning ladies didn't materialise he hoped I would invite some single or, even better, divorced women, preferably without small children, to the christening.'

The breeze caught Vuldom's hair and blew it over her face for a moment. When she brushed it away her expression had softened.

'Mother and baby doing well?'

'Very well.'

'You didn't make it back in time, did you?'

He gazed at her, wondering that she should ask this, then he thought instead of how he had walked into the hospital ward four hours too late, past a mother-in-law who had vouchsafed him only a chilly hello, and there was Lise with damp hair and tired eyes, but a beautiful smile and, beneath the quilt, a stomach which seemed to have shrunk to almost nothing. A small white bundle nestled in the crook of her arm. Poking out of the top of the bundle he saw a tuft of dark hair and a tiny wrinkled face with eyes screwed tight shut. He had wanted to say he was sorry, but had not known where to start. Then she had simply said:

'Oh, Per, it's wonderful to see you. I'm so glad you came home to us alive and well. Come and see our daughter. I'm afraid she

| 425 |

looks like you, the poor little thing, so I suppose I'll have to get used to that.'

And he had felt the tears welling up and had let them run and had not been ashamed of them – in fact it was a relief to cry.

Vuldom coughed.

'And the father?' she asked. 'How's he doing?'

He looked at her. And said exactly what he was thinking. At the end of the day that was usually simplest, also where Vuldom was concerned:

'Surprised by how quickly one becomes attached to such a little creature.'

'I know.'

'Those tiny toes, tiny fingers, the little bum, and then these huge eyes … I'm actually getting pretty good at changing nappies already.'

'Now don't you go getting too soft and sentimental,' Vuldom admonished. 'But you'll be taking your paternity leave, I gather?'

'Absolutely.'

'I thought so. Take an extra month. Over and above the holidays you've got coming.'

Toftlund looked at her. Her shrewd eyes were smiling more than her mouth.

'On what condition?' he asked.

'You stay with me?'

He considered for a moment.

'How soon do you need an answer?'

'I need it now.'

'Okay.'

'Okay what?'

'Okay. I'll stay with PET.'

'Good. It's where you belong.'

She held out her hand and he shook it. She walked off down the street and he watched her go: a slim, erect figure walking with a swift, almost gliding step. Without turning she called out:

| 426 |

'Say hello to the mother and baby for me.'

He smiled and raised his hand to wave, but she did not look round. Toftlund walked across to his car. He should not be driving with only one arm, but he could manage it without too much difficulty and only a little pain. Not since he was a child could he remember looking forward to anything as much as he now looked forward to coming home to Lise and the baby, and only at this moment did it actually dawn on him that his life had changed irrevocably, because now he was no longer alone, he was part of a family, and to his astonishment this made him feel a little apprehensive, but also happier than he would ever have thought possible.

Epilogue

IT WAS JUNE 10TH. Toftlund was running in the woods north of Ganløse. Ahead of him he pushed the fancy baby jogger in which he had invested. The baby was asleep and he took the smoothest paths before turning at his five-kilometre mark and beginning the run back. The wound in his arm had healed and the stitches had been taken out a while ago, but it still ached slightly when he ran. The scar he would always carry as an unpleasant reminder. It was a lovely summer's day, even if the sun was having trouble breaking through. The woods were a mass of green, the light from the partially clouded sky was bright and beautiful, but it was the scents he would remember. They were still so fresh and subtle as to be indefinable, but they included the fragrance of new-sprung flowers and of the withered wood anemones on the forest floor. When he reached the fringes of the woods he stopped, checked on Freya, who was sound asleep, and did his stretching exercises up against his usual oak tree. It was early in the morning, with no sound except the birdsong, so he jumped when a strange and yet well-known voice said in English:

'It tires me out just to watch you, Per.'

Toftlund froze in mid-stretch, turned round and saw Konstantin Gelbert standing behind him. Gelbert was wearing his usual designer jeans, together with a light-coloured shirt and blue tie. There was dust on his shoes. Toftlund's face lit up in a smile:

'Konstantin!' he cried and went to shake his hand, but Gelbert did not merely grasp the proffered the hand, he drew it to him and gave Per a hearty Central European hug.

'Good to see you so happy, Per.'

Toftlund was still out of breath, but managed to gasp:

'This is quite a surprise, Konstantin. Come on home and have a cup of coffee. You must meet my wife.'

'Ah, but I already have. Your lovely wife gave me coffee and told me that I would find you here. You're a lucky man, Per.'

'I know.'

'I hope you do.'

'What are you doing here.'

'I paid a routine visit to your charming Commissioner Vuldom yesterday. We have a lot to talk about in connection with Poland's integration with the rest of Europe.'

'Come on home and have another cup of coffee.'

'My car's parked at your house, but I have a plane to catch. However, if you will walk with me at a normal, human pace I will fill you in on a last little piece of the Maria Bujic story.'

'Great,' Toftlund said, although he did not mean it. He had been doing his best to put that story behind him. The baby saved him from having to say any more. She gave a little wail and looked up at him with those amazing blue eyes which were unlike anything he had ever known before. Her dummy had slipped out. He popped it back in her mouth, stroked her cheek and listened to her contented little sucking noises.

'Fatherhood suits you,' Gelbert said.

Toftlund glanced up. He felt vulnerable in his shorts and sweaty T-shirt next to Konstantin Gelbert, the cool chief of Polish counter-intelligence.

'Thanks.'

'I mean it.'

'I said thanks.'

Gelbert eyed him and grasped the handle of the pushchair, which at the moment functioned as a small pram in which Freya could lie down:

'May I? That way I can keep our speed down.'

'Be my guest.'

'It's very American. This jogging pushchair thing. What is her name?'

'Freya.'

'Very Nordic. Very beautiful.'

They had started walking, but Toftlund halted and said:

'It's good to see you, Konstantin, but why the hell are you here?'

Freya had begun to whimper again when they stopped moving, but Gelbert bent over the pram, said something in Polish and when he started pushing again the baby stopped crying.

'To tell you a small part of what now constitutes the end of the story,' he said, then went on:

'The bombings will cease today.'

'I listen to the radio, Konstantin.'

'It's the beginning of the end for Milosevic. The peacekeeping force is moving into Kosovo. I'm certain that next time round the Serbs will elect another president and Milosevic will have to stand down. After four wars and four defeats even his supporters have had enough. It may take a little time, but it will happen. Oh, by the way, the excellent Commissioner Vuldom asked me to say hello.'

'Thanks. Now get to the point, Konstantin!'

They emerged from the woods and walked down the road towards Toftlund's house. The occasional car went by, but otherwise traffic was light. The birds were singing fit to burst and Toftlund felt light and easy, despite the fact that the large sweat-soaked patch on his T-shirt was chill against his chest now that he was not jogging the last bit of the way home.

'There was a Serbian side to your investigation. We no longer believe this had anything to do with your little spy, her past or her half-sister. That is the official line.'

'I don't follow.'

'We won the war. Now we have to win the peace. In its present position the alliance can do without having a rotten apple being exposed in the media. The case has been laid to rest. America's,

| 431 |

and hence NATO's, view is that there is not, and never was, a Serbian spy within the system.'

'And you believe that?'

Gelbert pushed the pram along the side of the road, looking like a man in his element. He glanced round about him. Was clearly very happy with what he saw. The soft, pretty countryside, the freshly opened leaves on the trees, the blossoming bushes. The little nettle shoots unfurling. The peaceful, orderly Danish landscape with the clutch of new, functionalist, red-brick houses and a farm at the foot of a hill. They might have been taking a perfectly ordinary stroll on a perfectly ordinary Danish summer day.

'Per, I haven't been in this job very long, but one thing I have learned is that idealism and ethics are one thing, practical politics is something else again. We're the new boys in the club. If Washington and Brussels say that is how things are then I have to go along with that.'

'That's the easy way out.'

'No, it's not, it's hard. But it's also realistic. We're working in the real world. It has its own laws. Either I accept them, or I go back to my nice, safe academic world, free of all responsibility.'

'And Pavel Samson?'

Gelbert pulled up short, but when he did so Freya started grizzling. Once more he leaned over the pushchair and said something in his native tongue – which clearly seemed to have a soothing effect – because again the baby stopped crying. He strolled quietly on, saying:

'I know you feel guilty. Don't. It actually occurred to me that you might have been the real target. Or both of you. Pavel was trying to protect his old love by leading you up the wrong track. But it was all one to the Russian mafia. You were both expendable. Human life means nothing to those guys. Far better to take someone out than to take any chances. You swat a fly to stop it buzzing or producing more flies, don't you?'

'But still.'

'It wasn't your fault, Per.'

They walked on in silence. Toftlund had more questions he would have liked to ask, but in another way he did not really care. His life had fallen into another pattern, one that revolved solely around Lise and Freya. And the little everyday concerns, such as getting enough sleep with a new baby in the house.

He had not thought much about the case, but Gelbert had touched on a sore point: the fact that he felt guilty because he had got there too late. For more than one thing.

They reached the house. Lise was outside. Toftlund waved. It suddenly struck him how good she looked. When had he last regarded her as a woman? With desire in his eyes rather than protectiveness or concern? She had on a pastel-coloured T-shirt and a pair of blue shorts and her hair was held back by a hairband. Bare feet in a pair of sandals. She looked young and vulnerable and very attractive and he felt a surge of pride and happiness. Gelbert gave him charge of the baby jogger while he gallantly kissed Lise's hand before shaking Toftlund's and saying:

'Goodbye, Per. You're a very fortunate man. Make sure you appreciate it.'

Per lifted the baby out of her harness and passed her to Lise. Freya whimpered again, but quietened down when she felt Lise twiddling the dummy in her little mouth.

The driver in the new Polish Embassy BMW with the blue plates turned the key in the ignition. Gelbert opened the door to get into the back seat. Watching him, Toftlund had a sudden flash of insight – how it came to him he did not know. With a couple of bounds he was by the car and placed a hand on Gelbert's arm:

'Do you know what I think, Konstantin?'

'No, Per. What do you think?'

'I think it's most odd that there should have been so much speculation about the possible presence of a Serbian spy somewhere within the NATO organisation. Who was he? Where is he? And we're not the only ones who've been looking for him. It was taken very seriously. But now that the war has been won everybody seems to be in a great hurry to kill that story.'

Gelbert stood with his hand resting on the door. The driver stared straight ahead, giving a good impression of the three wise monkeys – seeing, hearing and speaking no evil.

'I think, Per, that you should tend to your child and your wife.'

Toftlund held on to his arm:

'But say this spy did exist?'

'So?'

'So, theoretically, it might be that some organisation has had a particular interest in having the case buried. And maybe it was clever enough to use another investigation as a smokescreen. Even if it cost the life of an innocent man like Pavel Samson. The thought suddenly struck me. Although it's just a theory, I suppose.'

'Theories are what academics are paid to propound. You and I inhabit a somewhat more concrete world.'

He made to pull his arm away, but Toftlund kept a tight grip on it, even though he could tell from Gelbert's eyes that they were reaching the stage where the driver would become something more than a mere driver.

'You used to be an academic.'

'I no longer enjoy that luxury.'

'But what if that whole story about Irma and Mira was just some old case, of no relevance today, which simply happened to crop up again. And what if the EU's new member, Poland, realised that this case might come in very handy as a means of saving itself from landing in the soup. That's what I'm thinking, Konstantin. You haven't been there long enough yet to get rid of all the bad apples you've inherited. And the last thing anyone wants is for Poland's loyalties to be called into question, not now, with the EU negotiations and the country's integration into NATO coming up. No one needs that, do they?'

'I have a plane to catch. There is no Serbian spy. Read the papers. It's official, straight from Washington.'

'And naturally we both believe that.'

'Forget the whole business, Per. The war is won, the past is dead, what matters is the future. We're talking about a new Europe. A different and better Europe. A Europe for all of us.'

Toftlund's hold on Gelbert's arm tightened slightly:

'Is he actually a Pole, this guy who passed information to the Serbs? Is he, Konstantin? He doesn't have a damn thing to do with all that other business I was looking into, does he? My case was just a blind, to draw attention away from the real issue. It just struck me, that's all. That you might have had more control over the final stages than it appears on the surface.'

Gelbert pulled his arm away, climbed demonstratively into the back of the car and grasped the handle. But he held the door open:

'The excellent Commissioner Vuldom hinted at something similar. She asked me to say hello. Hoped you were enjoying your holiday.'

'Thanks. And what conclusions did you two reach?'

'That we both wish for a continued, productive collaboration. That we both appreciate the fact that we live in difficult times, in which the important thing is to consolidate the bonus of peace which we have miraculously gained. And we are agreed that peace created by human beings can easily be destroyed by human beings.'

'Well, that all sounds very simple,' Toftlund said.

'Do you play chess, Per?'

'Not very well.'

'I'm a good chess-player. It's a game for those who are always thinking several moves ahead. If you do that you know that sometimes it's necessary to sacrifice a pawn or two, and possibly even a knight.'

'You play for Poland.'

'I told you in Warsaw that we had been given a window of opportunity. My job is not to close it, but to make sure it remains open.'

He pulled at the door. Toftlund hung onto it, but Gelbert said:

| 435 |

'We'll meet again, Per. And when we do we can discuss what's possible, what's unattainable and what's realisable; we can talk about our dreams, about the corruptness of power and the philosophical and practical necessity of discussing at one's leisure the great questions in life and the need for a moral conscience in the service of power. But right now I have a plane to catch.'

'What a load of bullshit, Konstantin. What will you do to him? If you know who he is?'

'Oh, we know alright. Now we do.'

'And?'

'And the case is closed. He'll disappear.'

'I see, and how do you feel about that?'

'What a childish question. I am not me. I am the interests of Poland. All else is between my and my garden which I rarely have time to tend these days. But right now you do. So, my friend, tend your little garden.'

Toftlund let go of the door and Gelbert closed it with a costly little bang. Toftlund followed the car with his eyes as it drove down the narrow road, through the roundabout and disappeared over the low hill. He walked back to Lise who was standing rocking the baby.

'What a great guy,' Lise said.

'Yeah. A great guy.'

'What's that supposed to mean?' she asked.

'Nothing. That he's a great guy. What did you talk about while I was on my run?'

'Oh, different things. He's a very well-informed man, Konstantin, and very charming.'

'No, tell me, what did you talk about?'

'About the war being over. About books a little. And about you, of course.'

'And?'

'We agreed that you're a good man, Per, but that you need to be taken in hand, given a bit of polish. That you're the soul of honesty, but maybe not all that sophisticated. That you're actually a clever guy, you just don't realise it yourself. That you understand a lot of things, but aren't capable of formulating them. It was so good. For the past month I've done nothing but babble baby-talk to Freya, discuss breast-feeding and burping with Pernille and my mum, and sleeping and weight curves with my husband. Which is fine, but it gets a bit boring talking about nothing but baby's bowel movements.'

Toftlund could not help smiling. He stroked first Freya's, then Lise's cheek. He loved touching them both.

'He was really easy to talk to,' Lise said and shook her hair, as if the hairband was pinching slightly.

Freya began to whimper. Her dummy had fallen out and her whimpers quickly turned to howls.

'I think she's hungry. Running does that to her,' he said and picked up the dummy. He stood with it in his hand, very close to Lise.

With the baby in her arms, she went up on tiptoe and kissed Toftlund on the lips. Lightly at first, but then he felt her tongue, and her breasts pressing against him. Then she pulled away:

'You're just fine, Per. In fact you're wonderful and we love you, but sometimes you talk the most awful bullshit.'

'He's not as simple as he looks. Konstantin, I mean.'

'Not many people are.'

She hugged the baby to her, pressed against him and kissed him again before saying:

'I don't want to hear any more about that case. Now you're going to go in and have a shower while I feed this little glutton and then you're going to come to bed with me.'

He looked at her:

'Is it okay?'

'Per, you great dope. I'm not sick. I was pregnant, I had the baby. I'm all healed. I'm a woman. I miss my husband. I'm still your wife and I want you. To put it bluntly, I'm horny as hell.'

She cradled the baby in one arm and with her free left hand she cupped his balls and hefted them, making him jump, so surprised was he by her words and her fondling hand, which he had not felt in such a long time.

'If you're up to it,' she said, eyeing him and giving his lips a little peck.

'Oh, I'm up to it,' he assured her.

'Hm, it certainly feels like it. So how about showing me?'

'Right now?'

'After she's fed. She'll sleep for at least a couple of hours if we're lucky. I can't wait to find out how much you've missed me.'

'Oh, I've missed you a lot.'

'Then show me, Per. Show me, my love.'

Thanks

I FIRST HAD THE IDEA for Teddy and his pictures back in the winter of 1998–1999, but I would like to thank the former Danish Foreign Minister, Uffe Ellemann-Jensen, who drew my attention to the monument at Narva and, by asking who could have erected it, put me on the trail of this story. Thanks also to the workers with the Danish Refugee Council and the Danish Emergency Management Agency in Albania who, in the spring of 1999, gave me some insight into the difficult job they do in that tormented land. Nor would this story have got very far without the clear, simple introduction to the Storebælt Bridge security systems provided by the obliging and efficient staff at the Operations Centre at Halskov. My thanks also to everyone else who has assisted me, not least to Jørgen Anton, who helped me more than he may imagine, and to Jan Stage for the story about Hoxha. To Otto Lindhardt for reading the manuscript and offering his advice. To Hans Henrik Schwab for being such an excellent editor. And as always to Ulla for her invaluable help and support. The final responsibility rests, of course, with me and to claim that this novel is not based on actual events would be absurd. It is, nonetheless, a work of fiction in which my freely invented characters inhabit a setting which could be real, but is, in fact, of my own creation.

Leif Davidsen, *Copenhagen, 2001*